BREAKING
MATTHEW

A NOVEL

Jennifer H. Westall

Healing Ruby Series

Volume 2

Jennifer H. Westall
Website: www.jenniferhwestall.com

Publisher's Note: This is a work of fiction. Names, characters, places, and incidents are a product of the author's imagination. Locales and public names are sometimes used for atmospheric purposes. Any resemblance to actual people, living or dead, or to business-es, companies, events, institutions, or locales is completely coincidental.

Book Layout ©2013 BookDesignTemplates.com

Ordering Information:
Available online at Amazon or Barnes and Noble.

Breaking Matthew/ Jennifer H. Westall. -- 1st ed.
ISBN 978-0-9908759-7-0

To my mother, Becky, who never stops cheering me on

"Then Peter got down out of the boat, walked on the water and came toward Jesus. But when he saw the wind, he was afraid and, beginning to sink, cried out, 'Lord, save me!' Immediately Jesus reached out his hand and caught him. 'You of little faith,' he said, 'why did you doubt?'"

—MATTHEW 14: 29-31

Matthew

I need to breathe, but I can't. I suck at the air, but the harder I try, the more impossible it seems. I hack up the muck stuck inside my lungs, the coppery taste of blood lingering in my mouth. My eyes water, the pressure in them building, and tears run down my cheeks. My chest burns. My heart races. I cough again, this time releasing the muck and finding precious moments of relief.

Rolling onto my side, my eyes don't quite focus on the bloodstained wall, speckled with fading brown smudges. The pail beneath me, just to the side of my bed, is splattered with dark red globs. I gulp down as much air as I can, but it's not enough, and I know the next breath will be even smaller.

This is it. Death has finally come for me. I can quit struggling, quit aching, quit lumbering through this nightmare. I want to let go and die in peace. But my lungs have a mind of their own, and they refuse to give up, fighting for air as if they don't realize they're doomed. My head throbs. I don't think I can take this. God, just make it stop!

But then I feel a hand on my back, smoothing out the pain as it circles over and over, moving closer and closer to the center. It widens again, circling and circling, pushing the pain with it, scattering the burn.

My frantic lungs gulp down air, before coughing up more of the blood drowning them.

I roll over onto my back, exhausted from the effort to breathe. Her face hovers over mine, her eyebrows pinched together with worry.

"You're back," I whisper between gasps.

"I promised I would be," she says.

I hear someone else talking, a man to the side of me, but I can't see his face. His words run together, and I feel the urgent need for air rising inside me again. I roll to the side, cough to make room for the air, suck in...nothing. My brain screams for oxygen, my chest too. I can't get any more in. I suck in just enough to cough out more blood.

And then everything stops.

The room blurs. Another hand, a larger one, is circling my back again. I close my eyes, and a cool tingle comes over my head. It spreads down my neck, down into my chest, like a million butterfly wings tickling each artery and vein. It sweeps over me, soothing the ache and filling me with peace. I wonder if this is what death feels like.

My lungs gasp for air, and I cough. A large, wet glob of blood surges out of them. I gasp again. This time there's more air, and I cough again. More air, and more air. My lungs soak it in like desert rain. The tingling continues, and even the coughing doesn't hurt as much as it did.

I roll over and fill my lungs with air, precious air!

Her face is beside me again, smiling with a glow that lights up her eyes. I can breathe. I can breathe.

I reach for her hand, but she's no longer there. I didn't see her move, but she's standing at the end of the bed now. Clumsily I push myself up to a sitting position and reach for her. But she's moving further away, like something's pulling her away from me.

With renewed strength, I throw off the covers and stumble onto the floor, muscles cramping, toes curling beneath me. Months have passed since I last touched the ground. I round the end of my bed just as she nears the wall. She reaches out for me, but before I can grasp her hand, she fades away into nothing. I scream.

"Ruby!"

CHAPTER ONE

Matthew

I sat up and dropped my feet onto the floor beside my bed, willing my heart to slow down. Focusing on one breath at a time, I looked around my bedroom in the gray light of early morning. No bloody pail. Clean wallpaper. A cool breeze drifted through the window with the smell of fresh rain. I looked to the end of my bed. No Ruby either.

It had been a long time since I'd had that dream. Over a year, maybe. Seemed to come to me often for a while there in the months following the tornado. I hadn't thought about that spring back in '32 for some time. Used to wonder if I'd ever go one day without thinking on all that mess. Took nearly a year to get all them sights out of my head—Hannah bleeding near to death, Ruby praying over her like she was possessed or something, and those words:

Matthew, I love you.

Sitting there on the side of my bed, in the same room where it all began, I knew it was time to get moving. Dwelling on Ruby took me to places best left behind. So I dressed and headed downstairs for breakfast. The aroma of Esther's cooking made my mouth water, and I sped up my pace to the dining room. Mother and Mary were already seated, but hadn't begun yet, so I took my place next to Mary and said good morning.

She gave me a tentative smile. "You look tired."

That caught Mother's attention, and she studied me more closely. "Didn't you sleep well, dear?"

"I slept fine." I smiled to reassure her, but she didn't look convinced. Thankfully, Esther brought the rest of the food to the table and distracted her.

Mary leaned over and lowered her voice. "You had another nightmare, didn't you?"

I began filling my plate with eggs and sausage, doing my best to ignore her. Mary was kind, and she meant well. I'd shared those awful nightmares with her when they'd first started in the hopes of lifting my guilt over turning my back on Ruby. But I could never tell Mary everything, and that meant letting her come to conclusions I couldn't correct.

"How long you home for?" I asked, hoping she'd allow us to move on.

She narrowed her eyes, but then she sighed and went to filling her plate as well. "Just through the weekend. I have an early class on Monday."

"Good," I said. "Vanessa and her parents are coming up to visit on Saturday afternoon, and she'll be glad to see you."

Mary's eyes brightened with her smile. "Oh Matthew! That's wonderful! I haven't seen her in ages! Is this a *special* occasion?"

I glanced at Mother who was back to paying keen interest to our conversation. Then I smiled back at Mary and took a bite of my biscuit. She swatted my shoulder and giggled, a sound I realized I'd missed greatly. Her laughter had always been like medicine to my soul when I needed it most.

"Mother," she whined. "You must know something. I can see it in your face. You have to tell me!"

"What's all this nonsense about?" Father said as he came in and sat down. He always entered a room like he was preparing to command forces into battle, even if it was just his own family. I was grateful for the interruption as Mother and Father went though their usual exchange of morning pleasantries. But it wasn't long until Father turned his attention to evaluating the merits of my activities for the day, and my defenses shot up.

"Where are you heading to today?" he asked.

"Calhoun's place." It was best to keep your answers short and to the point with him.

"This is the last one, right?"

"Yes, sir."

"So then you're through with TVA." Father had made no secret about his displeasure at my working for the Tennessee Valley Authority to build dams since graduation. But it was good experience, despite the low pay, and I refused to apologize.

"Yes, sir."

"It's about time, is all I can say."

"Now, Patrick," Mother scolded. "Leave the boy alone."

Father pointed his fork at her. "Now Francine, he's not a boy. He's a man. And he's got no business working for the government like some poor soul with no class or family name. Now I paid for him to go to college, even supported him when he wanted to major in Engineering instead of Business." The fork swung in my direction. "And I've done my best to let you be your own man, but it's about time you started making something of yourself."

I swallowed the food in my mouth, though it had lost its taste. "That's exactly what I'm doing."

He didn't seem to hear my response. "Now take your brother, Tom, he's doing things right. He worked his way up from sweeping the floors to opening up his own store down in Birmingham. That's how you do things. You don't sit around on your behind, living off the government, just waiting for a career to fall into your lap."

I slammed my fork down and stood. "I spent my entire summer in the mud building a dam up in Wheeler so people all over the state could have electricity in their homes. I'd hardly call that sitting on my behind!"

He frowned at me, distinctly unimpressed. "You didn't make nothing but pennies for all that effort, so don't pretend like you accomplished something."

And there it was. The only measuring stick that mattered.

"I gotta go if I'm gonna make it to the Calhoun farm on time." I nodded at Mary and Mother and headed for the door.

"Matthew, don't go yet," Mother called after me.

I didn't stop till I got around the door. I stood there for a moment, straightening my shirt. I could hear Mother scolding Father about it being no wonder I never came home anymore. A twinge of guilt hit me. It was bad enough to stay away for so long, but to let her think it was because of Father seemed a bit cruel.

Truth was, I could take Father's poor evaluation of me. I'd been doing that for years. I just couldn't take the chance on running into Ruby, and the longer I hung around Hanceville, the more likely it was to happen. That was why I'd saved the Calhoun farm for last. At least if I did see her, I'd be gone soon afterward. Then I could go back to pretending that year of my life never happened.

Calhoun's farm looked smaller than I remembered it. I was hoping I'd pull up and everything would look so different I wouldn't be able to remember anything. But God seemed to take small pleasures in tormenting me, and as soon as I caught a glimpse of the house, a string of images I'd fought for over four years to erase flashed through my mind.

I turned off my car and climbed out right where Calhoun's oldest son had sprawled across the ground after I'd landed a punch to his face. I could still hear Ruby screaming at us to stop. *Matthew, the storm!* Hail pelted my skin. The approaching tornado roared in the distance.

Closing my eyes, I forced the images out. Then I took a deep breath, opened my eyes, and went up the stairs to the front door. I knocked, and a few seconds later Calhoun pulled the door open. He looked just like I remembered him: tall and broad, skin weathered by the sun and wind.

"What can I do for ya?" he asked, stepping onto the porch and running his hand through his white hair. Before I could answer, his face went hard as stone. "Wait a minute. You're Patrick Doyle's boy. I know you. What're you doing here?"

"Mr. Calhoun, I work for the TVA, and I'm going out to all the farms that signed up with the Cullman Electric Cooperative to make sure your electricity is connected properly and everything's running to your satisfaction."

"Excuse me?" He looked at me like I'd said I'd come to rob him.

"Your electricity, sir. Is it running all right?"

He stared at me another minute, and my skin felt like it was burning up beneath my shirt. I knew his secret, and he knew that I knew it. Men can't talk normal with each other when secrets are staring at them. I had to look down at my feet.

"I reckon it's working just fine," he said. "Now, if you'll excuse me I have some work to do."

"I don't mean to trouble you any further, but I do need to take a look at the connections and verify that it's all set up properly. Then I promise I'll be out of your hair. If you could just point me in the right direction, I'd appreciate it."

His frown deepened beneath his huge mustache, and he walked past me to the end of the porch. "James!" he hollered across the yard toward the barn. "Get up here!"

That made my stomach knot up even more 'cause seeing James was just one step closer to seeing Ruby. "Mr. Calhoun, there's no need to bother James. Just point me in the right direction. I'll check everything out and be on my way."

Calhoun said nothing. Just stood there and waited on James to cross the yard. When he was a few feet away, Calhoun came back to the front door. "Show young Mr. Doyle here where the electricity's hooked up 'round back."

"Yes, sir," James said. He glanced at me, and I noted the surprise in his eyes. It quickly changed to something else. Maybe dread. I'd never noticed before, but James and Ruby had the same eyes—intense, fiery eyes that expected so much from me.

Calhoun excused himself and went back inside. I trudged down the stairs and offered my hand. He didn't hesitate to take it. "How are ya, James? Been a long time."

"I'm all right, I reckon." He gestured at the fields off to his right. "Been managing things here for a coupla years. How 'bout yourself?"

"Oh, I been getting along just fine." I didn't want to pretend there wasn't a mountain of vexation between us. I'd hurt his sister, no doubt about that. No telling how much he knew, but his discomfort was clear. "Why don't you show me the connection, and I'll let you get back to work. I don't want to inconvenience you."

He nodded toward the back of the house. "No inconvenience. It's just right around here."

When we cleared the side of the house, I stopped and looked out over the field. I could still see Ruby tearing out across it with a tornado literally bearing down on her. She'd made it into the woods just as James, her mother, and I had taken shelter in a ditch. I'd thought my heart would stop right there.

"It's over thisaway." James's voice broke through my memories, and I turned back to face him.

"How is she? Ruby, I mean. She doing all right?"

His mouth pressed into a line before he answered. "Good. She's real good. Works in town with Dr. Fisher most days. She helps deliver babies. Seems to have a knack for it. She delivered mine and Emma Rae's first young'un. Got another due anytime now."

"Congratulations. That's good." I shoved my hands in my pockets and rocked on my heels. I shouldn't have asked about her. Better to let the past stay buried.

"You planning on seeing her?" he asked.

I shook my head. "I'm leaving in a few days."

"Probably for the best." No argument there. "Well, I should get back to work." He pointed at the box with all the wires and connections. "I reckon you know what you're doing from here. I'll leave you to it."

"Thanks. You take care."

James turned and left me there with my memories still tapping on my mind, demanding attention I shouldn't give them. I pushed them back where they belonged and focused on what was right in front of me instead.

I knew I wouldn't be able to avoid her the entire time I was home, not when I was going to be around for more than two weeks. So I was surprised when that last Friday rolled around and I still hadn't seen Ruby in Hanceville or Cullman. I'd let myself start to think I was going to make it out of there without much more discomfort than a few bad dreams, but once again, God reached down and stirred my pot.

I walked out of the office of the Cullman Electrical Cooperative that afternoon feeling right proud of myself. I'd delivered my report to the board, explained the concerns I'd had with a couple of farms, and shook hands to officially close out my term of service with both the Co-op and the TVA. There'd been no major complications, and in a few days I'd be on a train for Nashville doing my best to "make something" of myself. I should've known something was brewing, like the dead calm before a tornado rips through your life.

I stepped out onto the sidewalk and soaked up the waning warmth of the sun on my face. I'd always loved fall. Loved the crisp air, loved football season. But it was fading, and winter would soon steal every leaf around, leaving a cold death over everything. I was glad to have the prospect of a new life beginning soon. Something to carry me far away from this place.

But then I saw her.

She was coming out of a house down the road a piece. Maybe a couple of blocks down. Dr. Fisher was in front as they crossed the yard. He opened the front gate and let her pass. Then he opened the car door for Ruby to climb inside. She should have, but she stopped and looked around, lifting her face to the air, like she was measuring the breeze against her cheek.

Then she turned toward me, covering her brow with her hand to shield her eyes from the sun. She was too far away for me to know for sure, but I thought she saw me. My stomach tightened. Should I go to her? Should I wave?

It didn't matter 'cause she got in the car before I could decide. Dr. Fisher climbed in too, and in an instant they were gone. The whole thing couldn't have lasted more than five seconds, but seemed like it could've been four years just the same.

I stood there for a moment, my head spinning. I should've waved or something. I should've gone over and spoken to her, told her how sorry I was for leaving things the way I did. But once again, without even trying, I'd disappointed her. Part of me wanted to track her down. She'd be heading back to Dr. Fisher's office at some point. I could easily make my way there and wait for her.

But I couldn't shake the lasting effects of what I'd seen that day four years ago. The thought of someone I knew, someone I cared for, having some strange power to make a person stop bleeding. That just didn't seem right. I couldn't say it was evil; I knew there wasn't an ounce of evil in Ruby. But that kind of power wasn't natural. And I couldn't wrap my head around it, even after four years of trying.

I made my way back to my car and cruised the streets of Cullman for a while, mulling everything over. I asked God to make things clear to me. 'Course, he didn't.

I ain't sure what I was expecting. Not a voice talking to me or anything, but something. Some kind of sign or clarity in my thoughts to tell me if I should go to Ruby and make things right. After all, if it wasn't for her, I'd probably be dead from T.B. Even if she, or her uncle, had used some dark power to heal me, God had allowed it. Maybe he'd even been the one to give her that kind of power. Was that even possible?

I'd searched the Bible as much as I could over the years. Couldn't find anything that sounded like what I'd seen. I mean sure, the disciples healed people, but that was different. They walked around in public; they healed out in front of everyone. And they healed people with sicknesses and demons. I didn't read anything about fatal injuries being healed.

I realized I was still aimlessly driving around Cullman, and when I turned to head back to Hanceville, I spotted my family's church ahead on the left. As I passed by, I remembered the times Ruby and I had spent there serving in the soup kitchen. I remembered how humbly she had served, how the broken men and women coming into that place loved her so much 'cause she treated them with dignity.

But I remembered also the warnings from Brother Cass. He'd told me to keep away from her. Said she was trouble. I'm not sure if he knew how true that was. I'd always wondered if he knew about her gift, and if that was the reason he'd spoken so poorly of her. It didn't matter anyway. I'd left both of them behind. I couldn't worship at a church where the pastor had such contempt for another person. Especially when he'd gone so far as to send that brute Chester to attack Ruby.

I focused my attention on the road ahead. Remembering that day, when I'd found her in the woods nearly beaten to death, made my whole body burn with anger. No matter what that old man thought of her, no matter if she could do something dark and mysterious, she didn't deserve that.

As I put more miles between Cullman and me and neared my parents' home, I pushed all those memories aside. It was best to leave well enough alone. Vanessa would be visiting tomorrow, and I was moving forward with my life. Dwelling on the past could only cause more heartache and nightmares.

Saturday evening, Mother and Father hosted a dinner for Vanessa's parents, who'd driven up from Montgomery to spend the weekend with us. I'd had my fun torturing Mary and Mother all morning, but once the Paschals arrived, Vanessa and I finally shared the news that we were engaged. You'd have thought I was announcing a run for President from the way my family reacted. Even Father seemed pleased with my decision, something I didn't think was possible.

As I waited at the bottom of the stairs, Mother and Mrs. Paschal beamed at me from the parlor where they were greeting the arriving guests. 'Course, the most important ones, to my parents at least, wouldn't arrive for a while yet. I could always measure a person's importance in this town by the order in which he showed up for dinner. Seemed silly to me. But appearances had to be maintained.

I glanced up the staircase to see Mary and Vanessa coming down together, radiating sunshine and beauty. They already looked like sisters. Acted like it too. I couldn't help but smile as I admired them and gave them a slight bow. "Ladies, you are both stunning."

Mary breezed past me, giggling as she headed for the parlor to join Mother. Vanessa stopped on the bottom stair so that her hazel eyes were level with mine. They sparkled as I lifted her hand to my lips. "You look so handsome in your suit!"

"Thank you, my dear. You did an excellent job of picking it out and forcing me to buy it."

She grinned and shook her head. "You'll be glad I did, trust me. I'll bet your mother's already pointed it out to mine no less than ten times."

"Well, they better enjoy it. Can't imagine I'll be wearing it again anytime soon."

I took her hand and led her over to the parlor to join the families and guests, introducing her as we made our way around the room. Despite my hatred for these dinners, I found myself enjoying the sight of Vanessa making her place in my world. I'd been hesitant for so long, wondering if we shouldn't just elope and head west. The thought of making my own way in the world away from Father's judgment called out to me. But there was Mary and Mother to consider, not to mention what such a betrayal might do to Father.

No, I'd dreamed of that freedom, but I could never act on it. Good thing I supposed, after seeing everyone gathered together and happy. I figured it was all for the best, and I was sure Vanessa would slide right into being a Doyle. I reckoned seeing as how our parents had been friends since before we were born, she might as well have been part of our family all along.

In fact, I was so content I hardly noticed when Brother Cass showed up. He strolled over to greet Mother and Mrs. Paschal before turning his fake smile on Vanessa and me. "Matthew! It's good to see you, son." He stuck out his hand, but I put mine on Vanessa's back instead. He didn't seem to notice. "And my goodness, Miss Vanessa, I hardly recognize you! It's been what? Four years? You've grown into a lovely young lady."

"Thank you, Brother Cass," she said.

"Will we be seeing you and your family for service in the morning? I'd be so pleased to have you all in the congregation once again."

"I believe so."

He turned his eyes on me then, the same gaze that had sent a cold shiver down my spine every time he'd come to pray over me when I was sick. Like he thrived on my suffering. "And you, Matthew? Will you finally be rejoining us for worship? I'm sure the Lord would love to hear your voice lifted up in praise."

"I'll be praising God on my own, as usual." I tried to hide my contempt. He was a preacher after all, and the child inside of me was still just the tiniest bit afraid he might call down God's wrath upon me.

"Well, keep in mind that God calls us to corporate worship—"

"God and I have been getting along just fine, Brother Cass. Every Sunday morning I take a nice long stroll and have a talk with him. I assure you, the Lord and I are on solid ground."

He cleared his throat but kept his smile in place, and nodded to Vanessa. "I'll just look forward to seeing you all tomorrow morning, then."

As he slid over to Father and Mr. Adams, Vanessa frowned at me. "Maybe it's time to put the past behind you and just go to church with your family."

"I'm sorry, but I refuse to sit and listen to a man like that tell me how to worship God. He ain't got the slightest bit of compassion in his heart."

"Well, all right then," she said, shrugging it off. "Who's that man over there talking with your daddy and Brother Cass? He seems familiar."

"That's Charles Adams. He runs the newspaper in town. Father's practically kept him in business the past couple of years."

"How's that?"

"A lot of businesses cut back on advertising with the economy so poor for so long. Father's stores take up a fair amount of ad space."

"I see. Anyone else I should know about?"

Mary appeared on Vanessa's left, scooping her arm under Vanessa's. "What are you two gossiping about over here?"

"Matthew was just informing me of who I should be mingling with if I want to move up in society." Vanessa winked at me. "Anyone else here that's remotely interesting? Mayor? Bank president? Judge?"

"Judge Woods is right over there, but he's not very interesting," I said. "Don't think I've ever seen the man smile in my life. Not sure why he comes to these things."

Vanessa leaned towards me, flashing her own wide smile. "Well, he may be boring, but you never know when you might need a judge in your pocket."

We had a good laugh, and I led her over for an introduction. Judge Woods and his wife were seated on a sofa near the front windows, both of them frowning as if they were in pain. He sipped on a brandy, while she nodded her head along with a conversation among some gray-haired women seated in the chairs nearby.

"Judge Woods," I said. "I'd like you to meet my fiancée, Vanessa Paschal. Vanessa, this is Judge Albert Woods and his lovely wife."

Judge Woods stood and shook her hand. Mrs. Woods barely made eye contact.

"It's a pleasure to meet you," Vanessa said. "I hear you're an excellent judge. Very fair and knowledgeable."

He lifted a thin silver eyebrow. "Likewise, Miss Paschal. I wish you the best of luck in your upcoming marriage."

"Thank you, sir."

We nodded and dismissed ourselves. Vanessa giggled as we turned away and headed back across the room. "You were right. Not very interesting at all."

CHAPTER TWO

Ruby

Saturdays were my favorite day of the week, 'cause those were the days I was free to just be myself. Dr. Fisher would let me borrow his car for the mornings, and first thing I'd do was drive out to see James, Emma Rae, and little Abner. I didn't care as much for seeing James on account of him being as cranky as ever, as if he packed every one of us on his shoulders every day and carried us through the desert or something. Sure, things were bad all over Alabama, but they were bad all over everywhere in 1936. Everybody we knew was hovering right above disaster, just one sickness away from death, one meal away from starvation, one drought away from losing everything. But we were also one prayer away from miracles, and those were everywhere too.

Just take little Abner's birth for one thing. He was turned all around inside Emma Rae, and I was pretty worried he wasn't going to come out without killing her. But I laid my hands on her belly, and I leaned down real close to where his head was, and I talked to him as sweet as I could. I told him how much his mother loved him already, how much he was going to love being in her arms, and how much I was going to love him too. And I told him he'd have to turn around to come out and see us.

Then I prayed. I prayed so he could hear me, and I asked God to help him turn around the right way. And I promise as soon as I finished that prayer, that little baby practically did a flip inside her. He came on out without any trouble, and he announced himself to the world with the most joyful noise I'd ever heard. I cleaned him up and laid him on Emma Rae's chest, and he got quiet pretty quick.

Now most folks wouldn't know it 'cause they weren't in that room, and they didn't talk to that sweet baby, but I knew it was a miracle. 'Course, by that time, I'd seen my fair share of miracles, so I knew what they looked like. Not everyone gets to see the things I did, so I knew what a privilege it was.

Well, every Saturday I'd drive over to see Emma Rae and Abner. James was usually already over at the main farm. I'd help with a few chores or chase Abner around while Emma Rae got some work done. Then we'd talk for a spell. She was about ready to deliver her second baby, so I'd ask her how things were going just to make sure she was progressing like she should. It was always a happy time for me, and that Saturday in late October was no different.

James was still at the house, so he gave me a hug as I came through the door. "On your own today?"

"Sure am." I pushed my chin up and dared him to start another argument with me about the merits of my driving.

He peered down his crooked nose at me, sending a warm shot through my chest, 'cause that was just how Daddy used to look at me when he thought I was up to something. "I reckon you're determined to go flying around this town in that car of the good doctor's till you kill yourself or somebody else. He ain't got no business letting you go out there on the roads by yourself."

"I didn't give him much of a choice. Besides, you worry too much. I can drive just as good as any man. You beat all I ever seen. Just 'cause I'm a girl don't mean I can't do the same things as you."

"Well, all right then, let's see you go out there and hook up the mules to the plow and get them fields taken care of. You go on out there and boss them field hands around and see what happens."

I put my hands on my hips and readied myself for a full on fight, but Emma Rae came out of the bedroom with Abner, and he tore across the living room toward me.

"Udee!"

I scooped him up and threw him into the air as he squealed. "Oh, look who I've got here!"

Emma Rae smiled as she waddled toward us, her belly looking like it was about to explode. She wasn't quite as together as she normally was, but who could blame her? With only a couple of weeks left in her pregnancy, she had to be exhausted.

"Sounds like we came out just in time," she said, raising an eyebrow at James.

James huffed, but he grabbed Abner from my arms and swung him around for another peal of laughter. There's nothing in this world like the laugh of a toddler to clear a room of all darkness, and Abner seemed to have a special gift for bringing light into any place. He squirmed in his daddy's arms till his shirt nearly came clean over his head. I reached over and tickled his chubby belly, relishing more of that sweet laugh.

James set him down, and Abner took off running. He hid behind a kitchen chair and peeked through the slats. James stomped his foot and pretended like he was going to give chase. Abner squealed again and took off for the back door. Emma Rae sighed, smiled at us, and then hurried after him.

"I'm heading for the fields," James called. "See you for dinner!"

"I'll be seeing you for dinner today too," I said.

He dropped his hand from the doorknob and turned back to me. "How's that?"

"Dinner. I'm coming with Emma Rae up to the big house today. She's helping her mother with something, so I said I'd play with Abner for a bit."

"You might not want to do that," he said, rubbing the back of his neck.

"Why not?"

He glanced over at Emma Rae as she came back through the door with Abner in her arms. "I ran into Matthew at the big house yesterday. I ain't sure if he's coming around again." He hesitated. "Maybe I shouldn't have said nothing, but I thought you should know."

I ignored the momentary spike in my heart rate. "Well, how is he?"

"Just fine, I reckon. Guess he's working for the TVA or something. He was checking the electric connections."

"That's good to hear." I nodded, wondering why such information should keep me from going over to the Calhoun place. Surely he wasn't likely to return?

"He asked about you."

Another spike. "And what did you tell him?"

"Told him you were just fine, that you been working with Doc Fisher and such."

Emma Rae came over and kissed James on the cheek. "I thought you were leaving."

He looked at me uncomfortably. "I am. Guess I'll be seeing you in a little while."

He headed out the door, and Emma Rae looked at me kind of funny. "You all right?"

"I sure am." Breaking the spell, I clapped my hands together. "Now what can I help you with this morning?"

She narrowed her eyes. "Who's Matthew?"

I waved my hand to dismiss her. "Oh, nobody you'd remember. He's one of the Doyle boys I knew a long time ago from school."

"Oh, I remember him! I overheard Daddy talking about him and Chester getting into an awful fight."

This conversation was quickly heading down a road I didn't want to travel. I tried desperately to think of something to change the subject. But it was like a dam had been busted wide open.

"I think Daddy said something about you too," she said. "Do you remember all that? I'm sure you do. He wouldn't say a word about it if I asked him directly, but I think that was about the time Chester quit and walked out on Daddy. I didn't even see him for nearly a year!"

The more she talked, the more my stomach churned. I preferred to think of Emma Rae as part of my family, and to forget all together that Chester was her brother. I couldn't see how in any sane world, a man so full of hatred as to attack a helpless woman, could be related to Emma Rae and Abner. I wished she'd stop talking.

"He only just started coming around now that me and James are talking of getting our own place to run." I was only half listening. "After the baby's born, of course. But I reckon Daddy and Chester will patch things up. Say, do you know what Chester and that boy were fighting over?"

I stared at her for what seemed like a length of time that would be considered rude by most people. I had learned a long time ago that lying was not for me. Not only was I bad at it, but I was determined to raise my character to a level that was deserving of the precious gift God had given me.

I couldn't lie. But I couldn't tell her the truth either. "Listen, Emma Rae. It isn't my place to talk about what happened in your family. If you want those answers, you need to talk to them."

But God help you if you ever get those answers.

As I was coming out of church on Sunday, I stopped to take in the glorious autumn breeze. It lifted the fallen leaves and carried them away to their resting places along the dusty roads that crossed paths in our small town. People trickled out of the churches onto the sidewalks and meandered toward their homes on foot or by car. Many stood around laughing and talking with one another.

I missed going to church as a family with my parents and brothers. After the service, Daddy would talk forever. Mother didn't mind so much, but I could tell when it was time to get him moving. Initially she'd gently rub her hand across his back while he just kept on talking, his booming laugh carrying across the lawn. But eventually she'd start patting him on the back, and he'd get the message. Then we'd head for home, and Mother and I'd finish preparing our big Sunday dinner.

Nowadays, I was on my own most Sundays. Dr. Fisher and his wife went to a different church. James and Emma Rae rarely made it into town 'cause it was such a hassle. They'd head over to the big house with the Calhouns and have their own service, with a big family dinner following. They'd invited me a few times, but I avoided the Calhoun place whenever possible. Too much poison in those memories.

Mother and Uncle Asa kept to themselves too. The year following the storm, he sold Grandma Graves's place in Good Hope and bought a small farmhouse just outside of town. Wasn't long till he and Mother married, which made many of my relatives uncomfortable to say the least. I guess some people just can't let go of the past. But I thought it was wonderful. I couldn't think of anything better than falling in love with someone a second time, after so much heartache. Theirs was a story of redemption, and it saddened me that so many of my good Christian neighbors and family couldn't see it that way.

I let out a deep sigh as I thought of them, wondering if I could catch a ride out to see Mother and Uncle Asa in time for dinner. I'd never get there in time if I walked. But just at that moment, I caught sight of Matthew Doyle approaching from across the street, and my skin went all tingly. He was coming right for me, and it was too late to pretend I hadn't seen him. My mind went in all different directions, but one thought was clear. He was the last person I wanted to speak to on such a beautiful day.

So I turned on my heels and headed for home with a deliberate pace I hoped communicated my intentions. I made certain not to look over my shoulder, but everything within me wanted to. Was he following after me? Had he really seen me? Had I really seen him? I thought I might have heard my name, but I wasn't about to turn around to find out.

When I reached the next intersection, I had to cross over to the side of the street I'd seen him on, and I couldn't stop myself from taking a quick glance down the sidewalk to see if he was coming. He was there all right; I hadn't imagined it. But he wasn't walking toward me any longer. He was just standing there on the sidewalk, looking at me with his hands in his pockets.

My feet seemed to stop of their own accord. Some little part of me wanted to go to him, to fix everything that had gone wrong. But I just stood there looking at him, and he just looked back at me. We might have stood there like that for hours, maybe only seconds. I wasn't sure. Sometimes, single moments have eternity wrapped up inside them. It was long enough for me to relive the heaviness in my chest from back when he'd looked at me like I was some kind of witch. It was long enough for me to remember my resolve to forget about Matthew Doyle. Then, just as he raised a hand to wave at me, I turned and persuaded my feet to start moving down the sidewalk again.

I made it back to Ms. Harmon's house, where I'd been renting a room for nearly a year. I hurried up the steps to the large wrap-around porch and glanced back to see if Matthew had come after me. He hadn't, and I think that might have been the first full breath I took since I started walking. I pushed open the front door as quiet as possible, preferring to take a few solitary moments in my room to settle my nerves.

But before I reached the stairs, Ms. Harmon pushed through the kitchen door and into the dining area to my right. She caught sight of me just as I reached out for the banister. "Miss Ruby, will you be joining us for dinner?"

I paused with my foot on the first step. "No, ma'am. I just came by to freshen up. I think I'll head over to Dr. Fisher's."

She stopped beside me with her eyebrows raised like she was expecting trouble. "Now, Miss Ruby, I hope you plan on being back here at a respectable time this evening."

I put both my feet on the floor and faced her, pulling my shoulders back like she expected from all the girls who rented rooms from her. I was in no mood for another lecture about how my appearance reflected onto her. "Yes, ma'am. I don't expect to be gone long."

She narrowed her green eyes. "Why, you're shaking. What's going on?"

I clenched my hands behind my back. "Oh nothing. Just a brisk walk home from church is all."

I didn't think she believed me, but at least she didn't press me any further. I excused myself as politely as I could and darted up the stairs to my room, closing the door firmly behind me. Only then could I concentrate on slowing my heart rate. But from behind closed lids, I kept seeing Matthew standing in front of me, his arm outstretched, my name on his lips.

I opened my eyes and crossed the small room to my bed. Sitting on its edge, I thought of those months after Daddy died—the harsh adjustment to life as a sharecropper, my shame when Matthew and Mary first saw the shack we'd moved into, my feeble faith as I'd floundered along the path of serving others. And then I thought of Hannah and the terrible state of her home when we'd met.

Maybe a visit with Hannah was what I needed. It had been several weeks since I'd been out to see her. Our talks always seemed to help right my perspective. And right then, putting some miles between Hanceville and me seemed like a wonderful idea.

As I drove west out of town toward the Colony, each passing mile relieved my tension a little more. Dr. Fisher had seemed reluctant to allow me to drive two days in a row, but my promise it would only be a short trip to visit friends had loosened him a bit. 'Course, had he known where I was going, he would've said no for sure. Despite his affection for Hannah, and his care for her after the tornado struck, he adamantly opposed our continued friendship. Some kind of malarkey about my safety.

So I didn't often tell him exactly where I was going, and he'd learned not to ask too many questions.

When I pulled onto the dusty back road that led to Hannah's house, I slowed my speed and offered smiles to a few of the neighbors as I passed. As usual, the colored folks looked at me with suspicion until they recognized me. Then there was the typical mixture of shaking heads and tentative smiles in return. None of them ever came down to Hannah's house when I was there, but she told me about the questions they'd asked over the years.

"Why she coming out here all the time?"

"You got to wait on her in your own home?"

"Ain't you scared?"

I laughed to myself as I pulled up into Hannah's yard. We'd decided long ago that we preferred a world where a colored girl and white girl could be friends no matter what others thought about it, and that was the world we were building for ourselves. One day at a time. One visit at a time.

I supposed she heard me drive up, 'cause she met me on the front porch with a big smile and a little shadow peeking out from behind her skirt. Before I'd taken two steps, Isaiah darted out from behind her and came running to me. "It's Miss Ruby, Mama!" He leapt up and threw his little tan arms around my neck, and I carried him back to the porch. When he pulled his face back, I looked into his sweet gray eyes and felt my spirits take flight again.

I set him down and hugged Hannah while she fussed at me and loved on me at the same time. "Now, Miss Ruby, you done surprised me! I ain't got nothin' but a bit a cornbread and milk today, and you gone show up on my doorstep!"

I tried to reassure her that I'd already eaten and didn't want anything but her company, but she wouldn't hear of it. They didn't have much in the way of food, but she'd try to feed me whatever she did have. I followed her into the kitchen and sat down at the table, as she went to filling a bowl with cornbread. When she took a pitcher of milk out of the icebox, and I saw how little was left, I insisted she put it back.

"I don't care for milk with my cornbread, Hannah. I'll just take some water."

She raised a finger at me and shook it. "Now don't be telling me no stories. I seen you eat plenty a cornbread with milk."

"Not today though. I'm just too full."

She put the pitcher back and came over to the table, finally dropping into the chair across from me. I always liked it when she let her guard down and relaxed. Over the years, it had taken less and less time for her to reach that point during our visits. I even noticed that at some point while we talked, she'd drop the "Miss" in front of my name.

"Where's Samuel?" I asked.

"No telling. That boy's aiming to put me in the grave before my time." She shook her head. "He said he was walking Millie Hatch home after church, but he should a been home by now. He probably found some other boys and went off to cause a ruckus."

I couldn't help but laugh a little. "My brothers were the same way when they were fifteen. He'll grow out of it."

She shook her head and looked more serious. "I wish that was all it was. I'm afraid he's heading down a dangerous path lately. Been talking—"

The door swung open, and Samuel stepped inside. He made eye contact with me, and I saw the hint of distrust he'd never been able to completely erase. But it was gone in a flash, and he gave me a smile instead.

"Hey there, Miss Ruby."

Hannah jumped up and went over to him, swatting at the dirt on his pants. "Mercy! Can't you even keep your Sunday clothes clean for half a day?"

She brushed the back of his shirt, and he slunk out from under her hand. "Mama, stop fussin'. It ain't no big deal. 'Sides, I'm just going right back out."

Hannah stepped back and put her fists on her hips. "Oh no, you's staying right here and visiting with Miss Ruby! Them boys down the road can wait."

"Mama," Samuel groaned. "I ain't got time—" But he didn't get any further 'cause she pinched the back of his neck. "Ow! All right!" He slapped her hand away and moved over to the empty chair at the table, which he dropped into with a loud sigh.

Hannah came over and took her seat as well, shaking her finger in his direction. "You see? This is what I'm putting up with every day."

I couldn't help but laugh a little. "I don't think you have too much to worry over. Seems like I remember my brothers causing a much bigger fuss than Samuel does." I smiled at him, but he slumped even lower in his chair. "Boys can be a handful when they're anxious to prove they're men."

Hannah huffed and crossed her arms. "Well maybe you can talk some sense into this one. Lord knows he ain't gone listen to me!" She dropped her chin, glaring at her eldest son. "You want to tell her what you were up to last month?"

"Mama!" he said. "Miss Ruby don't want to know about our business." He darted a glance at me from under dark, angry eyebrows.

"Well, somebody needs to knock some sense into that head of yours. Go on! Tell her what ya done. I just found out myself a week ago."

He stared at the table, picking at a flake of wood. Hannah turned her glare at me. "He went off picking cotton at the Calhoun farm. Not once, but three times! After all the trials we been through with that place, he wants to go and kick a hornet's nest!"

"Samuel?" I leaned toward him, hoping he'd make eye contact. "Is that true?"

He shrugged.

"Why?" I asked. "Why would you do that?"

"I just wanted to see for myself."

"See what?"

He shrugged again. I glanced at Hannah, wondering what was eating away at him. "See what?" I tried again.

"The life my other half is supposed to have."

It was dead silent in the room for a good minute. I sat back in my chair and wondered what I was supposed to say to that. Samuel continued picking at splinters from the table, glaring at them like they were the source of his anger.

"Just ain't right," he said. "Half of me should be walking around that farm like any other white person, able to say hidey to who I want to, look any man in the eye I want to, or just walk across any piece of land I so desire. Half of me is free." He looked at me sideways. "Should be, anyhow. I got just as much Percy Calhoun's blood in my veins as Chester."

I couldn't help but see the caramel-skinned little boy I'd first met years before sitting at the table with me, scarred from years of beatings dealt out by Chester Calhoun. The first time I'd met Samuel, he was stealing a chicken to feed himself and Hannah. I'd covered for him, but I'd seen the way Chester tormented him. So much of Samuel's anger and suspicion of me made sense once I'd learned about the abuse Chester was doling out on both him and Hannah. I'd felt his wrath myself, and I'd never forget it. I still suffered occasional headaches from the concussion Chester had given me.

"Samuel," Hannah said, covering his hand. "God made you in His own image, so you ain't half of anything. You're *all* His. Can't nobody take that from you. And you're going to grow up to be the man He wants you to be. Maybe He never meant you to be colored or white. Maybe He meant you to be the glue that's gone hold things together. So you don't let nobody tell you who you are. You ain't half Calhoun. You ain't half colored, or half white either. You's *all* Samuel."

I wasn't sure her words sank in, but I sure hoped they did. Underneath all that anger and mistrust, was a boy who loved his mother something fierce. I prayed God would give him peace and keep him from stirring up trouble with the Calhouns. I wanted to reassure Hannah, but

I shared her apprehension. I'd have to keep my eye out for Samuel whenever I went to visit James and Emma Rae. Maybe he'd listen to me, if not his mother.

I was certain no good could possibly come from his being anywhere near that farm.

And I was right.

Monday morning, long before sunup, Dr. Fisher woke me from a deep sleep. We'd learned pretty quick that early morning calls put Ms. Harmon in a bad temper for the rest of the day, so I'd installed a little bell attached to a string that ran out of my window and down the side of the house. He'd only had to use it a few times. Most early morning calls he just handled without me, but he knew I'd never let him hear the end of it if he didn't bring me along when it was time for Emma Rae to deliver. So when I heard the bell's light jingle, I jumped out of bed and dressed quick as lightning.

Dr. Fisher met me on the porch with a lamp. "Got a call from the Calhoun farm," he said. "Sounds like we best hurry. James says Emma Rae's progressing pretty fast."

That was all well and good, but Dr. Fisher didn't have a hurry-up bone in his body. He still drove the same ambling pace down the road, no matter what the emergency was. Sometimes I fussed at him, but it didn't do a lick of good. So I bottled up my frustration as he made his way down the dark roads.

By the time we reached the Calhoun place, I could make out the dim edge of dawn outlining the horizon. I'd hoped we were heading to James and Emma Rae's house, but Dr. Fisher parked the car in front of the big house. Putting aside my discomfort, I followed him up the front steps, across the front porch, and through the open door.

Mr. Calhoun stood just inside holding the door open for us. Our eyes met, and like always, I felt a shiver go down my spine as I saw an older version of Chester looking back at me. It never once failed. In one instant, I'd see his face contort into Chester's snarl, hear his gravelly voice swearing and threatening, feel the splitting pain in my head. But as quick as I'd see it, I'd close my eyes and turn away from Mr. Calhoun. That had been our greeting for the past four years.

James appeared, and ushered us up the stairs to the bedroom where Emma Rae was being tended to by her mother. Mrs. Calhoun jumped up from her chair beside the bed and pushed a tangled mess of auburn hair away from her face. "Oh, thank the good Lord you're all here now. Ruby, why don't you take little Abner and keep him outta the middle of things. Dr. Fisher, I have a fresh pitcher of water and clean rags ready."

Emma Rae pinched her face up and tried to talk between her labored breaths. "No, Mother...I want...Ruby with me."

I went to her side with one of the clean rags, dipped it in the pitcher on the bedside table, and gently wiped the sweat from her brow. "Don't worry. I'm right here."

Dr. Fisher's deep voice carried authority with it. "I'll be needing Miss Ruby. Why don't you take the child down to his father?"

I could practically feel Mrs. Calhoun's icy stare on my back. She called to Abner, and I heard the door close behind me. I smiled down at Emma Rae while Dr. Fisher did a quick exam. She gripped my left hand, while I continued to dab at her forehead with my right. "Just take deep breaths. You can do this."

She pushed out a string of hard breaths. Then during a short break in the pain, she said, "Will you pray?"

So I called down blessings on her and that little baby. I asked for their protection, for a quick and uneventful delivery. And then I held onto her as she pushed with all her might.

By the time Emma Rae lay sleeping with another baby boy in her arms, the sun was well above the horizon and streaming into the bedroom like it couldn't wait to greet such a precious creature. I washed up and told Dr. Fisher I'd be sticking around the rest of the day to help

Emma Rae and her mother. So he packed away all his supplies and headed back into town.

Since Emma Rae and the baby were asleep, and the men had returned
to the fields, I took the opportunity for a quiet walk around the property
to give thanks for my answered prayers. Heading across the grass toward
the barn, my mind full of thanks and praise, I could hardly contain my
joy at my new little nephew. I began singing 'All Hail the Pow'r of Jesus's
Name,' lifting my hands as I walked.

As I rounded the side of the barn, I saw James and Mr. Calhoun
standing with another man talking, so I quit singing. I was about to turn
and head the other direction, when James shifted to one side, and I got a
clear view of the third man with them. It was Chester Calhoun.

Before I could catch myself I gasped, but none of them seemed to
have heard me. They just kept right on talking while I stood frozen. Fear
snatched all my reason away, and I couldn't think of what to do. If I ran,
he'd see me. If I stood still, he'd see me. What if he came after me again?
My insides went cold, and goosebumps spread over my whole body. I
could hear his voice in my head, dripping with venom. *Look at you.
Treating them Negroes like they's equal to you. Like you don't know no better.*

I had to move. I took one step backward, as slowly as I could. Then
another one. I couldn't turn around 'cause I was sure as soon as I did,
he'd be on me, kicking me and beating me over the head. So I took two
more steps backward. Then two more. Finally, I was around the corner
of the barn, and I let out my breath. I leaned against the side of the barn,
bent over, and heaved like I'd just run a mile. My heart beat so loud in
my ears I couldn't hardly think.

Lord, please help me, I prayed. *I can't move. Help me.*

The Holy Spirit moved through me, and my fear quieted enough for
my reason to return. I slowed my breathing, and I stilled the voice in my
mind screaming for me to run. When everything was finally quiet, I
prayed again, asking God what to do.

As clear as day, I heard a whisper in the breeze. *Samuel.*

Samuel was on that farm somewhere. And I had to find him immediately. I took off running around the other side of the barn and toward the cotton field on the far west side of the property. Only the colored workers were supposed to go in those fields, especially when Chester had been running things. But I'd have to take a chance.

I reached the field in a couple of minutes and searched all over for the familiar caramel-colored skin that stood out among the rest. I had to force my mind to slow down and look carefully at each person out there. I ran up and down a few rows. I even asked a couple of the colored workers if they knew him, but the closest I got to an answer was an old man who shook his head and kept on tugging at the cotton plants.

I ran back toward the big house, thinking maybe I'd been wrong. Maybe I hadn't heard what I thought I'd heard. Usually, God's voice was as clear as could be. Quiet, but clear. Maybe my fear had made me imagine things.

I was about fifty yards from the barn when I saw Chester emerge from the house. I stopped where I was; my feet ready to tear off in any direction but toward him. He marched over to the barn, his massive arms swinging with purpose. I held my breath, hoping he wouldn't see me and would turn toward the fields so I could hightail it down to James's house and hide. But he held his course, so I waited, still barely breathing.

Yanking open the large side door, he stepped inside. I took a few steps back, trying to remember just which direction James's house was in. I looked around and got my bearings. South. I needed to run south. Past the barn.

CHAPTER THREE

Matthew

Early Monday morning, I walked Vanessa over to her parents' car while our folks said their goodbyes. She looked up at me with some apprehension. "Something's on your mind. I can tell. Is it the interviews?"

I nodded, grateful for the excuse. I hadn't told her about my attempt to speak with Ruby. "I want to make sure I can provide for us, is all. Father's just waiting for me to botch things up."

She smiled and ran her hand along the collar of my shirt. "I'm sure you'll do great. And your father will be very proud of you. You've worked hard to get yourself here, and everything's going to work out fine. You'll see."

I was reminded again of why I loved her. She knew me well enough to know when something was off, but she didn't push. She listened to me, encouraged me without criticism. She'd make a good wife and mother someday. I was blessed to have had her love for these past few years. My family adored her, especially Mary. We were a good match. *A good match.*

"I'll call you in a few days when I've finished with the interviews," I said. "Then I can start looking for a place for us to live."

Her eyes lit up. "Oh! Nashville is going to be wonderful!"

I kissed her on the forehead, and helped her into the car as her parents approached. I shook Mr. Paschal's hand and told him I'd see him soon. He wished me luck before climbing inside. Then I walked over to Mother. Together we watched them drive away.

Mother's eyes were damp as I put my arm over her shoulder. "Suppose it's my turn now," I said.

She squeezed my waist tight. "When can we expect you home again?"

"Soon, I promise. I'll be around a lot more often. I already told Mary I'd go see her at school. I know I've been a lousy son and brother, but I'm going to make it right, I swear."

"Oh honey, I can't tell you how happy that makes me. Why don't you come back next weekend after your interviews so we can all celebrate together?"

I grabbed my suitcase from beside the front door. I wanted so badly to make her happy, I might have agreed to just about anything at that point. "That sounds like a fine idea."

Her smile spread across her face, reassuring me all would work out as it should. I hugged her goodbye, walked over to my car, and threw the last suitcase in the back. Then I climbed inside and cranked it up. Only one more stop before heading to Nashville. It was time to make things right with Ruby, and this time I wasn't going to let her walk away.

"Why, Matthew Doyle!" Mrs. Fisher shouted through the screen door at me after I'd knocked a couple of times. "I haven't seen you in these parts in ages!"

She pulled open the door for me to step inside the foyer, but she didn't even wait for me to get my whole body inside before she threw her great big arms around me. I did my best to return the hug and still maintain the ability to breathe.

"Hidey, Mrs. Fisher," I managed.

She let go of me and shooed me through the foyer toward the sweet smells coming from the kitchen. "Come on in here and get you something good to eat. I got all kinds of breads and cookies sitting around just waiting on some young fella to finish 'em off."

"Mrs. Fisher, I really can't stay long," I protested. She kept herding me into the kitchen. I had to admit the smell was making my mouth water. Maybe I could just grab a few bites.

"Take a seat," she said, and placed a plateful of cookies on the table. "Have as many as you want."

I shook my head and laughed. "Thank you, kindly. They do look delicious." I sat down and helped myself to an oatmeal cookie while she gathered up two loaves of bread and another plate of cookies, and brought those over as well.

"To what do I owe the pleasure of your visit today?" she asked, plopping all the food in front of me.

"I was hoping you might be able to tell me where I could find Miss Ruby."

"Well, let's see here. She and Dr. Fisher tore out of here before sunup this morning, heading over to the Calhoun farm. Emma Rae was delivering her baby, you know. I reckon Dr. Fisher got back about a half hour ago and said Miss Ruby was staying at the farm for the day to help Emma Rae."

I shoved a cookie in my mouth and wondered if maybe it would be better to wait for another chance to talk to Ruby. The thought of heading back out to the Calhoun place wasn't appealing, especially with a brand new baby and Emma Rae needing her attention. I supposed I could come home the next weekend as I'd promised Mother. But I felt uneasy about waiting. I'd put off making things right for far too long, and if I waited another week, I might just talk myself out of it again.

I took a handful of cookies off the plate and pushed myself up from the table. "Well, thank you for the delicious cookies, Mrs. Fisher."

"You running off already, son?"

"Yes, ma'am. I got to head on up to Nashville today, so I should get moving. Give Dr. Fisher my best if you don't mind."

She came over and drowned me in her arms again. "I just praise the good Lord every time I see you looking so fine and healthy. You're a walking miracle, you know it?"

That was one way of putting things. "Yes, ma'am."

"You take care of yourself, you hear?"

"Yes, ma'am."

I managed to slide out of her arms and out the door. Driving toward the Calhoun farm again, an uneasy feeling worked its way through me. It was going to be hard enough to face Ruby and the mistakes of my past without having to revisit that place. I considered turning north the entire time I was driving. I kept telling myself I could just talk to her the next weekend, but something, some kind of force I couldn't explain, held my course steady all the way to the Calhoun place.

As soon as I pulled in front of the main house, that uneasiness in my gut multiplied a thousand times. People milled around the large oak trees in front of the house, and parked down between the main house and the barn were the sheriff's and coroner's cars.

I stepped out into the brisk breeze, figuring it was best to hang back and see if I could learn what was going on. So I meandered over to one of the trees where a couple of men were talking. I assumed they were some of Calhoun's field hands or sharecroppers from the surrounding land. When I approached, the older one tipped his hat to me.

"Mornin' fellas," I said. "Looks like quite a fuss going on 'round here."

"Sure is," the younger one said. He was filthy, covered in earth and sweat. He pointed toward the barn. "They all in a mess down there. If you got business with Calhoun, probably best to come back 'nother day."

"Any idea what happened?" I asked.

The older man mashed his white eyebrows down low on his forehead. "Some poor fella's died down at the barn, best we can tell. Someone said it's Calhoun's eldest son. We heard the old man hollerin' just a while ago. Sounded awful tore up."

The man had to be wrong. Chester wouldn't be on the farm! Calhoun had kicked him off the property and out of the family. Surely it couldn't be Chester? But I also couldn't help thinking that if it was indeed him, a part of me was glad he'd finally gotten what he deserved.

"Either of you seen James Graves?" I asked. I figured he'd know something.

The older one pointed off toward the barn again. "He's down there with 'em. Like he said, you'd do best to come back 'nother day."

I tipped my hat and bid them good day, then I wandered across the yard closer to the barn. Another group of men and women were standing nearby, the women clicking their tongues and shaking their heads. They were plenty sorry for Calhoun losing his son just when they seemed to be working out their differences. So I figured it must be true. I was about to turn around and leave, having made up my mind the conversation with Ruby would just have to wait. But one of their comments stopped me in my tracks.

"...just find it hard to believe is all, that a young girl like that could kill a full grown man."

A cold dread worked its way up my back and into my chest. I turned to the lady who'd spoken. "Excuse me, ma'am. Did I hear you right? Did you say a young girl killed Chester Calhoun?"

There was no mistaking the eagerness in her eyes. She stepped closer, lowering her voice like she was sharing a fantastic scandal. "Oh, yes. I saw her come out of the barn with the sheriff, and she had blood all over her hands and clothes. Looked a fright!"

"Do you know who the girl is?"

"I've seen her around before. Think the last name's Graves..."

Words continued to spill from her lips, but I didn't hear the rest of what she said. Imagining Chester attacking Ruby again, my blood went white hot and I ran straight to the barn, ignoring whatever else the woman was trying to tell me. I searched the area around the sheriff's car and the ambulance, but no one was there. Heading around to the back of the barn, I encountered the commotion.

Several more workers from around the farm, as well as neighbors from the area, were standing around talking in hushed voices, their eyes darting over toward Ruby. She was seated on a hay bale beside James, her eyes dazed and staring out into the fields. Her hands were stained red, and blood was smeared on her dress and across her cheek. My throat knotted up. I wanted to rush over to her, but I was afraid she wouldn't want to see me, and I had no idea what to say.

James leaned forward with his elbows resting on his knees, and his right leg bouncing up and down as he looked around at all the people gathering. Just as I was about to walk over to them, the back door flew open and slammed against the side of the barn. A deputy stepped backward through the door, followed by Sheriff Gary Peterson. I only knew him a bit from hearing Father talk about him. He had a reputation for being tough but fair. He and the deputy, who I recognized as a former classmate, carried a body between them. It was covered with a large blanket, an arm swinging lifelessly from underneath it.

With cryptic expressions they walked the body over to the ambulance and loaded it into the back. Then the sheriff went over to talk to Ruby. Her eyes were wide, and she shook her head vehemently throughout their exchange. I edged closer to them so I could hear properly.

"James, soon as she's up to it, I'm gonna need her to come to the office and explain all this in detail," the sheriff said.

James nodded. "I'll take care of it."

Sheriff Peterson stared down at Ruby for a long moment, studying her carefully. Then he spat some tobacco on the ground and headed back inside the barn. I came over to James and knelt down beside him. He looked at me like he didn't know who I was.

"What can I do to help?" I said.

His face flushed pink. "I don't know. I can't even think straight."

I looked over at Ruby, and she met my gaze with red-rimmed eyes. She covered her mouth with a bloodstained hand.

"What happened?" I asked.

She shook her head, and a tear slipped down her cheek.

James jumped up and began pacing, his boots kicking up dust. "We don't need this right now, Ruby," he growled. "Not this." He bent over and glared at her. "I swear you're determined to destroy this family."

"Hey," I said. "That's not gonna help anything."

He turned his glare on me. "How does this involve you? You think you can show up after all these years and jump into our business?"

I stood, and we faced each other at our full heights. "I just want to help, James. I ain't the enemy. Tell me what I can do to help."

He gestured toward Ruby and let out a frustrated puff of air. "You know as well as I do there ain't nothin' to be done with her. She's pig-headed and determined to do everything she can to get the white sheets after her! Now look what's happened!" He stepped closer and lowered his voice to an intense whisper. "You know Chester's one of 'em. No telling' what they're gonna do now!"

I looked down at Ruby, and her face drained of all color. She shook her head and whispered. "I couldn't...I tried, James. He just came at me...and I couldn't—"

Just then, the sheriff walked over holding something in a piece of cloth. He lowered his hands so Ruby could see. It was a medium-sized pocketknife covered in blood. "Miss Ruby, do you recognize this?"

She stared at it, her eyes widening like she was horrified. She looked up at the sheriff then down at the knife again. "I...I think...it's his maybe." Tears flowed steadily down her cheeks now.

I knew something wasn't right, but I couldn't scratch that itch in the back of my mind. "Sheriff, why don't James and I take her down to his place, clean her up and let her calm down. We'll bring her into town later today to tell you everything."

The sheriff looked at me like he thought I was up to something, but then he surveyed the growing crowd. "Guess we can do that. This place is 'bout to turn into a circus anyway." He turned to James. "You get her down to the office this afternoon, and let's get this cleared up. The sooner the better. For everyone."

"Yes, sir," James said, taking Ruby by the arm and helping her stand. She grimaced and clutched her side.

"What's wrong?" I asked. "Are you hurt?"

She shook her head, but it took her a moment to get her breath back. "Just some bruised ribs. I'm all right."

Her eyes met mine, and I held her gaze long enough for my chest to stir. "Maybe we should get Dr. Fisher."

"No," she said. "Really, I can tell they're only bruised. I want to get away from here."

I decided to drop it for the moment. As we pushed our way through the crowd, I noticed the sheriff watching us. He spat again, and then tipped his hat and stepped back into the barn.

Ruby sat in a rocking chair by the fireplace, staring at the fire James had built moments earlier. She clutched the blanket around her shoulders and shivered like it was the dead of winter. James and I stood in the dining area watching her and glancing at each other every minute or so.

I finally broke the eerie silence. "What in blazes happened up there?"

James closed his eyes and shook his head. Then he took a seat at the table and motioned for me to join him. "I ain't rightly sure. I was working in the cotton field when Luke Dalton runs up to me and says Ruby's hurt or something. I take off with him to the barn, and when we get inside, Ruby's sitting a few feet away from Chester's body. Blood's all over both of 'em, and Ruby's sitting there, still as a statue..." James ran his hand through his hair. "I go over and ask her if she's all right." Leaning forward, he held my gaze. "Then she looks right at me and says, 'I did it. I killed him.' Says he came at her just like last time and she killed him."

"So he did attack her again."

James raised an eyebrow. "Did you know about him being the one that beat her back several years ago?"

I nodded. "Didn't you?"

"No," he said, rubbing the back of his neck. "She never would say, and Mother said to quit asking her about it...Uh-oh, Mother. Guess I better let her know what's going on." He stood and began pacing again, looking like he couldn't decide whom he was mad at. "Sure makes sense of some things, though. I knew them white sheets were behind her getting beat up for helping those Negro folks. Looks like they got something else to hold against her now."

"But why would the Klan attack her again?" I wondered out loud. "She ain't still hanging around them folks, is she?"

"Lord only knows. I don't ask, and she don't say. But I guarantee you this all has something to do with them."

I looked over at Ruby and a wave of guilt washed over me. If I hadn't turned my back on her, maybe I could've been there somehow. Maybe I could've protected her from Chester. But I knew it wouldn't have made a lick of difference. There was no protecting her from herself. I'd known that when she was just fourteen years old.

I couldn't change the past, and I couldn't make up for being absent from her life. But maybe I could find a way to be there for her now.

"What can I do to help?" I asked.

James stopped pacing and sighed. "I have to get back to the farm. There's equipment lying around all over the place. The field workers are all standing around doing nothing but chewing over all this gossip, and the negro workers scattered to the wind as soon as the law showed up. I gotta go get that place back in order."

"I can stay with Ruby," I said.

"Can you drive her to town later and stay with her while she talks to the sheriff?"

"I got an interview in Nashville tomorrow. I was supposed to drive up there today. But the interview ain't till the afternoon. I reckon I can drive up tonight or early tomorrow morning."

"I can't thank you enough. It's bad enough I got to go put the farm back together, but I've hardly even seen Emma Rae and the baby at all today."

"The baby!" Ruby hollered from the other room. She shot up from the rocking chair in a panic. "I'm supposed to be taking care of the baby!"

James rushed over to her and wrapped the blanket back around her shoulders as she fought against him. "Now Ruby, I'll take care of Emma Rae and the baby. You just stay here with Matthew and let him take you to see the sheriff. We'll get all this straightened out today, and everything will be just fine."

She looked over at me with a deep sadness behind her dark eyes. A sinking feeling in my gut told me she knew as well as I did that none of this was going to be fine. But I pushed that feeling aside, and gave her a supportive smile. I had to believe that once she explained everything to the sheriff, and he understood the whole story, she'd be able to put this mess behind her, and maybe everything would be all right.

James shot me one more uncertain look before heading out the door. My stomach twisted as I realized I had no idea what to do. I barely knew the woman across the room from me. Suddenly embarrassed, I shoved my hands in my pockets. "I reckon you'll want to get cleaned up. Why don't I get some water warmed up for you?"

She nodded.

"Should I go fetch your mother?" I asked.

"She...she doesn't live on the farm here anymore. She and Asa have a little place out on Sand Hill."

"Asa?"

Her mouth gave the faintest smile. "They got married a couple years back."

"Oh. That's nice." It struck me how absurd pleasantries sounded at the moment. "I'll fetch you some water so you can clean up. Then I'll go see about helping out while you change."

I went out the back door and drew a couple of buckets of water from the well, brought them inside and set them beside the washtub in the kitchen. I turned and waited for her to move toward me, but she didn't budge. Just stared.

"You all right?" I asked.

She nodded, but a tear slipped down her cheek. "It just happened so fast."

"What exactly happened? What made him come after you again like that?"

She swiped at the tear, smearing a faint streak of pink blood. "I don't know...Just...I went in the barn, and there he was. He was in a state, hollering and cursing about finishing me off this time."

Her shoulders shook as she dropped her head into her hands. I felt like I might split in two. Didn't seem to be a thing in the world I could do for her. "Listen, I'm gonna step out while you clean yourself up. But I won't go too far. You call for me if you need anything. Then I'll get you over to the sheriff, and you can tell him exactly what happened. Then you can put all this behind you."

Ruby lifted her eyes to the ceiling, a hopeless expression on her face. "Oh, it's never going to be over. Mr. Calhoun let everybody know. He's going to see to it that his son gets justice."

CHAPTER FOUR

Ruby

As I sat in the chair in Sheriff Peterson's office, my mind turned in circles. Clutching the cup of water in my hands, I tried to block out the images from that morning. I focused instead on the books off to the side of his desk that were stacked on the floor, the seven or eight boxes with papers in them, and a large map of Cullman County on the wall above. I traced the red lines of the map with my eyes.

But then the lines started resembling rivulets of blood. I closed my eyes and prayed for help.

"Well now, Miss Ruby," Sheriff Peterson said as he came into the office with a cup of coffee. "Let's get down to it and get you out of here quick as we can."

I turned in my seat to face him across the desk, nodding my head in agreement. My throat was raw, and I had no desire to form words. He took a sip of his coffee then leaned back and laced his fingers across his chest. My stomach twisted and rolled as he looked right at me.

"So, you feeling like you can explain everything to me now?"

"Yes, sir," I said. "Where do you want me to start?"

"Just start from the beginning, honey. What were you doing at the Calhoun place this morning?"

"Well, Dr. Fisher and I went out there to help Emma Rae deliver her baby. She's my brother's wife, you know." He nodded and kept on looking at me like he wanted more. "Well, the baby was fine, and Emma Rae was resting, so I decided to go outside for a bit and get some fresh air. I walked around for a while. Then I decided to look for James, and I went into the barn. I looked around and didn't see him, so I turned to leave, but Chester was standing between me and the door."

My heart raced. His eyes narrowed, like he knew I'd left something out. I clasped my hands together in my lap and prayed again for the strength to find some way to tell the truth without actually telling the truth. *Lord, I hate lying. I'm so sorry. But it just has to be all right this one time.*

"Then what happened?" Sheriff Peterson asked.

"He said I needed to be taught a lesson. Said he knew I went out to Colony to look after...colored folks...and he called me some vile names." My cheeks flushed, and I hoped he'd believe it was because of my recollecting such harsh language. "I told him he'd best leave me alone, and I tried to run for the back door of the barn. But he caught me by my hair and flung me around onto the ground."

He nodded his head and offered a "Hmmm."

"Then he kicked me in the ribs. I couldn't breathe for a moment or two. He yanked me up by my hair again, slapped me, and threw me against the hay bales. And quick as I could blink he was coming at me, so I screamed and kicked at him as hard as I could."

I tried not to look directly at Sheriff Peterson's eyes. He leaned forward in his seat, and it creaked real loud. "Did you see the knife?"

I shook my head. My throat tightened, and I wasn't sure I could talk much longer. "Not till...after."

"Then what happened?"

"Well, he kind of fell onto me. I was still pushing and kicking at him with all my might, and he rolled off to the side onto another bale. That's when I saw he had the knife in his chest."

"So did you stab him?"

"No, sir. At least, I wasn't trying to. I guess I may have kicked it or something in the tussle."

"Then what happened?"

"He fell onto the floor, and he pulled the knife out. He was bleeding all over everything. He kept on hollering at me that he was going to kill me. I didn't know what to do. He fell over again, and I tried to help him. I tried to stop the bleeding, but he grabbed me again and slapped me." My voice steadied somewhat as I got to the parts that I knew were the truth. "He told me not to touch him, but then he passed out so I tried again to stop the bleeding. I think that's when Mr. Dalton came in. He tried to help me, but we couldn't save him. Then he went and got help."

Sheriff Peterson leaned back in his chair and laced his fingers together again. "Miss Graves, seems to me like you was defending yourself, and you did a mighty fine job considering." His thick black eyebrows knitted together. "Just a thing or two I don't feel right sure about. Now, you said Chester Calhoun told you he was going to teach you a lesson for…" He glanced down at his notepad. "…Going over to the Colony to look after colored folks." He glanced back up at me. "How would he have known about your activities there?"

I dropped my gaze. "I'm not sure."

"I see. And lastly, Miss Graves. Chester Calhoun was a very large man. And yet, you somehow managed to fend him off. You must be pretty strong for a young lady."

The bottom fell away from my stomach. He knew. Maybe not everything. But he knew something wasn't right. I shivered. "I guess, I was just so scared that…I don't know…I don't know how I did it."

"Well, I may need to ask you a few more questions over the next coupla days. You do what you can to make sure you tell me everything. And if you think of something that might be important, be sure get in touch with me."

"Yes, sir," I said. I pushed myself out of the chair, relieved to finally be getting out of there.

But as I went through the doorway, Sheriff Peterson called out to me again. I turned to see him come around to the front of his desk. "I know this is a lot to take in, Ruby. I want you to know that the best thing you can do is be honest, tell everything you remember, and stick to the truth."

He'd said that twice. Maybe he didn't believe me after all. Maybe no one would believe me, and all this was for nothing.

I got into Matthew's car outside the sheriff's office and folded my hands in my lap. I gazed down at my feet, wishing I could make myself so small that no one see would me. I didn't want to cry anymore, but I couldn't seem to stop. Something was bound to erupt out of me sooner rather than later if I couldn't get control of myself.

Matthew got in beside me, saying nothing as he cranked up the car. He'd hardly said much of anything since James had left us at the house a few hours earlier. But he looked at me every once in a while. Looked at me with this mix of wonder and heartache. It didn't last long; just a moment or two. I figured he was working out in his mind the quickest way to be rid of me again.

"I'm sorry about Sunday afternoon," I said.

"You ain't got nothing in this world to apologize to me for, Ruby." He clenched the steering wheel, released it, then clenched again. "It's me that owes you an apology. Been trying to find a way to say I was sorry for some time now, but I just can't seem to do it." He took a glance over at me. "I mean it. I'm awful sorry about the way I treated you after the tornado. I was wrong. I aim to do whatever I can to make it up to you."

That released a flood of tears, which was just plain humiliating. I swiped as many of them as I could. He handed me a handkerchief, and I managed to catch some more. He waited for me to get myself under control again, watching me the whole time with curious eyes.

"Where do you want me to drive you?" he asked. "Back to James's house?"

"No, I think it's best if I go home. Can you drive me back to Hance-ville? Back to Ms. Harmon's place?"

"You sure?" he asked. I nodded. "All right then."

He pulled out onto the main road, heading south. I let the buildings blur in my vision. My eyes ached. I leaned my head back against the seat and closed them against the pain. "Thank you," I said, not sure if it was even loud enough to hear.

Once again, Matthew seemed content to let the silence sit between us, and I was grateful for it. Seemed like the wrong time for amends, but it was hard to deal with the present without dealing with the past. I wasn't eager to face either one. So I tried to send my mind off on a more pleasant path of remembrances. Like when I was little, and Daddy would take the boys and me down to the creek not far from our house, and we'd fish and swim all afternoon. There wasn't anything in this world as refreshing as sinking down into that cool water on a hot afternoon.

But those thoughts were only happy for a short time. They always led to sadness eventually, wondering when I might see Henry next, or what life might've been like had Daddy lived. I certainly wouldn't have gotten myself into such a fix as I was in. I hoped and prayed with all my might that Sheriff Peterson had accepted my explanation of the events. If anyone found out the truth...well, I couldn't even think about that.

About that time, we pulled up to Ms. Harmon's place, and Matthew shut off the car. He turned in his seat and faced me with a grim expression. "Ruby, what happened out there this morning? Why did Chester come after you again? You mixed up in something?"

"What? No. I mean, I'm not mixed up in anything. I just went into the barn and there he was, and he attacked me." I clenched my hands to stop their shaking.

"Something don't seem right. You telling everything the way it happened?"

"You think I'm lying?"

"No, now I didn't say nothing like that. But…it just don't make sense, is all. I mean, has Chester come after you since that first time?"

I shook my head. My face flushed red hot. I needed to get out of that car before everything came flying out of me. Flinging the door open, I took a huge gulp of air as I clambered out. Then I shut the door and leaned back against it. A searing pain shot through my head, the same one I got every couple of months since the concussion.

Matthew came around the car, looking at me like I was about to keel over. "You all right? You need me to fetch Dr. Fisher?"

"I'm fine. I just need to lie down for a while. I don't want to talk about this anymore." Walking past him, I started up the front porch steps. His footsteps followed close behind, and when I reached the top, I turned around. "I'm fine, really Matthew." He stopped just below me. "Thank you for taking me into town, and for driving me home. Thank you for…well, for being here. And I accept your apology. All's forgiven." I turned and crossed the porch to the front door.

"Wait a minute," he said. "Ain't there anything else I can do? I don't want to just drop you off and leave you like this."

"You have an interview to get to, right? A job in Nashville or something?"

He shoved his hands in his pockets. "Right."

"You should put your mind on your future. I hope you find what you're looking for."

His face fell. He seemed like he wanted to say more, but I knew if I didn't lie down soon, I'd pass out from exhaustion. So I went inside, and left him standing there. Maybe we'd both be able to move on and forget the past. I wanted to fall asleep and forget the present as well.

Ms. Harmon was flustered by my lack of information and desire to go to bed, but she eventually quit asking questions long enough for me to escape to my room. By the time I slid under the sheets I felt almost desperate for sleep, and it wasn't even seven o'clock in the evening. But as soon as my head hit the pillow, and my eyes closed out the world, all I could do was think about what had happened that morning.

I could hear the shouts of anger, smell the hay and feed, feel the scrape of the dirt against my cheek as I fell. I saw Chester slump to the ground, over and over. I'd tried to save him. Hadn't I? I'd prayed for the power to heal him, to stop the blood. But I'd felt nothing of God's presence in that barn. Maybe it was my fault. Maybe I hadn't really wanted to save him.

I tossed and turned with that weight on my mind for long into the night before I finally fell asleep, still begging God for answers and forgiveness. When I awoke the next morning, I heard my mother's voice drifting around downstairs, mixed in with Ms. Harmon's. My stomach tightened as I thought of how I'd explain the mess I'd gotten myself into this time. Already I could hear the lecture and see the disappointed shake of her head. But I knew she'd also hold me close, and eventually she'd tell me everything would be all right.

So I pushed myself out of bed, washed my face and changed my dress. My hair was hopeless on the best of days, but especially this morning. I gathered it best I could and plaited it down one side. That would have to suffice. As I reached the top of the stairs, I heard Uncle Asa's deep voice, and my spirits lifted.

I practically ran down the stairs and straight into his arms. "Oh, Asa, I'm so glad you're here!" I soaked up the warmth of his hug before gathering my wits and finding Mother. I hugged her too, though it was more reserved. "You too, Mother. I'm so glad to see you."

When I pulled away from Mother, I could see the slight disapproval in Ms. Harmon's gaze, but I didn't care. I'd work on the finer points of being a proper lady some other time. I looked between Mother and Asa, both afraid and relieved. "I suppose you've heard?"

Mother held onto my shoulders and looked me over from head to toe. "James told us what happened yesterday. Are you hurt?"

"I'm fine. A bit sore is all."

"Oh, Ruby," she said, pulling me into her arms again. "Thank the Lord you're all right. But mercy, why can't you stay out of trouble?"

Asa chuckled behind me. "Too much Graves blood in that one." Mother and I separated, and she glared at him. "'Course, from what I understand that troublesome gene may be stronger on your side of the family. Those Kellum brothers—"

Mother cleared her throat and darted her eyes at Ms. Harmon. Asa clamped his mouth shut. Ms. Harmon raised an eyebrow. "I'll just go and make sure breakfast is ready. You all take your time. Miss Ruby can join us when she's ready." Then she disappeared into the kitchen.

Mother and I took our seats on the sofa. Asa moved beside Mother, but kept on standing. As soon as he was out of her line of sight, he caught my eye and mouthed, "You all right?"

I shook my head sadly. "Mother, I'm sorry if I've caused you any worry."

She leaned toward me and lowered her voice. "What exactly happened out there yesterday? James says this man, Chester Calhoun, was the one who attacked you before. Is that true?"

I nodded and looked up at Asa. I hoped he saw the gratitude in my eyes for his silence after so many years. "I don't know how to explain everything. It all happened so fast."

"Well," she said, "I don't know how you were able to fend that man off except by the grace of God. He's facing his judgment now."

My skin prickled and I looked up at Asa again. I wished I could talk to him alone, especially about why God wouldn't heal Chester, but that would just upset Mother. Even after years of knowing the truth, she was still clearly uncomfortable with my gift. She never once asked about it, and I knew better than to mention it. But Asa would understand. There had to be some way to get him alone and talk things over with him.

A few minutes later there was a knock at the front door, and when Ms. Harmon opened it, I heard Matthew's voice asking after me. Ms.

Harmon showed him into the sitting room. He was wearing a dark suit with his hair combed back away from his eyes. The changes in him were subtle—lines around the corners of his eyes, a lift to his shoulders that commanded respect. The boy I'd cared for had grown into a man.

Ms. Harmon gave me the warning glance she gave the other girls when one of them had a gentleman caller. *No nonsense in my house.* I didn't know how she could think such a thing at a time like that, especially with my mother and Asa right there in the room. I reckoned it was just habit by then.

Ms. Harmon excused herself again, and Matthew greeted Mother and Asa before turning to me. "Just wanted to look in on you before I headed up to Nashville. How are you this morning? Did you get any sleep?"

"I managed a little," I said. I figured reassurances were the quickest means for allowing him to escape.

"Is there anything I can do for you?"

"No, I'll be all right. I'll head over to Dr. Fisher's office in a bit to make myself useful. I want to go and check on Emma Rae and the baby later."

Mother huffed. "Now that's just plain silly. You need your rest after such an ordeal. You get a bite to eat and go back to bed. I'll help Emma Rae with the baby today. Besides, that may not be the place for you to be right now."

"Mother, really, I want to get my life back to normal as soon as I can."

Another knock on the front door sent Ms. Harmon blustering through the room, mumbling about a circus. When she pulled the door open, she gasped. I looked up as Sheriff Peterson stepped inside with a look on his face that sped up my heart.

"Morning," he said to the room, clearing his throat. Then he looked directly at me. "I'm afraid I got some difficult news, Miss Ruby. Seems Mr. Calhoun's rather upset about things. Mrs. Calhoun, too. They been over at my office this morning causing a stir and making some pretty serious claims against you."

"Like what?" I asked.

Sheriff Peterson rubbed his hat between his fingers. "Well, first, I ought to tell you that I'm going to have to place you under arrest—"

The room erupted, everyone shouting over each other and wanting to know how this was even possible. Mother about came unglued, while Asa and Matthew peppered the sheriff with questions about what the Calhouns had said and declarations of how absurd this was becoming.

It took a few minutes for everyone to calm themselves, and I realized they were all looking at me. "I...I don't understand," I said, my voice faltering. "Wh-what are you arresting me for?"

He let out a long sigh before he said the worst thing I could've imagined. "Murder."

Matthew stepped between the sheriff and me. "Now wait a minute. You don't actually believe she *murdered* Chester, do you?"

"Don't matter what I believe. I got to follow the law. And for now, the way things are, this is what's got to happen."

"This is ridiculous!" Asa cried, pacing in front of the sofa. "A young woman gets attacked and defends herself, and you want to arrest her for murder? This makes no sense! What did Calhoun say? He's just upset! How can you arrest Ruby based on something he's saying?" He came to a standstill in front of the sheriff and waited expectantly.

Sheriff Peterson shook his head, glancing at me. "Listen, I know this is tough, but I don't think we need to go into all the details right this second. Let's go down to my office and talk things out in private."

As my eyes darted from face to face, my gaze fell on Ms. Harmon's horrified expression. As soon as I was out those doors and before I even arrived in Cullman, the rumors of my arrest for murder would reach the entire county. The sheriff was right about one thing. This needed to be dealt with in private.

I pushed myself up from the sofa and resolved to stay calm. I'd made a choice I would have to see through to the end, even if it meant going to prison. "All right then. Let's go."

Mother jumped up beside me and grabbed my arm. "Ruby, you can't be serious! You didn't do anything wrong."

"I have to go, Mother. What else can I do? It'll be all right." I walked over to the sheriff. "I'm ready."

Stepping forward, Matthew took hold of my shoulder and looked at me like he might just sweep me up and run me right out of there. "Don't you say nothing, you hear? You don't say nothing to nobody till you have a lawyer with you." He looked back at the sheriff. "Where's she going for now?"

"I'll have to take her over to the jail."

Matthew pulled me into his arms so fast, my breath caught in my chest. "I'll get a lawyer there right away. We'll get all this straightened out today, I swear."

He let me go, and Mother clung onto me next. Asa wrapped his arms around both of us, promising things would be all right soon. I didn't know how to tell them that this was how things had to be. That from now on, nothing would ever be the same again.

CHAPTER FIVE

Matthew

I knew it would take a little while to get Ruby through the process at the jail, so I drove as fast as I could over to Father's office in Cullman. It was a few blocks over from the courthouse, tucked into the second floor of a two-story brick building just above our family furniture store. It was in a prime spot—the stores and other offices along the main street were the more upscale businesses in town—which is why Father preferred that location. He could've saved himself a heap of money by having the store and office just two blocks over, but he refused. I heard him arguing with an officer from the bank about it once. As usual, Father made his point and stood his ground.

When I pulled up outside the store, I figured it was time to stand my ground as well. I rushed through the door to the right of the store entrance and jogged up the stairs. Era, a distant cousin on my mother's side of the family, wagged her finger at me from behind her desk, stopping me in my tracks.

She pointed to the slightly ajar door across the room, from which I could hear voices. Father was in a meeting. I'd have to wait. As much as I wanted to barge in there and get help to Ruby as quick as possible, I couldn't forget the consequences of interrupting Father during a meeting, which had been drummed into me since childhood.

"How long's he gonna be, you think?" I asked.

She shrugged her thin shoulders. "No telling. It's Mr. Adams, and they been at it for some time. Sounds serious."

I crept over to the door for a quick listen. It did indeed sound serious. Father's voice was steady, but it had that slow cadence he got when he was set on a position. "—been the same price for ten years, and I ain't paying no more than I paid last year."

"Patrick, you have to understand," came Mr. Adams's nasally drawl, "I have to increase ad prices to keep my head above water!"

"I do understand. But I'm a businessman, and I have to make the best decisions for my customers that I can. Now if I have to pay more for advertising, then I have to raise the prices of my goods. And you should know, these times are not made for raising prices. I'd be hurting my own business, just like you're doing now. Out of respect for my customers, I cannot pay another dime more for advertising."

Mr. Adams gave a great big sigh. "But Patrick—"

"Let's not squabble over it anymore," Father interrupted. "You do what you must. Raise the price of the ads. I'll do what I must. I'll take my business elsewhere. In fact, I reckon most folks around here know the Doyle name and the quality of our goods without much advertising. I might just cut that out of the budget all together and save my customers even more."

There was silence for a good minute. Then Mr. Adams caved, his voice tiny and defeated. "All right, then. I'll keep your advertising prices the same this year. But only yours. And you can't go around telling people your price is different from theirs. You do, and I'll deny it. Then we really will be done doing business together."

The chairs scraped across the floor. I figured they were shaking hands, and pictured that look of triumph on Father's face I'd seen so many times in situations like this. Sliding quietly back across the room, I took a seat in a chair across from Era. A couple of minutes later, Mr.

Adams shuffled through the door like a dog with his tail between his legs. He didn't even look at me as he mumbled a quick "Good day" to Era.

I hoped with a fresh victory on his plate, Father'd be softened up enough for my request. But in all honesty, I knew what was coming. At least, I thought I did.

I closed his office door behind me. "Morning, Father."

He barely glanced up from the papers he was reading on his desk. "I thought you left for Nashville this morning."

"Something's come up I need to talk with you about."

"Oh? What's that?"

"The sheriff just arrested Ruby." I waited for him to look up with some decent amount of concern, but he turned one paper over and started reading another. "Calhoun's saying what she done was murder, but it wasn't. It was self-defense. Now the sheriff's taking her down to the jail." I paused again. Nothing. "I want to help her out. She ain't gonna be able to pay her bond or afford a decent lawyer. Surely we can help—"

"We?" He finally looked up at me. "I thought you said *you* wanted to help her out. What's this *we* business?"

I'd only asked Father for money once in my entire life. That was enough to know I'd never do it again unless it was an absolute emergency. "Her bond hasn't been set yet. I figure it might be a couple thousand. I can cover that with my savings. But a lawyer might run more than I can muster. I'd pay you back every penny and interest if need be."

"You'd pay me back? What about Ruby? Would she pay you back?"

"No, sir. I couldn't ask her to do that."

He stood and walked around to the front of his desk, leaning back onto it as he gave me a look that made me feel about four inches tall. "So let me make sure I understand this. You want to use your pitiful savings—the money you been saving up since you were a teenager, money I gave you while working in my stores—to get Ruby out of jail and get her a lawyer? And you have no intention of Ruby paying you back a dime?"

"That about sums it up." I rubbed my hands together, trying to wipe off the sweat.

He crossed his arms and let out a long sigh. "Son, I've done the best I can to raise you with a good head on your shoulders, with a sense for smart decisions, but I have to tell you this is the dumbest thing you've ever said." Heat rushed up my neck and face, as he shook his head and kept on going. "Now, I'm going to try to pretend you didn't just come in my office and say those things, and you get yourself on up to Nashville. You need to concentrate on getting a job and providing for your future wife and family."

"Father, I respect what you're saying, but I can't leave Ruby in a bind like she is. She did a lot for me when I was sick—more than I could ever explain—and I owe it to her to look after her at a time like this. Just like she looked after me."

"Was she looking after you when she caused you to hemorrhage so bad you nearly died? All for what, a basketball game?"

"She's the one who stayed with me day after day, cleaning up after me, keeping me company, giving me faith that I could survive! I'd be dead if it wasn't for Ruby."

He stared at me for a long moment before heading back around behind his desk. Keeping his back to me, he stared out the window at the patch of grass behind the building. I could only hope he was considering my words, so I waited for him to turn around. When he did, his face was grim.

"My decision on the matter is final, Matthew. I won't be able to give you any money. And if you forgo your interviews in Nashville, throw away two perfectly fine job opportunities—especially in these times— well, I reckon I'll have to withdraw all financial support until you demonstrate a more responsible attitude."

"Now wait a minute, what financial support are you speaking of? I've been on my own for years now, working and saving my own money."

"Who do you think paid for that degree of yours? Who took you down to the bank and opened that savings account with you when you were fourteen years old?" His voice hit a new octave. "Who bought that car you drive everywhere your heart desires, except to come home and see your poor mother? Me! I did all those things! I provided the roof you lived under, the roof you still live under when you're here. Do not disrespect me!"

I waited for him to cool off, gathering my thoughts and deciding on my course of action. Should I just give in and do what he said? Do the responsible thing and go get a job, or defy him and stick by Ruby's side? I said a quick prayer in my head for wisdom.

Lord, help me decide what to do. I can't just abandon Ruby. Not after I already walked away from her once. Give me courage to do what's right.

I raised my chin and met his gaze. "I can't leave Ruby. She needs my help, and I'm going to make sure she has all she needs. I reckon I'll just have to take the consequences that come."

Father's eyes hardened. "I reckon you will."

My mind reeling, I headed over to the jail, which was just behind the courthouse. Sheriff Peterson sat at the desk in the lobby, bent over some paperwork. He glanced up as I came in.

"Where's Ruby?" I asked.

He nodded toward the door to my left. "Just got her settled in. Her mother and uncle are back there with her now."

As much as I wanted to go straight to her and make sure she was all right, I figured this was a good time to see if I could get some answers. "So what happens next?"

He shot me a withering look and glanced at the clock on the wall to my right. "We'll get her some dinner. The solicitor's over at the courthouse now. Should be back soon enough, and we'll know if we have an indictment." He went back to writing things on his papers like it was just another day for him, which only made my blood boil.

"I still don't understand how she can be charged with murder. She was just defending herself."

"That's probably true—"

"Probably?"

"—but look, we gotta follow the law here. Now, there's enough testimony and evidence to move forward—"

"What evidence?" I stepped closer and leaned onto the desk.

"I ain't at liberty to say."

I realized I'd get nowhere with impatience and anger, so I made a deliberate effort to keep my voice calm. "Listen, I know you have to do your job. I ain't trying to get in the way of that. But she means a lot to me. She means a lot to many people in this town. She's no criminal. Seems like if a person's getting arrested for murder, they should know what evidence is speaking against them."

He put down his pen and leaned back in his chair, looking me straight in the eyes. "All I can say is that she's got things working against her. If you're truly her friend, you tell her to tell the whole truth so we can put this all behind us."

The whole truth. Therein lay the problem. Ruby's story had holes in it, and the sheriff knew it. But if Ruby was determined to keep quiet, there wasn't nothing on God's green earth that could change her mind. No question about that.

"Can I see her?" I asked.

"Sure, sure." He walked over to the rusty door on my left, pointing into the back room. "She's in the last one on the right. Just knock on this door when you're ready to go."

He closed the door behind me, and I made my way down a narrow path between four cells—two on each side. On my left, a man lay on a cot snoring, his right arm and leg dangling to the floor. Just ahead of me, Asa and Mrs. Graves looked in on Ruby, held behind bars like a trapped and wounded animal. Mrs. Graves sat in a chair, her back rigid as she swiped at a tear. Asa stood behind her, his hands on her shoulders.

When I reached them, I could see why they were so upset. Just looking at Ruby—knowing what she'd go through to help people in need—made my head swim. She was the absolute last person I'd have ever thought to see behind bars.

"You doing all right?" I asked.

She stood in the middle of the cell with her arms wrapped around her stomach, like she wasn't quite sure of what to do with herself. "I'm fine. I think it's Mother who might need some tending to."

Mrs. Graves dismissed her with a wave of her handkerchief. "No, I'll be all right. It's you I'm worried about, sitting in this place like a common criminal. It's ridiculous."

Asa met my gaze over Mrs. Graves's head. "Matthew, would you mind staying with Ruby for a bit while Lizzy and I go get some fresh air?"

"I don't want to leave her till we know if they're going to indict her," Mrs. Graves said. "Maybe they'll dismiss this ludicrous charge, and we can all go home."

Ruby stepped over to the bars and knelt down. "Mother, please. Uncle Asa's right. You need to get some fresh air. Matthew can stay for a bit. I'm just fine, really."

"Yes," I said. "I'll stay until we find out something for sure. And then I'll come let you know. Don't worry, I promise I'll stay with her. She won't be alone."

I glanced down at Ruby to see her large brown eyes staring up at me with just a hint of doubt. A stab of guilt ran through me. Reckoned I deserved that.

Mrs. Graves stood and took Asa's elbow. "Just a short walk, all right?"

"Of course," he said.

I watched them leave, Mrs. Graves clinging onto her husband's arm, then I stole a look at Ruby to see if she really was all right. She observed her mother and Asa's departure with a stoic calmness that surprised me. In fact, I realized that since the moment the sheriff told her she was under arrest, she'd almost seemed…relieved. Almost as if she was ready and willing to head off to prison.

After the door closed, she went over to her cot and sat down on the edge. "You don't really have to stay. I just wanted Mother to get out of here before she fainted or something. I know you must have a lot to do."

"I meant what I said. I ain't leaving."

She sighed as she met my gaze, an acknowledgment of our mutual inflexible natures. I took a seat in the chair her mother had left. After a few minutes of silence, I started getting antsy. "I still don't understand how you ended up in jail for defending yourself," I said. "What exactly did you tell the sheriff?"

She shrugged as casually as if I'd asked her about the weather. "Just told him what happened."

"Well he seems to think you left some things out."

"I told him everything."

"You sure?"

She glanced at me. Then she dropped her gaze to her hands in her lap, saying nothing more. In the past, when she didn't want to tell me something, she'd go completely silent. About drove me crazy sometimes. I'd never known her to tell a lie. But then again, I had to wonder if I really knew her anymore.

"Ruby, what exactly happened in that barn?"

"I told you already." She fidgeted with her hands.

"Why did you even go in there? Did you see him go in there first? Was he already there when you went inside?"

Ruby threw her hands up and began pacing back and forth beside the cot. "Good grief! You sound just like the sheriff! I told him the same thing I told you. I went into the barn looking for James 'cause I'd just left Emma Rae and the baby. He wasn't in there. When I turned to leave, Chester was coming toward me, and he attacked me. Just like he did before in the woods."

"How did he end up with a knife in his chest?"

She stopped pacing and put her hands over her eyes. "I'm not sure. I can't remember it exactly. He had the knife and came at me, so I kicked my feet at him. I must have kicked the knife into his chest or something."

And there it was: the gaping hole in her story. The whole thing sounded fishy, even to me, and even knowing Chester had attacked her before. How was she ever going to convince twelve jurors to believe that story, if it came down to that?

The door swung open and Sheriff Peterson stepped inside with a man who looked vaguely familiar. I'd seen his silver hair and mustache somewhere before, but I couldn't quite place them. He had to be about my father's age. Maybe they knew each other. As the two men approached, Sheriff Peterson called out to Ruby. She came over to the bars, her face revealing the smallest hint of worry. I stood and nodded to the sheriff.

"This is Solicitor Charles Garrett," Sheriff Peterson said. "He'll be prosecuting your case, Miss Ruby."

"So the grand jury indicted her?" I said. "You have to be joking!"

Mr. Garrett raised his eyebrows. "And just who are you?"

"Matthew Doyle. I'm Ruby's friend."

"Doyle?" Mr. Garrett glanced at Sheriff Peterson. "Patrick Doyle's boy?" I nodded, and he seemed to consider that for a moment before turning his attention to Ruby. "Miss Graves, you've been indicted on a charge of murder. You'll be assigned a lawyer by tomorrow morning. Bond's been set at four thousand."

Ruby let out a small gasp at the same time my head nearly exploded. "What? That's insane! There ain't no way she should have that high a bond."

"I assure you, Mr. Doyle, that the bond is perfectly within reason given the charge," Mr. Garrett said. "Now if you will excuse us, I have some questions I need to ask Miss Graves."

"No, that's not how this is supposed to go," I said. "I ain't no expert, but I know she should have her own lawyer here if she's answering any questions."

Mr. Garrett exchanged a look with Sheriff Peterson, who put a hand on my shoulder. "Now listen, son. Miss Ruby's in good hands, and she's gonna be just fine. I'll look after her myself. It's just a few preliminary questions. Nothing to get worked up over. Now, why don't you go on and fill her mother and uncle in on the situation? I'm about to have to close up for the evening anyhow. You can come on back in the morning and visit."

As he talked, my muscles tightened beneath his hands. I wanted to punch him in the mouth. Did he think I was stupid or something? I pointed a finger at Ruby. "You ain't got to answer any of their questions, you hear? Don't say nothing till you have a lawyer with you."

"All right, son—" Mr. Garrett started.

"Don't call me son. I know what you're trying to get away with, and I ain't gonna stand for it." I looked at Ruby again. "I'll have you out of here in a jiffy. You just stay strong, and don't say nothing."

I pushed past the sheriff and Mr. Garrett for the door with only one thing on my mind. With or without Father's help, I was getting Ruby out of that cell by the next day.

When I got home that afternoon, I went to Father's office to use the telephone. I rang the Paschal's home in Montgomery, reaching their butler, Abe. He'd served them for so many years, his hearing was about gone, so I had to holler a bit before he got Vanessa on the phone. We usually had a good laugh about it, but not this time.

"I need to discuss something important with you," I said, trying not to sound too ominous.

"Why, sure." Her voice, usually light with happiness when we spoke, had an edge of tension to it.

"I didn't go to my interviews in Nashville. I'm still in Cullman."

"Why? What's going on?"

"Do you remember Ruby Graves from a few years back?"

"Who?"

"Ruby Graves. She was good friends with Mary in school, and she tended to me while I was sick with T.B. I believe you met her once when she was over at the house."

"Oh, yes! I remember now. That sweet little girl who walked through the woods to your house sometimes."

I paused, unsure of how to explain everything. "She was attacked yesterday morning while out at the Calhoun farm."

Vanessa gasped. "Oh no! I hope she's all right."

"She ain't hurt or anything. But while she was trying to fight off her attacker, he was killed. His family's had her arrested, and now she's sitting in jail accused of murder. It just ain't right."

"That sounds terrible for her." I could hear the question in Vanessa's voice. What did that have to do with us?

"We ain't been close for some time now, but Ruby doesn't deserve this. She needs help, and I figure the least I can do is pay her bond. I mean, she shouldn't have to sit in there like a criminal."

I was pretty sure once Vanessa heard the whole story, she'd understand and encourage me to help Ruby. After all, she'd worked right beside me at the bread lines in Tuscaloosa over the past couple of years. She had a heart for helping the less fortunate. It wasn't the same kind of devotion Ruby had. But then again, who *did* have that kind of devotion? All the same, Vanessa was kind, so I was shocked at her response.

"Doesn't she have family and friends who can help her?"

"Not with the kind of money she needs. The judge set her bond at four thousand dollars."

"Four *thousand*? Why Matthew, that's nearly your entire savings! What about our home? What about *our* future?"

"Sweetheart, I'll save the money for the house again."

"How? You didn't go to the interviews, so you don't have a job. How can you save up money when you aren't earning any?"

"There'll be other jobs. Have some faith in me."

I could hear her breath tremble. Was she crying?

"Matthew, you're a good man, with a good heart. If you feel the right thing to do with your money is to help Ruby, then I won't argue. I just hope she appreciates what we're giving up for her."

"I have no doubt she'll be grateful," I said. "And listen, maybe it's a good thing I didn't go to those interviews. I can take a closer look at some jobs around Montgomery now. Wouldn't you like to stay close to your parents?"

That seemed to brighten her spirits. "Oh, do you mean that? Maybe Daddy could find a place for you in his company for a while. Just until you find something you really want."

It hit me that I was falling into the trap we'd been dancing around for the past several months. I had no intention of working in the lumber business, or sitting behind a desk for that matter. I'd made that clear. And I knew once I started working for her father, I'd be trapped there for the rest of my life. But I'd gone and put myself in the position of needing to keep her happy.

"I reckon that's an option to consider," I said.

I spent a few more minutes encouraging her cheerful mood with talk of the wedding. Flowers and guest lists didn't interest me much, but I felt better knowing she was supporting my decision. Once we hung up the phone, I was feeling much better myself. As long as Ruby didn't say anything incriminating tonight, she'd be safe at home by tomorrow.

I left Father's office and headed down the hallway toward the foyer and front stairs. As I neared the end, I heard voices that sounded like they were coming from across the foyer, probably from the sitting room. If Father was home, it would be best to avoid him, so I intended to make my way up the stairs unnoticed. But as I hit the third step, I heard my name. Something about how I was ruining more than my own future.

I went back down the steps and moved over to the doorway that opened into the sitting room where Mother usually entertained her friends in the afternoons. But it was Father in there talking this time, and I could hear his heavy footsteps pacing the wood floor.

"You babied him too much," he said. "He never learned to be tough and face the realities of life. Now he's throwing away jobs like there's one around every corner!"

I could hear Mother's soft reply, but I couldn't make out the words. Whatever it was, it didn't please Father too much. He raised his voice even more.

"I'm serious, Francine. It's time for him to grow up and act like a man. I will not continue to support a son who is lazy and refuses to earn his keep. I reckon I'll have to teach him a lesson or two yet."

Then Mother's voice rose to where I could hear it, something I hadn't ever heard her do before. "He hardly ever comes home as it is now! Patrick Doyle, if you run him off again, I promise I will never speak to you as long as I live!"

"Don't put your threats on me, woman! This is my house, and I'll be treated with the respect I deserve. Who do you think provides this nice house and those fine clothes of yours? Who pays for your servants? Do you think you'd have any of this without me? All I ask for is a little respect from you and our children. Is that too much?"

There was a long pause, and I debated on whether I should go in and give him a better target than Mother. But then he kept on going.

"Now, I am not going to allow Matthew to throw away his future. I will make him see reason if it's the last thing I do. He will not disgrace this family, or the Paschals for that matter."

I backed away from the door and headed up the stairs. Once inside my bedroom, I closed the door and sat on the edge of my bed pondering Daddy's promise. I'd seen him worked up many a time before, but never had he seemed so determined. I couldn't understand how my helping Ruby would disgrace our family, let alone the Paschals.

Lord, help me reason with him before this gets out of hand. Soften his pride and make him see that helping Ruby's the right thing to do. And if he won't see reason, give me the courage to stand up to him.

CHAPTER SIX

Ruby

I spent my first night in jail moving from one uncomfortable position to another. I prayed on my knees until they ached. Then I sat on the edge of my cot to pray some more. I lay down for a bit, even closed my eyes. But sleep wouldn't come, so I went back to praying. My heart cried out to God, and my spirit was so disturbed that I ended up right back on my knees. In fact, at one point, during the darkest moments I'd ever had in my life, I found myself flat on my face. I sobbed with all my might, begging God for His presence, aching for some kind of assurance that I'd done the right thing. It seemed like the harder I begged, the more alone I felt.

By the time morning light began to creep into my cell, I was empty. I'd prayed with my most fervent words. I'd cried out from deep within my spirit. I had surrendered myself to anything God wanted from me. But I got nothing in return. Not that I blamed Him. I was filthy from head to toe with sin. But I'd tried so hard to make it right. Why hadn't God let me heal Chester?

I jumped at the sound of the door slamming closed. I figured Sheriff Peterson was bringing my breakfast, so I turned and sat on the edge of my cot. But it wasn't the sheriff who sauntered up to the bars of my cell. It was that old goat, Brother Cass. I didn't think my spirits could've sunk any lower than they had already, but the sight of that man—after begging so hard for a sign from God—made my chest ache.

Brother Cass strolled over to my cell door with a smug sort of frown that I could imagine held a sick pleasure behind it. In his hands he carried a newspaper, which he used to tap the bars. I thought about laying back down on my cot and ignoring him until he went away, but I'd promised God long ago that I wouldn't hold a grudge against him for sending Chester after me the first time. And God had blessed me over the years by allowing me to avoid running into Cass except for maybe a few occasions in Cullman. Even then, we'd simply ignored each other, and I'd assumed he'd left his pursuit of my demise behind. I wondered what he was doing here now. Was this really God's answer to my prayers?

"Well, Miss Ruby, you seem to have gotten yourself into quite a jam here."

It still amused me to hear such a deep voice coming from such a small man. I mustered up as much politeness as I could manage and walked over to the door. "I suppose so. What can I do for you today, Brother Cass?"

"Why there's nothing in this world you can do for me, darling. The grace and mercy of our Lord and Savior is all I ever need. However, I believe it is you who is in dire need of that mercy now. Though you have resisted my guidance thus far, I am here to offer you a chance at redemption. God is allowing this time of trial in order to bring about your repentance."

"And just what is it I need to repent of?"

He glanced back toward the door and lowered his voice. "It is my understanding that you have continued in the ways of dark mysteries under the guise of healing. Surely you must realize that God is punishing you for such evil rebellion. Not to mention your shameful behavior toward the Negroes."

My soul was exhausted, but somehow I managed to find a bit of fight left inside me. "Since when is healing folks and providing food and clothing to the poor considered shameful? You are a spiteful man who would not know grace, or mercy, or compassion, if Jesus himself walked right up to you, took your hand, and showed you someone in need. You'd simply preach at them about whatever sin you believed they committed and tell them to do better. That isn't God's love."

His face reddened. "Young lady," he huffed, "I'll not concern myself with your misguided notions of my character—"

"Nor I with yours."

He shook the newspaper at me. "I have done my best to keep my distance from your fiery tongue and your evil sorcery, but as I suspected, another innocent life has been ended because of the Graves arrogance!"

"Innocent?" I cried. "Chester Calhoun was far from innocent—"

"And you took it upon yourself to mete out justice, did you?"

"What? No!" I threw up my arms and turned my back on him, stomping over to my cot. I should've known better than to speak to that man. I crossed my arms over my chest, determined not to say another word.

Brother Cass studied me with a satisfied tip to his mouth. "As for your *other* activities, I happen to know that you have been carrying on with Negroes, not just providing food and clothing. Why, it's all right here!"

Carrying on? What was that supposed to mean? He shoved the paper between the bars, baiting me with its contents. I was tempted to take it to see what he was talking about, but I knew that was exactly what he wanted me to do. Instead I lay down and covered my eyes with my arm.

"I don't have any interest in whatever stories are being told about me. I know the truth. I know who I am, and what I've done. I thank you for your concern for my soul, but I assure you it's in good hands."

"Ruby Graves, you are a vile, rebellious Jezebel. I am horrified that you have once again dragged the good name of the Doyle family into your sinful behavior."

So that was what had him in a fuss. He'd always hated my friendship with Matthew and Mary. "I'm not dragging anyone into anything. Matthew is a grown man who can make his own decisions. Now, please excuse me, but I'm pretty tired. I'd like to get some rest."

"You better get used to confinement. The rest of your time on this earth may well be spent in a cell, and unfortunately for you, the afterlife will be much, much worse than you can ever imagine."

I closed my eyes and listened to the sound of his shoes clopping away, pushing his words as far away from my thoughts as possible. Once again, I prayed that man would find some measure of compassion, and that God would control my tongue when speaking to him. As much I despised any interaction with him, he was a powerful influence in Cullman, and it would not be wise to entice him into a campaign against me.

Only a short while later, Matthew strode up to my cell like a man on a mission. His dark eyes blazed with that familiar intensity I'd seen before when he was set on making things happen. Despite my predicament, my heart did a little flutter. Something I hadn't felt in so long; I'd nearly forgotten the sensation. I set it straight right quick though. There'd be no more schoolgirl crushes on Matthew Doyle.

"Morning," he said, gripping the bars. "You all right? What happened last night? Did the sheriff and solicitor grill you? What did you say?"

I walked over to him, offering a smile to slow his onslaught of questions. "Good morning to you too. Yes, I'm all right. I didn't get much sleep, but I feel just fine. They asked me the same questions the sheriff already asked me. Now, what are you still doing here? You should be heading to Nashville."

"I postponed them."

A sigh of exasperation escaped my lips. "And you lecture me about being stubborn, while you shove the same beam into your own eye."

His brow wrinkled. "What's that supposed to mean?"

"Don't you read your Bible? It's from Matthew. Surely you at least read *that* book?"

Gripping the bars, Matthew's head dropped between his shoulders. "Can we skip the sermon this morning? I'm getting you out of here, today."

"Don't you spend one dime of your money on this circus, Matthew Doyle."

He looked up at me with wide eyes. "What? You want to stay locked up in here? I have the money. Let me help you."

I shook my head 'cause I knew if I tried to speak, my words might betray me. It was true. I didn't want to spend one more night in that place, but I couldn't allow myself to be indebted to him either. I could see he was going to dig in his heels, so I'd have to dig mine in just as deep.

"Ruby," he said. "Don't be ridiculous. Go home. Sleep. You should be with your family through this."

"If you have even an ounce of respect for me, then you'll forget all this mess, get on up to Nashville, and move on with your life," I said, ignoring the heaviness in my chest and the sting in my eyes. "I don't need your money, and I won't accept it."

The door opened, and Sheriff Peterson approached with a very large man in a dark suit following close behind. When they reached us, Sheriff Peterson stepped aside. "Miss Ruby, this here's Norman Oliver. Judge Woods appointed him to represent you."

Mr. Oliver tipped his hat. The sheriff turned to Matthew and clamped a hand onto his shoulder. "Why don't we give Miss Ruby and Mr. Oliver some time to get acquainted?"

Matthew stiffened, but he didn't shrug the hand away. He met my gaze, sending another rebellious flutter through my stomach. "I'll be back soon."

Before he was out the door, the sheriff was unlocking my cell to let Mr. Oliver inside. "Y'all take all the time you need," he said. "I'll be right outside. Just holler when you're done."

Mr. Oliver stuck out his hand as the sheriff walked away. "Well, I wish it were under better circumstances, but it's nice to meet you, Miss Graves."

I shook his hand. It was damp. "Likewise."

He motioned toward the chair in the corner. "Shall we sit and talk a while?"

I nodded and took a seat on my cot. He pulled out the chair in front of me. I was afraid it was going to collapse as he sank into it, but it just groaned a bit. He took out his handkerchief and wiped it across his brow.

"Well now," he said. "It's my understanding you're being charged with the murder of Chester Calhoun. So how about you tell me everything that happened, and we'll decide how we should proceed."

I closed my eyes to set myself right. I wondered how many times I was going to have to tell this story. And I wondered what might happen if I slipped up, even just once. *Lord, give me wisdom and help me to be as truthful as I can be.*

So I opened my eyes and started my story again. I explained how I went into the barn looking for James, and how Chester had come at me. I told him the hateful threats that spewed from Chester's mouth—that part was as clear as daylight in my mind. I told him how Chester had flung me around and come at me with a knife, and how I'd somehow managed to kick at it so it lodged into his chest. That part wasn't so clear, and I could see it bothered Mr. Oliver. But he let me keep on talking. Then I told him about trying to help Chester, and Luke Dalton coming into the barn, and all the chaos that followed.

Mr. Oliver studied me before he spoke. "I'm a little unclear on something. Why would Chester come after you in the first place?"

I twisted my hands in my lap. That was the tricky part. How to explain anything without explaining everything. "Chester attacked me once before. About five years ago."

"Five years ago? How old were you?"

"Fourteen."

"Why on earth would a grown man attack a fourteen-year-old girl?"

I shrugged, unable to lie, unable to tell the truth. "He's always been violent. My family was working as sharecroppers at the Calhoun farm back then. He managed his daddy's place. He kept things under control by using force. I did some things he didn't like, and I knew things about him he didn't want anyone else to know. That's all I can say about that."

He rubbed his brow again. "Well, there's no way we can say you didn't kill him. If he did try to hurt you, then it was self-defense. But that's extremely hard to prove, and you run the risk of being found guilty of murder. And in that case, you could possibly face the electric chair."

A chill ran down my spine, and I was pretty sure my heart stopped for a few beats. "The chair? For this?"

"Like I said, only if the jury thinks you planned it and did it on purpose. Unfortunately, that seems to be what the prosecution is going to try to show."

"How could they possibly show that if it isn't true?"

"I haven't seen all the evidence yet, or talked to any witnesses. I only have your words to go on right now. But Mr. Garrett is thorough and excellent with juries. I'm not sure how, but he will go after you. He will dig up every secret you have."

Every secret...

My heart thudded in my ears as I realized the enormity of what was at stake. The electric chair? Was I going to die for this?

And what if my secret came out? Would God take my gift from me, like He took it from Asa? Maybe He already had. Maybe that was why He didn't heal Chester. He knew all along this would be the end of me.

"What do you suggest?" I asked.

Mr. Oliver leaned toward me onto his elbows, his hands clamped together. There was something in his eyes that made my heart quicken. "Listen, you're a young girl with a bright future ahead of you. If you plead guilty to a much lesser charge, say manslaughter, then most likely the judge will give you the minimum sentence. Considering the circumstances, it might be just a couple of years."

"It might be. But it could be a lot more."

"Well, yes. For manslaughter it could be up to twenty-five."

Twenty-five years. Covering my face with my hands, I forced myself to breathe slowly. No matter what happened, it seemed I was heading off to prison. How had I gotten myself into this? *Breathe in; breathe out.* My throat ached, and a few tears slipped down my cheeks. I heard Mr. Oliver clear his throat.

"Miss Ruby, I know it's hard to think about going to prison. But we should consider that it would be a lot better than facing the electric chair."

Coming back up for air, I wiped my face on my sleeve and tried to still the tremor in my voice. "You're p-probably right. But...can I have some time? To think about it?"

"Oh, sure," he said, his expression clearing of concern like the sun emerging from behind the clouds. Heaving himself up, he put the chair back in the corner of the cell. "I'll speak with Mr. Garrett and make sure we can proceed, if that's what you decide. And I'll get all the paperwork ready."

I suddenly felt too tired to stand. "Thank you," I managed.

He stepped over to the cell door and called out for Sheriff Peterson, who appeared within seconds. Then Mr. Oliver bid me a last farewell, and I fell back onto my cot to release the tears I'd been trying to hold off.

"Oh, God!" I sobbed. "Is this what Your will is for me? What do I do? Please give me Your peace, Your strength, Your grace. I'm empty and so afraid!" I pulled my hands into my chest, trying to hold back the fear threatening to take over my mind.

Nothing came. No words of comfort. No whisper of love or encouragement. I ached for His voice, but there was nothing.

CHAPTER SEVEN

Matthew

When I came out of the courthouse, it was drizzling just a bit. The bank was only a few blocks away, so I decided to pull my coat a little tighter and walk. It gave me a chance to ponder my options—leave Ruby to sit in jail all alone, or pay off her bond and endure her anger? It wasn't really much of a debate. I'd known what I was going to do from the outset, but her resistance had given me pause. I was already in need of forgiveness for turning my back on her. Should I risk even more of her ire?

I said a quick prayer and decided I'd just have to ask for more forgiveness. I'd borne her wrath many times in the past, and this was for her own good. She'd see that as soon as she got back home with her family. And she'd see that I wasn't going to leave her to fight this battle on her own. Then she'd forgive me. Maybe.

I entered the bank and waved at Judy Hathorne behind the counter. She'd gone to school with my older brother, Frank, and her husband had died a few years back. Father had put in a good word for her and helped her get a job at the bank so she could feed her two kids.

"Is Mr. Campbell in?" I asked her.

She smiled and pointed toward the back corner. "He's at his desk."

I thanked her and headed that way. Parker Bank & Trust was about the only reliable bank in town the past several years. There'd been one that closed all together in '33, and a small building and loan that did its best to stay afloat, but like many businesses, it struggled to keep its doors open. Father had never put his money anywhere but Parker's, and he hadn't allowed any of his kids to either.

As I approached Mr. Campbell's desk, he smiled and waved me over. "Why, Matthew! I haven't seen you in here in some time. How are things going?" He stood and extended his hand. Mr. Campbell was an old friend of my father's and about his same age. His face was lined with years of worry, which I presumed to be over the stock market.

"Just fine and dandy, thank you," I said.

He motioned toward the chair on the other side of his desk. "Take a seat. What can I do for you?"

I perched on the edge of the chair and pulled the passbook for my savings account out of my coat pocket. "I just came in to close out my savings account."

The lines on his forehead deepened. "I don't understand." Then he smiled. "Oh, you mean you want to update your passbook with yesterday's withdrawal? That isn't necessary, son, but I'll zero it out for you."

"Yesterday's withdrawal? What are you talking about?"

He tilted his head like a dog trying to make sense of a command. "This account was closed yesterday."

"What? How is that possible? I have the passbook right here. I should have just over four thousand dollars in there."

My head spun with questions. That was every penny I'd saved up since I was fourteen years old. I'd worked in Father's stores, gotten odd jobs around town. Surely it wasn't just gone.

Mr. Campbell looked down at the passbook and back up at me with a perplexed expression. "Why, your father came in here yesterday and closed out the account. Said you had a new job lined up in Nashville, and you'd be moving your account to a bank up there."

I let this sink in for a moment. Why hadn't he mentioned anything about this to me? "Are you sure?" I asked.

"Well, I spoke to him myself. He didn't have the passbook, but he had the account information and well...He and Mr. Parker go way back. And Mr. Parker approved the transaction since he was the primary account holder."

"*He* was the primary account holder? That was supposed to be changed years ago when I went off to school!"

"Well...I don't know anything about that. According to Mr. Parker, your father was the primary. I suppose you'll need to speak with Mr. Doyle about all this and get it straightened out. I'm sure it's just a misunderstanding."

I groaned, knowing it was most certainly not a misunderstanding. It was a deliberate move to place me under his thumb. Did he think he could just hold my money as ransom over my head to force me to do what he wanted? My blood raced hot through my skin.

"I apologize for any confusion," Mr. Campbell said. "If I can be of any further service, I'd be happy to help."

"I want to speak with Mr. Parker," I said.

"Unfortunately, he isn't here right now."

Pushing myself up from the chair, I slammed my hand onto the desk, and Mr. Campbell jolted. "This is completely ridiculous! You're telling me that my father can just waltz right in here and steal money from my account with the bank's blessing?"

Mr. Campbell glanced nervously around the room. When he spoke he lowered his voice to nearly a whisper. "No one said anything about stealing."

I paced in front of his desk, rubbing the back of my neck to ease the pressure building. Mr. Campbell was right about one thing. I was going to have to talk to Father and find out exactly what was going on.

I stormed right past Ruth and into Father's office, heading straight to his desk. Flinging all caution and childhood fears to the wind, I shoved my finger at him, demanding an explanation. "What kind of game are you playing at?"

He kept on writing, his expression remaining unchanged. It occurred to me that he had been expecting this very confrontation, and I was probably playing right into his hands.

"You may think you're a grown man," he said eventually in a steady, calm voice. "But you will not come bursting into my office and disrespect me."

I was in no mood for submitting to his control. "Where's the money?"

He dropped his pen and leaned back in his chair, his eyes narrowing as they met my own. "What money are you referring to, son?"

"*My* money! The money you stole from my savings account yesterday."

"Stole? I believe that account was in my name, and that I personally deposited every penny into it."

"I worked for that money, and you knew I was saving it up to buy a house for Vanessa and me."

He leaned forward and smiled. The smile did not reach his eyes. "Well, then you go on up to Nashville, and get yourself a job. You and Vanessa can pick out whatever house you like. I'll see to it the money gets paid to the cost of the house. In fact, I'll even throw in some extra to help you kids settle in."

Control. It always came down to control. "No, thank you," I said, gritting my teeth. "I'd like the money returned to me, that's all. I'll determine how it's spent."

He sighed and folded his hands over his chest. "And I suppose you intend to spend it on that wretched girl who's in jail for murder."

"I intend to spend my own money any way I see fit."

"That's what I was afraid of. You see, I can't just stand by and allow you to throw away your future on someone so worthless. She deceived us all once before, and she used your good name to smuggle food away from hardworking men who needed it. She's a liar, and now she's a criminal. I won't have our family name dragged through the mud."

Realization mixed with exasperation made my volume rise. "That's what really matters here, isn't it? Not the fact that she's innocent! Not that someone decent and kind needs our help. Not that she practically *saved my life*. But that *your* precious family name might be tarnished!"

"It's your family name too!" My father's voice finally reached the tone he used when demanding obedience. "I've worked hard all my life to secure a future for each one of my children, and I'll not apologize for it. Nor will I stand by while one of them tosses it aside as if it had no meaning. You are a Doyle, and you will act like a Doyle!"

I stared into his eyes, so hardened they were blind to the truth. "I don't want any part of being a Doyle if it means being like you."

"Really? Oh well, then, you're more than welcome to change your name! March right over to that courthouse and do it if you like. But that will not change who you are on the inside, and no matter what you do, you will always be my son. You want to come in here and fight me?" He chuckled and shook his head. "You're more like me than you realize."

"I'm nothing like you. I want nothing to do with controlling the people I love. I would never force someone to do what I want rather than allowing them to make their own choices."

"Is that so?"

The corner of his mouth tipped as he stared into my soul. I couldn't stand one more second of being in the same room with him, so I left as quickly as I'd come in. Once I was down on the street again, I stomped through the rain back toward the courthouse where my car was parked, continuing my argument with him in my mind.

I was nothing like him. *Nothing!* But his words cut into me, digging into my motives for wanting that money in the first place. Maybe I was trying to force Ruby into accepting my help, but that was different. He was pushing me to do what he wanted; be who he wanted me to be. It had nothing to do with loving me. It was *not* the same!

By the time I got back to Ruby's cell, I thought I might just come right out of my skin. How could I explain that I'd failed her once again? That she'd have to stay in this awful place for who knew how long?

She was standing on the other side of the cell, her face turned toward the light coming through the small window, her hands lifted by her side. Her eyes were closed, and her lips moved with what I assumed to be a silent prayer. I was intruding on something private, a conversation I knew was none of my business, but I couldn't pull my eyes away. She practically glowed from the inside out.

A tear slipped down her cheek, and she tilted her head back. "Your will be done, Father," she said. Then she opened her eyes and saw me watching her. She smiled.

"Are you all right?" I asked.

She smoothed her hair. "I uh…just finished talking with Mr. Oliver a little while ago."

"Well?" I said.

She stared at the floor, saying nothing for a little while. Eventually she walked over to me, resting her hands on the bars in front of me. I thought about placing my hands over hers, but that seemed too close, too intimate.

"I'll be fine once this is all settled."

"What did Mr. Oliver say?" I didn't think I could keep it together much longer.

"He seems to think I can plead guilty to manslaughter and get a lighter sentence."

"What?" I stepped back from the bars. "Plead guilty? That's crazy! You can't plead guilty to something you didn't do!"

She touched her palm to her forehead. "You don't understand—"

"Make me understand, Ruby. Explain to me how you ending up in jail for something you didn't do makes any sense at all."

"I am not innocent in this!" She pointed into her chest. "What I did caused that man to die! I'm the reason he's dead!"

"That man was a sorry excuse for a human being, and he got what he deserved! Don't throw your life away because of him."

She shook her head and stepped back. "No, I'm not going to put my family and everyone else through a trial. I'll take responsibility for this. That's the only way."

"The only way for what? For you to end up in jail? You can't be serious. I'll get you out of here, I swear. Then we can fight this together." I had no idea how I was going do that. I'd have to get my money back from Father, but I'd figure something out.

"You will do no such thing! You get yourself up to Nashville, go to your interviews, and start your new job."

"Don't start that again. I'm not going anywhere."

"Mr. Oliver says if I plead guilty to manslaughter, the judge will take it easy on me. Maybe I won't even have to go to jail. I could get some kind of probation."

"I don't think you should trust that man. I think I know him from somewhere. I can't remember exactly where, but my gut says something's not right here."

"You think he's lying to me?"

"I ain't saying that. I don't know exactly. But I don't think you should plead guilty. That ain't the truth. Ruby, I know we ain't been close for a long time, but I never knew you to be a liar."

Her face flinched slightly, and I could see my words hit a nerve. "I'm not trying to lie. It's just...I thought if I could make this easier, then everyone could get on with their lives."

"Make it easier for who? Look, I don't know what happened at the Calhoun place, but I know for certain there ain't gonna be nothing easy about any of this. I don't think the Calhouns are gonna just let you get off easy. They already got people in the town believing you committed murder. The paper's printing all kinds of lies. You got to see reality here before you get yourself in a mess of trouble." I could see her struggling with my words. "For once, Ruby, just listen to me. Do not plead guilty. Let's get you out of here and start working on a defense."

She closed her eyes and dropped her forehead onto her hands. "Matthew, please don't make this any harder than it is already. I cannot accept your money."

"I'm trying to help you!" How could she be so stubborn at a time like this? It was becoming increasingly clear that Ruby hadn't changed one little bit. I pounded my fist on one of the bars.

Then she met my gaze with damp eyes that pierced right through me. "I know you're trying to help. You just can't fix this."

Looking down at those eyes, I saw the same girl who'd filled me with hope during my darkest hours. The dreamer, who believed in me no matter what. The fighter, who never let me wallow in my sorrow. My chest tightened, and I prayed that somehow, now that she was in need, I could give her hope as well.

"Ruby, don't give up. You can fight this. You won't be alone, I swear." I covered my heart with my hand. "I will not let you down when you need me this time. Don't plead guilty."

"All right," she said, throwing her hands out to the side. "I won't plead guilty. But I won't let you spend one dime on this, you hear?"

"What? How else—"

"Not one dime!"

"So how else are you gonna get the money to get out of here?"

"That'll be my concern, not yours. Now there's nothing more for you to do, so get on up to Nashville and do your interviews."

"I already told you. I'm not going anywhere, so quit trying to get rid of me."

She huffed and went back over to her cot, throwing herself onto it. "Fine. Do what you want. But I'm exhausted. I'm going to rest for a while." Then she turned to the wall and pulled a blanket over her head.

I watched for a few moments as she tried to hide the tremor in her shoulders. "Ruby?"

No answer.

"Are you ever going to forgive me?" I asked.

No answer. I stood there and waited—for what, I wasn't sure. But the cell was so quiet, I could hear the drip of the pipes in the walls. As I turned to leave, her voice drifted through the air.

"I don't know."

That afternoon I drove out to the Graves farm just outside the city limits of Hanceville. It was a pretty little piece of land with a small but sturdy house in the middle. A small wood was off to the east, with a creek that ran alongside the house. And off to the north, behind the house, were several acres of farmland that had been recently laid by in preparation for winter.

When I drove up, Asa was over at the barn, chopping wood. He straightened and waved to me as I got out of my car, strolling over to meet me at the front porch with an outstretched hand.

"What brings you out here today?"

"I was hoping I could speak with you and Mrs. Graves about Ruby."

"Sure, sure. Come on inside."

He ushered me into a cozy living room with a bedroom off the back. Over to my left was a table with four chairs, and a neat little kitchen just beyond. Mrs. Graves gave me a half-smile as she worked at the stove.

"Why, Matthew," she said, her voice tired. "Come on in and have a seat." She probably hadn't slept much the night before either.

I took off my hat and slid into a chair at the table. As I did, I caught sight of the newspaper on the floor nearby. I leaned over and flipped it to the side with the front-page article about Ruby.

"You haven't burned this yet?" I said.

Mrs. Graves frowned. "I plan to. Soon as I get done fuming over it. The nerve of that man." She shook her spoon in the air.

"Which one?" Asa said, taking the chair to my right.

"All of them," she said. "Mr. Adams, old man Cass, and whoever that rotten excuse for a journalist is who wrote the thing. Curse all of them!"

"Has Ruby seen it?" Asa asked me.

I shook my head. "Thankfully, no. I didn't even mention it."

Mrs. Graves wiped her forehead with her apron and went back to stirring her pot. I read the headline again. *Hanceville girl charged with murder; Claims self-defense.* A picture of the scene at the barn was next to the article. Ruby sat on a hay bale with her bloody hands covering her face. All of it seemed rather tame at first glance, until the reader got into the fourth paragraph, where an unnamed source explained how it couldn't have been self-defense based on the evidence at the scene. No facts, of course. Nothing to back up his claim, but the paper printed it anyway.

But that wasn't even the worst of it. Brother Cass had spoken with the writer, painting a picture of a troubled young lady who used to steal from the soup kitchen at his church. He even hinted at Ruby participating in secret ceremonies connected to witchcraft.

"I tell you what," I said. "I don't understand how Brother Cass can stand in that pulpit every Sunday and preach the Lord's words, and then turn around and attack a sister in Christ."

Mrs. Graves pointed her spoon at me. "Don't you get me started on that man. Maybe it's time I had a talk with him myself." She locked eyes with Asa, and her anger melted. "He wasn't always like this. Maybe I could reason with him."

"You know as well as I do he ain't gonna listen to reason," Asa said. "He's gonna take all his anger he's built up at me and push it right onto Ruby's shoulders."

"What exactly is Cass so angry about?" I asked. "I thought he just didn't like Ruby, but it seems like it goes much deeper than that."

Asa gave a sideways glance to Mrs. Graves. "There's a long story there, son. I'll just say this. His niece passed away many years ago, and he blames me for it." He dropped his head and muttered, "Rightly so, I reckon."

"But what does that have to do with Ruby?"

Mrs. Graves's spoon took aim at Asa. "This is precisely why I didn't want Ruby getting mixed up with your ideas in the first place."

"I know," Asa said. "Maybe you were right. But there ain't no going back now." He looked over at me. "You know about Ruby's gift, don't you?"

"Asa!" Mrs. Graves stiffened.

"Well, he does. Ruby said so."

The hair on my neck prickled. I'd never said a word about Ruby's *gift* to a single soul. I still clung to the small possibility I'd imagined everything I'd seen. But I figured it was about time to face the truth, and maybe get some answers.

"I saw her do it once...I think...with that colored woman."

Mrs. Graves threw down her spoon. "I can't listen to this." She turned and walked out the back door.

Asa let out a deep sigh as he watched her go. "Grace was her best friend." I must have looked at him funny, 'cause he backed up a bit to explain. "Brother Cass's niece, Grace, was Lizzy's best friend growing up. We all ran around together as kids. Anyway, there's a long story as to how things got all messed up, but I was angry, and when Grace needed me, needed my gift, I refused to help. Brother Cass blames me for her death."

"Forgive me for being dense," I said. "But I still don't see what that has to do with Ruby."

"Son, when you were sick, Ruby came to me for help. She was desperate. I didn't think I could help you, but she wouldn't hear none of it.

She marched me right over to your deathbed and we prayed over you. That was the first time Ruby truly experienced what healing was all about."

A cool shiver went down my spine as I recalled that night. My nightmare, the one that haunted me whenever I came home, always started with that night. Strange thing was, it never started as a nightmare. It started as a sweet dream of releasing the monster inside my lungs. It only turned awful when I lost Ruby.

"After that," Asa continued, "Brother Cass figured Ruby was the same as me. He figured her for a fraud. He never even gave her a chance."

I glanced down at the paper again, finally putting together all the comments Brother Cass had made about Ruby early on, before I realized what a snake he was. He knew all along, at least on some level, and he'd judged her as evil.

"What about the rest of this article?" I asked. "The stuff about the colored folks. Any truth to that?"

"Honestly, I ain't sure how close she is to them anymore. She keeps that to herself. I think the idea of her being romantically involved with one of them is garbage, but I wouldn't be surprised if she was still visiting that woman she was helping before." Although Ruby's mother was no longer present, he lowered his voice. "Frankly, I'm concerned it could get out of hand."

"What do you mean?"

"There's been some hints that Ruby's a target now, and maybe even us. I ain't sure. Just overheard things in town yesterday. Some people are saying Chester was a member of the Klan."

"That explains a lot. Especially why he'd go after her that first time. Maybe he found out she was still helping them and he wanted to teach her a lesson again. Maybe he heard the same rumor about her being involved with one of 'em. Who knows?" I drummed my fingers on the table, trying to figure out what I could do to help. If it were Ruby out here, and me in that cell, she'd have already figured everything out and returned me safely to my home. She'd save me just by her sheer will. Why couldn't I do the same?

"Ain't there any way to get her the money she needs to fight this without ruffling her pride?" I asked.

Asa shrugged. "Now, you solve that problem, and you just might be a miracle worker yourself."

"What about her brothers? Would they be willing to help any?"

Asa sighed and shook his head. "Nobody's heard from Henry in months. He could be anywhere from Mississippi to California. Last I heard he was playing ball in the summer for a semi-pro team in Texas. I think during the fall he works with the Civil Conservation Corps somewhere."

"And James?"

"James is a mess. He's all worked up about being in the middle of everything. He ain't gonna be any help."

And then it hit me. "What about her church? Would they support her? What about the people in Hanceville she's helped over the years?"

"You mean ask 'em for money?"

"An offering. We could get the church to have a special service. An all-day singing or something. Churches love those kinds of things. They could take up a special offering to help Ruby."

"I reckon they'd do it, but I don't think that little church could come up with so much as a hundred dollars. Maybe not even fifty. People are hurting right now. No one's got anything to give."

I wasn't listening to his doubts. I'd lit on something I knew would work. And I was prepared to be as determined and persistent as Ruby. "You let me worry about how much money people can donate. You and Mrs. Graves get the singing organized and start letting people in the community know about it. We'll get that church filled to the steeple with people. You watch!"

CHAPTER EIGHT

Ruby

Another day began with me still in jail, and I wondered if God was ever going to speak to me or work His power through me again. I'd prayed most of the night, till I passed out from exhaustion. I'd never felt God's absence like this, and it was slowly becoming about the loneliest feeling I'd ever had.

I was grateful to see Matthew when he showed up after breakfast. I was even more grateful when he handed me a gift through the bars. "Here," he said. "Your mother wanted you to have this."

I took Daddy's Bible and ran my hands over the cover. Then I opened it up to the front where Daddy's name was written inside in his messy scribbles. My throat tightened, and I had to push back my tears. I missed him so much.

"Thank you," I said. "You don't know what this means to me."

"I think I have an idea," he said. His smile warmed my heart, and chased away the lonely ache in my chest. I'd been trying so hard to push Matthew away, but that morning it just felt nice to have the company.

"How's Mary doing?" I asked, realizing we hadn't talked about anything but my troubles for days.

"She's doing real well. Real well. She's going to college, but I think she spends most of her time studying the young men there rather than her books."

"Not surprising."

"No," he said, chuckling. "She's turned out to be a lovely young lady."

"I'm sure she has. She was always kind to me. She was a good friend." I hung my head, ashamed I'd pushed Mary away after Matthew had left for college. But I simply couldn't figure out how to be friends with someone and keep my secrets at the same time. I still hadn't.

"How about you?" he said. "You ever hear from Henry?"

"Oh yes, just about every couple of months or so. He's doing well for himself. Playing baseball out west and working for the Conservation Corps. He's helped build several projects."

"Have you written to him? To let him know what's going on here?"

"No. What could he do about it anyhow? I keep asking him in my letters when he's coming home again, but he doesn't really answer. Just says he's very busy."

"Well, I can't judge him," he said. "Been a pretty lousy brother myself. I can't say I visit often either."

"Why is that?" I asked, more for my own understanding of Henry than anything else. "What's so hard about coming home?"

He kicked his foot against the bottom of the cell bars and shoved his hands in his pockets. "It's complicated. Father don't make things easy. He has his own ideas about who I should be and what I should be doing, and I don't have any use for those ideas. When I'm away, I'm free to make my own choices and be my own man." Then he blew out a big breath. "Then there's you."

"Me?"

"I've been pretty mixed up ever since I saw…well, you praying over Hannah. I didn't handle it well, and I guess I was ashamed of myself. I hated the thought that I might run into you and have to face what I done." He held my gaze a while, as if searching for something. "I still don't quite know what to make of you, but I want you to know how sorry I am for leaving you the way I did."

My heart had just about stopped beating altogether. I scolded it and set my mind right again. Seemed like I had to do that a lot when I was around Matthew. Had I learned nothing from that painful goodbye? I had to find a way to forgiveness that didn't land me right back in the briars of loving him.

"I know you're sorry, and that you want to make up for it. I appreciate all you've done for me."

He dropped his gaze to the floor. "But you won't forgive me."

"You said it yourself. I can't lie. I thought I'd forgiven you a long time ago. But seeing you again made me realize that I hadn't." I paused, feeling terrible for having to tell him the truth. "I want to. Just give me a little time, all right?"

He nodded and cleared his throat. "Of course. I understand." He looked around like he wasn't sure what else to say. "How are you doing this morning? You get any sleep last night?"

I shrugged, not wanting to worry him any more than necessary. "Enough."

"You're still planning on telling that lawyer of yours that you're pleading not guilty, right?"

"Of course," I said. I walked over to my cot and slid Daddy's Bible under the pillow. Then I turned back around and forced a smile. "Nothing to worry about. I'll talk to Mr. Oliver today when he comes by."

"I don't know how you do it. How can you stay so calm about all this?"

I nearly laughed as I plopped down onto the cot. "Truth is, I don't feel calm. I haven't had a moment's peace since all this happened. In fact, I've been struggling with my own faith." I knew I shouldn't say anything, shouldn't open myself up to Matthew. But he was the only one who knew everything about me. I couldn't seem to help myself. "I keep praying for God's help, to feel Him with me. But it seems like I'm just talking to the walls. He doesn't answer."

Matthew pulled the chair over from against the wall and sat down, leaning toward me like he was ready to study me. "Does God talk to you? I mean, out loud or something?"

"It's more like a quiet thought in my mind. Something I know I didn't think myself. And there's a calm peace that comes with it. Like a gentle breeze."

"Must be nice to hear from Him like that. To know exactly what He wants from you. He'd have to write it in the sky with the clouds for me to get it. Might not get it even then."

"He speaks to you too. I'm sure of it. In a way that's just meant for you. You just have to learn how to listen."

He grinned. "I reckon I'm not a good listener then."

"I wish He'd speak to me now," I blurted, barely able to keep my voice even. "I ache for Him to give me some kind of direction. It hurts almost as bad as when Daddy died." My legs felt jittery, so I stood and began pacing the cell.

"It's going to be all right," he said. "You just stay the course, and keep explaining what happened. The truth is going to come out, and everything will be just fine."

That's what I was afraid of. Except when the truth came out, things would never be fine again. I was going to lose everything. My gift, my family, and most certainly my freedom. I wondered for a moment if it wouldn't be better to just tell Matthew everything. If God wasn't going to speak to me, maybe Matthew could help me figure out what to do.

But just as I was about to open my mouth, the door to the lobby opened, and the sheriff walked through. I clamped my mouth shut. A man in handcuffs trailed behind the sheriff, with Deputy John Frost right behind.

Sheriff Peterson walked the man in handcuffs into the cell next to mine. He looked like he'd been dragged out of a pond and all the way to the jail. His clothes were tattered and filthy, and after only a few steps into the room, his stench permeated the whole place. Sheriff Peterson shoved the man into the cell next to mine. The man looked over at me with dark, dead eyes. He started to look away, but then he looked at me more closely, like he was figuring out who I was.

My skin crawled, and I had to look away. I made eye contact with John, and he gave me a slight nod. "Hidey, Ruby," he said.

I smiled back. "Hi there, John. You been doing all right?"

"Sure have."

Sheriff Peterson looked between John and me. "I take it you two know each other?"

John motioned toward Matthew, who waved back at him. "We was all in school together over in Hanceville a few years back."

"Well, isn't that nice," the sheriff said. John's smiled faded, and he stiffened. Then Sheriff Peterson looked over at me. "I got to take care of business on the other side of the county. Deputy Frost here'll be keeping an eye on things for the rest of the day. Holler if you need anything."

They turned for the door, but just then Matthew jumped up from his chair and started toward them. "Is that who I think it is? That's Emmitt Hyde, ain't it? You can't put him next to Ruby."

Sheriff Peterson turned to him with a grimace. "Now, just what do you think he's gonna do? Squeeze through the bars or something? You need to go on home and get out of my business, son."

"Matthew," I said, "what are you doing?"

He stepped back to the door of my cell and pointed at the man again. "Don't you know who that is?" I stared at him in confusion, unable to answer. "That's Emmitt Hyde," he continued. "He's been all over the papers for years now. He's been traipsing all over the surrounding counties stealing what little the farmers have around here."

I looked over at the man again. He'd sat down on his cot and was staring at Matthew and me like he'd like to come over and choke us. I turned back to Matthew and saw the concern growing in his eyes. "It'll be all right. There's nothing to worry about."

"He's bad news, Ruby. He even attacked a couple of farmers over in Morgan county when they caught him stealing. Put both of 'em in the hospital."

My legs felt a little wobbly beneath me, but I was determined not to show an ounce of fear to anyone, least of all Matthew. But when he leaned down and looked me directly in the eyes, my resolve weakened for a second.

"Please Ruby, just let me post your bond. Let's get you out of here and figure out how to face this together. Nothing good's gonna come from you staying in here."

I did waiver, just for a brief moment. But I knew I couldn't put my heart in his hands again. So I shored up my resolve. "I'll be fine."

He slammed his hands against the bars before turning away from me. "It's the same old thing with you as always! 'I'm fine,' you say. Well, look at you." He stepped back over to the bars. "You *ain't* fine. When are you gonna get that through your thick head?"

"I reckon we both have thick heads then," I said, my blood heating up. "'Cause you sure love acting like I need saving all the time. I don't need you to rescue me!"

"That's great! 'Cause I ain't doing it. You want to handle this on your own? Be my guest."

With that, he strode straight past the sheriff and out the door. I watched him go, regret washing over me. My eyes welled up for just a second, but I pushed away the ache in my chest, knowing it was best for both of us that he go.

Sheriff Peterson raised his eyebrow at me. "You need anything, Miss Ruby?"

I shook my head and he closed the door. I stole a quick glance at Mr. Hyde. He was smiling like a cat about to pounce on a mouse.

Mr. Hyde stayed quiet most of the day. I figured it had something to do with finally getting something to eat that almost resembled a meal. He scarfed down his stew and bread like a dog. Then I noticed him looking eagerly at me as I ate mine. He didn't ask for it, though. I expected him to, but he didn't. He just stretched out on his cot and closed his eyes. I thought he might have fallen asleep, but his breathing wasn't quite right for a man who was sleeping. It was too shallow.

Shortly after supper, John came to let me out for my evening washing and to relieve myself. There wasn't a washtub big enough for a bath, but there was a small bowl in a little bathroom that was filled with water for me each night. I cherished that washing more than anyone could know. It was one of the few things that kept me feeling human.

After removing my dress, I leaned over the tub and splashed some of the water over my face, letting the grime of the day trickle away. I scrubbed my face clean and then as much of my body as I could manage in the tiny space. Then I put my ragged dress back on. I hoped Mother would bring me a clean one the next day. Between the makeshift baths and not having any place to take care of myself, I knew I looked terrible. I loosened my hair from its braid and pulled a handful around in front of me. It felt like straw in my hands. It shouldn't matter, but I hated looking so poor with Matthew coming around every day. No wonder he felt so sorry for me.

I resigned myself to doing what I could, ran my fingers through my hair several times, pinned it back up, and then let myself out. John escorted me back to my cell. I could feel Mr. Hyde's eyes on me the whole time. It made my skin feel like there were a thousand tiny chiggers crawling all over me. I walked over to my cot and sat as far away from his cell as I could.

"Come on, Emmitt," John said. "I reckon it's your turn now."

They disappeared for a while, so I closed my eyes and concentrated on my prayers. Seemed like only a few minutes had passed when I heard them coming back. Mr. Hyde came through the cell door and stopped right in the middle of his cell. He looked over at me, and I could've sworn he looked even more menacing with his black hair slicked back. His eyes bulged out, and his jaw jutted forward. If he'd washed himself, it sure didn't make a lick of difference. He still smelled to high heaven and back.

John closed his cell door and left us there to ruminate in the stench. Mr. Hyde shuffled over to the bars separating our cells and leaned onto them, his hands dangling into my cell. The black grime surrounding his nails made me wonder what kind of hardship they'd seen. I couldn't help but have some compassion for him. He didn't look much different than the poor souls I'd once served at the soup kitchen, except he had this awful darkness that just seemed to sit on him.

When I was younger, I figured out I could see this sort of light around people. Not like a bright light that shone all around them; not like they were glowing or anything. But if I looked at people with my heart, if I saw the brokenness that weighed them down, and God showed me His love for them, then I'd start to see them in shades of light. Some people, like Mary, were as bright as the sun, warming me from the inside out every time they were near.

But others, like Chester, were as dark as storm clouds, and I did everything I could to keep my distance from them. That was what I saw when I looked at Mr. Hyde through the cell bars. He was dark, so dark I could hardly stand to look at him. He sneered down at me, and I tucked my knees up to my chest.

"What's it like being with a Negro?" he asked, his voice dry and rough.

"Wh—Excuse me?" I stuttered.

"Well, you know, I just thought you might be able to tell me the difference. I mean, I imagine it's almost like being with an animal or something."

"I have no idea what you're talking about."

"Why, sure you do. I'm pretty certain I read about it in the newspaper yesterday. You and your Negro boyfriend killed that white man when he caught you—"

"Now you listen here!" I pushed myself up from my cot, my anger overcoming my fear of him as I marched right up to where he stood and shoved a finger in his face. "I may be a woman, but I am not scared of you! Now you best get your filthy mind and body on back to your cot! I have never in my life—"

"Oh, don't get so bent out of shape!" His eyebrows shot up and to my surprise, he stepped away from the bars. "I didn't mean no harm or nothing."

"Don't you have an ounce of dignity? Don't you have one iota of self-respect?"

His face went blank, and I imagined he was trying to figure out what an iota was. But then he furrowed his brow and came right back at me. "Don't go throwing your big words around at me, young 'un. I done raised one smart-mouth child of my own, and I ain't gonna take it from you. I'll turn you over my lap quicker than you can say jack rabbit!"

We stared each other down, all the while my heart thumping in my chest like a racehorse's hooves. What was I thinking? Getting this man riled up at me was about the dumbest thing I'd ever done. But something seemed to change in him, and he lost the sneer he'd had earlier. He shook his head and went back over to his cot, sitting down so hard I thought it was going to break.

I eased back over to my cot and curled up under the blanket. Maybe something I'd said or done had reminded him of his own children. Maybe he had just a tiny glimmer of light inside of him, buried under all that anger and disappointment. I closed my eyes and tried not to think of that sneer. Instead, I prayed for Mr. Hyde, that God would go into his heart and find that tiny ember, and he'd light Mr. Hyde on fire with his compassion. But if he couldn't change Mr. Hyde's heart, I prayed he'd protect me from his wrath.

Mr. Hyde didn't say anything else for a while. I sat on my bed and scooted up against the wall, opening Daddy's Bible on my lap to the Book of John. It was my favorite book, the one I turned to for comfort. Then I started reading out loud, 'cause that made it even more real to me. As I reached the fourth chapter, I was beginning to feel the comfort I'd been seeking, and I'd completely forgotten where I was, and what my troubles were. I was with Jesus as he sat by the well in Samaria.

"There cometh a woman of Samaria to draw water: Jesus saith unto her, Give me to drink. (For his disciples were gone away unto the city to buy meat.) Then saith the woman of Samaria unto him, How is it that thou being a Jew, askest drink of me, which am a woman of Samaria? for the Jews have no dealings with the Samaritans. Jesus answered and said unto her, If thou knewest the gift of God, and who it is that saith to thee, Give me to drink; thou wouldest have asked of him, and he would have given thee living water.

"The woman saith unto him, Sir, thou hast nothing to draw with, and the well is deep: from whence then hast thou that living water? Art thou greater than our father Jacob, which gave us the well, and drank thereof himself, and his children, and his cattle?

"Jesus answered and said unto her, Whosoever drinketh of this water shall thirst again: But whosoever drinketh of the water that I shall give him shall never thirst; but the water that I shall give him shall be in him a well of water springing up into everlasting life."

Resting my voice, I laid my head back against the wall and closed my eyes. *Lord, please speak your words of life to me now. Don't leave me here all alone.*

"You're wasting your time."

I looked over at Mr. Hyde sprawled across his bed. He hadn't moved in hours. I'd figured he was asleep. "I apologize if I woke you, Mr. Hyde."

He slid his arm away from his face and sat up on his bed. His dark eyes bore into mine. "Why you waste all your time praying and reading that malarkey? Don't you know God's abandoned you?"

"He hasn't abandoned me. And He hasn't abandoned you either."

He pushed out a half laugh, half cough. "He's definitely abandoned me. Long time ago. Not that I care. I don't need Him anyhow." He pointed at his chest. "I take care of myself. I don't need God doing nothing for me." He shook his head. "Living water. Why that's the dumbest thing I ever heard."

I wondered what had happened to make him so bitter and angry. And despite our earlier confrontation, my heart softened for him. "I have that living water in me," I said. "You can have it too. You don't have to keep living like you are. There's still hope."

He waved me off with his hand and leaned back against his wall. "God done took everything I had. What is there left to hope for?"

"You're still alive, aren't you? You haven't lost everything yet. There's still time to get to know Him."

He closed his eyes, and I figured he was done talking to me. I was about to go back to reading when he started talking real low. "My Caroline would be about fifteen now, I reckon. She died about five years ago, and she was just ten. So yeah. About fifteen."

"What happened to her?"

"Scarlet fever. Got her and her momma both. Little Caroline died first, on Sunday. My Rachel followed her two days later. Said she couldn't stand the thought of her baby being all alone without her." He gave a chuckle that wasn't much more than a sob. "I tried to catch it too, just so I wouldn't be left here all alone. But I reckon God didn't want me around, and I can't say I blame him. So I been stuck here. Doing what I can to get by."

I hesitated, wondering if I'd just draw more of his ire if I spoke. But then I stood and walked over to the bars separating our cells. "I lost my little brother to the Spanish flu when he was three. One of the worst times of my life. My parents' too. My daddy nearly went mad with grief."

Mr. Hyde picked at his blanket like he wasn't listening, but I kept on going. "Then a few years ago, my daddy died from diabetes. I prayed like everything for God to heal him, and when he died, I thought it was because I didn't have enough faith. But I learned that death is part of life. Losing people is part of loving them. You can't have one without the other."

Mr. Hyde sniffed and finally looked up at me. "That's all well and good for you. But I ain't got nothing left. You still got folks who love you. Like that boy in here fussing over you. Bet your momma still cares for you too. Don't nobody care if I live or die."

"I care." I hoped as he looked at me, he could see that I meant it. "Jesus cares. Maybe if I pray with you—"

"Young lady, I'm sure you're a fine person, and maybe you didn't do what they say you did. Anyway, I hope not. I thank you for trying to be kind to me. But all I want is to see my girls again. To be the man I was before all this happened. And there ain't nothing in this world anyone, not even Jesus, can do to make that happen."

"Mr. Hyde, if it's all the same to you, I'd still like to pray for you."

"Go on, then. I reckon you got the right to pray as you want. But it'll be a waste of time."

I dropped my head and closed my eyes. "Lord, I thank You for putting me here next to Mr. Hyde just when he needed to hear a word of encouragement from You. I ask You to take his hardened heart, and fill it with Your hope. Give him the peace of knowing his girls are safe in Your loving arms, and that if he only trusts in You, he can be with them again someday. Give him the strength to let go of his anger, and all the despair he's endured. Show him Your love and mercy and forgiveness. Jesus, I pray in Your name. Amen."

When I looked up again, Mr. Hyde sat on the edge of his bed, his shoulders slumped forward, his chin on his chest, and tears streaming down his face. He lowered himself down until he was lying on his side facing the wall.

Mr. Hyde didn't say anything else to me the rest of the night. He just curled up on his bed with his back to me. I figured there was nothing more I could do for him except to pray. So when I went to bed, I prayed for him over and over, begging God to show Himself to Mr. Hyde. And to speak to me again too. Then I prayed for Mother and Asa, that they wouldn't be too burdened with trying to help me. I hated the anguish I was putting on Mother.

Then I prayed for Matthew. I prayed God would lead him away from me and toward the future God intended. I prayed for strength to keep my heart from being broken all to pieces again, while still being able to forgive. Somehow.

CHAPTER NINE

Ruby

I eventually drifted off to sleep, dreaming of Matthew as if I hadn't just prayed for God to take him out of my thoughts. At some point during the night, I heard my name.

Ruby.

My eyes flew open, and I sat up. Mr. Hyde was asleep, and no one was in the cell room with us. But I knew beyond any doubt, someone had called my name. I sat there for a moment wondering what I should do, but then I decided there wasn't anything for me to do about it. So I lay back down and closed my eyes again.

Ruby.

This time I kept my eyes closed and didn't move.

Ruby, the door is open.

I waited for more, 'cause that didn't make much sense. But nothing else came. I wondered if maybe I'd heard the voice wrong. What door was open? Was there some journey God was getting ready to send me on? Or maybe he was talking about Mr. Hyde? Maybe the door was open for me to talk to him more about God's power to change his life. I certainly couldn't make heads or tails about it, so I eventually drifted off to sleep again.

The next time I awoke, it was still dark, but I could hear sobs coming from Mr. Hyde's cell. They were quiet sobs, and he mumbled something to himself about "be seeing you soon." I wondered if he was praying.

But then I felt something uneasy inside me, like something dark had come in there with us. Something was very wrong. I pulled the chain to the light bulb above me. Then I got up and walked over to the bars between us, straining to see Mr. Hyde in the dim light. When my eyes and mind finally put the scene together, my heart raced to life. Mr. Hyde was sprawled across the bed on his back, his arm hanging off the side and blood dripping from his wrist.

I rattled the bars and screamed at the top of my lungs. "Help! Someone help! John? Please help!"

A moment later I heard shuffling around in the office outside the door. I screamed again. "Help! Mr. Hyde's hurt! Please!"

Mr. Hyde didn't move the whole time I was making my ruckus. I wondered if he was already dead. John burst through the door and fumbled around to find the light switch. "What's going on in here?" he called.

"It's Mr. Hyde! He's injured!"

The big light finally came on, and John looked in on Mr. Hyde. He unlocked the cell and rushed over to him, trying to feel his neck for a pulse. "I need to call the Sheriff."

"Is he alive?"

John stood and ran out of the cell. "Yes, barely."

"Then let me help him! I'm a nurse. I can bandage the wounds while you get help."

He stopped and looked at me like he was considering it for a moment. "Probably best you stay in there. I'll take care of this."

Then he was gone. I stood there and watched the life drain out of Mr. Hyde, my mind racing over what I could possibly do. He needed bandages. Fast. If only I could've gotten out of my cell! I paced back and forth for a moment, praying God would help Mr. Hyde. Then I forced myself to stop moving, to still my thoughts and listen for God's word.

Ruby, the door is open.

I opened my eyes and looked at my cell door. It was cracked open.

I raced through it and went into Mr. Hyde's cell, kneeling beside him and ripping off a strip of my dress. I wrapped it around his wrist. Then I reached for his arm furthest away, and I saw it was also cut and seeping blood. A shard of metal, maybe a piece from the bed, clanged to the floor. He'd cut his arm long ways, up the vein. I wouldn't be able to stop it with a simple wrap.

I closed my eyes again, and I stilled my thoughts. *Lord, what would you have me do?*

The air around me went perfectly still, and the most wonderful peace flooded my heart. I took ahold of Mr. Hyde's wrist and I prayed along with the words God laid on my heart. Not my own words, not from my own mind. But words He spoke through me. Words of grace and hope. Words of healing.

As the Spirit began to fade, I looked down at Mr. Hyde's wrist. No more bleeding. I tore two more strips off my dress and wrapped them around the wound. Then I felt his neck for his pulse. It was weak, but he was still alive. He moaned as his eyes fluttered open.

"Mmm...gonna...see my girls," he mumbled.

I knelt down to his ear and whispered. "Not yet, my friend. Not yet."

I heard commotion out in the sheriff's office, so I checked the bandages one more time before darting back into my cell. I closed the door behind me, and it clicked shut. Not a second later, John came barreling back into the room with strips of cloth. He knelt beside Mr. Hyde and picked up his right arm. He looked over the bandage. Then the left arm.

"Ruby?"

"Yes, sir?"

"You been out of your cell?" He stood and walked toward the bars that separated us. His black hair was all a mess, and his eyes were wild.

I didn't want to lie, so I just shrugged my shoulders and dropped my gaze to the floor. He left Mr. Hyde's cell and came over to the door of my cell. He shook it. Locked. He stood there for what seemed like the longest time, just staring at me. I finally lifted my eyes back to his. He was looking at the bottom of my yellow dress.

John went back over to Mr. Hyde and lifted one of his arms, studying the yellow bandage. He pulled it back just a bit, and then he dropped the arm. He turned wide, dark eyes back to me.

"Ruby, he ain't even bleeding." He took a few steps toward me. "What did you do?"

I spent the rest of the morning hours on my knees. One minute I was begging God for Mr. Hyde to be all right. The next, I was singing praises that I'd felt His spirit move in my heart again. I'd longed for it so deeply. And what a blessing it was! My heart was so overwhelmed with joy; I couldn't hold back my tears. So I sobbed, and sang, and sobbed some more.

"Ruby, what's wrong?" I turned when I heard Matthew's voice behind me. His face was stricken; his eyes nearly frantic. He looked around and froze when he saw the blood on the floor of Mr. Hyde's cell. "What's going on? Are you all right? Where's Mr. Hyde?"

I stood and came to the edge of my cell, wanting to pour out all my joy on him. But I caught myself just in time. He wouldn't understand. "I'm fine. Really. I was just praying and spending time with God."

"You're crying. And there's...there's blood." He gripped the bars in front of me.

I wiped away my tears and shook my head. "It's okay now. Last night, Mr. Hyde tried to kill himself."

"What? Did he try to hurt you?"

"No, no. I swear, I'm fine. I'm better than fine. It's all okay. He's going to be okay."

Matthew stared at me, a flicker of fear crossing his face. "Ruby, what exactly happened in here last night?"

I wasn't sure how much to tell him, but I also knew he'd find out most of it anyway. "Mr. Hyde cut his wrists with a shard of metal from his bed. John was out front, so I called for help. He came in here and saw that Mr. Hyde was in bad shape. Then he called for the sheriff, and they took him over to the hospital."

Matthew let go of the bars and rubbed the back of his neck. It seemed he was having a hard time looking at me. "Did you...um...did you heal him?"

"No." Relief flickered in his eyes, until I finished with the truth. "God did."

He dropped his hand as if he'd been burned. "What were you thinking, Ruby? You can't be doing that kind of thing in here!" Shaking his head, he went to pacing along the bars. "Look, I don't pretend to understand everything about your...your gift. But it's a bad idea to be doing that in here. Especially with Cass after you again."

"I don't see how this has anything to do with Brother Cass or my case. A man was in trouble. I helped. It's as simple as that."

"No, it ain't simple at all. This explains why Mr. Garrett was out front, talking to the sheriff. I knew something was up."

"It might not have anything to do with me."

He blew out a puff of air, still pacing just beyond the bars. I reached my hand out and grabbed his arm. "Hey. What are you so afraid of?"

For a moment Matthew looked down at my hand clamped on his arm, before slowly bringing his eyes up to mine. My heart thumped wildly.

"You, Ruby," he said quietly. "I'm afraid *for* you. Don't you realize that everything you do right now is going to be twisted against you? You have to think about your future. You have to stop this. At least until the trial is over."

"Matthew Doyle, don't you even believe in your own healing anymore? Don't you remember?"

He leaned his forehead against the bars and closed his eyes. "Yes. I remember."

"Then you know healing comes from the Spirit of God. It's not something I do at my choosing. I'm only the vessel. I can't ignore God's calling. He tells me when He's going to heal. It's all from Him."

Matthew sighed and pushed away from the bars. "Of course it is. I get that, okay. I just don't want you to jeopardize your future."

"You still don't believe in me, do you?"

He shoved his hands in his pockets and looked everywhere but at me. "I don't know what you mean."

"You don't believe this power is from God. You think Cass is right about me."

Mention of Cass's name seemed to trigger something in Matthew. "Hey, that ain't true!" Frowning, he shook his finger at me like he was scolding a child. "Don't you say nothing like that again, you hear me? That old goat don't know nothing about you."

I waited for him to answer the rest of my accusation, but he didn't say anything else. That told me everything I needed to know.

The door opened and Mr. Garrett walked toward my cell. Mr. Oliver was close behind. They stopped just beside Matthew.

"Miss Ruby," Mr. Garrett said, "I need to ask you a few questions about last night."

"Yes, sir," I said.

Matthew pushed up close to the bars again. "Don't say nothing."

Mr. Garrett turned to Matthew with his chest puffed out. "Son, I think you should go now. I need to speak with Miss Graves and her lawyer alone. You have no part in this."

Matthew shook his head and muttered under his breath. "I'll be back in an hour. Remember, don't say nothing."

After the door closed behind Matthew, Mr. Garrett asked me to explain exactly what happened the night before. Contrary to what Matthew thought of me, I knew my position was precarious, and the less I said the better. Especially until I was certain of whether or not I could trust Mr. Oliver.

"What does this have to do with the charges against me?" I asked.

Mr. Garrett leaned forward. "I'd appreciate it if you'd let me do the asking, and you do the answering."

"It's a legitimate question, Charles," Mr. Oliver said. "If you intend to bring new charges against Miss Graves, then do so. But what happened in the cells last night has no bearing on her case, and you know it."

Mr. Garrett's icy stare travelled from me to Mr. Oliver. "Does she have something to hide? I'd think if she was completely innocent of any wrongdoing, then explaining the events that took place here would be of little consequence."

"Look, it's real simple," I said. "Mr. Hyde cut himself. I saw he was hurt. I called for help. Deputy Frost came in and looked him over before calling for the sheriff. I simply bandaged his wrists using strips torn from my dress."

Mr. Garrett's mouth slid into a grin. "Then you left your cell?"

Mr. Oliver put a hand up to silence me. "She answered your question. That's enough. She'll answer no more."

Mr. Garrett looked at me like he knew he'd won something, but I wasn't quite sure what game we were playing. Then he turned to Mr. Oliver. "Well, as long as we're all here, we might as well discuss the plea deal you asked about."

"I'm not pleading guilty," I said.

Mr. Oliver's eyes widened, but he didn't contradict me. Mr. Garrett actually looked pleased. "All right then. I suppose I'll see you in court."

Then he bent over and took a look at the lock on my cell door, after a while straightening and calling for the sheriff. Before leaving, he offered me another victorious smile.

"You know, Mr. Hyde was very lucky it was you next to him, what with you being experienced with wounds and all. Some might call it a miracle he survived."

I kept my mouth shut, feeling a cold dread work its way up my spine. What if my secret wasn't so secret? Would he try to use my gift against me somehow?

Mr. Garrett's words hung in the air after he left, along with the growing realization that I couldn't trust anybody in the whole wide world. I turned to Mr. Oliver and gripped the bars. He wiped the sweat from his brow with his handkerchief.

"I need to know something," I said.

"Yes, ma'am."

"Just where do we stand? You and me, I mean. Are you on my side?"

"Well, of course I'm on your side," he said carefully, putting the handkerchief back in the breast pocket of his suit. "Why ever would you ask that?"

"Have you been talking to Brother Cass about me?"

"Brother Cass is the preacher at the church I attend, and yes, he has shown interest in your case. But I promise you I have told him nothing that isn't public record. And I won't tell him anything at all if you don't want me to."

"That man despises me. Has he tried to get you to do anything against me?"

There was a split second of hesitation. "No, not really. He's just shown some interest in your case. I assumed it was innocent curiosity at first, but after what he said in the paper, I came to the same conclusion you just mentioned. It's true, he does seem to have a negative opinion of you. But I promise that will in no way affect my work on your case."

"Mr. Oliver, do you believe me? Do you believe I was defending myself?"

"It doesn't matter what I believe, honey."

"It matters to me. If you don't believe me, then how can you speak for me?"

He ran his hand through his thinning hair. I could see he was torn. Over what, I wasn't quite sure. After a few moments, he met my gaze again. "Listen, Ruby. If I'm going to do the best job I can to defend you, then you have to tell me the whole truth about what happened in that barn. There can't be any surprises. It only takes one little detail you left out for Mr. Garrett to paint you as a liar, and then you're through. I want to believe you, because you seem like a nice girl with a kind heart. But I'm not convinced you've told me everything. So it's not a matter of whether or not I believe you. It's a matter of whether or not you trust me enough to tell me the whole truth and nothing but the truth."

My stomach churned as I considered telling the whole truth. Could I trust Mr. Oliver? I doubted it. And I couldn't take the chance. No matter what, I had to hold onto my secrets. I'd never tell anyone what really happened in that barn. Ever.

"I've told you everything," I said.

He didn't look convinced, but he didn't question me further. "All right then. Let's talk about our strategy moving forward. Given the unusual nature of this case, I'd recommend that we not ask the jury to consider manslaughter as an option. It's murder or nothing. And no one in their right mind would convict you of murder with the evidence they have."

"But what if they do?"

Mr. Oliver fell silent for some time as he considered my question. At last he spoke. "Then you'd most likely go to prison for a very long time." He looked up and held my gaze, the possibility he had not mentioned left hanging in the air between us.

But I couldn't bring myself to utter the words "electric chair" any more than he could. I dropped my eyes, hugged my waist and prayed for wisdom. "Do we have to decide this now?"

"No. We can decide any time before the trial starts. But I'll tell you, in my experience, when the jury has the option of finding someone guilty of manslaughter, they usually take it. It's hard to convince twelve men that you're completely innocent of any wrongdoing. But it's also hard to convince them that you're completely guilty."

"All right, Mr. Oliver," I said, still unsure about the whole thing. "I trust you. We'll do what you think is best."

CHAPTER TEN

Matthew

I just knew Mr. Garrett was going to twist something awful out of Ruby healing Emmitt Hyde. I wasn't quite sure how, but I was even more convinced that I had to get her out of that cell as soon as possible. I tried talking to Father again. But things ended up even worse than before, with me becoming so infuriated that I moved all my things out of the house and into my brother Frank's house in Cullman. Probably worked out for the best anyhow. I was closer to Ruby for the time being.

I spent the rest of the week helping Dr. and Mrs. Fisher, Asa and Mrs. Graves talk to folks about going to the special service at Ruby's church on Sunday. We were met with enough support and encouragement for me to get my hopes up just a bit. Asa cautioned me against it, especially when Mr. Hatchet, the owner of the drugstore, said he'd overheard talk of the Calhouns busting up the service. But I was not going to be swayed. I refused to fail Ruby again. And I prayed like I'd never prayed before. Surely, if anyone had God on her side, it was Ruby.

When Sunday rolled around, the little sanctuary was filled to the brim with folks. Some were even standing in the back. Before things got started, I spoke with Asa and Mrs. Graves, outlining my hopes for enough money to get Ruby out of jail. They didn't share my optimism.

"Of course we're praying for the best," Mrs. Graves said, "but these folks have so little to give. Seems like people are worse off now than ever."

"But look around," I said. "Something about Ruby moves people. Everyone we talked to had some story to share of when she helped them out in a time of need. Surely they can manage to return her kindness?"

Asa patted me on the shoulder. "You done all you could, son. And we're mighty thankful. But it's in God's hands now, and we just have to pray. Put your trust in Him. Not in these poor folks."

He sounded just like Ruby. "Is James not coming?" I asked, trying not to be too obvious about shifting the conversation.

"He says he don't know which way to turn," Mrs. Graves said. "He's all in a fuss about being in the middle of things. Says he can't stand to see his family torn apart. I don't believe he'll show up."

I figured as much. "What about Henry? Any word from him?"

"No, nothing."

My anger flared. How could her brothers leave her hanging out in the wind like that? She deserved so much better.

The music started, so we turned to the front and sang the opening song. I managed to control my nerves through announcements and prayer requests, more singing and more praying. Then a lot more singing, and a lot more praying. I kept my thoughts on Ruby, praying for a miracle, at least the kind that made sense. When the general offering plate was passed around, I couldn't help my hope that people would save their money to give when the plate came around for Ruby. Seemed like an awful thing to hope for, but I did nonetheless.

About the time the offering was completed, I heard a bit of mumbling from the back of the church on the opposite side from where I sat. I turned my head along with the others to see what was going on, and my stomach dropped. Mr. and Mrs. Calhoun made their way across the back of the church, sliding in between some others near the back windows. I could tell by their hard-set jaws they were not there to support Ruby. All I could do was pray they weren't there to sabotage her either.

Brother Harbison took the pulpit and welcomed everyone to the service. He looked around the sanctuary with a kind smile, and thanked the visitors for coming as well. Then he reminded folks that there would be a special offering at the end of the sermon to support Ruby's family. It was all I could do to keep from looking back at the Calhouns, though I'm sure many others didn't restrain themselves.

Brother Harbison began by reading from the fifth chapter of Acts, describing when several of the Apostles were arrested and thrown in prison. An angel from the Lord came to them, opened the doors, and told them to go preach the words of life in the temple. So they did. And when the chief priests and teachers of the law found out they were no longer in the prison, they had the Apostles brought by force before them.

"And did the Apostles act out of fear for their lives?" Brother Harbison said. "No. They stood up to the religious leaders of their time, even unto death. In fact, the leaders were so infuriated by the Apostles' determination to lay Jesus's death on their heads that they rose up to kill them too!" He looked around the congregation with accusing eyes. "How many of you would be so willing to stand by your faith, that you would die to preserve it? How far would you go? How much would you sacrifice?"

An uneasy sensation worked its way over me as I considered the questions. I had no doubt about Ruby. There didn't seem to be a thing in this world that could knock her off her faith, not even death. How did she do that? I was filled with too many doubts and questions. I'd blow over in a strong wind. I knew it.

Finally, Brother Harbison finished with the end of the chapter. "And when they had called the apostles, and beaten them, they commanded that they should not speak in the name of Jesus, and let them go. And they departed from the presence of the council, rejoicing that they were counted worthy to suffer shame for his name. And daily in the temple, and in every house, they ceased not to teach and preach Jesus Christ."

Brother Harbison took a long pause and seemed to consider his words before moving on. "Now I know there are many in our community who are suffering, so I do not say this lightly. But take note of the mindset of the apostles. They *rejoiced* because they were counted worthy to suffer. *Worthy* to suffer. Think on that for a moment. Is suffering some kind of badge of honor? Is it something we should consider a blessing?" He paused again. "Maybe it is, in certain circumstances. Now I don't believe the Scriptures are talking about suffering from the consequences of our sin. But suffering because we refuse to back down from our faith? Now that is an honor, and a blessing. And we should pray for the honor to suffer for the name of Jesus."

I closed my eyes and wished he'd talk on something else. I wished he'd focus on the angel setting those apostles free. Or how God was going to support Ruby in her time of need, just like he did for the apostles. I could think of many other avenues that sermon could have traveled. But there was nothing I could do about it. I just hoped it wasn't God trying to tell me that Ruby was about to suffer even more than she already had.

Finally, Brother Harbison concluded the service. We sang a hymn, and he asked everyone to be seated. Then he took a quick, nervous glance toward the back corner of the sanctuary where the Calhouns still sat. "Now, we must turn our hearts to one of our dear sisters. As you all know, Miss Ruby is currently in jail awaiting trial. I'll not go into the details of her case, as that's for the Lord to sort out. But many of you have been cared for by Miss Ruby and know that she has a heart for the Lord's service. I ask you to pray and consider what you can do now to support her and her family in this time of need."

I was surprised he didn't make a more impassioned plea. I wanted to take the pulpit myself and explain exactly who Ruby was, exactly who Chester was, and exactly what he'd done to her before. These people needed to know, so they could reach as deep into their shallow pockets as possible. But Brother Harbison only lifted his hand and said a quiet prayer.

When he finished, he looked around at the faces in the congregation with a tight smile. "Now Mrs. Graves, will you please come forward and share with us what your family's needs are."

Ruby's mother eased her way past a couple at the end of the pew, strolled down the aisle and stood in front of the pulpit. "I want to thank all of you for coming out today. I know how hard these times are on many of you. We are grateful for any amount that the Lord chooses to provide today. Of course, we're praying to receive enough to cover Ruby's bond, but anything will help her. We just ask that you pray and give as the Lord leads you." She made her way back to her seat, her head low like she was embarrassed.

Then Brother Harbison spoke again. "Would anyone else like to add anything before we take up the offering?"

Two older gentleman rose from their seats and approached the front of the sanctuary with tiny straw baskets in their hands. I dropped my head and leaned onto my knees to pray. This was it. Time for God to work that miracle. But a rough, deep voice came from the back of the church.

"I'd like to say something, Pastor." I knew that voice. It was Mr. Calhoun.

"Of course," Brother Harbison said.

I turned my head to see Mr. Calhoun come about halfway down the aisle before he turned to face everyone. He held his straw hat over his chest as he spoke. "I'd like to ask all of you to remember my son, Chester Calhoun, today as well. We ain't here to ask for your donations. The good Lord has provided for our needs. But I do ask that you pray for wisdom before you reach into your pockets. Now, Chester was no saint. We all know that. But he didn't deserve to die, especially like that. And all we want for him is justice."

My stomach rolled with every sentence out of that man's mouth. It was all I could do to keep from jumping out of my seat and telling him to hightail it out of there.

"Let me just say this," he continued. "Miss Graves was well-known to keep company with Negroes, and her associations have brought a great deal of shame on this community. I pray you'll all ask yourself if you really want to give support to someone who'll put Negroes ahead of her family and her community."

I couldn't stand it anymore. I pushed up from my seat and pointed my finger at that hypocrite. "How dare you come in here and speak lies against Ruby! You accuse yourself with your own words, Percy Calhoun!"

Asa pulled roughly on my arm, yanking me down in my seat.

"He ain't gonna say those things about Ruby," I protested to him, loud enough for everyone to hear.

"Now, let's everyone settle down," Brother Harbison said over the rising tide of voices.

Mr. Calhoun turned and grabbed Mrs. Calhoun from where she stood in the back, marching themselves out of the church. He shot an angry glance over the crowd at me, and I hoped he caught the meaning behind my stare as well.

Brother Harbison got everyone quieted down again. He called for reflection and prayer, and then we passed around the straw baskets. I tried my best to calm myself, but I could tell the whole atmosphere had changed with Calhoun's words. I didn't even need to know the final count of the donations at the end. God had once again left Ruby to languish without his support. And I'd have to find some way to bridge the gap.

Once the church had emptied and the money had been counted, it was official. The people Ruby had so faithfully poured her heart and soul into had managed to cobble together a measly seventy-nine dollars and fifty-seven cents.

Words could not begin to describe the fury and frustration coursing through my veins. In one fell swoop, I knocked the basket and all its contents to the floor. "What kind of game is God playing at here?"

As I paced the front of the sanctuary, Asa kept his cool. "Now listen, Matthew. Surely you didn't expect this little congregation of poor folks to raise four thousand dollars today."

"It's not that. I just thought that if we prayed hard enough—and after everything Ruby's done in His name—I just thought He'd work a miracle or something."

"Don't go getting all upset," Asa said. "We have to remain strong in our faith. There's a reason for all of this. We have to trust in the Lord."

Stopping dead in my tracks, I pointed my finger at him. "You spout all this high theology, and talk about miracles and faith, but when we need Him the most, when someone who has the ultimate faith in Him needs His help...what happens? He doesn't show up! I don't understand. It's like He asks everything of her, and gives nothing in return."

Mrs. Graves was busy cleaning up my mess. She straightened and tried to reason with me. "Listen, Matthew, I know it's hard to look at the circumstances and see God's hand, especially in the middle of the storm. Most times, we don't see His perfect plan until long after the dust has settled. Now, Ruby cares for you, and she needs you to stay strong. She can't carry the weight of her own doubts and fears and add yours to it as well."

I forced myself to consider her words, knowing she was right. But how was I supposed to face Ruby and tell her I'd failed her again?

On Monday morning I met Asa and Mrs. Graves at the jail to tell Ruby about the church service. Mrs. Graves had a clean dress in her hands, which only underscored the fact that Ruby was set to spend a lot more time in jail if I didn't figure out a way to get back the money Father took from me.

Sheriff Peterson was seated at his desk as we came in, and he came around and shook all our hands. "Mr. Oliver's meeting with Ruby right now. You all can wait here, or come back in a while if you want."

We agreed to wait, so I went outside to take in the fresh air and think through a plan to confront Father. 'Course, everything I came up with seemed to be no good. Talking had gotten me nowhere, so that was out. But maybe he'd put the cash where I could find it, if I just thought hard enough. Where had I seen him put money before? I couldn't recall him keeping cash stored in any particular place. Seemed like he always put it in the bank—he expected his money to earn its keep as much as anyone else. I couldn't very well break into the bank.

Maybe he had a safe of some kind in his office? I couldn't remember seeing one. Maybe a lock box in his desk or something. But if that were the case, I'd have to find the key as well. I didn't like the idea of sneaking around Father's office, but I was having trouble coming up with any other ideas. He was adamant that the money belonged to him, and the only way I was going to get it back was to take it.

After I'd exhausted all my ideas, Mr. Oliver finally came out into the parking lot. He stopped when he reached me, and we shook hands. "Asa says you were able to raise a bit of money yesterday."

"Not nearly enough."

"No, but it's a start. It may not cover her bond, but she'll need other things before the trial. A nice dress for starters. But we can cover all that next week."

"Next week?"

His shoulders sagged. "I tried to get the trial pushed back so I could have some more time, but the judge set the date of the trial to a week from Wednesday."

I was dumbfounded. "That's...why? I don't understand. That's only a little more than a few weeks to prepare for trial. What's the hurry?"

"Honestly? Seems like some important people in town are pushing things along. I don't like the feel of it. Nothing technically illegal, mind you. But still, seems like Ruby has some powerful enemies."

"Cass," I muttered.

He nodded. "And I hate to say it, but your father seems to be pulling strings as well. I can't put my finger on anything specific yet, but his name came up when I was speaking with Mr. Garrett."

"How? What's he done?"

"There's a rumor going around he's willing to pay for evidence against Ruby."

I couldn't believe what I was hearing. Surely it wasn't true! I knew Father didn't want me helping Ruby, but would he go so far as to railroad her? And why?

"Mr. Oliver," I said. "Is there anything I can do to help you? Do you need some kind of assistant or something? You don't have to pay me or anything. But Ruby deserves the best defense you can give her, and I plan on making that happen."

"Well, now that you mention it, I believe I'd be grateful for some help, son."

The weight I'd been carrying from my failure thus far seemed to lighten a bit. "What can I do?"

"I've only had time to go over the evidence from the scene briefly. Why don't we meet back here after dinner and pick through it together? Maybe between the two of us we can get a better idea of what the prosecution is going to throw at us."

"Terrific. I'll meet you back here this afternoon, say around two."

We shook hands again, and said our goodbyes. Then I headed into the jail and back to Ruby's cell. By the time I got there, Asa and Mrs. Graves had explained everything that had happened at the church service the day before. I thought at first Ruby was sad, which nearly broke my heart. But her damp eyes looked on me with admiration in them.

"You did all that for me?" she said.

I went to her and rested my hands on the bars next to hers. "Of course. I told you I was going to get you out of here, and I meant it. I ain't giving up on you. I'm just sorry it wasn't enough."

"It was enough," she said. "It was exactly enough. I don't want to take any money from anyone. Especially the poor folks in my church. I'd have felt just awful if they gave more than that."

"If it hadn't been for Calhoun—"

"No, Matthew. Don't worry about that. Thank you for trying. And for not just throwing your own money in there to make it happen. I'm even more grateful you trusted God."

I shook my head, completely baffled by her attitude. "But He didn't come though. I did everything I could think of, and I prayed and prayed. He didn't answer."

She smiled. "Yes, He did. Matthew, just because things didn't happen the way you wanted doesn't mean you didn't get an answer." She placed her hand over mine, sending a tingle of warmth through me. "You'll see. It will be exactly what we need when we need it."

Standing there with her, looking into her faith, I could almost believe what she said. Maybe she was right. Maybe I could trust God to take care of her, even in jail.

I stayed with Ruby even after Asa and Mrs. Graves left. I even brought her a hamburger and a Coca-Cola from the Busy Bee Café for dinner. Something had changed in her toward me. It was like a wall had come down between us. She almost seemed happy, which I found odd considering her circumstances.

But it was also infectious. By the time I met Mr. Oliver out in the lobby, I was downright optimistic that Ruby was going to be all right. We'd show everyone the truth, and she'd be fine.

After shaking hands again, Mr. Oliver and I walked over to the sheriff's desk, where he sat reading the day's newspaper. Mr. Oliver cleared his throat. "Excuse me Sheriff, but I need to take a look at the evidence in Miss Ruby's case for a while. Mind bringing it up here?"

Sheriff Peterson dropped his feet to the floor with a thud. "Sure thing." Then he headed through a door behind him.

I turned to Mr. Oliver with my newfound optimism. "So what else can I do to help you?"

He sighed and took out his handkerchief, once again wiping his brow. Seemed like he sure was hot all the time. Or maybe just nervous. "I'd sure be grateful if you get Ruby to open up with me. I've tried to explain to her that she has to be upfront about what happened in that barn, and I'm not convinced yet that she's told me everything."

I couldn't argue with him there. I too had my suspicions she wasn't telling everything. Lots of things still didn't add up. Like how she could have come away with minor injuries from a man almost triple her size. He'd nearly beaten her to death a few years back.

"I need some more information to better understand her," Mr. Oliver continued. "Whenever I speak with her, she's very careful about her words, only saying exactly what she wants me to know. No more, no less. It's like she's already made up her mind to go to prison. Something's off. I was hoping you could help me figure it out. Maybe get her to tell us the whole story."

He broke off as Sheriff Peterson returned with a box and set it on the desk. "That's everything we got. It can't leave this office though, you hear?"

Mr. Oliver waved him away. "I got it." He picked up the box and took it over to a table near the back corner of the room, yanking on the chain for the solitary light bulb hanging over the table. As he whipped out a pad of paper and a pen, he glanced up at me. "Let's see what we got here, son. Mind writing down some notes as we look through it?"

"Not at all." I took the pad and pen and took a seat in a chair at the table. "I'm ready when you are."

He pulled out a bag with a blood-soaked shirt inside. "Chester's shirt. Ripped where the knife must have gone through."

I wrote that down. "How does this help Ruby? I don't think there's any question that she stabbed Chester, and I think that's all you'll get from the evidence."

"You never know," Mr. Oliver said, placing the shirt back in the box. "Plus, this will give us a better idea of how Mr. Garrett might go after her." Next he pulled out an envelope with pictures of the scene after deputies had arrived. "Let's have a look here." He spread the photos out on the table. "See anything that jumps out at you?"

"Not right away." I scanned the scene for anything to tell me something Ruby might have left out. It was apparent a struggle had taken place over a wide area of the barn. Footprints over the top of one another, smears of blood in the dirt, blood on a stack of hay bales. The struggle must have taken several minutes. How had she fended Chester off for so long?

I picked up the photo of the body and looked closer at it. Chester lay on his back, with smears of blood across his chest. Had Ruby tried to heal him? That might explain why so much blood was on her hands. She'd only said she'd tried to *help* him. But how had she gotten blood on her face and in her hair? From her hands or his? Maybe none of that mattered.

I realized I had no idea what to look for. I was useless. Mr. Oliver studied the pictures as well, pointing out the extended area of the struggle, as I had noticed. I wrote down his observations. He wondered the same thing I had. How had Ruby come away with barely a scratch on her, yet covered in blood?

Frowning, I picked up another photo of the body, this time from a different angle. The knife lay on the ground a few feet away from the body. Something about it tickled my mind. I knew that knife.

"Is the knife in that box?" I asked.

Mr. Oliver looked over the edge and reached inside. "Sure is." He pulled out a knife with a small wooden handle, still smeared with Chester's blood.

I pulled it out and examined it close up, turning it over and over in my hand. I definitely knew this knife. "Where did Ruby say the knife came from again?"

"She said Chester had it." He gave me a curious look. "Why?"

I turned it again and looked at the end, where initials had once been etched into it. Only part of the "G" remained. I knew exactly where this knife had come from, and it wasn't Chester Calhoun. I knew whose knife it was, 'cause I'd been there the day she'd given it away as a Christmas gift. The knife with her father's initials on it. And I knew now exactly why she was so careful about what she was saying, and why she had no real injuries.

Ruby didn't kill Chester.

Samuel did.

CHAPTER ELEVEN

Matthew

I debated with myself over confronting Ruby with what I suspected, but in the end I had to know the truth. When I walked up to her cell, she was sitting on her cot with her daddy's Bible open on her lap. She looked up at me with a smile that made me pause. She had lied. *Ruby*. The girl who never lied.

She'd been terrible at it, and I'd always known in my heart she wasn't telling the whole truth. But had I suspected that she was actually lying? Something inside me shifted. She wasn't the perfect angel I'd created in my mind, someone I could never relate to. She was human. She was fallible. And I loved her.

I loved her.

Ruby tilted her head and looked at me curiously. "I thought you'd gone home for the day."

"I was helping Mr. Oliver with your case. I told him I'd help out. We were looking through all the evidence."

"Oh." She pushed the Bible onto her cot and walked over to where I was standing. "Are you all right?"

My stomach tightened. I had to look away. I glanced around the jail, and it dawned on me that Emmitt Hyde had never returned to his cell after going to the hospital. "Where's Mr. Hyde?"

135

"His bond was paid, so they released him."

"How did he come up with the money?"

She shrugged and averted her gaze.

"Ruby?"

She grinned at me, her eyes glowing with joy. "Don't be mad, okay?"

"Ruby, you didn't—"

"But it was a miracle! I had to! Did you know his bond, after the fees and everything, came out to exactly seventy-nine dollars and fifty-seven cents?"

I dropped my head, knowing I shouldn't be surprised in the least. "That money was for you!"

"It was the Lord's money all along. Not mine."

She was more frustrating than I could bear. But I realized there was nothing I could do to get the money back, and that we had a much bigger issue to deal with, so I decided not to argue about the money anymore. "Okay, fine. I understand. But we need to discuss something else right now."

I walked toward the corner of her cell furthest away from the door out to the lobby and motioned for her to follow me. Her mouth tipped into a grin. "What is going on with you?"

I steeled myself for the fight I knew was coming. "Was Samuel in the barn with you?"

The color drained from her face. "Wh—No. Why would you ask that?"

I lowered my voice to barely above a whisper. "I saw the knife, Ruby. The one you gave him for Christmas." She stared at me with unblinking eyes. "He was there. Did he kill Chester? Just tell me the truth."

She dropped her gaze to the floor, but said nothing. I couldn't stand just waiting for her to say something. I was about to bust wide open.

"Ruby. Please. Just tell me the truth about what happened in the barn. You can trust me."

She raised her eyes back to mine, and I could see they were filled with fear. "All right," she whispered. "But please, you have to promise you won't say anything to anyone."

"Ruby—"

"Promise!" she said. "Or I won't tell you anything, and on top of that, I will never speak to you again!"

I reached through the bars with my palms up. "Give me your hands." She hesitated, but then placed her hands on mine, and I gently gripped them. "I promise. I won't say anything."

Her shoulders shook as she took a breath. "I was out for a walk after Emma Rae delivered her baby, and I saw Chester talking with James and Mr. Calhoun. I was overcome with fear; I could barely move. Eventually I managed to turn around and go to the other side of the barn to calm down and to pray. And I had this awful feeling that Samuel was around somewhere. So I tried to find him so I could get him to leave."

"Why?" I asked.

"He's all turned around about being half Calhoun. He's been hanging around the Calhoun property, picking cotton, trying to work out where he fits into everything. So I went looking for him to see if he was there. You know how Chester used to beat him?"

I nodded.

"I just wanted to protect him."

Her eyes welled up, so I let her have a moment to gather her thoughts again. "Then what happened? Did you find him?"

"I came back to the barn, and I saw Chester go inside. I wanted to get away from there, so I was going to run down to James's house, but that would take me past the barn. So I froze. I couldn't move. That was when I saw Samuel. He was about fifty feet away from me, and he was watching Chester go into the barn with the most awful look on his face. I just knew he was going to go in there and stir up something with Chester. I ran over to him and tried to talk to him. And I finally got him to listen to me. He said he'd go on home."

"But he didn't, did he?" I asked.

"He was walking away from the barn when Chester came out and called him over to move some feed out of the barn for the animals. He didn't recognize Samuel at first, but when he did...You should have seen the look that came over Chester. It was like pure evil. He was *happy* to see Samuel."

I squeezed her hands, knowing she must have been so frightened in that moment. I'd tangled with Chester myself, and I knew for certain there was nothing but evil in that man.

"He hadn't seen me because I was still off to the side of the barn, and he only had eyes for Samuel at that point. He made Samuel go into the barn and start moving feed sacks around. I crept in after them and stayed in the shadows."

"Ruby, why? Why didn't you go get help?"

"Help from who?" she said. "Who would care if Chester was mistreating a colored boy? I was his only help. And I had no idea what to do. So I hung back in the shadows under the loft and prayed Samuel wouldn't lose his head."

"All right," I said. "Go on."

"Chester started saying awful things to Samuel about his mother, calling her terrible names. Then he said something about how he'd be so happy to run into her again 'cause she was so feisty. Oh, Matthew, Samuel just lost it. He went after Chester and they started brawling all over the barn. Samuel held his own for a little while. I think Chester was trying to beat him to death, but Samuel kept on fighting.

"But then Samuel pulled out his knife, and Chester just laughed at him. He said he was a dead man for sure now, that he'd be strung up in a tree before the end of the day."

She pulled her hands out of mine and hugged her waist. "Matthew, I knew he was right. The moment Samuel stood up for himself, he was a dead man. And I had to do something. So I ran out from under the loft and jumped on Chester's back. I told Samuel to run for it."

"Did he?" I asked.

"No. Chester flung me off and said he was going to kill me just as soon as he was through with Samuel. Then he kicked me in the ribs."

I winced and tried to imagine that monster hurting her again. I had to tell myself he'd finally gotten what he deserved.

"But then Samuel came at Chester again, and this time they were fighting over the knife. They fell against the hay, and Chester hollered real loud. He started cursing and stumbling around. That was when I realized he had the knife in his chest. He pulled it out, and blood shot out of him. He screamed at both of us that he was going to kill us."

She closed her eyes. "I tried to help him. I prayed for God to let me heal him. I ran over to him and put my hands on his chest and started praying whatever words I could. But it didn't work. And he grabbed me by my hair and told me to keep my sorcery to myself. Then he slapped me away. I couldn't get near him. I couldn't stop the blood."

I was amazed. "Ruby Graves, I think you're the only person in the world who'd try to save a man who was trying to kill her."

She shook her head. "I couldn't, though. And I didn't know what to do. I told Samuel to get out of there. That he needed to get out of town. I told him not to say anything to anybody. That Chester had attacked me, and I'd defended myself."

I leaned back against the wall and tried to think clearly about what all this meant. "Ruby, I know you had good intentions, and you want to protect Samuel, but you have to tell the truth about this."

"I knew you were going to say that," she said. "But you know as well as I do what'll happen to Samuel as soon as I tell the truth. There won't be a trial for him. No one will be interested in the truth. They'll just see the color of his skin and condemn him. I can't let that happen."

"So you'd rather risk going to jail for murder? Do you understand what that means?"

She met my gaze. "Yes."

I couldn't bear it. I gripped the bars and rattled them in my hands. "You are so infuriating sometimes! No one in their right mind would do this, Ruby."

"I have to."

"Why?" I yelled.

She hugged her waist again. "Because he's my friend. And he doesn't deserve to die."

My throat ached as I looked into her eyes. "Neither do you."

I was a mess when I left the jail that evening. I walked up and down the streets of Cullman trying to figure out what to do with what Ruby had told me. Should I tell Mr. Oliver? Or maybe Sheriff Peterson? Ruby would never forgive me this time if I betrayed her. I'd promised to keep my mouth shut. But how could I stand by and let her go to prison for murder?

I tried to focus on positive thoughts. Maybe she'd be able to convince a jury she'd killed Chester in self-defense. It was plausible. She'd have to become a much better liar in the next week. But if she stuck to her story, and if we could show that Chester had attacked her once before, she might just stand a chance.

But what if the jury didn't buy it? Even Mr. Oliver knew Ruby wasn't telling the whole truth, and if they thought she was lying…Every time I thought of Ruby going off to prison—or worse, the electric chair—my whole body felt like it was on fire. I couldn't lose her again.

That thought brought me around to what I'd been avoiding all afternoon. I knew now I loved Ruby, and I was going to have to deal with that. I wasn't sure how. I was engaged to Vanessa, after all. I loved her too, and she deserved to be treated right. Besides, did I really have a future with Ruby? That seemed impossible. Sure, she'd loved me at one time when she was a child, but she'd changed so much. She was completely devoted to her calling. I doubted she'd ever love me again after I'd rejected her.

After walking around for nearly two hours, I realized I was no closer to answers than I'd been when I started. I leaned back against a building and closed my eyes to pray.

Lord, what would You have me do? Speak to me the way You speak to Ruby. Show me how to hear You and to trust You.

I opened my eyes and waited. Nothing came. I didn't hear a thing. But I did see something. I was standing across the street from Father's office. Maybe I couldn't figure out everything, but I could definitely work on one thing. I could figure out a way to get my money back.

By that time it was nearly dark, so I waited in a restaurant down the street until I knew both Father and Ruth were gone for the night. Then I made my way back. Father locked the store up tight every night, but the small door that opened to the stairs leading up to his office was never locked. So I was able to walk right into the reception area where Ruth sat.

I figured his office door would be locked, and I was right. But I was fairly certain Ruth had an extra key hidden somewhere. I searched as best I could without disturbing how she had things arranged in her desk. I came up empty.

I switched on the light to see better; then I sat behind her desk and looked all around the room. If I were Era, where would I put an extra key to Father's office? There was a plant in the window, so I checked underneath it. Nothing.

Then I noticed a small picture near the back of her desk, almost hidden behind a stack of papers. It was a young man in army uniform. I'd heard from Mother once that Ruth had been engaged to a soldier, but he was killed accidentally while training. I figured that had to be him.

I ran my hand along the back of the picture and felt a bump. When I pulled the back off, there was a key. I couldn't believe it. I'd actually found it.

I hurried over to Father's door and unlocked it, heading straight for his desk. I sat in his chair and ran through the same exercise again. If I were Father, where would I stash a little over four thousand dollars? I pulled the drawers out with no luck, checked the pictures of Mother and my siblings, dug through a plant near his window. Nothing.

Dropping my head into my hands, I wished I were a better investigator. I knew for certain that was not my calling in life. I decided it was unlikely the money was in his office, but I wondered if maybe there was a clue to its whereabouts. Maybe a receipt from the bank or something. If Father could waltz up and withdraw my money, maybe I could return the favor. So I started paying closer attention to papers in his desk.

I was careful to keep them in order and replace them as I'd found them. Most were purchase orders, receipts, and transactions from estate sales. I recognized all the names from my years working for him. I found his ledger book and took a quick look through it to see if he'd made any deposits that equaled what he'd taken from me. But everything seemed in perfect order.

When I got to the bottom drawer, I found an envelope buried beneath several folders. I rifled through the folders, pausing when I reached the last one and found two groups of documents with my name on them. They weren't withdrawals from my bank account though. In fact, I wasn't certain exactly what they were. But from the language on the documents, I could swear these were land deeds in my name. I hadn't bought a single piece of property in my life. How did my name get on these? I turned to the last page in each group, and there on the line for the purchaser's signature, was my name, just as if I'd signed it myself. But I'd never seen it before.

"Well, Father," I muttered to myself. "What are you up to?"

I set the deeds aside and pulled out a booklet from the envelope that had been underneath the folders. It was another ledger. But as I looked through it, I didn't recognize the names. Each name had a symbol beside it with an amount listed beside that. Some were marked out, some had amounts subtracted beneath the original amount. I turned the page and found even more. And then I saw several entries by the name Robert Paschal.

I copied a few of the entries onto a sheet of paper, wondering if it was money Father owed to people. If so, then it was clear he was deeply in debt. And over twenty thousand of it was to Vanessa's father alone. What was he thinking?

I returned everything to its place, except for the two deeds. Those I took with me. If I was right, and this was land in my name, then I'd just have to beat Father at his own game. I was going to pay a little visit to the Building and Loan the next morning.

CHAPTER TWELVE

Ruby

After I told Matthew everything, I tossed and turned all night. I couldn't shake the feeling that I'd just sold Samuel down the river. At the time, I'd felt relieved to share the truth so I wouldn't feel so alone. But as the night wore on, my conscience wrestled with the terrible burden I'd placed on Matthew's shoulders. Could I trust him to keep his word?

So I wasn't too surprised the next morning when he didn't come by to visit me. It was the first day since I'd been locked up that not a single soul appeared at my cell. The quiet of the morning worked on my mind, sending it to all sorts of awful places. What if I was never free again? What if the jury found me guilty and sentenced me to the chair?

I could deal with the idea of death. God and I had come to an understanding when I was running from that tornado. No, it wasn't death I feared. It was the pain that would come before death that set my stomach on edge.

Sometime after dinner, the door to the lobby opened, and Asa and Mother came in to see me. I was so happy to see them, I nearly ran across the cell.

"Mother, Asa, what are you both doing here today? I thought you weren't coming back until Thursday."

"I told them to meet me here so they could pick you up," Matthew said from the doorway. He strode over to my cell with a huge smile on his face. The sheriff followed behind him with a set of keys dangling.

"What's going on?" I asked.

"You're going home. Your bond's been paid."

"What?" I stepped back from the door and looked from one happy face to the next. Then I landed on Matthew. "Didn't you hear a thing I said before? I can't accept your money."

"Well thankfully, the fine county of Cullman has no problem accepting my money."

He looked so proud of himself. He hadn't understood anything. "Matthew, I can't. Please don't force this on me."

His smile faded, and he turned to Asa. "Would you please talk some sense into her? I know that's asking a lot, but would you please try?"

"Ruby, honey," Asa said. "Take a moment and think about what you're doing. God is providing for your needs. Who are you to decide that it's not good enough? Be mindful of your pride. Matthew cares for you, and God has given you a friend in your corner who has the means to help you. Don't dismiss that help so carelessly."

I let out a deep sigh. "You mean the world to me. And I understand what you're saying. I just don't think it's wise for me to be indebted to others. Even if they are friends, and even if their intentions are noble. God already provided for my needs at the church service on Sunday. His provision is enough."

Matthew's head dropped between his shoulders. "There's just no getting through to you."

Footsteps echoed in the empty cell room, and I turned to see Sheriff Peterson coming toward us followed by Mr. Oliver. The sheriff stuck a key in the cell door and gave it a turn.

"Well, everything's in order," he said. "You can't leave the county, but you're free to go home until the trial."

"I'm not leaving," I said.

Sheriff Peterson looked at me like I was mad. Then he looked over at Mr. Oliver. "Did I miss something?"

Matthew raised his head to regard the older man. "Can I talk to Ruby alone for a minute? We just need to get some things straightened out."

"Sure," the sheriff said, leading the others back out to the office.

As Matthew came into my cell, I realized it was the first time in weeks we weren't separated by bars. I took a few steps back and steeled myself. "You aren't going to change my mind."

"I know. Believe me, I haven't forgotten who I'm dealing with. But I have something to say, and I wanted to say it without the others present. So just listen to me for a minute, all right?"

"All right."

"First, can I ask just why you're so set against me? Maybe if you explain to me why you can't accept my help, I can find a way to be your friend without making you mad at me all the time."

Rocking on my heels, I tried to think of an answer that made sense. "I already explained. I can't be indebted to you. It makes me..."

"What?"

"...Vulnerable."

He took a step toward me, and my stomach took a dip. "I swear, Ruby. I ain't never gonna hurt you again."

I dropped my gaze to the floor. I couldn't look at him. I'd lose myself in loving him again, and I'd wind up right back where I was before.

"Look," he said, closing the gap a bit more. "Do I owe you anything for helping me when I was sick?"

I shook my head.

"Remember the day you saved me? When I was dying, and you ran for Asa?"

I did remember. I'd been desperate. If I'd lost him...

"You wouldn't let me give up, Ruby. I was ready to die. But you wouldn't give up on me. And I ain't giving up on you now. Let me help you. This ain't about keeping score, or you being indebted to me. You're afraid I'll let you down again. But I'm telling you, Ruby, I'm right here. I ain't going nowhere."

I shook my head and took another step back, doing everything I could to keep my breathing steady. "I'm not afraid."

"So what is it then? You're the only one allowed to help people? You can pour every ounce of yourself out for others, but can't nobody help you? Especially me, right? 'Cause I messed up. 'Cause I made a mistake over four years ago that you can't forgive."

My whole body was shaking. Why'd he have to stand so close to me? He took my hand and ran his thumb over my palm. "Come on. Let's get out of here and start making things right again. Please."

I studied his hand, memorized the warmth of it. I let myself look up into his eyes, and I wondered for one tiny second, what it would be like to kiss him. I was such a stupid girl.

"All right," I said, pulling my hand away from his. "I'll accept your help this time. And…I forgive you."

His face lit up, and he pulled me into a hug so hard, I could barely breathe. Unable to stop the nervous laugh that escaped me, I wrapped my arms around him too. He pulled my shoulders back and laughed as well.

"Holy moly!" he said. "Did I just win an argument with you?"

"Don't get used to it."

He threw his arm over my shoulder and guided me toward the cell door. My heart still raced, despite my desperate attempt to control it. I knew this feeling too well, like the ground had suddenly been snatched away, and I was falling toward oblivion. But this time was worse. So much worse. Because I wasn't a little girl with a crush anymore. I was a grown woman, and I was in love with Matthew Doyle all over again.

Matthew treated all of us to a late lunch at the Busy Bee Café, my favorite place for a hamburger. It was after the dinner rush, so it wasn't too crowded, but the ten people or so inside all stopped eating and stared at me when I came though the door. Every single one of them.

I tried to pretend like I didn't notice. I walked over to the booth near the windows and took a seat beside Matthew. I could tell Mother had noticed too. She made eye contact with me to check if I was all right. I smiled to let her know I was.

The table next to ours had a newspaper on it, and the bold headline across the top said: "New evidence in Calhoun murder points to co-conspirator; police searching for suspect."

I hadn't heard anything about that, so I reached for the paper. Matthew grabbed my other arm and pulled me tight against him. "Don't do that. Trust me. It's all garbage."

"Do they really think that? About the co-conspirator?"

Matthew looked around at all of us and lowered his voice. "Mr. Oliver thinks the prosecutor will try to show that you went into the barn with the intent to kill Chester in order to cover up your relationship with a...well, with a colored boy."

"How could they even come up with that theory?" I asked. "That's completely ridiculous!"

"Probably from the Calhouns," Mother said. "They're talking to the paper, riling people up about you being friends with coloreds, and that you're conspiring to start a rebellion against the laws that keep them separate from us."

I didn't know what to say. "When did this turn into a circus?"

Mother reached across the table and covered my hand with hers. "Let's not waste our energy on the fools around here who believe everything they read in a newspaper. Let's focus on the positives. You're finally out of that horrible cell, and we can spend the next week getting ready. We've got a nice little sofa you can stay on until all this is cleared up."

"No, Mother. I want to stay where I am, at Ms. Harmon's place with the other girls. I'll be fine there."

Mother's smile faded. "That shameful woman told us to get your things out of her house the day after you were arrested. I'm so sorry, honey."

With Ms. Harmon kicking me out, the newspaper making me out to be a murderer, and everyone staring at me like I was a sideshow at a carnival, I wondered how I was ever going to turn this around. Would I lose my job with Dr. Fisher as well? Who would want a criminal tending to them?

I reckon Matthew saw the dismay on my face, 'cause he patted my hand. "It's better for you to be with family right now anyway."

I put on my best smile for the rest of our meal, but I'd lost my appetite. I only half ate my hamburger, and it didn't taste nearly as good as it usually did. Matthew paid the bill and walked us out to Asa's truck. The joy of my getting out of jail had left us pretty quick. I hugged Matthew and thanked him again for his generosity.

"Don't even think about it ever again," he said. "I mean it."

Asa climbed into the truck, and Mother called for me to come get in. I realized Matthew was holding my hand.

"Why don't I drive you?" he said. "I'm heading that way anyway, and then you three wouldn't have to squeeze into that old truck."

I looked over at Mother, who gave me a small smile. "All right. We'll see you two at the house."

She got into the truck, and Asa waved as they drove past us. I followed Matthew over to his car behind the cafe. The sickness in my stomach from earlier had been replaced with butterflies. Maybe everyone else in the county thought I was a cold-hearted killer, among other things, but Matthew believed in me. And maybe that was enough.

He pulled open the passenger door and held my hand again as I stepped up into the car. I noticed the back seat was full of luggage, and my heart dropped. He came around and opened his door.

"Where are you going?" I asked.

He looked at me funny and chuckled. "To your Mother and Asa's place. Right?"

I tipped my head to motion toward the back. "No, I mean this. Your bags are packed. Are you going to Nashville or something?"

Closing the door, he turned and looked at me. "Do you really want me to go?"

I fidgeted with my hands in my lap. I knew the best answer would be "Yes." But the truth was much more complicated. "I want you to do what's best for you. I want you to be happy."

"That almost sounded like an answer, but you know, it really wasn't. Do *you* want me to go?"

"Do you want to go? I wouldn't blame you if you did."

He sighed and dropped his head onto his hands as they gripped the steering wheel. "Ruby, I ain't going to Nashville. That's over. I don't even want those jobs anymore. I done told you, I ain't leaving you." He turned to faced me. "I'm going to be here with you, going through this with you, the whole time."

A blush crept up my neck and cheeks. "Thank you."

He smiled before turning back to the wheel and starting the car. As he pulled out into the street and headed for Hanceville, I realized he hadn't answered my question. "Wait a minute, so what *is* the luggage for?"

Matthew explained that he'd been fighting with his daddy so much, he'd finally moved in with his brother. "Besides," he said. "It made it a little easier to come see you every day."

"You didn't have to do that," I said. But deep down, I was so grateful he had. I had to admit that his visits gave me something to look forward to each day.

"Anyway," he said, "I figured with you getting out and moving back to Hanceville with your family, I'd go back and stay with my parents. If I do a good job of avoiding Father, I'm sure I can keep my sanity until your trial is over."

"You never know what could happen. You should work things out with him while you still can."

He stared at the road in front of him, saying nothing for a solid minute. "My family ain't like yours, Ruby. Your father loved you, and you always knew that. You could trust him, and you loved him as much as he loved you."

"Your family is full of love! I've seen it myself. Your mother loves you, and Mary adores you. I don't know your daddy as well, but I'm sure he loves you too. You should have seen how upset he was when you were sick."

Matthew swallowed hard. "He don't really love me, Ruby. He just wants to control me. There's a difference."

"All fathers are hard to get along with. Mine was, for sure. But I know your daddy loves you. And even if you two disagree, you need to try to find some common ground. Trust me. When he's gone, you'll regret all the disagreements."

He shook his head, his knuckles turning white as he gripped the steering wheel. "You don't know him. And frankly, I'm starting to realize that I don't either. He isn't a good man, Ruby."

He looked over at me with anguished eyes, and I wished I could help him see the power of forgiveness. His daddy was difficult—I'd experienced his forceful personality a few times—but I'd witnessed his anguish when Dr. Fisher had told the family that Matthew had only weeks to live. For whatever reason, Mr. Doyle kept his love locked up tight, but it was definitely there.

The rest of the ride to Asa's and Mother's house was quiet and uneventful, so I spent it praying for Matthew and for the trials ahead. I knew that I wasn't the only one about to face hard times, and I prayed God would strengthen all of us.

As soon as Matthew pulled his car down the dirt road that led to the property, I could tell something was wrong. Mother was standing in the yard, waving her arms around as she talked to Asa, who knelt beside something in the ground. Matthew pulled up beside Asa's truck, and I jumped out of the car.

"What's wrong?" I said as I approached Mother.

She was crying, and could barely form a sentence. "Those...animals!"

Matthew knelt beside Asa, and I went to see what they were looking at. It was a small wooden cross, like the kind graves were marked with. Only this one was sticking out of the front yard. A small piece of paper was nailed to it.

I tried to read it, but Matthew yanked it out of the ground and threw it across the yard. "If they want a fight, then they're going to get one."

"What did that say?" I asked.

"Nothing!"

Asa stood and turned to me, placing his hands on my shoulders. "Ruby, let's get your mother inside and calm her down. Everything's going to be all right."

"Look," Matthew said. "I have my things in the car. I can stay here, and you and I can take shifts keeping watch."

"That isn't necessary," Asa said. "I'm sure this is just to frighten us."

"You think so?" Matthew yelled. "It's working!"

This was too much. "What did the paper say?" I screamed at them.

Matthew and Asa stared blankly at me, so I stomped across the yard and picked up the cross.

"Ruby, don't," Matthew called.

"Don't tell me what to do!"

I looked down at the small piece of paper and read:

"Here lies Ruby Graves
A young woman who never
Learned her lesson...
1917-1936"

My stomach swam, and I felt the earth shift beneath me. I might've fallen right over if Matthew hadn't come beside me and put his arm around my waist.

"No one's gonna hurt you ever again, I swear."

"You got that right," Mother said. She'd marched over to us and was standing in front of me with her fists on her hips. "I'll tell you right now, if that good-for-nothing Klan wants to play like this, then they got another thing coming to them. I think it's time they got a dose of the Kellum clan!"

I reckoned it was wrong of me, but deep down I was just a bit excited that Mother's brothers were coming to stay with us. I'd never met them properly, since she'd always been adamantly against their way of life. In fact, I'd only actually seen them once, and that was right after Daddy died, so I wasn't in the frame of mind for paying attention. I did remember that they were dressed mighty fine, and they were all carrying guns beneath their coats. And I also remembered how the entire room went quiet when they entered. You see, the Kellum brothers were infamous around northern Alabama.

I didn't know all this when I was younger, but my uncles were moonshiners. They had stills stashed all over Rickwood Caverns over in Walker County, along with hideouts and plenty of firepower. Mother wouldn't tell me much, but Asa had filled me in when I was sixteen and determined to find out about my family.

Anyway, I couldn't help the small sense of excitement I felt when Mother returned from her trip out to her brothers' place near the caverns. It was the only time in my life I ever remembered seeing her drive herself anywhere. She wouldn't even let Asa go with her. Said they'd never show themselves if they saw him.

So on that following Thursday, when their trucks rolled up to the house, I had a strong sense that something big was going to happen.

The house was already full, what with Matthew refusing to leave. He'd slept the past two nights out on the porch with Asa, which must have been freezing cold. I'd slept in the bed with Mother, while Asa and Matthew took turns sleeping and keeping watch. All this commotion combined to make me feel even more like a carnival sideshow.

I was trying to read on the sofa, and doing a poor job of it, when I heard the trucks pull up. I glanced out the front window and saw four men in long coats get out of two trucks. Soon after I heard several pairs of boots shuffling across the front porch. Mother came from the kitchen and pulled the door wide open.

A tall bearded man stepped into the living room and hugged Mother with such affectionate force that he clean picked her up off the floor. "Lizzy!"

To my surprise, she hugged him back, and even seemed to enjoy him swinging her around like that. Two other men stepped inside, and they threw their arms around her too. She ushered them further into the living room.

"Ruby," she said. "These are your uncles." She gestured to each one, starting with the first through the door. "This is Roy, Eddie, and Thomas."

They all smiled at me as I pushed myself up from the sofa and went to shake their hands. But we just ended up in one great big hug. I loved it. They smelled like dust and leather, and seemed just as excited to meet me as I was to meet them.

Roy looked to be the oldest. His beard was gray, and I saw gray hair peeking out from under his hat. He had the same eyes as Mother. I couldn't tell who was older between Eddie and Thomas. Eddie was a bit taller, with a loud laugh and dark curly hair. Thomas seemed more reserved. He smiled at me and hugged me just as the others did, but he seemed content to let Roy and Eddie do most of the talking.

After a couple of minutes of welcoming them into her home, Mother stopped and looked around. "Wait, where's Franklin?"

Roy's smile hardened into a serious frown. "Frankie done got himself into some trouble, and police are looking for him over in Walker County. He figures it's best to lay low. He headed out to the barn with a bedroll."

The front door opened, and Matthew and Asa came inside. Mother introduced everyone again and they all shook hands, though the greetings this time were much more guarded. Matthew in particular looked uncomfortable. He kept wiping his hand on his shirt in between handshakes.

He glanced over at me with wide eyes as the group made its way into the kitchen and dining room. Asa pulled out a chair for Mother, and Roy, Eddie and Thomas took the other three. Roy wasted no time getting down to business.

"Lizzy filled us in on what's been going on around here. Maybe not every detail, but I think I have a clear picture. So what can we do to help?"

"I'm not sure there's much you can do," Asa said. "But Matthew and I've been keeping watch at night for anything suspicious, and it's been quiet so far."

"We can definitely help out with keeping watch," Roy said.

"Yeah, that's our specialty," Eddie said.

Mother leaned onto the table and pointed her finger at them. "Now listen here," she said, her tone serious. "There won't be any of your foolishness while you're here. I came to you because I was afraid for Ruby, but I don't aim to heap more trouble on top of trouble. You understand?"

Roy put his hands up, weathered palms on display. "No trouble from us, Lizzy. We left every drop of 'shine at home. We're just here to protect Ruby, like you asked."

The sound of wheels on the dirt road made everyone at the table freeze. But seconds later, they were up on their feet. Roy and Eddie headed for the window in the living room, while Thomas moved to the wall on the other side of the table. He pushed aside the curtain to peer outside. Matthew grabbed my hand and pulled me toward the bedroom.

I thought my heart might beat right out of my chest. Were the police already here for my uncles? Maybe it was the Klan coming. I imagined a violent confrontation, and immediately started praying.

"Sit on the floor between the bed and the wall," Matthew said.

He made sure I was settled, and then he went to stand beside the doorway. It got so quiet, I could hear the tires spin to a halt outside. Then heavy footsteps crunched on the porch. Mother's voice rang out through the house.

"It's just James!"

Matthew leaned his back against the wall and blew out a long breath. "This is crazy." Concern in his eyes, he walked over and offered me a hand up. "You all right?"

I nodded, unable to form any words.

"Come on," he said.

We walked into the living room just as Mother finished introducing her brothers to James, who had only come as far as a couple of feet into the house. He stood with his arms crossed and his brow mashed down as he looked everyone over.

"Mother, did you invite them?" he asked.

"Yes, I did."

"Why? I thought...aren't you just inviting more problems for Ruby? She's already in enough trouble as it is. We don't need more criminals holing up here."

More criminals? Was that how James saw me? As a criminal?

Roy stepped toward James, and I saw a flicker of fear in James's eyes. "Don't worry about your mother or sister," Roy said. "We ain't bringing no trouble. Just want to be here in case someone tries something."

"Well, that's reassuring," James muttered.

Roy turned to Asa. "Why don't we finish our discussion, get some plans in place, and then get everyone settled?"

The men all moved toward the dining table again. Matthew took my hand and squeezed it. "You all right with all this?"

"Do I have much of a choice?"

"I don't reckon. But I don't want you to feel uncomfortable either."

My head was swirling with feelings, so I wasn't sure how to answer. I just knew I didn't want Matthew to let go of my hand. But he did.

"It's going to be all right," he said. Then he kissed the top of my head and followed the others to the table.

My legs felt just a bit wobbly as I followed. Mother was already pulling food out of the cabinets, so I went over to help her prepare something for all these men to eat. Meanwhile, Asa and Roy took over planning shifts for them all to keep an eye on things. When I glanced over at them all gathered around the table, I noticed James was the only one away from the action. All the others were either seated or standing at the edge of the table, leaning over as Roy used his fingers to draw imaginary maps on the table. But James stood over by the wall, his arms still crossed, his face still angry.

I was sliding the biscuits out of the oven when I heard Thomas say something that caught my attention. "Look, this is all well and good, but I think we're avoiding the obvious solution here."

"What's that?" Roy asked.

Thomas gestured over toward me. "If they are railroading Ruby into a murder conviction, why are we just waiting around? We can take her out to the caverns for a while, get her set up with a new name and all, and she can just—"

"No!" Mother said, slamming a pot of beans onto the counter.

Thomas stopped talking, and all the men turned wide eyes at Mother. "She is not going to become some fugitive like you three. She didn't murder anybody, and when the jury hears the truth, all this will be straightened out."

Thomas drummed his fingers on the table. "Look, I didn't mean to upset you, Lizzy. But we have to think about the reality of what Ruby's facing here. Even if she's found not guilty, she may still have a target on her. It might be best to consider it as a last resort."

"I think he's right," Eddie said. "We got some experience at hiding out. Might be best to plan for it, just in case."

James pushed away from the wall. "I can't listen to another word of this garbage." He marched over to the doorway that opened into the living room and faced the table. "This is about the most ridiculous thing I've ever heard. Ruby is the one who created this mess because she has to go around saving the world, even Negroes. Now, we've got you all coming in here like it's the wild west, preparing for hiding out from the law, and Lord knows what else! I can't be a part of this."

That was enough for Matthew. His eyes blazed as he pointed an accusatory finger at James from across the room. "You can't be a part of this? You haven't been a part of anything! You haven't so much as shown your face to Ruby since she was arrested, or even asked her how's she's doing."

"You got no right to blame me for anything!" James yelled. "I have a family to protect, a wife who lost her brother—"

"That brother tried to kill your sister!" Matthew roared back.

Asa stood from his chair and held out his hands toward Matthew and James. "Boys, let's try to stay calm."

James turned his fiery glare on Asa. "You are not my daddy, and you have no say in what I do."

Eddie jumped up from his chair. "Why are you even here? You ain't no Kellum. You ain't even part of this family! Why, your mother was a Cass!"

Mother gasped and flew over to the table. "Eddie, you shut your mouth!"

Eddie slumped back into his chair like he'd been slapped. Mother turned to James, who stared at her with incredulous eyes. "What is he talking about?"

"James," she said with a shaky voice, "it's a long story. Just come on back in here and let's talk about this."

James backed away. "No. Just tell me the truth. Is he saying you're…you're not my mother?"

No one said anything. The men around the table had all dropped their heads and were studying the floor or their hands. I didn't know what to do, but I felt compelled to try.

"James, please don't leave," I said, walking toward him. "We're family, and we need to stick together. Everything can be explained."

"You…you know about this?" he said.

I stopped beside Mother, whose eyes were wide in shock. Clearly Asa had not informed her what he'd shared with me in confidence, all those years ago. "I—I found out by accident. Just come back and listen."

He shook his head. "I don't want any part of this."

Then he stormed out the door and drove away.

CHAPTER THIRTEEN

Matthew

I took Ruby out the back door while the others went back to planning things. She buried her face in my chest, and I held her while she cried. I could've punched James right in the mouth for tearing her apart like that. He'd always treated Ruby more like a burden than a sister. But I didn't dare say anything against him.

Once she'd settled down some, I sat with her on the back steps. "Listen, James is gonna be all right," I said. "He never seemed too attached to the family."

She wiped the last tears from her face and looked out over the fields. "No...You're right, I know James will be fine. But what if I never get to see little Abner again? He's my nephew, and I love him like crazy."

"I know everything seems all messed up right now, but let's not worry too much about the future. Let's focus on the next week or so. You don't need to be concerning yourself with all the fuss going on in there. You need to be going over in your mind what your story is, and exactly how to answer the questions that are going to come up."

"You're right about that. I don't know how I'm going to be able to sit in front of all those people and lie. What a mess I've gotten myself into!"

"You know...you could just tell the truth."

161

She shook her head. "You don't understand. I can't put Samuel in that kind of danger. Just look what's happening to me. It would be a hundred times worse for him, and there would be no uncles or friends to stand up for him."

I had a feeling she'd throw herself right in between Samuel and any mob after him. I had to consider that maybe that would be even worse. So I decided to shift topics.

"You got a meeting with Mr. Oliver soon to get everything straight, right?"

"Monday morning."

"Are you going to tell him about Samuel?"

She shook her head again. I didn't really expect she'd say yes, but there was always hope.

"I'll come over and pick you up and drive you into town," I said.

Ruby's eyes darted over to me. "You aren't staying here?"

"I figured with all these bodies around, I should go on back to my parents' house. Your uncles are more than capable of keeping you safe." The disappointment on her face made my insides warm. She wanted me to be with her, something I'd not yet gotten used to. Was it safety she yearned for? Or was it me? "But if you want me to stay with you, I will."

"No, you should be with your family. I'm sure they want you home."

I hated the thought of leaving her, but what I really needed to do was to find out what was going on with Father, and if he was indeed trying to build up evidence against Ruby. It was time for us to have an honest conversation. I especially wanted to know why he was putting my name on land deeds. And I'd have to face his fury over selling them to get the money for Ruby's bond.

I gave her a hand up and walked with her back into the house. The meeting had broken up, and her uncles were taking bedrolls out to the barn. I found Asa sitting with Mrs. Graves on the sofa. They held hands, and I could see Mrs. Graves had been crying as well.

"I'm going to head on back and stay at my parents' place now that you have more help," I said. "I have some family matters to tend to, but I'll be back Monday morning to take her to her meeting with Mr. Oliver. I promise I'll be right by Ruby's side through this."

Asa stood and offered me a hand. "Thank you so much for everything. I really don't know how to show you how grateful we are."

"There's no need. And if anything comes up, I'm just a few miles away. But I got a feeling once word gets around that Ruby's uncles are here for a visit, you won't be getting any more suspicious messages."

"I hope you're right."

Mrs. Graves stood and gave me a hug, thanking me as well. "You are such a blessing to all of us."

Ruby walked me out to my car. We stood there staring at each other with awkward half smiles. "You sure you don't need me to stay? I could come back later tonight."

"No, really. I'll be fine."

I shouldn't leave her. *I shouldn't love her.*

"Try and stay out of trouble, just for one night," I said.

She laughed. "I'll do my best, but I can't promise anything."

I got into my car and waved goodbye as I turned around to drive up the dirt road. When I turned left to head back toward Hanceville, she was still standing right where I left her, watching me drive away.

I spent the ten-minute drive home wondering what in the world I was doing. I wasn't just falling for Ruby; I was betraying Vanessa. And I was setting us all up for pain if I didn't do something about it. Was a future with Ruby even possible?

Thomas was right about one thing. Once the trial was over, and Ruby was cleared, that didn't necessarily mean she was safe. I could take her away from Cullman. She'd always wanted to travel and see the world. We could move west. I could make a life for us. But how?

Father was sure to cut me off completely if I married Ruby. I'd have no job, no money, and no family to help us out until I could get those things. I'd be ensuring a life of poverty for us, at least for a while. But I wasn't afraid of being poor. I'd never cared for money anyway. Too many expectations came with it. But Ruby deserved a life so much better than she'd had so far.

And what about Vanessa? I did truly care for her, though I had to admit it was completely different from the way I loved Ruby. Vanessa and I were a good fit, and we never fought. I couldn't remember the last time she had a cross word for me.

I turned onto the dirt lane that wound along our property and caught a glimpse of the stately white house I'd grown up in. Giving it all up would be as easy as breathing. But hurting the people I loved? Mother. Mary. Vanessa. Could I hurt them so deeply as to cut them out of my life? Because I knew deep down, that was where the path with Ruby would lead.

When I pulled my car in front of the house I noticed another car already parked in my usual spot. It was the Paschals' car. I'd have to face Vanessa and her family a lot sooner than I'd thought.

I trudged up the steps, dreading both conversations I'd be having that evening. When I opened the door, Vanessa was the first to greet me. She came toward me with her hands outstretched for mine. "Sweetie, I hope you don't mind our surprise, but I couldn't sit around waiting any longer."

"What are you doing here?" Stumbling to cover the disappointment she must have heard in my voice, I took her hands and kissed her on the cheek. But her smile faded all the same. "I mean, of course, it's wonderful to see you, but it's quite a long trip from Montgomery."

Mrs. Paschal stepped toward me and offered her hand, which I took immediately. "Mr. Paschal had some business to complete with your father that needed his attention, and Vanessa and I just couldn't pass up the opportunity to see you. All of you."

I glanced at Mother and studied her for a moment. She never was very good at disguising her plots, and this one stunk to high heaven of her meddling. But perhaps it was true. I had seen Mr. Paschal's name in the ledger I'd found in Father's office. Perhaps they did have some business to attend to, and maybe it wasn't as underhand as it had seemed from that book. Still, I had to wonder, how did she know I'd be coming home today?

Mother reached over and hugged me. "Thank the Lord you came home," she whispered in my ear. Then she pulled away and took Mrs. Paschal by the elbow. "Come, let's get some tea and leave these two lovebirds to talk."

As soon as they left the room, my nerves tightened. Something strange was going on. "Vanessa, how long have you been here?"

"We arrived yesterday, late in the afternoon. Your mother said you were helping your brother with some repairs to his house and had to stay there last night."

I nodded, deciding the truth would be difficult to explain. "Would you like to take a walk?"

"That would be nice."

I ushered her out the door, and we headed around to the back of the house for the path that encircled part of our property. A cool breeze whipped up the dry leaves, and it occurred to me I should've asked if she needed a coat. "Are you cold?"

"Not too much," she said. "It's a beautiful day. The trees are magnificent this time of year. I think the bright yellow is my favorite. How about yours?"

I hadn't even noticed the trees, and had no desire to talk about them. I shoved my hands in my pockets and tried to think of what, if anything, I should say about Ruby.

"I'm sorry I haven't called in a while," I said. "Things have gotten rather intense around here."

"Yes, I've heard."

"What have you heard?"

"Your mother says you've been spending a great deal of time at the jail with Ruby, and that you went behind your father's back to pay her bond. He's very upset."

That was an understatement. "Father and I have never exactly gotten along. You know that. But it's worse than ever over Ruby's situation."

"Why are you sacrificing so much for her?" She stopped and looked me right in the eyes. "Matthew, are you in love with her?"

And there it was, the direct question, with no room to avoid the truth. "Listen, I want to be honest with you, but I hope you'll give me a chance to explain. The last thing I want to do is hurt you."

Her eyes widened. "So it's true."

"I can explain everything. I do care for Ruby deeply. She's a very close friend—"

"Who you haven't spoken to in over four years, but suddenly is the most important person in the world." She narrowed her eyes and crossed her arms over her chest. "Have you loved her all this time? Is she the reason you don't ever come home to see your family?"

"No, it's not that. I can't explain everything—"

"You just said you *would* explain everything! So which is it? You can explain, or you *can't* explain?"

I was getting this all wrong. I hadn't been prepared for this conversation. I still wasn't even sure of what I wanted. Everything was so complicated. "I just meant that I would try to explain, and that I would be honest with you."

"Are you breaking off our engagement? Are you destroying our future for some farm girl who's probably a murderer?"

"Now hold on a minute! I'm trying to be honest with you. And she didn't murder anybody."

Vanessa uncrossed her arms and took a long, deep breath. "Look, you're just confused. Coming home makes you crazy. We both know that. You just need to get away from here and get some perspective."

"I can't—"

"You said you'd look for jobs in Montgomery. Daddy can give you work until something better comes along."

"Vanessa—"

"We can move past this. Once you get away from all this, you'll see—"

"Vanessa! I'm not leaving. I promised Ruby I wouldn't leave her again, and I'm not going to break that promise."

She stared at me, silent and unblinking, while the leaves swirled around us. I felt sick. How could I have handled this so poorly? At last she took a step back and hugged her arms around her waist. Closing her eyes, she tilted her head back, as if she was soaking up the last warmth of the sun.

"I'm sorry," I said. "You're a beautiful, kind, and gracious woman. I don't deserve you."

Vanessa lowered her head and opened her eyes. The pain and confusion I saw in them was almost unbearable. "I...I don't know what to say. I can't believe this is happening." She turned and glanced at the house behind us. "I'll speak to Mother this evening, and we'll be gone tomorrow."

"You don't have to do that."

"What?" she said, with a strange, high-pitched laugh. "Should we stay here? That's absurd."

"You're still friends. We're all still friends. My family, and yours. It doesn't have to be such an awful thing, does it?"

She sucked in a breath and smiled, though I could tell it was forced. "Of course. We're all still the best of friends. The best." Then she spun on her heels and headed back up the path for the house.

As I watched her go, I wondered if maybe I shouldn't have just stayed at the Graves's farm. I had a feeling that things at this house were only going to get worse.

Supper that evening was about the most awkward meal I'd ever sat through. Mother and Mrs. Paschal chatted away as if nothing was going on, while Vanessa sat beside me in complete silence. Father hadn't spoken one word to me since he'd arrived home just before supper. Though he did take the opportunity to shoot daggers at me with his eyes every now and again. He and Mr. Paschal both remained quiet, so the women filled the conversation with gossip. As I listened to their chatter, I began to get the impression that Vanessa had not yet mentioned our conversation to her mother.

"Well now," Mrs. Paschal said as she glanced around the table. "Since we're all here together, we could get a few things settled about the wedding."

I felt Vanessa stiffen. I'd been right. Why hadn't she said anything?

Mother's face beamed over at me. "We're all so excited! What do you think of having the wedding in Cullman? I mean, you still have family in these parts, and we'd love to host an engagement party!"

Mrs. Paschal shot a glance at Mr. Paschal. "I hadn't thought of that, honestly. Of course, there are some beautiful locations around Montgomery for a wedding reception. And it would make a lovely trip for you and your family."

The two women shared polite smiles, but I could see Mother's disappointment. I didn't want to think how upset she was going to be when she found out there wasn't even going to be a wedding. My head pounded, and I couldn't swallow another morsel.

I pushed away from the table and stood. "I, uh...think I'm coming down with a headache. I'm going to head up to my room and rest for a bit."

"Oh honey, are you not feeling well?" Mother said.

"Sit down," Father commanded. "You'll stay until we finish our meal. Then you'll accompany me to the library for a smoke. That should set your head straight."

I didn't miss the pointed look he gave me with that last sentence. I sat back down, resigned to endure uncomfortable conversation about a wedding that wasn't going to happen, followed by an argument that would most likely resolve nothing. Thankfully, everyone finished eating soon afterward, and Mother and Mrs. Paschal departed for the sitting room to continue their grand plans.

I took Vanessa by the elbow before she could leave with them. "Why haven't you said anything?"

She looked up at me with weary eyes that seemed a bit puffy. She'd been crying. "I, I don't know. I didn't know what to say. She's so happy." She looked like she might start crying again, so despite the awkwardness of the situation, I pulled her into my chest.

"Don't worry about it tonight," I said. "Why don't you go lie down? We can deal with all this in the morning. There's no rush."

She relaxed against me and mumbled into my chest. "Thank you."

Then she turned for the door and headed into the sitting room. I took a moment to steel myself for what waited for me in the library. But when I arrived, I was surprised to find Mr. Paschal smoking with Father. Apparently he meant to torture me further with anticipation. I should have seen that coming.

"Come in," Father said, handing me a cigar. "It's about time you joined the real men in a smoke."

"I prefer not to," I said. "You know what the doctors say about my lungs."

He raised an eyebrow. "I was under the impression you had super-human lungs that were miraculously healed."

My face flushed hot. "I think that was meant as a joke, not as permission to smoke."

He took the cigar and placed it back in the humidor on his desk. "Very well then. We can still attend to important matters. Take a seat."

He gestured to the large wingback chair next to Mr. Paschal, who puffed gently on his cigar like he had not a care in the world. I got the impression that I was the only one in the room who didn't know exactly what was going on.

Father took the leather armchair across from mine, sucked on his cigar, and then leaned back and crossed his legs. "Now, let's clear the air about your latest business transaction."

"Certainly," I said, though I was surprised we were going to do this in company. "Why don't you explain to me why there was land purchased in my name without my knowledge?"

"Son, you are still very inexperienced in life and in business. There are rules about taxes and property that are frankly, beyond your understanding."

"So educate me."

He sucked on his cigar again and blew the smoke toward the window. "That would take quite some time, and I don't want to bore Mr. Paschal with our family business. But here's what you need to understand. Mr. Paschal has been kind enough over the last couple of years to do business with me. He and I support each other in many ways—financially and personally. The land you're so interested in, wasn't exactly yours."

"The name on the deed said otherwise," I said.

"If you want to play ball with the big boys, son, you have a lot to learn." He paused and considered me. "I admit, I was angry when I realized what you'd done. But I must commend your decisive action, uninformed as it was. It's precisely what I would've done at your age."

I glanced at Mr. Paschal, who still appeared only mildly interested in all this. "Look, I understand you're upset with me, but I did what I had to. You had no right to take the money out of my savings account. Seems to me things are pretty even."

He leaned forward and shook his head. "Oh no, son. That's where you're very wrong. You see, Mr. Paschal and I had plans for that land in the future. Plans that had the potential to make a good deal of money. So you didn't just cost me what I paid for the land, you cost me *and* Mr. Paschal every penny we would've earned in the future."

"Then go down to the Building and Loan and buy it back. I'm sure it will still be worth about the same."

"Don't worry, Matthew," Mr. Paschal said, his voice deep and gravely from the smoke. "Your father and I are several steps ahead of you...on many things."

What was that supposed to mean? The whole conversation was beginning to make the hairs on the back of my neck stand up. I didn't want to have anything to do with whatever the two of them were concocting. I suspected it was less than ethical, if not outright illegal. I stood to leave.

"Well, I suppose with that being cleared up, I'll head off to my bedroom."

"Sit down," Father said. "We have another matter to clear up as well."

"Look, I'm not a child anymore. I'm done talking with you. All you want is control over every aspect of my life." I turned and took a few steps for the door.

"You know your little farm girl is going to be convicted for murder, don't you?"

I turned back around. "I'm not going to be baited into another argument about Ruby."

Father gestured toward his guest. "Don't you think Mr. Paschal deserves to know what you've been up to? How you're running around town making his daughter look like a fool?"

Heat shot up my neck and face as I tried to think of any reasonable explanation. Mr. Paschal scowled at me, his dark brow protruding as if he could rip me to shreds. Maybe Mrs. Paschal was still in the dark, but Mr. Paschal was *completely* informed.

"I've spoken with Vanessa, sir," I said to Mr. Paschal. "I haven't hidden anything from her, and I've tried to treat her with the utmost respect."

Mr. Paschal blew out a puff of smoke and turned his icy glare to Father. "I'm tired, Patrick. I'm going to leave you to handle this situation properly. It may require methods best kept between you and your son." He buried his cigar in the ashtray beside him. Then he stood and walked past me without another glance.

"What methods is he referring to?" I asked once the door had closed.

Father glared up at me, his contempt no longer masked by manners. "You are a stupid, arrogant boy. You have no idea what you're doing."

I threw my hands out. "Once again, why don't you enlighten me?"

He stood and made his way around the large cherry desk, dropping his cigar into the ashtray and leaning onto his fingers, his usual pose for scolding me. "I've done everything I could to provide a secure future for you, but you've made it clear you have no desire to be a part of this family. I'm going to explain this to you in terms even you will grasp. If you abandon your responsibilities to Vanessa and your promises to the Paschal family, and you continue to publicly embarrass both of our families, I will have no choice but to completely cut you off."

"What makes you think I want anything of yours?"

"Not only will you be cut off, but I will do everything in my power, which you know to be substantial, to ensure that Ruby is put away for life, if not sent to the electric chair."

I took a step back, unable to believe what I was hearing. "You'd condemn an innocent person just to spite me? Are you *insane*? Do you have no integrity at all?"

"You can judge me all you want, but the facts are what they are. And I will follow through with my promise."

"So now you have the power to convict people of crimes?" I yelled. "You're a monster!"

"From what I understand, the girl is far from innocent. And the fact that you would associate our good family name with someone who carries on with Negroes is appalling. And this isn't the first time. Now, I tolerated your behavior several years back because your mother assured me it was simply a period in your life you'd outgrow. But this is far more serious. And I will not tolerate it this time."

I stepped forward and made sure to meet his gaze with all the force I had. "Ruby didn't kill anyone, and I intend to stick by her side every step of the way until she's proved innocent. You may have some sway in this community and Cullman, but you cannot thwart God. If anyone has ever had God on their side, it's Ruby Graves."

I turned and strode toward the door, refusing to engage in his game any longer. As I pulled the door open he called across the room. "You will regret this decision, Matthew. It will cost you more than you can bear."

"The only one demanding a price here is you. But I reckon a son is pretty cheap to you." I slammed the door and headed straight out to my car. I hadn't even unpacked my things. I reckoned even the Graves's porch in a freezing hailstorm would be warmer than this godforsaken place.

CHAPTER FOURTEEN

Ruby

When Matthew's car arrived back in our driveway the very same night, I had to admit I was glad. Having him nearby for the past few days had been like a dream, and I hadn't wanted to wake from it. Oh, I knew it was pointless. My affection for Matthew had always been more rooted in my dreams than reality. But it was a nice distraction from the quicksand that surrounded me. His steady presence kept me from going under the weight of the bleak future I faced.

In fact, things between us had been so easy lately, I didn't think twice about going to him with my request the next morning. After breakfast, I followed him out the back of the house under the pretense of getting the broom for sweeping. He and Asa had planned to head off into the trees for the morning to find more wood for the coming winter. I put my hand on his arm before he went down the stairs.

"Can I ask you for something?" I said.

"Sure." His easy smile warmed my heart. "What can I do for you?"

"I'd really like to know how Samuel's doing, and see Hannah and Isaiah." His face dropped to a frown, making me pause. "I, uh, I was hoping you might drive me out—"

"Have you completely lost your mind?" Matthew looked around like someone might be spying on us. Then he grabbed my elbow and pulled me down the stairs toward the clothes line and lowered his voice. "Absolutely not. What if someone sees you? Have you even thought about that?"

"Of course, but who would see me? No one cares about where I go, especially in Colony."

"Ruby, you can't be that naive. There are people in this town that want to see you put away for life. Why do you think your mother went after her brothers? For entertainment? You can't give the Klan anything!"

"I understand that, but it's killing me not knowing if Samuel's all right. I think about him every day, and I pray for him every night. I just want to make sure—"

"Ruby, if someone sees you and connects Samuel to Chester's death, then you've as good as sealed his hanging. Not to mention your own. You can't be that foolish."

My pride flared, even as I knew he was right. "Fine! If you don't want to take me, then I'll just find my own way. I'm sure I can borrow Asa's truck or Uncle Roy's."

"You'll do no such thing."

"I'm not one of your servants you can order around, Matthew Doyle."

He walked several paces away from me before turning back. "Look, I ain't trying to start a fight with you, and I ain't ordering you around. Lord knows you're going to do whatever you set your mind to. But I've never known you to put Samuel and Hannah's safety in jeopardy. I'm just asking you to consider this idea carefully before you run headlong into the fire."

He was right. I knew it in my head. But it drove me mad to have to face it. "All right," I said, my voice cracking. "I won't go. I just can't stop worrying about them."

He came back to me, putting a gentle hand on my shoulder. "Aren't you the one with all the faith?" he said. "Don't you know your scriptures?" His head tilted slightly, a grin spreading across his face. "Be anxious for nothing, but in everything by prayer and supplication, with thanksgiving, let your requests be made known to God; and the peace of God, which surpasses all understanding, will guard your hearts and minds through Christ Jesus."

I closed my eyes and breathed in the peace God had sent through Matthew's words. God was Hannah's provider, just as much as He was mine. I had to trust Him to take care of them, and do what I knew had to be done in the meantime.

I opened my eyes to find Matthew still smiling at me. "Thank you," I said. His hand was still on my shoulder, and I reached up to take it in mine. "Once again, you're the voice of reason when I seem to forget all my common sense."

He let out a quiet chuckle and rubbed his thumb against the back of my hand. "Who would've ever suspected such a crazy thing as Ruby Graves listening to me? What's gotten into you?"

I couldn't name what had gotten into me, but I sure could feel it coursing through me. *Lord, please set my head right. Take my thoughts off Matthew and set them back on You.*

I dropped his hand and took a step back. "I have a lot of work to get done today, and I reckon you do too. I'll see you for dinner."

I could tell my sudden distance confused him. "Did I say something wrong?" he asked.

"No. I just have a lot on my mind. I need to keep busy." I'd nearly reached the back porch steps.

"Ruby, if it'll make you feel better, I could drive out and check on Hannah and Samuel."

Everything in me wanted to fly into his arms. "You'd do that for me?"

"Of course. I know it's got to be hard on you. Maybe you could write a note or something, and I could give it to Hannah."

I was pretty sure my delight was plain to see. "I'd be so grateful. Really, I would. But..." My enthusiasm died with the realization that Matthew could be in as much danger as I was. How selfish it would be to ask this of him. "I can't let you risk your safety for me like that. If something happened to you…"

We gazed at each other for a long moment, long enough to stoke my hope once again. But there was something else. I was beginning to see that he didn't look on me like he used to, like I was a little girl needing protection. There was something more behind his eyes, a yearning that looked much like mine. Could he possibly feel the same as I did?

He cleared his throat and broke the spell, looking toward the trees where Asa had disappeared several minutes ago. "I reckon I ought to get to work. But I mean it; if you want me to, I'll head out there this evening and find out if they're all right."

I shook my head. "No, you're probably right. Best to keep them both as far away from this mess as possible. No sense in risking their safety just to appease my mind."

"All right, then," he said. "I'll see you for dinner."

He took the ax from the wood block and slung it onto his shoulder, walking toward the tree line. I couldn't keep myself from watching him for a while. Seemed like every step he took, my heart thundered. What if he did love me in return? I could wind up spending the rest of my life in prison, without him. Then what?

There was nothing else for it. I'd have to continue keeping my emotions in check until the trial concluded and I knew exactly what I'd be facing. There just wasn't any room for What Ifs.

As I hung the wet laundry on the line later that afternoon, I did my best to keep my mind off my worries for Samuel, but it just wasn't any use. One terrible scene after another played out in my thoughts, and I asked God over and over to give me peace. But peace didn't come.

I went over every detail of what I remembered of the day Chester died. The only thing I could think of that pointed to Samuel was the knife. And no one else knew it even existed except Matthew. I felt certain I could deny ever having seen it before. But what if someone else figured it out? What if the solicitor had found someone who'd seen Samuel come out of the barn? Surely the sheriff would've questioned me about it if that were the case.

While my mind spun round and round the possible outcomes, I heard the motor of a truck coming down the dirt road. It was coming pretty fast, so I figured it was my uncles. They'd taken off just after breakfast. No one asked them where they were going, and they didn't offer any explanations.

I secured the last sheet to the line and walked around the corner of the house. Sure enough, Uncle Roy's truck slid to a stop in front of the barn amid a cloud of dust. A few seconds later, Franklin came stomping out of the barn, pointing his finger at them and yelling things I couldn't make out. But I could tell it was something to do with them leaving him behind. I still hadn't seen him up close, but I could tell he was quite a bit younger than the others. He might not have even been in his thirties yet.

From what I could tell, Roy stopped to listen for a moment before he dismissed Franklin with a wave of his hand. Then Eddie must have teased him, 'cause Franklin flew into a fit of swearing. Eddie laughed and disappeared into the barn. Roy yelled at both of them to shut up. That part I could hear clear as day.

Franklin huffed around in the dust, making his way toward the back of Asa's house. When he reached the fence that encircled the pasture, he kicked the bottom rail right hard. It shuddered, vibrating for several feet in both directions. He turned around and leaned against the fence, finally noticing me.

"Sorry about the ruckus," he said. "I'm just a little restless."

I walked over to the fence with a little apprehension. There was a wildness in his blue eyes that set my nerves to attention. He had a cut over his left eyebrow, and a busted lip that was on the mend, but still swollen. I reckon I was staring, 'cause he grinned a little and pointed to his lip.

"Got this from Roy when he heard the law was after me. I got a little careless."

I held up my hand. "I don't...I mean, Mother would be upset—"

"Oh, of course. I mean, I didn't do nothing bad. It's not like I killed someone or something." His mouth clamped shut, and heat spread up my face. Franklin's eyes widened. "Oh no! I didn't mean nothing by that. I mean...what you done...now that was something. I'm right proud we're related, to tell the honest truth."

I couldn't help but smile at him, which seemed to ease his discomfort. "You're Franklin, right? The baby of the family?"

He smiled and tipped his hat. "The one and only."

"So how come you don't come up to the house?"

"Oh that," he said in a flat voice. "Roy dragged me out here under the notion we needed to help keep the family safe—which I'm all for—but then he goes and tells me I got to stay in the barn out of sight the whole time. I might as well have stayed in our place down in the caverns. At least there, I could've had something to drink now and then."

He turned around and leaned his elbows onto the top rail and looked out over the fields. "I don't mean nothing against you or Lizzy," he continued. "Just feel like I'm trapped here waiting on something to happen. Makes me feel crazy inside. Like I got ants all over me or something."

"I feel that way too," I said. "Like I'm just waiting for something to happen. I'm trapped here until the trial starts, and then what? I might be heading off to prison for the rest of my life."

"Naw, that ain't gonna happen. Roy and Eddie know how to deal with things like this. They can get you somewhere safe, where the law won't find ya."

"Oh no, I couldn't do that. Just take off running. That just doesn't seem right. Besides, if it's God's will for me to go to prison, then that's where I'll go. Many of the saints in the Bible went to prison for periods of time. If it was bearable for them, it'll be bearable for me."

Franklin was looking at me like I'd gone bat crazy. "You really believe all that nonsense?"

"Of course. Don't you believe in God?"

"Well, of course I believe in God," he said. "I just don't think He's interested in my life is all. And I can't imagine He'd send a nice young girl like yourself off to prison. What's more, I can't believe you'd be so calm about it."

I leaned onto the rail next to him and took in the faint orange and pink streaks forming above us as the sun dipped low. How many more sunsets would I get to see? "I wouldn't exactly say I'm calm."

He turned to me with a mischievous glint in his eyes. "Say, you wanna get out of here for a bit? Maybe go for a ride?"

My first thought was to jump at the chance to get away, even for just a little while. But I could hear Matthew in my head blessing me out for even thinking about it. Still, if Franklin was with me, I'd be all right. He knew how to protect himself.

"Won't Roy be upset with you?" I asked.

"I don't care one little bit if he's upset with me."

"Where would we go?"

He grinned. "Where do you want to go?"

Franklin drove fast, making my stomach lurch a few times around curves. It wasn't as bad once we hit 69 going south. The road was a bit smoother then. But my stomach still wouldn't settle, especially once we made it through Bremen. The closer we got to Colony, the faster my heart raced.

"What're you after in Arkadelphia?" Franklin asked. "I happen to know there ain't nothing interesting to do there."

I gripped my hands together in my lap and prayed he wouldn't turn the truck around. "I only meant we needed to head *toward* Arkadelphia. I don't want to actually go there. We'll need to make a few turns before we get that far."

He raised an eyebrow and looked at me like I was amusing. "Whoo, Ruby got a secret boyfriend or something? And here I thought you were sweet on that boy staying at the house!"

"No, it's not that. I just have a friend I need to check on, that's all."

"A friend, huh? All right. If you say so."

"Take this turn up ahead," I said.

"Nah, you don't mean that one. That's the road that goes to Colony."

I rubbed my palm with my thumb. "That's the road I mean to take."

He took his foot off the gas, and we started slowing down. Then he pushed on the brake and brought us to a halt on the side of the road. "You want to say that again? I think I misunderstood."

"I aim to go to Colony tonight to check on a friend."

"That's what I thought you said." He shook his head. "Are you nuts? There's only two reasons white folks go to Colony—liquor or...well...anyhow, neither of 'em are reasons you should be mixed up in."

I wasn't about to get this close and not see Samuel and Hannah. "That's about the most ignorant thing I've ever heard. Colony is a perfectly fine little town. Did you know they have their own gin? Their own stores? A school? They have everything! And they're just as normal as you and me."

"You done lost all your marbles."

"Well, if you won't drive me, I reckon I can walk the rest of the way."

"Walk?" He threw his head back and laughed. "You must be nuts. You can't walk. It's nearly dark. What do you think one of them Negroes is gonna do to you if they catch you walking all by yourself? The only ones out after dark are the ones looking for trouble."

"Look, I've been out here plenty of times. I know my way around."

"Oh, you do?"

"Yes, I do. I come here to visit my friend Hannah almost twice a month. We've been friends for years. And I intend to visit with her.

Now you can either drive me over to her house, or you can explain to my mother why you let me walk all along these back roads—"

"All right!" He furrowed his brow at me. "I'll drive you where you want to go, and I'll wait in the truck for ya. But we go straight there, and then straight back to your mother's house. Ya hear?"

I nodded.

Franklin put the truck back in gear and made the turn I'd indicated. We rode in silence, with only my directions and the growing tension filling the air. The trees hid the last bit of sun from the road, making it hard to see, even with the lights on. I pointed to the dirt road Hannah lived on. "Take that left."

Franklin stopped, but didn't make the turn. "You sure about this?"

"Definitely."

"Ruby, I think we best turn around and go back home."

"You turn this truck around, and I'll jump out. I once jumped on and off a moving train to get where I needed to go. You think I'm scared of a little old truck?"

He turned wide eyes to me. "You really are as crazy as people say."

"What people? Who says I'm crazy?"

He just shook his head and made the turn. "I'll give you ten minutes. That's it. Then I'm out of here. I mean it."

"Fine. The house is up here on the right. You can pull around on the other side of that bush so the truck isn't easy to see. That's what I usually do."

He pulled to a stop where I'd pointed. "Ten minutes. You hear?"

I jumped out of the truck and ignored his reminder. What was he going to do? Drive back to Mother and admit he'd left me here? I'd take whatever time I needed.

Crossing the yard, I climbed the steps to the front door, taking care to keep my footsteps light. When I knocked quietly, I heard feet shuffling. I didn't want to frighten Hannah, so I figured it was best to let her know who was at her door.

"Hannah," I said, leaning as close to the door as I could. "It's me, Ruby. Come let me in."

There was more shuffling, and then the door cracked open. Hannah peered out at me, and I was reminded of how she'd looked at me when we first met, like I was a bobcat that might suddenly jump her.

"Ruby Graves, have you lost yo mind?" she whispered. "Why you bringing trouble to my doorstep?"

"Hannah, please let me in, just for a minute. I had to see you."

The door swung back, and I half expected to see the broken, beaten down woman I'd found in the shack on Mr. Calhoun's property all those years ago. I was grateful to see she was unharmed.

She quickly closed the door behind me and grabbed me by the elbow. "Now, I don't know what you hope to accomplish here, but if you done changed yo mind about telling those folks about Samuel—"

"No!" I said. "Oh, Hannah. No, I would never do that to Samuel." I threw my arms around her neck, unable to hold back my tears. "I'm so sorry. I won't stay long. I don't want to cause you any trouble. I just...I had to know if he's all right."

Her body softened, and she hugged me in return. After a few moments, she pulled my shoulders back. "He done packed up and went off to my sister's place in Georgia. But he told me everything about how you was there for him and tried to help him."

Relief flooded over me, and I sank into the nearby chair at the kitchen table. "Praise the Lord. I was hoping you had some relatives he could go to."

Hannah took the seat across from me, and I got my first good look at her. She looked like she was barely keeping it together. Her eyes had dark circles under them, and her thin hands shook as she reached across the table to pat mine.

"I can't...Miss Ruby...there just ain't any words to express..."

"Please don't fret over it. I'll be all right. God is my provider, my comforter, my healer. He'll keep me in the palm of His hand."

She brought her hand back to her forehead. "I don't know how you keep your faith so strong in something like this." Then she grinned. "'Course, I am talking to the same girl that ran right at a tornado."

"Now, look. I did no such thing. I ran away from the tornado, and I was trying to get to you."

"I know." Her eyes filled with grateful tears. "You always run to me in the middle of the storm. I reckon you're our guardian angel." Water spilled down her cheeks. "But I fear this storm so much more than the tornado."

God's words in Isaiah flooded my heart, and I shared them with Hannah as they came.

"Fear thou not; for I am with thee: be not dismayed; for I am thy God: I will strengthen thee; yea, I will help thee; yea, I will uphold thee with the right hand of my righteousness.

"Behold, all they that were incensed against thee shall be ashamed and confounded: they shall be as nothing; and they that strive with thee shall perish.

"So you see," I concluded. "We have nothing to fear. God is with us. He's with Samuel. All is well."

The drive back to Asa and Mother's wasn't nearly as exciting as leaving had been. Franklin didn't smile at all. In fact, he didn't say one word the whole time. I was just so relieved Samuel was out of harm's way, I figured I could face the wrath I knew was waiting on me.

"Thank you," I said as we pulled off 69 and neared the last turn of our journey.

Franklin just stared ahead of him like he'd done for the past several minutes. I wondered how he must feel. There he was, hoping to take a quick drive to relieve his anxiety, and all I'd done was add to it. Maybe he was wondering what kind of wrath he was facing as well. Maybe another busted lip.

"I'll take the blame for all this," I said. "I tricked you, and blackmailed you into taking me. It's my fault."

"You do that a lot?" He asked. "Take the blame for things you ain't actually done?"

"I did trick you a bit, and I threatened you to make you—"

"That ain't what I'm talking about." He glanced sideways at me. "You're taking the blame for this murder too, ain't ya?"

My stomach dropped. "I don't...know what you mean."

"I read what they said about you in the paper." He looked at me a bit longer this time. Studied me before looking ahead at the road again. "I ain't saying I believe it. But I see things. I seen you hug that Negro woman before we left."

The hairs prickled on the back of my neck. What if he told someone where he'd taken me tonight? Matthew was right. I was so foolish. "I still don't understand what you mean."

"All right," he said, letting out a defeated sigh. "I won't push."

By that time we'd pulled up to the house, and the headlights swept over Matthew sitting on the edge of the porch. I could see both relief and anger flash over him. Franklin turned off the engine as my uncles, Mother and Asa all filed out of the house.

Roy headed straight for Franklin. "What in the blazes were you trying to do? Get both of you killed? Get thrown back in jail?"

I walked around the front of the car and met Mother with a hug. "I'm sorry if I worried you, it was all my—"

"We just got a little cabin fever," Franklin broke in. "We got to talking and just needed a little drive is all. Nothing to get bent out of shape about."

Everyone looked at me as if they were waiting for me to verify Franklin's story. "I...I reckon. Just a drive." I met Matthew's gaze and saw he wasn't buying one word of it. How did he always know?

"Listen," Franklin continued, "me and Ruby didn't mean to worry y'all. We just went up to the gas station and got a couple of Coca-Colas. Then we rode around to get some fresh air."

Roy shoved a finger in Franklin's chest. "You went out in public?" He grabbed Franklin by the ear and started pulling him down to the barn. Franklin didn't even put up much of a fight. I said a quick prayer that Roy would go easy on him. I couldn't believe he hadn't let me tell them the truth.

Mother squeezed my shoulders. "How about next time you want to go for a drive, you let one of us know. I'm sure Matthew or Asa would have been happy to drive you somewhere. We were worried sick, honey."

"I'm sorry. It won't happen again." I glanced at Matthew, still standing on the porch, now leaning against the post with his hands in his pockets. He hadn't said a word to me.

Asa patted my back as he passed us. "I reckon we best be getting in bed soon. Early day tomorrow."

Mother followed Asa inside, and Matthew met me at the top of the steps. The front door swung closed, giving us a moment alone. I had no idea what to say. "I'm sorry if I worried you. It was all my fault. I shouldn't have—"

He put a hand up to stop me from talking. "I think it's best if I don't know what you were up to tonight. I'm pretty sure I know anyway, but we don't have to talk about it."

My heart sank at the disappointment in his eyes. "All right."

"You done now? Satisfied? No more...*drives?*"

I nodded. "I found out what I needed to."

"Good. You need to get your head on straight and start concentrating on your defense. The trial's gonna be here before you know it."

He opened the front door and went inside, leaving me alone with the stars. I looked up into the clear night sky and thanked God once more for protecting Samuel. I knew I could face what was ahead, win or lose, with peace in my heart that I'd done the right thing.

CHAPTER FIFTEEN

Matthew

The next few days went by so quick I barely kept up with them. I was troubled over what Father had said, but I couldn't believe he'd have any meaningful influence over the trial. So I didn't say anything to Mr. Oliver or Ruby about it. I didn't want to add any worries. Besides, after that stunt she pulled, I wasn't saying a whole lot to her anyhow.

I spent most of the time helping Asa around their property, chopping wood, repairing fences, tending to animals. It was hard work, the kind I'd never really had to do much of. Every once in a while, I'd have to take a break. I'd lean against a fence post or a stump, take a swig of water, and I'd catch Ruby watching me from the porch or a window. Sometimes, it was like a thousand words passed between us in single moments. Did she know how much my love had grown for her? Was it written across my forehead? How would I possibly let her go if she was found guilty?

Ruby's uncles didn't hang around much during the day. I figured Franklin must've told the others where he and Ruby really went, 'cause Roy kept looking at her funny, like he wasn't sure of what to make of her. And he pulled Asa and me aside the next day to encourage us to keep Ruby close by. Asa and I nodded and shared a glance. We knew better.

I noticed that despite the fact I was sleeping on a porch, I was wiped out every night by dark, and I slept better than I ever had before. I didn't even mind the blisters on my hands too much. When I wasn't toiling around the farm, I talked with Ruby about the trial. I tried to convince her to tell Mr. Oliver everything, especially since Samuel had seen Chester attack her the first time. She wasn't even willing to entertain the thought of Samuel coming within a mile of the trial. When I tried to push the issue, she simply quit talking to me for the rest of the afternoon. I kept wondering how we were going to prove that Chester attacked her without any eyewitness account. I just prayed the jury would take her word for it.

Oh yes, that was another thing we did. We prayed. I hadn't prayed like that ever before in my life. Ruby would take my hand, close her eyes, and start talking to God like they were as close as family. Like He was sitting right there with her. I could've sworn I actually *felt* a presence when she prayed.

I realized after I'd felt it a time or two that it was the same feeling I'd had the night I was healed from my tuberculosis. It was hard to put words to, but once it washed over me, once it filled me to overflowing, I knew it was the same. And I let go of all my doubts that Ruby's gift was anything but pure. I still didn't quite understand it, and I had to admit it still made me uncomfortable, but being with Ruby was like being with an angel.

Now, I know how that sounds. I've heard other men say some lady was an angel, but I'd wager none of them had ever come so close to the real thing. I knew beyond a doubt that I had, and I was better for it. 'Course, that didn't change her stubborn nature one little bit. But I began to see that her stubbornness came from a sense of what was right, and she clung to it no matter what. I had to respect that. But still, such devotion might come at a price.

By the time the morning of the trial came, I could hardly believe it had been a week since I'd left my family home. It didn't even seem like I belonged there anymore. But I couldn't shake the feeling I didn't belong in Ruby's world either.

I waited with Ruby and Mr. Oliver in a conference room down the hall from the courtroom. We didn't say much, but the air in the room was stifling, despite the cold downpour and drop in the temperature that had come over the town the night before. Ruby sat at the end of a long table, her hands in her lap, her eyes mostly closed. I suspected she was praying.

Mr. Oliver sat around the corner from her, looking through notes, mumbling to himself. I figured he was going over his opening remarks. He was dressed in a dark suit, but he'd already removed his jacket and loosened his tie. The beginnings of sweat stains crept down his back.

I couldn't sit. I thought my insides were going to jump right out of my body. I'd never even been inside a courtroom, so I had no idea what to expect. I'd asked Mr. Oliver some questions, but I didn't want to distract him from his preparations, so I kept my curiosity to myself. I lingered in front of the door, listening to the squeaks of shoes in the hallway as people crowded into the courtroom.

Mr. Oliver took out his watch and glanced at Ruby. "It's about time. We should go inside."

Ruby nodded, and they both stood. Panic surged over me as I realized that whatever happened on that day was going to determine if I was going to lose Ruby forever. I had the urge to grab her by the hand and make a run for it. Maybe we could settle down in a tiny little town in Texas, or Oklahoma, where no one would ever look for us.

Ruby and Mr. Oliver moved toward me. I put my hands up to stop them. "How 'bout we say a prayer before we go out there?"

Ruby smiled, steadying my jitters. "That would be nice." She reached for my hand. "Go ahead."

I was sure I'd sound like a dimwit compared to Ruby, but then I also knew she'd hate the thought of me comparing my prayers to hers. She'd scold me and tell me to just open my heart, and say whatever my spirit led me to say. So that's exactly what I did.

"Lord, we come to you now asking for Your mercy and strength. We know You are present with us, even in our struggles—most assuredly in our struggles. Be with Ruby today, and give her confidence to speak boldly. Give Mr. Oliver sound wisdom in his words. And we pray that each witness will speak truthfully. We know that justice will prevail. It's in Your Son, Jesus Christ's name that we pray. Amen."

"Amen." Ruby squeezed my hand. "Thank you."

We followed Mr. Oliver out of the conference room and down the hallway to the courtroom entrance. People swarmed the hall, and each and every one of them stopped to stare at Ruby. She offered them a gentle smile in return. Even in facing such difficulty, she could find grace and kindness for others. I could hardly believe it, but then I hadn't really expected anything else.

We entered the courtroom, which from the rear looked more like a church. The pews were filling up with people as if they were getting ready to hear a good sermon. I followed Ruby down front. Her mother and Asa were already seated on the front row just behind the table on the left, so I joined them. Ruby came around in front of us and hugged them both while Mr. Oliver set up his yellow pad and folders.

At the other table, Mr. Garrett and a young man I didn't know had turned to speak to the Calhouns, who were seated directly behind the solicitor. They threw glances in Ruby's direction, but mostly they spoke quietly with Mr. Garrett. In the rows behind them, I saw the sheriff, an older gentleman I believed to be the coroner, a couple of men I didn't recognize, and in another row behind them sat Brother Cass. Of course he'd want a ringside seat to Ruby's demise. I was disappointed, but not too surprised, to see that James was nowhere to be found. I reckoned they hadn't been able to reach Henry either, but I didn't want to bring it up. I ached for Ruby. She deserved so much better than this.

The good news was that I didn't see Father anywhere either. Hopefully he'd be more concerned with work than getting involved in Ruby's trial. From the spectacle forming all along the rear and sides of the seating area, he'd be the only one in all of Cullman working today. That was due in large part to the sensational articles that had run in the paper over the last few days leading up to the trial. I had to wonder if Father's hand had been in that, given his relationship with Mr. Adams.

The clerk called us to order, and everyone stood as Judge Albert Woods entered the courtroom. I stiffened, recalling how he'd wished Vanessa luck in our forthcoming marriage at my parents' dinner party. He seemed like such a serious man. In fact, I couldn't recall a single time I'd ever heard him laugh. He looked around the room, stuffed full of spectators, and frowned. Then he called court into session, and the dreary process of selecting a jury began.

As jumpy as I'd been earlier in the morning, by the time we'd worked our way to twelve jurors, I could've taken a nice, long nap. 'Course, there wasn't a single soul on the jury that could relate to Ruby. Each and every one of them was a farmer—businessmen had a knack for getting struck down or dismissed. And each and every one of them was more than fifty years old. I didn't know any of them. But there was one fellow, Richard Moore, whose name stood out. I couldn't figure it out exactly, but I knew his name from somewhere. After trying to dig through my brain for several minutes, I gave it up.

Once the jury was seated, I took a look at them as a whole. I figured for sure it would work in our favor to put a bunch of old farmers up there. They wouldn't want to see a poor young girl, maybe much like their own daughters, sent to prison for life. Once Ruby sat before them and explained her story, they'd see the truth. I started to think we stood a good chance. That is, until Mr. Garrett got underway with his opening statement.

Mr. Garrett wasted no time painting Ruby as a troubled girl, one who would steal from soup kitchens, lash out at those she loved, and worst of all, that she loved Negroes. "As you fine gentlemen will come to learn, Ruby Graves was, in fact, in love with a Negro boy, meeting him secretly inside the Calhouns' barn. And when she realized that her abominable affair had been discovered, she sought to kill Chester Calhoun to protect herself from further discovery."

That was when it hit me. These were exactly the right kind of men to convict Ruby.

The first witness for the prosecution was Luke Dalton, a man who'd worked on the Calhoun farm for several years, and the first person to come upon the scene. He seemed mighty uncomfortable as Mr. Garrett's questioning got underway. He leaned forward and gripped his hands between his knees, furrowing his brow as he was asked to remember just what he saw when he entered the barn.

"Well," he said. "I was headed to the barn to fetch some straps for the mules when I heard a woman's voice. She sounded upset."

"Upset how?" Mr. Garrett pressed.

"I couldn't make out her words, but I reckon it sounded like she was cryin', maybe speakin' to someone too. I couldn't be sure."

"So then what happened?"

"I opened the door and I seen Chester laid out on the ground on his back. Looked like he'd just fallen there. Arms kinda spread out. Miss Ruby was kneeling beside him. She was looking down at Chester with this blank sort of stare on her face. I noticed there was blood on her hands and some on her face, and I saw where Chester was bleeding onto the ground underneath himself."

"Was Miss Graves doing anything at the time?" Mr. Garrett asked.

"No, sir. She was just kneeling there. She looked mighty upset, like she'd been crying."

"Did you see the knife?"

"No, sir."

"All right then, what happened next?"

I went over to Chester to see if he was alive. He wasn't breathing. I asked Miss Ruby if she was all right. She nodded and asked me if I'd fetch her brother. I could see she wasn't hurt, so I ran out the door and out to the north field to find James. I told him his sister was in trouble and he needed to get to the barn. Then he took off, and I ran to the main house to let Mr. Calhoun know what was going on."

Mr. Garrett paused and scratched his chin. Strolling over to Mr. Dalton, he leaned casually on the railing in front of him. "Can you explain what you meant when you said Miss Ruby wasn't hurt?"

Mr. Dalton blinked and then turned his gaze on Ruby, like he needed to see her to remember what she'd looked like. "She had blood on her face, but I didn't see no cuts or nothin'. Same on her hands."

"Did it look like she'd been hit or punched about her face? Any bruising?"

"No, sir. I couldn't see nothin' where it looked like she'd been injured. 'Course, I wasn't exactly studying—"

"That'll be all." Mr. Garrett looked satisfied and took his seat.

Mr. Oliver didn't get out of his chair. He glanced at his yellow pad and then up at Mr. Dalton. "How long have you known Miss Graves?"

"Oh, I'd say about five years or so. Her family started sharecropping at the Calhoun place 'bout two years after I moved my family there. And her brother James has run the place the last three of those years."

"How *well* would you say you know Miss Graves?"

"Pretty well."

"Did she help deliver any of your children?"

Mr. Dalton's face flushed pink. His eyes travelled over to Ruby. "Yes, sir. She helped Sarah—that's my wife—with our youngest just over a year ago."

"And what's been your experience with Miss Graves? Is she hotheaded? Rash?"

Mr. Dalton shook his head. "Naw, she's about the kindest soul I ever been around. Wouldn't think she'd hurt a flea. Sarah says she don't ever want anyone but Miss Ruby delivering her babies."

I couldn't see Ruby's face, but I could see from the relief on Mr. Dalton's that she must've been smiling at him.

"No more questions," Mr. Oliver said.

My shoulders relaxed in relief that the first round was over. I already felt like I needed to go run a couple of miles around town. My knee bounced involuntarily up and down as I took a quick look at the jury while Sheriff Peterson was called up front and sworn in. I couldn't make heads or tails of how Mr. Dalton's testimony went over. But I figured it sure didn't hurt nothing.

Mr. Garrett was out of his seat once more, slowly pacing in front of Sheriff Peterson as he described pretty much the same scene Mr. Dalton had. He too said that Ruby had no major injuries, but that she had blood on her hands and face. I'd hoped that fact would escape too much notice, but I should've known Mr. Garrett would hammer the point home with the jury. That would prove to be trouble if Ruby wavered in her story at all.

"When did you first take Miss Graves's statement?" Mr. Garrett asked.

"She gave a short statement at the scene. Then she came down to my office a few hours later and explained in more detail what had happened." Sheriff Peterson looked much more comfortable in the witness stand than Mr. Dalton had, probably on account of him having to testify all the time.

"Why don't you tell the jury, in your own words, what Miss Graves said to you in that first interview?" Mr. Garrett had stopped his pacing right in front of the jury box. It was a subtle, but brilliant move. It made it that much easier for the sheriff to speak to him and the jury at the same time.

"She said that she'd gone into the barn looking for her brother, James. That he wasn't in there, and when she turned around, Chester Calhoun was coming at her, saying he was gonna teach her a lesson. She said she struggled with him for a bit, and he tossed her about. He kicked her in the ribs; then he flung her against the hay bale and came at her with a knife."

Mr. Garrett put up a hand to stop him. "Now say that again. What did she say Chester did?"

"She said he flung her around a few times, kicked her in the ribs, and tossed her against the hay bales."

"All right. Continue with Miss Graves's statement, please."

"Well, she said when he come at her with the knife, she kicked at his hand and fought him off. That was how the knife ended up in Mr. Calhoun's chest."

"When you spoke with Miss Graves, did she appear to have any injuries to her hands?"

"No."

"No bruised knuckles?"

Mr. Oliver stood. "Objection. Counsel has already established Miss Graves's medical condition and that she had not sustained any major injuries."

"Sustained," Judge Woods said.

Mr. Garrett continued as if he hadn't been interrupted at all. "Sheriff, did you find any evidence at the scene that would corroborate Miss Graves's story?"

Sheriff Peterson cleared his throat. "Only that it was apparent a struggle had occurred for a lengthy period."

"How long would you say is a lengthy period?"

"Several minutes. The signs of struggle covered a wide area of the barn."

Mr. Garrett turned to face the jury when he asked his next question. "Did you discover evidence that contradicts Miss Graves's story?"

"Yes."

"Can you please describe that evidence?"

"We found several sets of footprints, and were able to narrow down a few prints from the fight. There were a set of boot prints, a smaller pair of prints that looked like ladies' shoes, and a second pair of boot prints that were smaller than the first, but larger than the ladies' prints."

The crowd behind me began to mumble, and Judge Woods tapped his gavel. Mr. Garrett, appearing surprised by this revelation, approached the witness stand and leaned toward the sheriff. "But how can you be sure those prints were from the scuffle, and not from other farmhands coming in and out of the barn? Or your own deputies, for that matter?"

"Well, when people scuffle in the dirt like that, it gets all scraped around. Old footprints would get rubbed out from the boots and bodies moving all along the floor. And that was the case for the most part here. There were older boot prints around other parts of the barn, but where the fight took place there was large areas where the dirt had been pushed around, and a fresh boot print was on top. Therefore, we concluded the print had to have been made either during or after the fight had taken place."

"You mean like this?" Mr. Garrett went to his table and pulled out three pictures from the envelope I'd gone through with Mr. Oliver. He showed them to the sheriff, who agreed they were from the barn right after he'd arrived on the scene. Then Mr. Garrett took the pictures over to the jury so they could pass them around.

The courtroom had grown deathly silent, and I saw a couple of the men on the jury nod their head as they looked at the picture. My palms started sweating. There'd be no way to explain away the extra set of boot prints.

Once the pictures were returned, Mr. Garrett continued his questions. "Now, Sheriff, based on these pictures here, what can any reasonable man conclude—"

"Objection!"

Judge Woods leaned forward, looking pointedly at Mr. Oliver. "Sustained. Mr. Garrett, please make sure your questions only ask the witness for *his* conclusions."

Mr. Garrett tried again. "Sheriff, can you please, based on these pictures, explain to us what conclusion *you* came to?"

"I concluded that Miss Graves was not the only person fighting with Chester Calhoun."

Mr. Oliver wiped his forehead with his handkerchief before he stood and approached the witness stand. "Now, Sheriff, is it possible that the second set of boot prints you're referring to could have come from Luke Dalton? Or maybe Ruby's brother James when he came to help her?"

"I was able to find these prints a good distance away from the commotion that followed Mr. Dalton's entry. They were secured as soon as we saw them, so none of my deputies made those prints either."

"Did you take everyone's shoes that had been in the barn and compare them to the prints?"

Sheriff Peterson's mouth tipped wryly. "No."

"So you are *guessing* that the prints belong to Chester and Miss Ruby and...who?"

"Another person we weren't able to identify."

"Sheriff, exactly how many people entered that barn after the fight took place, but before you secured these footprints?"

Sheriff Peterson leaned onto his knees and seemed to consider this for a moment. "Let's see, there was Mr. Dalton, James Graves, Mr. Calhoun, and two of my deputies."

"And how are you certain that these footprints don't match up to any of them?"

"Like I said before, these footprints were located on the other side of the barn from where Chester died. Those folks who came into the barn didn't go to that side."

The line of questioning quickly became futile. The sheriff wasn't giving an inch on his conclusions, and the more Mr. Oliver pushed, the more certain the sheriff sounded. I was relieved when Mr. Oliver concluded his questions, but I was certain the sheriff had scored huge points for the prosecution.

The clerk called the coroner to the stand, whose testimony, thankfully, turned out to be so dry I saw a couple of the juror's heads drop before they bounced back awake. The coroner, Mr. Hankal, was an older gentleman who'd been coroner in the county for nearly thirty years. I felt sure he must have testified many times before, because he seemed rather bored by the whole thing.

"When the knife entered Mr. Calhoun's chest, it sliced into a major artery: the aorta. Although the wound itself was not large, Mr. Calhoun bled profusely into his chest cavity, which resulted in death."

Mr. Garrett sat at his table, leaning back as though he were as bored as the rest of the onlookers. "Were there any other signs of trauma to the body?"

"There was a bruise forming on the left side of his face consistent with being punched."

"Are you certain of that?" Mr. Garrett asked.

"Yes, sir. There was a fresh bruise forming on the left side of his jaw when I examined Mr. Calhoun at the scene. When I later examined the body at my office, it had deepened."

Mr. Garrett turned toward the jury and gave them a pointed look. My stomach sank again. No one in his right mind would believe little ole Ruby could have punched Chester hard enough to bruise him without injuring her hand in the slightest. This was quickly becoming a lost cause, and I was about to lose her forever if God didn't step in and turn things around.

I bowed my head and prayed while Mr. Hankal was dismissed, and the clerk called Mr. Calhoun to the stand. Surely he would be the last witness. And surely his testimony would actually help our case. He knew what Chester had done to Ruby all those years ago, and he'd have to stand before God and everyone and tell the truth, which is what he swore to do before taking his seat in the witness stand.

"What is your relationship to the victim?" Mr. Garrett began.

"He was my oldest son," Mr. Calhoun said, his large shoulders slumped forward.

"Tell us in your own words what you saw when you came to the barn that morning."

Mr. Calhoun rubbed the back of his neck before answering. "Luke Dalton come up to the house a-hollering 'bout Chester being hurt down in the barn. I took off after him. When we got there, Chester was laying on the ground on his back." Mr. Calhoun paused. He looked over at the jury with tortured eyes. "He was...gone...already. I checked him. He wasn't breathing or nothin'. There was blood...on his chest, on the ground a bit too."

"Did you see Ruby Graves?"

Mr. Calhoun turned his gaze to Ruby. "She was sitting on the ground a few feet away, leaning on the hay bales. James was there beside her. Neither of them said anything. I asked 'em what happened. Ruby said Chester had come at her, tried to attack her. Said she'd fought him off. Then she broke down and started cryin'."

"Did she say anything else about what happened?"

"No. Sheriff Peterson and his deputies arrived after a while. I went up to the house to comfort Mrs. Calhoun and my daughter."

"Did you walk around the barn at all?"

"No."

"Did you walk over to Ruby when you talked to her?"

"No. I stayed beside Chester until the sheriff arrived."

Mr. Garrett stood from the table and walked toward the jury box again. I knew now he did this whenever his line of questioning was particularly important. "Mr. Calhoun, the defense is going to try to convince us that your son, Chester, attacked Miss Graves once before. Are you aware of any such attack?"

This was it. Old man Calhoun was going to have to fess up. I rubbed my hands together and sat forward on the pew.

"No, sir," Mr. Calhoun said. "I don't have any knowledge of Chester ever attacking Miss Graves before."

Shock and anger surged through me. Ruby turned her head and caught my gaze. I could see she was asking herself the same question I was. How could he sit up there under oath and lie?

When Mr. Oliver finally stood to begin his questions, I wanted to jump right up there beside him and question Mr. Calhoun myself. I'd get that lying piece of trash to tell the truth.

"Do you remember," Mr. Oliver began, "March 21, 1932?"

"A course I do," Mr. Calhoun said. "That was the day all them tornados came through."

"Do you remember the conversation you had with Ruby Graves and Matthew Doyle on your front porch that day?"

"I remember 'em both coming up there and accusing Chester of attacking Ruby."

"And how did you respond?"

"I called up Chester to come over there and clear things up."

"And did he?"

"He came on over," Mr. Calhoun said. "He denied everything. And I believed him. I never saw no proof he done anything to Ruby."

"Did he not admit to you that he'd been attacking and raping a young colored woman—"

"Objection!" Mr. Garret said. "That is irrelevant to Chester's history with Miss Graves."

"Your honor," Mr. Oliver said. "It speaks to Chester Calhoun's temperament and pattern of attacking young women."

"I'll allow it," Judge Woods said.

Mr. Garret returned to his seat, and Mr. Oliver asked the question again. "Did your son admit to attacking and raping a young colored woman who lived in the woods on your property?"

Mr. Calhoun raised his chin and looked Mr. Oliver right in the eye. "No, he did not."

"Liar!" I found myself standing among the spectators, my finger pointed at Mr. Calhoun.

A gasp ran through the rest of the courtroom, followed by hushed whispers. Judge Woods beat his gavel, silencing the crowd. He pointed his gavel at me.

"Young man, you will kindly take your seat, and there will be no more outbursts in my courtroom. If you cannot control yourself, you will be removed."

I sunk back onto the pew, horrified that I might have just inadvertently hurt Ruby's case. I raised my gaze until I found Mr. Calhoun. He was looking down at his hands, a blank look on his face. Mr. Oliver dismissed him, and he slunk toward the pews behind Mr. Garrett. I willed him to look at me. Just once, so he could see that I knew who and what he was. But he kept his eyes resolutely on his hands.

I swore to God that when my turn came, and I was on that witness stand, everyone in that courtroom would know Percy Calhoun was a liar.

CHAPTER SIXTEEN

Ruby

I sat in the courtroom that morning mostly in a daze. It was the most surreal thing to sit and listen to everyone talk about me, about my life and things I'd done, like they knew me. How had I become the center of such a mess, when really, I wasn't worth all this trouble?

After Mr. Calhoun was dismissed, the clerk called Irwin Cass to the stand. I couldn't believe my ears. For a brief moment, Mr. Oliver seemed just as stunned. But then he lumbered to his feet and roared his objection.

"On what grounds?" Judge Woods asked.

"Your Honor, this witness was not present during the events that took place at the Calhoun farm. He has no knowledge of the evidence. His testimony bears no weight. Mr. Garrett is simply trying to prejudice the jury against Miss Graves."

Mr. Garrett turned to the judge as if he were offended. "Your Honor, I can assure you this witness has testimony that directly refutes claims made by the defense about Miss Graves's character."

Judge Woods looked between the two lawyers with weary eyes. "Let's take a fifteen minute recess and discuss the matter in my chambers." As both men opened their mouths to respond, he slammed the gavel down. "Fifteen-minute recess!"

Mr. Oliver followed Mr. Garrett through a door off to the right of the bench, while the crowd behind me began to shift and murmur. I turned in my seat just as Matthew leaned forward onto the rail separating us.

"How are you holding up?" he asked.

"I'm all right. How about you?"

He shrugged and tried to smile. "Pretty bored, so far."

Just about everyone was standing by this point, so we both stood too. Mother reached over the rail and gave me a hug. "I think Asa and I will go stretch our legs. Stay strong, honey. We're almost through the worst of it."

She and Asa headed out the double doors behind a few others filing out. Glancing around, I caught the stares of several people in the crowd, their brows furrowed as they discussed my guilt or innocence. My stomach tightened.

"I'm going to the restroom," I said. "I'll be back in a few minutes."

Matthew shoved his hands in his pockets and looked over the courtroom with restless eyes. "Don't be long."

I made my way along the aisle and through the double doors without meeting anyone's gaze, but I could feel the weight of their judgment as I passed. It seemed as though everyone in there, or nearly everyone, was convinced I could commit murder.

I went into the restroom hoping for a few moments alone, but there were several ladies already there, powdering their faces. They stared at me as I eased by them. One woman, whom I'd never seen before in my life, looked down her nose at me and muttered, "Should be ashamed of yourself."

"Excuse me?" I said.

She huffed and gestured toward the other women in the small room with us. "Everyone here knows you murdered that poor man. You should be ashamed of yourself."

My throat tightened, and I started to turn for the door, but I stopped at another voice from behind me. "In case you've forgotten, we live in a country where a person is innocent until *proven* guilty."

The young lady speaking stepped toward us. She wore a fine dress that spoke of wealth, and she carried herself with the confidence of someone who was used to commanding attention. Something about her seemed familiar.

The first woman, lifted her chin and gave my defender the same scowl she'd given me. "Well, I can hear as well as anyone in that room, and I heard the evidence. That's enough proof for me. She killed that man. Or helped someone else kill him. All the same to me."

I wanted to speak up, to explain everything. But I caught myself. I'd just make things worse. People were going to believe what they wanted to believe. So I stepped aside and let the woman pass. Several others followed her out the door, leaving me alone with the young lady who'd spoken up for me.

"Thank you," I said.

She smiled, and again it struck me that I knew her from somewhere. "Those old hags just like gossip to chew on and spit out. I wouldn't worry too much about what they think or say."

"At this point, it's the men on the jury I'm worried about. I can't help but wonder if they think the same thing." I turned to the mirror above the sink and stared at my reflection. "They look at me and see a person capable of murder."

I closed my eyes and shut out the sudden image of Chester dying on the barn floor, and how I couldn't save him. Or maybe I just hadn't wanted to enough. Did that make me a murderer?

I opened my eyes and turned back to the young lady. "You seem familiar. Do we know each other?"

"Oh, forgive me!" she said, extending her hand. "We met a long time ago at the Doyle home. I'm Vanessa Paschal. My family is old friends with the Doyles."

Vanessa. Yes, I remembered her. "What are you doing here, at the trial?" As the words tumbled out of my mouth I realized that sounded rather rude, but I didn't know how else to ask. "I mean, I thought you lived in Montgomery with your family."

"I just wanted to come up and offer Matthew my support. He's been so distraught over this whole thing."

"Yes, I've noticed." My mind raced to connect Vanessa with Matthew. "Are you and Matthew...are you...together?"

Vanessa smiled and raised her left hand, a ring glistening on the fourth finger. My stomach twisted, sending a wave of nausea through me. I tried to force a smile.

"Congratulations."

She looked down at the ring and adjusted it on her finger. "We were supposed to move to Nashville after the wedding. Matthew promised me this beautiful little house there. We had so many plans, but then..."

The full picture of what Matthew had sacrificed struck me so hard, I had to take a step back. "I'm...I'm sorry."

"Well, I understand how important you are to him. He's always said you were like a little sister to him. And when he said he wanted to use our savings to pay your bond, I'll be honest: it took me by surprise. But I supported him, because I know he cares for you. I mean, a house can wait. *You* are much more important...to both of us."

She came over to me and pulled me into a hug. I was afraid I was going to vomit all down the back of her fancy dress. "I had no idea," I managed to squeak.

She pulled away from me and looked on me with pity in her eyes. "I'm sure he didn't want to burden you. That's Matthew, isn't it? Always thinking of others before himself."

I couldn't think of anything else to say. I wanted her to leave so I could gather my thoughts. But she kept on talking as if we were friends.

"The sad thing is, his father's being so terrible about the whole thing. I'm sure he told you about it." I stared at her, not knowing how to begin to answer. "No? Well, let me tell you, it's tearing their family apart. Mr. Doyle has completely disowned Matthew, cut him off from everything, and his poor mother has been sick about it."

"He hasn't said anything." I gripped my stomach as it knotted again, and felt a bead of sweat trickling down my back.

"Oh, listen to me, going on about Matthew and me, when you have your own terrible circumstances to face. Please forgive me. I shouldn't burden you with all this. Matthew would be so disappointed if he knew I'd let on about his troubles. You won't say anything, will you?"

I shook my head. I couldn't imagine what I might say anyhow. She reached around and hugged my neck once more. "Oh, I pray all this will be over soon and we can all go back to our normal lives." She pulled away and turned for the door, stopping as she gripped the handle. "I really do hope everything works out for you, Ruby, and that you get the justice you deserve."

"Th-thank you."

She walked out of the restroom, leaving me to wonder how I'd been so wrong about everything. Why hadn't Matthew told me he was engaged? How could he give up his future in Nashville? I covered my face with my hands, guilt weighing so heavy on my shoulders. I could never pay him back in a hundred years. I should never have accepted his help. Deep down, I'd known this all along. But once again, I'd let my heart run away with fantasies.

Leaning over the sink, I grasped the edges as it swam in front of my eyes. As the nausea gradually abated, I forced myself to accept reality. I was most likely going to prison. Matthew would move on with his life with Vanessa. And if Cass got his way, and told everyone about my gift, I'd probably lose that too.

Lord, help me remember Your words...I count all things but loss for the excellency of the knowledge of Christ Jesus my Lord: for whom I have suffered the loss of all things...

I lifted my head and looked my reflection in the eyes. "Ruby Graves, you are a child of the King of Kings, and the Lord of Lords. Nothing else matters. Everything is in His hands."

I did my best not to look at Matthew as I took my seat in the crowded courtroom. The spectators were settling in, and both Mr. Garrett and Mr. Oliver had returned to their tables. I took my seat next to Mr. Oliver, catching his worried glance.

He leaned toward me and whispered. "Cass is testifying. What is he going to say that I need to know about?"

I shrugged. What did it matter at this point? "Probably that I'm a witch who stole food from the soup kitchen."

His eyes widened. "Is...any of that true?"

"I can explain everything."

"We don't have time now. We'll have to do the best we can."

"All rise!" We both stood as Judge Woods entered and took his place, calling court back to order.

Judge Woods eyed both lawyers over the rim of his glasses. "I have determined that the witness may testify, but only to events of which he has personal knowledge. Be mindful, Mr. Garrett, of wandering into speculation."

I stole a quick glance at Matthew, Mother, and Asa. This was going to be painful for all of us, and they each met my gaze with apprehension. I turned back around just as Cass passed between the two tables. Even after stepping up to the witness stand, he was still a good inch or two shorter than the clerk. He placed his hand on the Bible and swore to tell the truth. I was certain I heard a huff from behind me, but I couldn't tell who it was.

"Please state your name for the record," Mr. Garrett began.

"Irwin Cass."

"And what is your position?"

"I'm the pastor at Cullman Church of God."

"Thank you, pastor. Now can you explain to all of us in your own words, how you came to know Miss Graves?"

Cass cleared his throat and looked over at me as if I were a misbehaving child, and he was reluctantly informing my parents of my misdeeds. "I first met Miss Graves at the home of Patrick and Francine Doyle, when their youngest son Matthew was ill with tuberculosis. She was working for the Doyles at the time, cleaning and such. I spoke with her briefly about her conversations with young Mr. Doyle. Cautioned her about encouraging false hope. He was extremely ill at the time, and I was counseling the poor boy over his soul. Miss Graves sought to undermine my teachings, and we had a rather unpleasant conversation about it."

"What was your impression of Miss Graves's temperament?"

"I've always found her to be hot-tempered, quick to lash out with her tongue."

"Was she ever dishonest?"

Cass frowned. "Unfortunately, yes. Several times, in fact. After much prayer by many saints in our church and community, and after a time of repentance on his part, young Mr. Doyle was finally healed of his affliction. While the rest of us praised God for this miracle, Miss Graves attempted to claim that she'd been the instrument of his healing."

The courtroom became so quiet, I could hear the folks behind me breathing. My own heart raced loudly in my ears, and heat surged up my neck. I could feel every eye on me. My secret was about to be proclaimed to everyone in that room.

"You mean to say," Mr. Garrett said, "that Miss Graves believed she'd healed Matthew Doyle?"

"Yes. She as much as admitted she'd attempted some kind sorcery to heal him. Bloodstopping I believe some folks call it. She believes herself to be a bloodstopper."

"Objection!" Mr. Oliver stood and pointed a finger at Cass. "Your Honor, this is entirely speculation on Mr. Cass's part."

"I respectfully disagree," Mr. Garrett said. "Brother Cass is testifying to his personal interactions with the defendant. He is not speculating. He is repeating his conversations."

"I'll allow it," Judge Woods said.

Mr. Oliver sat down and wrote a note on his yellow pad. *Is any of that true?* He slid the yellow pad in front of me as Mr. Garrett went back to questioning Cass.

"Was there ever any other time when Miss Graves was dishonest with you?"

"Yes. Some time after Matthew was on the mend, Miss Graves was able to convince the Doyle family to allow her to join them in serving in the soup line organized by our church to feed the poor. She came and worked at the church nearly every Saturday for several months."

I slid my response in front of Mr. Oliver. *He's not completely lying. Just twisting the truth. He's very good at that.*

"Wasn't that a good thing?" Mr. Garrett continued. "Doesn't the church want volunteers to help in the soup line?"

"Of course, when it's done with the right intention of serving God and serving our neighbor. But that was not Miss Graves's intention at all. In fact, I discovered she was using it as an opportunity to swindle cans of food away from our ministry so that she could take it to a Negro harlot she'd become acquainted with."

There were a few gasps behind me, and the spectators began murmuring amongst themselves. Judge Woods tapped his gavel to quieten them.

"How can you be sure of this?" Mr. Garrett asked.

"Why, I caught her in the act. She admitted she was taking the food to the Negro woman and her bastard child."

That time the murmuring continued through several hard taps of the gavel. As difficult as it was to listen to Cass disparage me, this particular part didn't bother me as much. I'd never been ashamed of helping Hannah and Samuel, and I prayed God would give me peace over it. I knew

I'd do the same thing again if I had the chance, so I lifted my chin and looked Brother Cass right in the eye as he attempted to shame me. I'd show him that God's love knew nothing of skin color, or situation, or money, or power. And I hoped that I'd get the chance to tell everyone in that courtroom the same thing.

When all was quiet again, Mr. Garret proceeded. "Brother Cass, have you had any interactions with Miss Graves since that time?"

"Only recently, when I visited her in the jail shortly after she was arrested. I was attempting to offer her spiritual guidance and a chance to repent of her sins. It was my understanding she was continuing to practice her sorcery, passing it off as healing. When I learned of the circumstances of her arrest, I concluded that it was possible one of her bloodstopping rituals had gone terribly wrong. I felt a duty to offer her the chance to turn from such darkness."

"And how did Miss Graves respond?"

"With the same vitriol I'd experienced from her time and again. She accused *me* of having no compassion. Then she admitted to her continued practice of her *witchcraft*, or whatever she calls it. And that she continues to associate with Negroes of the worst sort. Nothing has changed, I'm afraid, despite my earnest prayers for her soul."

Behind me, I could hear Matthew muttering under his breath. I was surprised he hadn't had another outburst. Mr. Garrett stated he had no more questions, and Mr. Oliver took a worried glance at me before he stood and approached the witness stand. In all our conversations to prepare for trial, we'd only discussed Cass in passing, and never as a potential witness. He'd have no idea what truths Cass had twisted. All I could do was pray that God would guide Mr. Oliver's questions.

"Besides your recent visit to the jail," Mr. Oliver began, "when was the last time you spoke with Miss Graves?"

"Well, let's see now." Cass looked up at the ceiling. "It was right after the tornadoes in '32. Miss Graves was lurking around the hospital—"

"So it's been nearly five years?"

"That sounds about right."

"The last time you spoke with Miss Graves was when she was a four-teen-year-old girl?"

"Objection!" Mr. Garrett called out. "The witness has answered the question."

"Move along, Mr. Oliver," Judge Woods said.

"How long did you speak with Miss Graves at the jail?"

"About fifteen minutes or so," Cass answered.

"Let me understand this clearly. You're basing your entire assessment of Miss Graves on your limited interactions with her as a child and a fifteen-minute conversation you had with her five years later?"

Brother Cass blinked as if he were surprised Mr. Oliver even had to ask. "Why, yes. But as I said, it was apparent she hadn't changed—"

"No further questions, Your Honor." Mr. Oliver returned to the table with an air of confidence, sitting down and propping his leg over his knee. He appeared unfazed.

Mr. Garrett stood and announced that the prosecution was resting its case. Judge Woods pulled out his pocket watch and gave it a quick study. "Very well. We'll take an hour recess for lunch and then begin with de-fense testimony at one-thirty." He slammed the gavel down, and the whole room rose simultaneously.

Mr. Oliver leaned over to me, dropping his confident demeanor. "We need to head to the conference room *now*."

Mr. Oliver paced back and forth in front of me as I sat at the table in the conference room. Matthew stood to my right, leaning onto the table with his head bowed as Mr. Oliver peppered us with questions.

"So this healing thing," Mr. Oliver said, looking at Matthew. "It's re-al? She healed you?"

"It's not that simple," I said.

"I need it to be simple, Ruby," Mr. Oliver said. "I have to try to ex-plain it to a bunch of farmers."

"She's a faith healer," Matthew said. "That keeps it pretty simple. No need to explain the particulars. People know all about faith healers."

Mr. Oliver threw up his hands in frustration, still pacing. "Wonderful! Well, that explains everything, then."

"Mr. Oliver," I said. "Please, could we do our best not to focus on my gift? It's...very personal. I've never shared it with anyone but Matthew and my uncle, and for it to come out like this, well, it's more than I can bear."

He stopped pacing and faced me. "Believe me, Ruby, I'd love to forget all of this and simply focus on the facts of the case. Unfortunately, it is becoming increasingly clear that you haven't told me everything. I can't defend you when I'm unprepared for witnesses." He let out a frustrated sigh and leaned onto the table as well. "I know you've been holding back because of this *gift* of yours, but is there anything else, anything at all, you haven't told me?"

I shook my head.

Matthew pounded his fist into the table, sending a shock through me.

"Come on, Ruby!" He turned fierce, terrified eyes to me. "Your life is at stake! Tell him everything!"

My eyes welled up, and my throat tightened. "My life isn't the only one at stake!" I couldn't bear to look at him any longer, so I covered my face with my hands, trying to hold back sobs.

"Wait a minute," Mr. Oliver said. "What are you talking about? Ruby, you have to trust me. No matter what you tell me, it stays within these walls unless we decide otherwise. But I'm swimming with one arm behind my back here."

"Ruby, please," Matthew said, his voice straining. "Tell him. Maybe he can help."

"It's too late. He's gone." I dropped my hands and met Matthew's gaze. "He's gone." Something subtle, but powerful all the same, shifted between us. My hands began to shake in my lap. I willed Matthew to stay silent.

"Ruby, who's gone?" Mr. Oliver asked. "What is going—"

Matthew straightened and faced Mr. Oliver. "She didn't kill Chester."

"Matthew! No!"

"She's protecting a young man, Samuel, a mulatto, who was also in the barn. The same one who saw Chester attack her the first time. Chester attacked Samuel, and he's the one who killed Chester. Ruby tried to save Chester's life, but...but Samuel's the one who killed him."

All the color drained from Mr. Oliver's face and he dropped heavily into a chair behind him.

"You promised," I said. "You promised you wouldn't say anything."

Matthew bowed his head and closed his eyes. "I'm so sorry, Ruby. But I just can't stand by and watch you do this to yourself." Then he too fell into a chair.

The three of us looked at each other as if we'd all been pummeled in a boxing match. What was there to do next? I was laid bare. I could only pray Mr. Oliver would keep his word better than Matthew had.

"All right," Mr. Oliver said, scooting up to the table. "Who's this...Samuel?"

CHAPTER SEVENTEEN

Matthew

Ruby stewed in the chair beside me as I explained to Mr. Oliver exactly who Samuel was, about his mother, Hannah, and the relationship between the three of them. She'd huff and sigh, object and try to correct me. But in the end, I was pretty sure Mr. Oliver got the picture. He leaned back in his chair and looked up at the ceiling for a few moments, tapping the ends of his fingers together over his chest.

"Having the boy testify would be tricky—"

"He can't testify," Ruby said. "He's not even in town anymore. He's gone."

Mr. Oliver stood and resumed pacing, talking to himself as if he hadn't heard Ruby at all. "Yes, definitely tricky. We'd have to get a continuance. The jury is unlikely to believe the word of a Negro boy. And this would most likely add fuel to the prosecution's claims about your relationship with the Negroes."

Ruby threw her hands up. "And what is wrong with my friendship with them? I'm not ashamed to call Hannah and Samuel my friends. She's the kindest person I've ever known."

Mr. Oliver stopped pacing and held up his palm to stop her. "The nobility of your actions is not in question here. But I'm not about to turn this into a trial on society and its treatment of Negroes. That's a dangerous road for you. If you are determined to take the blame for this, then we need to focus on proving that you were defending yourself against an attack from a man with a history of violence toward you. That sure would be a whole lot easier if the Negroes could testify to the first attack."

"They have names," she muttered.

"Excuse me?" Mr. Oliver said.

"They have names. Hannah and Samuel. They are people, identified by their names, not their skin color."

Mr. Oliver dropped his chin and looked at me. "Is she always like this?"

I nodded. "Especially when she's right."

Mr. Oliver grabbed his yellow pad from the table and began writing furiously. "Listen, we can deal with this. We just have to focus on convincing the jury that Chester attacked you. Matthew, you'll testify first. I'll have to address the healing, but let's keep that to a minimum. You'll acknowledge she was there, but that God healed you. Then I'll go into Chester's first attack. I'll ask you to describe how you found her."

Scraping her chair back, Ruby stood and walked to the window, keeping her back to me as she stared out. "We have to leave Samuel's name out of this."

"I'm not sure we can leave his name out of your account of the first attack," Mr. Oliver said. "But I won't ask about his involvement in the incident at the barn. Although, I wouldn't feel I'd done my duty to you if I didn't advise you that telling the truth in this case is your best chance to avoid prison...or worse."

Ruby shook her head. It was all I could do not to go over to the window and start shaking some sense into her. "She ain't gonna listen to reason."

"I can see that," Mr. Oliver said, turning his attention back to me. "I'd like to refute Brother Cass's testimony, but I hesitate to impugn a respected pastor in the community. Is there anything he said you can directly contradict?"

"Definitely. The soup kitchen garbage for sure. Ruby's no thief."

"All right, then we'll move on to Dr. Fisher. He'll confirm your injuries from the first attack. I've also notified James that he'll be called on to testify, but I haven't seen him in court. We may have to fetch him."

"I don't know if he'll help us," I said. "He's awfully torn, and he's upset at the family right now, especially Ruby. Blames her for all the problems."

Mr. Oliver frowned. "Wonderful." He stood and approached Ruby at the window. "You'll testify last. The way things are going, we may ask for a recess until tomorrow for your testimony. I want you to be fresh, and I want the jury to have a chance to forget about Cass's testimony."

Ruby nodded and hugged her chest. "No mention of Samuel, right?"

"Right."

Then she turned to me. "No mention of Samuel. I mean it, Matthew. Keep him out of this."

"All right," I said. But I knew it was going to be the hardest thing I'd ever done.

Walking up to the witness stand set my nerves on edge. I placed my hand on the Bible and swore to tell the truth, the whole truth, and nothing but the truth, knowing if I did, Ruby would never speak to me again. As I took my seat, I met her gaze and saw the fear there. I couldn't hurt her, but I couldn't lose her either. *Lord, tell me what to say.*

I scanned the courtroom for a friendly face, but instead I found the face of my father near the back. He frowned as our eyes locked. What was he doing here? Had he spoken with Judge Woods? Someone on the jury? I shook the thoughts from my mind and concentrated on Mr. Oliver as he approached the witness stand. I had to get this right.

All seemed to go as planned as Mr. Oliver questioned me. I explained to the jury exactly what had happened the night I was healed, and how

Ruby had never once claimed she'd done it herself. She'd always given glory to God for that, and I could say that as the honest truth. Then I explained how Mother had given Ruby permission to take the leftover jars of food for a needy family. I told them how much Ruby had been loved by the downtrodden folks that came into the church—how caring and gentle she'd been with them.

"Ruby's always been that way. She gives more of herself than she has, and she never asks for anything in return. Anyone who knows her—really knows her—can see the light inside of her."

The most difficult part was talking about the day I'd found her in the woods, nearly beaten to death. Remembering that scene still made my blood run hot.

"Tell us about how you found Miss Graves that day," Mr. Oliver said. "What was her condition?"

I cleared my throat and focused on speaking clearly. Everything was riding on this. "I'd come home from college that weekend and went over to visit with her. Her mother seemed worried that she didn't know where Ruby was, so I went looking for her. I knew she'd been taking food to Hannah and Samuel down in the woods, so I headed in that direction."

"And who are Hannah and Samuel?"

"A colored woman and her mulatto boy that lived in a shack on the edge of Mr. Calhoun's property at the time."

"All right then, so you went looking for Ruby, and then what happened?"

"I didn't know exactly where to go. I wandered around for a bit, until Samuel came out of the woods. He hollered at me that someone was hurt and to come quick."

"How old was the he?"

"About nine or so."

"And what was Ruby's condition when you found her?"

"She was unconscious. Her head had a deep gash in it, and her face was all bruised up. Her leg also had a large gash, and it was bleeding pretty bad. I tried to rouse her, but she was completely out. I was afraid she was dead."

I met Ruby's gaze for a moment, remembering the fear that had engulfed me in those moments in the woods. Had I loved her then?

"What happened after that?" Mr. Oliver asked, snapping my thoughts back to the present.

"I carried her home. Her brother James went for Dr. Fisher, and he came out to the house and treated her. She was laid up for nearly a week. I went to see her several times before I had to go back to school."

"Did she ever tell you who beat her so badly?"

"Not at first. She eventually told me it was Chester Calhoun."

"Why do you think she waited so long to tell you?"

"'Cause she knew I'd be angry, and that I'd confront Chester about what he did."

"And did you?"

I found Mr. Calhoun sitting next to his wife on the first bench in the gallery, and made eye contact. "I sure did. I went up to the Calhoun place with Ruby, and we told Mr. Calhoun what had happened. He didn't want to believe us at first, but once Chester got there, and we started arguing about it, Chester admitted he'd been beating and raping Hannah."

"And are you certain Mr. Calhoun heard this?"

"Oh yes. He heard him." I looked directly at Mr. Calhoun. "Chester laid into his father for doing the same thing. Said he knew Samuel was his half-brother."

Mr. Oliver's eyes widened. I hadn't told him that part, and maybe I shouldn't have said anything at all, but I wanted the world to know what a hypocrite that man was. Whispers and muttering broke out among the spectators, and Mr. Calhoun glared at me, a red flush creeping up his neck. Mrs. Calhoun glared at him, and removed her hand from his arm.

Mr. Oliver tried to regain control of the interview. "Mr. Doyle, can you explain what happened after that?"

"Yes, sir. Chester threatened Ruby, saying that he'd finish the job next time, and so I laid him out."

"You punched him?"

"I sure did. We brawled for a bit, until he'd had enough and drove off. But that was the day of the great tornado, and when we noticed the bad weather coming on, everyone headed for shelter."

"Thank you, Mr. Doyle," Mr. Oliver said. "No more questions."

Mr. Garrett rose and approached the stand with a polite smile. "Mr. Doyle, I only have a couple of questions for you. Did you actually *see* Chester Calhoun ever lay one hand on Miss Graves?"

My stomach sank. "No."

Mr. Garrett gave a pointed look to the jury. "And this boy, Samuel, where is he? Why hasn't he come forward to support this story of an attack."

I glanced at Ruby, aching to tell everyone in there the truth. "I don't know."

"Mr. Doyle, how did you feel about Ruby's friendship with the Negro woman?"

"Excuse me?"

Mr. Garrett paused and narrowed his eyes. "How did you *feel* about Miss Graves visiting with the Negro woman?"

"I...I don't know. I was worried about her."

"And did you encourage her to give up the friendship at any time?"

"Yes, I did, but I don't see—"

"No further questions." Mr. Garret returned to his seat with a satisfied smirk, and I left the stand with very little hope that I'd done Ruby any amount of good.

As I took my seat behind her, she turned to me for just a moment. "Thank you," she mouthed silently. I nodded, still wondering if I'd made the right choice. All I could do was pray that the jury would see as much of the truth as we could tell them, and that God would protect Ruby.

Dr. Fisher was called to the stand next. He ambled across the floor and offered a warm greeting to Judge Woods. "How's that grandbaby of yours?"

Judge Woods lifted a corner of his mouth, the closest I'd ever seen to a smile. "Just fine. Just fine."

Mr. Oliver approached the stand after Dr. Fisher had taken his oath. "How long have you known Miss Graves?"

Dr. Fisher beamed over at Ruby like a proud father. "Oh, I was there when she was born. Came into the world just a-hollering. Been her doctor ever since."

"Did you treat Miss Graves when she was so badly injured in the fall of 1931?"

"Yes, unfortunately I did."

"What was the extent of her injuries?"

"Well, let's see. She had a bad concussion, a couple of broken ribs, a deep laceration on her forehead, another on her leg. I had to bandage her up pretty good."

"Was her life in danger?"

"Oh yes. We kept a close eye on her those first few hours. She had a fever, and I wasn't sure how much damage she might've had to her brain. Not to mention her blood loss."

"But she recovered fully?"

"For the most part. She still suffers occasional headaches that I believe are a direct result of the concussion."

Mr. Oliver walked over to the jury box and leaned against the rail, taking a tack from Mr. Garrett. "What is your relationship with Miss Graves at present?"

"She works as a midwife for me, and helps me take care of patients."

"And what is your opinion of Miss Graves's character?"

Again, Dr. Fisher smiled at Ruby. "Why she's the most dedicated caregiver I've ever known. All my patients adore her. Many ask for her by name, especially the delivering mothers. She calms them and serves them with complete devotion. I trust her completely."

"Thank you, Dr. Fisher. No further questions."

Mr. Garrett rose and took position on the opposite side of the courtroom near the clerk. "Dr. Fisher, did Miss Graves ever say who attacked her in 1931?"

"No, she didn't ever tell me who did it."

"Did you see the attack?"

"No."

"Have you ever seen Chester Calhoun lay a hand on Miss Graves, or anyone else for that matter?"

"No."

"You have, however, responded to an injury inflicted *by* Miss Graves, have you not?"

Dr. Fisher paused, and his brow furrowed. Mr. Garrett walked toward him slowly, purposefully. "It's been some time, so perhaps you've forgotten. Let me help you. Did you respond to a call for help at the Graves residence in the spring of 1927?"

"Why, um, yes. I...I believe so." Realization hit Dr. Fisher, and his face went slack.

"And what was the nature of that call?"

"Um, well...Young Henry, Ruby's brother, had been cut along the neck and was bleeding badly."

"And was his life in danger?"

Dr. Fisher frowned. "Well, I suppose at the time it seemed rather serious—"

"Yes or no, please, Doctor. Was his life in danger?"

"Yes."

Mr. Garrett turned and faced the spectators, rocking on his heels in anticipation. "And can you please tell us exactly how Henry Graves was injured?"

Dr. Fisher looked over at Ruby, his eyes pleading for forgiveness. Instinctively my heart sank, even before he answered. "Henry was injured because Ruby had thrown a knife at him."

Mr. Garret took a moment to soak in the collective gasp he'd been expecting. Then he turned and headed for the jury box. "Can you please repeat that?"

Dr. Fisher sighed. "From what I understand, Henry was teasing her, and Ruby threw a knife at him."

Each and every one of the men on the jury turned and looked at Ruby as if he was finally convinced of her guilt. Rage flooded over me, and all I wanted to do was rush up to the stand and tell them that she hadn't done this, to explain everything until they saw the truth. But I couldn't.

Mr. Garrett rested, and Dr. Fisher left the stand, his shoulders sagging as if he now bore a heavy load. Ruby watched him leave, and as he passed by the table, I caught the gentle look of understanding she gave him. It stabbed me right in the gut. Maybe I could be recalled to the stand. Maybe I could still stop this horrible train wreck from happening. I leaned forward to tap Mr. Oliver on the shoulder, hoping to convince him to let me testify again.

On the table, I saw several lines of notes between him and Ruby on his yellow pad.

Is this true?

Yes.

How could he have found out about it?

James.

Mrs. Graves held her head up high and scanned the gallery with a defiant glare as Mr. Oliver approached her for questioning. I'd never felt such solidarity as I did in that moment as she dared anyone in that courtroom to say a bad word about her daughter.

"Can you describe the incident that occurred in your home between Ruby and Henry when they were children?" Mr. Oliver asked.

"Yes, sir. It's true, Ruby had a temper when she was younger, but that's true of many children. And she did throw that knife at Henry. He'd been teasing her, and she lost her temper. She didn't mean to hurt him, and as soon as it happened she felt just awful. I never saw anything like the turnaround I saw in her from that day on."

"How so?" Mr. Oliver asked.

"She was much more self-controlled. I don't reckon I ever saw her lose her temper like that again. Now, she could be impulsive, and down-right pig-headed at times, but she never lost control again."

I glanced at the jury throughout Mrs. Graves's testimony. It didn't appear to help much. Most of them had set their face to a frown and weren't about to budge. When Mr. Garrett stood to question her, I was certain things could only get worse.

"Now, Mrs. Graves, were you aware that your daughter was taking food to a Negro woman in the woods of Mr. Calhoun's property?"

"I knew she was taking food to a needy family."

"Yes, but did you know that the woman was a Negro?"

Mrs. Graves sighed like she was dealing with an argumentative child. "No. I wasn't aware of that part."

"When you did become aware of it, what did you say to her? Were you supportive?"

"I was afraid for her."

"Did you tell her it would be best if she stopped going down there?"

"Yes, I did. I was concerned for her safety. And rightly so."

"And how about now?" Mr. Garrett asked.

Mrs. Graves shifted in her seat. "I'm not sure what you mean."

"How do you feel about Ruby going off to Colony every month to visit her Negro friends?"

A blush crept into Mrs. Graves's cheeks, and she glanced over at Ruby. "I reckon I'm still afraid for her safety. As much from the white sheets as from anyone she might meet in that town."

In the end, Mrs. Graves didn't do much harm, but she didn't appear to do much good either. I was convinced the only way to save Ruby at this point was to tell the jury everything about what really happened in that barn, even if it meant she would never speak to me again. After Mr. Garrett took his seat, I tapped his shoulder. He leaned back, and I whispered to him about recalling me to the stand.

He glanced at Ruby, who shook her head. Mr. Oliver frowned at me. "I can't do it, son. I'm sorry."

I fell against the back of the pew and sulked as Mr. Oliver rose and requested a continuance to the following day since Ruby's testimony was last, and would most likely take longer than we had remaining in the day. The judge agreed, and dismissed everyone. I was fuming by this point, and couldn't stand to be in that courtroom one moment more. So without a word to anybody, I got out of there as quick as I could, seeking the sanctuary of my car.

As I drove, I went over all the testimony of the day, trying to find a shred of hope that Ruby wouldn't be found guilty. But it seemed like everything had worked against her. I pounded my hand into my steering wheel, yelled curses at God for abandoning her, and prayed with all my might He would still work things out for her.

By the time I pulled up in front of the Graves farm, I was worked up so bad, I could hardly think straight. Slamming my door shut, I stomped around the yard, kicking up rocks and throwing sticks to get out all the pent-up frustration inside me.

A few minutes later, Roy approached me from the barn. "You look like you're fit to be tied. I take it things didn't go well?"

"Not at all," I said. But then something clicked in my head. There was a solution standing right in front of me. "Say, you still willing to get Ruby out of here? Take her somewhere safe she can hide out for a while?"

Roy's eyebrows shot up, and he scratched at his beard. "That bad, huh?" He glanced around like someone might be listening. "Come with me."

I followed him into the barn, where he called out to his brothers to come join us. They'd turned the barn into their own little hideout, setting a slab of wood on an upturned wagon wheel to use as a card table, and fashioning beds out of hay bales. The four of them gathered around the table, rubbing sleep out of their eyes like they'd been up all night.

"What's going on?" Eddie asked.

"Matthew here says the trial ain't going so good," Roy said. "Wants to know if we can help Ruby hide out or something."

Eddie rubbed the back of his neck. "Well, you know, we pitched that idea a few days back, but Lizzy wouldn't have none of it."

"Lizzy don't ever speak to us much anyway," Franklin said. "I say we do it."

Roy put his hands up. "Now hold on just a minute. What exactly are we talking about here? We'd like to help, honest. But Ruby don't seem like she wants to take this road. And we ain't in the business of kidnapping folks."

He was right about that for sure. Knowing Ruby, that was exactly what was going to have to be done. "Well, for argument's sake, let's say I can get Ruby on board. What would we need to do? What does running from the law entail?"

Eddie leaned forward on his knees. "For beating a murder charge? Name change for sure. Change of appearance; cutting her hair or something. Moving up north or out west. She'd have to hide out for a while till things cooled off. Then hit the road. A lot to go through for a girl her age and no experience with such things."

"Not if I'm with her," I said.

CHAPTER EIGHTEEN

Matthew

By the time everyone arrived back at the Graves farm, I'd left the barn and was chopping wood at the back of the house. The sky was dark and fat spots of rain were beginning to fall. I welcomed the damp coolness on the back of my shirt as I swung the ax, and swung again. Ruby's uncles continued to discuss possibilities, while I satisfied my anger by envisioning all those people who'd stood against Ruby—Cass, Father, Mr. Adams at the paper, Mr. Garrett. I saw their faces as I swung away, and it appeased my anger, but it didn't calm my nerves.

Ruby didn't say anything to me. Asa came out to check on me, but left me to do my killing on my own for a while. When I'd exhausted myself and came inside, Ruby was asleep on the sofa, and Mrs. Graves was preparing supper. I looked around for something else I could do, some measure of help I could give, but I found nothing. So I went outside to draw water from the well and wash up.

As we took our seats around the table for supper, Ruby didn't even look at me. She kept her head down as we all took hold of our hands, and Asa prayed over the meal. "Heavenly Father, we thank You for all the blessings You've bestowed upon us, especially this meal. Please allow it to nourish our bodies, just as You nourish our souls. We ask Your favor as we face the days ahead, and peace in knowing that we are safe in Your hands."

There was anything but peace in my spirit. God seemed to have no interest in keeping Ruby from going to prison, which I could not understand at all. I'd prayed for understanding, prayed for His help, but He didn't speak to me like He did to Ruby. I was at a total loss.

None of us spoke much during the meal, and I noticed Ruby pushed her food around the plate more than anything. Within a few minutes, she declared herself full.

"You've hardly eaten a thing," her mother said. "You need to keep your strength up."

"I'm all right," she said. "Just tired, and not very hungry. Please excuse me."

She left the table without even cleaning up her plate, something I'd never seen her do, and headed straight out the door without another word.

"I'm going to go talk to her," I said, leaving my plate as well. I hoped Mrs. Graves would forgive me this one time.

Ruby was making her way toward the path into the woods, and I ran to catch up with her. "Where are you going?" I asked as I caught her near the edge.

"Just for a short walk," she said, her gaze bouncing from one thing to the next, but never falling on me.

"In the rain?"

She looked down the path and then back at the house. "I suppose. It's only a little drizzle."

She folded her arms over her chest and started down the path. The sun hung low in the sky, casting a rose-colored glow beneath the clouds. As soon as we entered the shade of the trees, the temperature dropped. She pulled her coat tighter around her shoulders.

"Are you cold?" I asked.

She shook her head.

I continued beside her, unable to bear the silence, but unable to form the words I so badly wanted to say. "I know you're angry with me for telling Mr. Oliver your secret, but I can't apologize. I can't stand you being angry with me either. So you're going to have to find a way to forgive me, even though I'm not sorry."

She still said nothing, pushing my frustration to near madness.

"Ruby, talk to me."

"You broke your promise," she finally said. "I shouldn't have trusted you."

It killed me to hear her say that. I'd worked so hard to earn back her trust. "I'm sorry I hurt you. But please try to understand. I just...I can't lose you."

She stopped walking and looked up at me with indignant eyes. "That's the most ridiculous thing you could've said. *Lose* me? I'm not yours to lose. If anything, you should be more concerned about losing your fiancée."

"My what?" I stepped back, completely taken off guard. "What are you talking about?"

"I saw Vanessa, and her ring. You gave up a job and a home in Nashville, and now your family is falling apart. You shouldn't even be here. You should be at your parents' house, working things out with them. You've sacrificed everything. For what? Because you felt guilty? Because you *owed* me something from five years ago?"

"No! This is crazy. I...I'm not engaged. I broke it off with Vanessa over a week ago. How did she—? I don't understand. I'm not marrying Vanessa. And I don't want a life in Nashville. I'm here for *you*. Not because I owe you anything, even though I do." I stepped closer and reached for her face, unable to stop myself any longer. "I owe you more than I could ever repay, Ruby. But that's not why I'm here."

I hesitated, afraid to say what I'd wanted to for days now. Her eyes teared up, and she covered my hands with hers. "So, you're not getting married?"

"No." I rested my forehead on hers. "I could never marry anyone else. I love you, Ruby. Only you." I lifted her face to mine and looked into the most beautiful eyes I'd ever known. "Can't you see that? With all your talent for seeing the needs of others, for seeing right through me...How could you not see how much I love you?"

"But Vanessa said—"

"She's hurt, and she lied to you. I'm sorry about that. I wish I'd known she was there. But I promise you: I'm not sacrificing some imaginary future you've concocted. I would gladly give you every dime to my name. I'd walk away from my family in a heartbeat. All I want is to be with you."

I touched my lips to hers, my whole body aching with joy when her lips moved with mine. I was gone, for good. Completely ruined. I pulled back and looked down into her eyes. "Ruby, I won't lose you. There's still time to fix this mess. Just get on the stand tomorrow and tell the truth."

"I'd be sentencing Samuel to death. Maybe even Hannah, if they couldn't get their hands on him. I can't do that."

"Then let's run away. Your uncles can help us. We'll leave tonight, and we can make a new life for ourselves. Just you and me."

She stood on her tiptoes and kissed me again. "I love you too. I do. But—"

"No, no. No 'but'. Just say yes. Choose me." I kissed her again. "Choose me, Ruby. We can go to Texas or California. Start over. I'll be with you forever."

"I believe you," she said, stepping back and taking my hand in hers. "But it's crazy. And if we got caught...and my mother would just die..."

"Forget everyone else!" My voice shot up louder than I'd meant it to. "We can make it work."

"You'd be miserable. When would we ever see our families again?"

"I'd be with you. I'd be the happiest man in the world. And believe me, as long as we were together, and you were safe, I wouldn't care if I ever saw my family again."

"You don't mean that. What about Mary? Your mother?"

I had to admit, I'd miss Mary and Mother, but I couldn't even think about them when it seemed that this might be my last chance to save Ruby. She was so close to agreeing. Saving her was all that mattered.

"Listen to me," I said. "I don't care about everything I'd leave behind. Don't you get that? I just need you."

"No, Matthew. You need to listen to yourself. I'm not all you need. We have to trust God, that He'll work everything out for our good. Just because things seem bleak now, doesn't mean our faith should waiver. I know this is hard for you, because you want to make things happen just as you think they should. But God has a bigger plan for both of us. More than just loving each other." She reached for my face, touching my cheek so gently. "Don't give up your faith to be with me. In the end, it won't be worth the cost."

I pulled her to me once more, wishing I could stand there forever holding her against me. Some part of me knew she was right, because she was always right. But I couldn't accept it. All I could do was hope and pray that God would stand up for her in that courtroom, that He would use her words to work in the hearts of those men on the jury. I hoped that Ruby's faith was enough for both us, because all I could find in my heart was fear.

As I sat on the pew, exhausted from a sleepless night and waiting for Ruby to take the stand, it felt like I was sitting on a pincushion. I didn't know how I was going to be able to sit still through her testimony. I hadn't tried to convince Ruby again of either telling the truth or making a run for it. She'd made up her mind, so I tried to keep my focus on praying for her.

Father sat in the back of the courtroom once again, this time with Mother beside him. It pained me to see her looking so upset, but I didn't go to them. I also spotted Vanessa this time, just behind Mother and Father. I planned to confront her about her lies, but that would have to wait. I couldn't think of anyone else but Ruby.

When the clerk called Ruby's name, it seemed like everyone in the building went completely still. Here was what they'd all been waiting for, a chance to hear from the one person who'd actually been in the barn when Chester Calhoun died. The courtroom was even more packed that day than it had been the previous, with folks lining the walls and spilling into the hallway outside. Even Judge Woods had looked around in surprise as he'd called court in session.

Ruby took her seat, closed her eyes for the briefest moment, and moved her lips in what was most likely a prayer. Then she placed her hand on the Bible and swore to tell the whole truth. Everything in me wished she meant it.

"Miss Graves," Mr. Oliver said, standing just in front of her. "There have been many accusations laid against you from this witness stand. I'd like to take you through each one, and give you the opportunity to respond. Let's begin with your brother's injury when you were a child. How old were you at the time?"

"I was ten." Her voice was steady, calm. She didn't seem fazed in the slightest by being in front of all those people.

"And did you, in fact, throw a knife at your brother?"

"Yes, I did. I was washing up the dishes after dinner. He'd been picking on me, and I got angry at him. I had it my hand 'cause I was washing it, and I threw it. I don't think I actually meant to strike him. But it did. And I felt horrible about it."

"Have you ever physically attacked anyone in your life, other than that one moment of anger?"

"No, sir. I learned a valuable lesson that day about controlling my temper. I gave it up to God, and asked Him to take it from me. From then on, I never lost control of my temper again."

One of the men on the jury, a black-haired man near the back gave a slight nod. I clung to that small grain of hope. How could anyone listen to Ruby for more than five minutes and not see that she wasn't capable of murder?

Mr. Oliver walked toward the jury box. "And how about the incident at the soup kitchen? Were you stealing cans of food?"

"No, sir. I spoke with Mrs. Doyle, who had invited me to work there each Saturday, and I explained to her that I knew of a family in desperate need of help. I asked her about the extra jars of food in the pantry, and she agreed to let me take them to the family in need. The incident Brother Cass is referring to happened on a Saturday when Mrs. Doyle wasn't there. He jumped to the conclusion that I was stealing, and never let me explain otherwise."

"Very well. Now let's get to the events that took place in the fall of 1931. It's your claim that Chester Calhoun attacked and savagely beat you. Can you describe that event to the jury please?"

Ruby swallowed. Although she seemed outwardly calm, I noticed a slight tremor to her fingertips. "It was a Saturday afternoon, and I'd gone down into the woods behind the fields at the Calhoun place. I was walking down the path when I heard something behind me. I turned around and Chester was standing on the path."

"Now, had you had any dealings with Chester up to this point?"

"Only a little. He was in charge of all the workers and sharecroppers, so he oversaw my work most days."

"Did you ever witness him being cruel to other workers?"

"Yes. Especially the colored workers. I gave a dead chicken to a colored boy once, and Chester tried to beat him for it. Accused the boy of stealing, and told me he'd be watching me."

"Did he ever show any signs of aggression toward you after that?"

"Not until the day I saw him in the woods."

"And what happened when you saw him?"

Ruby fidgeted in her seat. I could see she was working out how to tell the truth and leave out Hannah and Samuel at the same time. "He told me I shouldn't be helping colored folks, that he was going to have to teach me a lesson. And that it was better that lesson come from him than from a bunch of men in white robes coming after my whole family."

Mr. Oliver fell silent. He must not have been expecting that answer. Several seconds passed before he continued. "Then what happened?"

"He came at me. I tried to run, but I stumbled. He kicked me. In the ribs, in the head. He swore at me while he kicked me. Called me awful names I'd rather not repeat." Ruby's face flushed pink, and from what I could tell, hers wasn't the only one.

Mr. Oliver cleared his throat and shifted his weight. "Why didn't you report the attack to the police?"

"'Cause I knew nothing would happen to him, and I was afraid if he attacked me again, he'd kill me."

I took a quick survey of the jury. Most of them looked on Ruby with sympathy. Maybe it was working. Maybe God was answering my prayers.

"All right, Miss Graves, let's move on to the events that took place in the Calhoun barn a few weeks ago. Now explain to us in detail, what happened that day?"

"Well, I was at the Calhoun place to help their daughter, Emma Rae, deliver her baby. She's married to my brother James, and he's the foreman for Mr. Calhoun. When they were resting, I decided to take a walk and get some fresh air. As I came around the side of the barn, I saw James talking with Chester Calhoun, and I froze. It was as if no time had passed at all, and I was standing on that path again."

"So you were afraid?"

"Yes."

"What did you do?"

"I got away from them as quick as I could without Chester seeing me, at least I thought I had. I went out into the fields to gather my thoughts and calm down. All I wanted to do was get away from there. So I looked around for James to see if he'd drive me back into town. I couldn't find him, so I checked in the barn. When I turned around, Chester had come into the barn after me and was standing behind me, just like he'd been on that path."

Ruby stopped talking, and her gaze drifted off. She closed her eyes, and her shoulders pinched up. Pain spread over her face, and all I wanted to do was grab her and run her out of that courtroom.

"He came at me again, just like before, saying I still hadn't learned my lesson. I tried to run, but he grabbed me by my hair and threw me down. Then he kicked me in the ribs again. I was able to roll away from him, and I ran across the barn, but in my panic I ran toward the corner that didn't have a door, so I had to turn around. I tried to get past him, but he threw me against the bales of hay. Then I saw he had a knife in his hand. He stabbed at me, and I leaned back on the hay bale and kicked at his hand as hard as I could. He hollered pretty loud. That was when I saw that the knife had gone into his chest."

She was doing great. The jury hung on her every word, and I could see that they believed her.

"He fell to the ground," she continued, "and he pulled the knife out of his chest. I jumped off the hay bale and tried to help him, but he wouldn't let me."

"What do you mean, you tried to help him?" Mr. Oliver asked. "What did you do?"

"He fell onto his back, and he was hollering something awful. I knew he was bleeding to death, so I kneeled over him and pressed my hands over the wound. But he slapped me across my face and told me to get away from him. That he was going to finish the job." She looked over at Mr. and Mrs. Calhoun, tears coming into her eyes. "I really did try to help him. I didn't want him to die."

The stillness in the room was absolute. There were no sounds and I couldn't even hear anyone breathing around me. She'd done it. She'd convinced them. I was sure of it.

As soon as Mr. Oliver took his seat, Mr. Garrett popped from his like he'd been waiting on this moment his whole life. That made me more than a little nervous. He approached Ruby with a an eager stride and leaned against the rail around the witness stand.

"Miss Graves, do you believe yourself to be a faith healer of some sort?"

"Objection!" Mr. Oliver called out. "Miss Graves's faith has nothing to do with the facts of this case."

Mr. Garrett put his hands out like he was baffled. "Your Honor, they have everything to do with it. Miss Graves's faith guides all her actions."

"I'll allow it," Judge Woods said.

Mr. Oliver had been expecting to lose on the ruling, but he'd wanted to make his point. At least that was what he'd said the day before and it explained why he hadn't brought Ruby's faith into his own line of questioning. I could only hope his decision helped Ruby instead of making it look like she was afraid to talk about it.

Mr. Garrett repeated the question, and Ruby gave him a polite smile. "I've been witness to a few miraculous healings, Mr. Garrett. But I don't claim to be responsible for them. Only God can heal."

The black-haired man nodded again. I was certain he was on our side. Mr. Garrett considered Ruby for a moment before he turned and walked toward the jury box. "When you went to Mrs. Doyle to ask about the extra food from the soup kitchen, you said you were taking the food to a family in need, correct?"

"Yes, sir."

"Did you tell her the *family* you spoke of was actually a Negro woman and her illegitimate son?"

Ruby's brow furrowed, and she sat up a bit straighter. "No, I did not. Because that shouldn't matter—"

"And later, when you were at Mrs. Doyle's home, did she not come to you and explain that you wouldn't be able to take any more of the extra jars of food?"

"Yes, but I didn't take any more—"

"Why, you yourself said Brother Cass saw you taking another jar of food, and confronted you about it."

"Yes, but I wasn't taking it. I had picked it up, and I was wondering why a perfectly good jar of food—"

"So you had it in your hand?"

"Yes, but—"

"Miss Graves, we are only after the truth here. I'll ask you to please keep your answers to 'yes' or 'no' unless I ask for a further explanation. Now, did you, or did you not, pick up a jar of food from the pantry after Mrs. Doyle had told you that you could no longer take the left-over jars?"

Ruby sighed. "Yes."

"Now, in your work with Dr. Fisher, do you often travel to Colony to provide medical care for Negroes?"

"Objection!" Mr. Oliver stood and pointed at Mr. Garrett. "Once again, Your Honor, this has nothing to do with the facts of the case. Mr. Garrett is simply trying to bias the jury against Miss Graves."

"Overruled."

I dropped my head and prayed I'd be able to hold myself together. The judge was letting Mr. Garrett do whatever he wanted, and Mr. Oliver's objections were beginning to seem desperate.

"Answer the question please, Miss Graves," Mr. Garrett continued.

"I do travel to Colony, but not usually for medical reasons. They have their own doctors and midwives there."

"You seem to know a lot about the area. How often do you go there?"

"Once a month, usually."

"And who drives you?"

"I drive myself. Dr. Fisher lets me take his car."

I heard muttering behind me, and one lady whispered, "Why would anyone in their right mind drive to Colony?"

Someone else whispered, "That's where her boyfriend lives."

I whipped my head around, but I couldn't tell who'd said it. Everyone was watching Ruby answer Mr. Garrett's next question.

"I go there to visit friends."

"So let me understand," Mr. Garrett said. "You are *friends* with Negroes?"

"Yes."

"Have you ever dated a Negro boy?"

"Objection!"

At this point, I wished Mr. Oliver would just stop objecting so the whole thing would get over with faster. Of course, the judge overruled him, and Ruby's face once again flushed pink.

"No, I've never dated anyone as a matter of fact." Our eyes met for the briefest of seconds, and heat surged through me. I'd never felt so completely helpless in all my life.

"You've never dated a Negro boy, and yet you visit friends in Colony once a month? Is that correct?"

"That's what I said."

"Miss Graves, once again, please simply answer 'yes' or 'no' when—"

"Yes."

Ruby shot daggers from her eyes at Mr. Garrett, but I was certain he didn't notice or care. "Miss Graves, was there someone else in the barn with you on the day Chester Calhoun died?"

"No."

"How do you account for the other set of boot prints?"

"I don't know. I never noticed them. But I can tell you that dozens of workers go in and out of that barn every day. Those footprints could have come from any of them."

"You said earlier that you tried to help Chester Calhoun. That you put your hands on his chest and tried to stop the bleeding, correct?"

"Yes."

"Did you try to heal him?"

Ruby went still, and her eyes widened for just a second before she regained control. "I prayed for him. I asked God to heal him."

"But God didn't heal Chester Calhoun, right?"

"No."

"He died."

"Yes."

"And you're the person that stabbed him?"

"Yes."

"Because he found out your secret, right?"

"No!"

"He walked into the barn and caught you with your Negro boyfriend, right? Those were the other set of footprints."

"No!"

Ruby's answer was drowned out by the eruption of the crowd behind me. I stared at Ruby, and she found my gaze. We shared a sickening moment of knowing whatever good she'd done to get the jury to believe her, Mr. Garrett had just unraveled.

"Order!" Judge Woods yelled as he pounded his gavel on the bench. "You will all be removed if you can't control yourselves."

Mr. Garrett moved over in front of Judge Woods. "Your Honor, I have no further questions."

"Very well," Judge Woods said. "Miss Graves, you may take your seat. Mr. Oliver, do you have any more witnesses?"

I wanted desperately to leap over the railing and take the stand one more time for Ruby, but it hit me then that the truth wouldn't even matter anymore. As soon as she said a word about Samuel, the solicitor would twist it into an ugly confirmation of Ruby's supposed boyfriend.

"The defense rests, Your Honor." Mr. Oliver stepped aside to allow Ruby back to her seat.

I couldn't even offer her a reassuring smile as she glanced at me. It was over. She was sunk.

CHAPTER NINETEEN

Ruby

I felt the eyes of the entire courtroom on me as I walked back to Mr. Oliver's side. I kept my head up, though, as hard as it was. I saw the judgment in everyone's eyes, but I knew in my heart that I'd done the right thing. Samuel was safe. And that was all that mattered.

As I moved behind Mr. Oliver to my seat, I caught Matthew's eye and tried to reassure him with a smile. But all I saw there was despair. I prayed God would shore up his faltering faith.

Mr. Oliver took his seat alongside me, and the judge asked both lawyers if they were ready to proceed with closing statements. Mr. Oliver leaned over and lowered his voice.

"Would you like to take a few minutes to gather yourself? I can ask for a recess."

"No," I said. "Let's just get this over with."

He turned to Judge Woods. "Your Honor, we are ready to proceed."

"We're ready as well, Your Honor," Mr. Garrett announced, the confidence clear in his voice.

"Very well, then. Mr. Garrett you may proceed with your closing statement."

Mr. Garrett strode across the room to the jury box and took up his position right in front of them, speaking as if they were an informal

243

gathering of friends. "Gentlemen, what we have here is a sad state of affairs all the way around. Ruby Graves is a troubled young woman with a volatile temper, a tendency to hide the truth, and a dangerous delusion about some...magical ability to stop a person's bleeding. Not to mention an unhealthy affection for Negroes. Unfortunately, this all came together as a tragic end for Chester Calhoun—a cherished son, a beloved husband and father, and an upstanding member of this community."

Behind me, I could hear Matthew muttering again. But at least he wasn't shouting at Mr. Garrett.

"The defense," Mr. Garrett continued, "has attempted at every turn to impugn the character of Chester Calhoun with unfounded accusations, but do not be fooled by Mr. Oliver's sleight of hand. The facts of this case are simple, and all I ask of you is that you use your common sense to draw conclusions based on those facts.

"Sheriff Peterson has stated, and presented you with evidence, that a third person wearing men's boots was involved in the vicious fight that resulted in Chester Calhoun's untimely death. Moreover, the coroner explained how fresh bruises were on Mr. Calhoun's face consistent with being punched. According to several witnesses, including herself, Miss Graves had no injuries to her hands. And if you read the record of Miss Graves's own testimony here, you'll not find one mention of her having hit Chester Calhoun. Her entire account was based on fleeing, not fighting back. So I ask you, gentlemen. Who punched Chester Calhoun?"

Mr. Garrett paused to let this sink in. He strolled in front of the jury box, keeping the men's eyes on himself. Then he looped his thumbs through his vest and frowned as if he was just then considering the meaning of all this himself.

"There is only one logical explanation for all this evidence. Only one conclusion that makes any sense at all." Spinning around, he pointed a finger directly at me, and my stomach dropped. "Ruby Graves was in that barn that morning with another man, and together, the two of them savagely attacked and killed Chester Calhoun."

Again, he paused, letting his statement sink in. I wondered for a moment how my mother was handling all of this. I thanked God she had Asa to lean on, 'cause I had a feeling things were only going to get worse.

"You may be asking yourself why this happened?" Mr. Garrett continued. "Why would Miss Graves want to kill Chester Calhoun? Why would she continue to insist she was the only one there? Again, all we have to do is look at the evidence and testimony of those closest to her to understand what was going on in her mind at the time. By her own testimony, as well as her mother's, Dr. Fisher's, and that of Brother Cass, we can be certain that Miss Graves has a history of carrying on inappropriate relationships with Negroes, despite warnings from family and friends. The only logical reason to kill Chester Calhoun would be to protect the shameful secret he had discovered in that barn...her affair with a Negro."

There was much shifting and muttering in the pew directly behind me. I reckoned my only three supporters in the entire gallery were preparing to leap over the railing to my defense. It gave me a moment of relief to know that in the sea of suspicion and condemnation behind me, I had three life preservers that wouldn't let me drown. I could handle Mr. Garrett's assumptions, and I knew I'd be all right soon enough.

Mr. Garrett strutted back to the center of the courtroom, as if he were taking position for his final act on stage. He turned and addressed the jury with outstretched hands, pleading for their understanding.

"Now gentlemen, you've been chosen for the unsavory job of deciding the fate of this troubled young woman. Although it is sad to see such a young life ruined, do not let her youth keep you from evaluating the truth of the evidence in front of you. You must decide, based on the facts and drawing from your common sense, whether she is innocent or guilty of first-degree murder. Those are your only choices here. And

246 | JENNIFER H. WESTALL

although it is a difficult task to be sure, you must do your duty to God and your community."

With that, Mr. Garrett walked back to his table, and took his seat. He folded his hands together and looked expectantly at Mr. Oliver. As my lawyer took a moment to wipe his brow, then stood and lumbered in front of the jury box, I prayed for him, asking God to guide his words as he spoke for me.

"Gentlemen, Mr. Garrett is right about one thing. You do have an unsavory task before you, and I'm sure no one envies your position. Now, Mr. Garrett has encouraged you to look at the evidence in this case, and to use your common sense. I would encourage you to do the same. However, it is the *lack* of evidence I'd like you to consider.

"Now, with all due respect, Mr. Garrett's case against Miss Graves rests upon the assumption that a bruise and some footprints in the barn *prove* there was a third person involved in the altercation. Gentlemen, no such proof exists. We don't know how or when Chester received that bruise. There's no telling how many workers are in and out of that barn each day, and there's no way of knowing whose boots made those prints, and when they were made. Now, we can make guesses on what we think may have happened. Chester may have been in another fight where he was injured in the jaw. Perhaps the footprints were made by deputies examining the scene. Perhaps by Luke Dalton, or James Graves. Or even by someone in the barn during all the commotion before the police arrived. We'll never know for sure about these things. But my guess would be very different from yours, and your guess might be very different from the next fellow's, and so on.

"Now the laws of our country state that a person is innocent until they are *proven* guilty. A bruised jaw is not proof. An unidentified footprint is not proof. It's guesswork. And to follow that guesswork with wild accusations of inappropriate relationships and witchcraft is not only ridiculous—it is irresponsible! Are we to convict an upstanding member of our community—a young woman ready to give her time and efforts to help others—of a most heinous crime based on guesswork and speculation? Now, I respect Mr. Garrett as much as the next fellow. He is normally a fine solicitor. But he has not proven his case against Miss Graves. And yes, you do have a duty to God and to your community. You have a duty to set the highest standards of the law. To ensure that only the guilty are punished, and the innocent are set free. Do not take that obligation lightly. For who knows when it will be your turn to sit in that chair, and to be tried for a crime you did not commit. All I ask is that you apply the same level of scrutiny to the evidence that you would want if you were in Miss Graves's place."

Mr. Oliver walked back to our table, and it seemed as though the entire courtroom took a collective breath. I heard shifting behind me, coughs, and warnings to children to sit still. I glanced at the jury, making eye contact with only one—a black-haired man near the top row who seemed to be studying me. His dark eyes looked distraught before he dropped his gaze to his lap. All the others were looking up at Judge Woods as he gave them instructions.

Then the men who would decide my fate filed out of the room.

No one left the courtroom. Even after the jury had been out several minutes, the pews remained packed with spectators, and every one of them kept glancing at me as they talked with their neighbors.

"You'd think these people would want some fresh air," I said to our small group gathered next to the defense table.

"Brood of vipers," Asa muttered.

I looked at him in surprise. It was the first negative thing I'd heard him say during this whole ordeal. He put an arm around my shoulders and squeezed, speaking quietly into my ear. "Don't be afraid, you hear? You put on God's armor. *For we wrestle not against flesh and blood...but against the ruler of the darkness of this world, against spiritual wickedness in high places.*"

I thought of Brother Cass placing his hand on the Bible and swearing to tell the truth, of him being the one to incite Chester against me in the first place all those years ago, and it was hard to fight the bitterness in my heart against him. Now there, indeed, was spiritual wickedness.

I hugged Asa in return and thanked him and Mother for their support. Mother leaned over the rail and hugged my neck. "No matter what happens, I love you, and I believe in you." She pulled away and wiped the corner of her eye with a handkerchief.

"I want to assure all of you," Mr. Oliver said, "that if they come back with a guilty verdict, we can appeal it to a higher court. There's no reason the evidence in this case should warrant a conviction."

Matthew locked eyes with me. "How are you doing? What can we do for you?"

It seemed everyone was convinced I was about to go down in flames. "I'm all right. I wouldn't mind a bit of fresh air. Might be the last I get for a while." I managed a small smile, but no one else did.

"I'll walk outside with you," Matthew said.

"We will too," Mother added.

So the four of us made our way through the crowd that had spilled out into the aisle between the pews, and then squeezed through the crowd in the hallway as well. I kept my eyes to the floor, not wanting any more looks of condemnation that day. I'd put on a brave front earlier, and it had taken all my energy.

As we reached the front door, a small crowd of men, a few of them with cameras, pushed their way toward us. A light flashed in my eyes, and I stopped in my tracks.

"Ruby!" One of them yelled. "Are you nervous about the verdict?"

Another light flashed, blinding me for a moment.

"Ruby! Who was the other man in the barn? Ruby! Ruby!"

Matthew maneuvered me behind him. "She doesn't have anything to say right now. Please leave us alone."

We backed away, but the group surged forward, still shouting questions. Asa and Mother stepped in front of them. Asa raised his hands to drive them back. "Miss Graves won't be answering any questions at the moment. If you'll direct your questions to me, I'll be happy to answer what I can."

Asa exchanged a glance with Matthew, who took my hand and led me down a side hallway and into the small conference room where we'd met with Mr. Oliver the day before. He closed the door behind us and leaned against it with his eyes closed.

"So much for some fresh air," he said.

He opened his eyes and reached for my hand, pulling me into his arms. I laid my head on his chest. Memorized the sound of his heartbeat, the warmth against my cheek. We stood like that for several minutes, neither of us with words for these last quiet moments.

When I pulled away from him, he rubbed his face and neck, groaning with exhaustion. "Ruby, this is our last chance. Are you sure? We could still find a way to get out of here. I'm sure of it. I'll go with you—"

"Shh," I said, reaching for his hands and pulling him away from the door. "No more talk of running. Let's just pray. All right?"

He nodded and kissed the top of my head. "Anything for you."

The door behind him opened, and Mr. Doyle slid through the opening. He frowned at us, and Matthew gripped my hand a little tighter.

"I think you might be lost," Matthew said.

"No," Mr. Doyle said, his eyes glancing down at our entwined hands. "I need to speak with you, son."

"I have nothing to say to you."

"Then you can listen. It's important."

"I told you already, I don't want anything more to do with you."

"Matthew," I said, moving between him and his daddy. "Maybe you should try to work things out."

"There's no working things out with him. It's his way or nothing. I choose nothing."

I looked over my shoulder at Mr. Doyle, whose eyes had not softened toward me one bit. Then I turned back to Matthew. "You owe it to yourself to forgive him. Not because he deserves it, or because he's seeking it, but because holding on to your anger will only hurt you. I'm not saying you have to give in to him, but find a way to forgive."

He rested his hands on my shoulders and touched his lips to my forehead. "All right. You win. I'll try. But I ain't promising anything."

I stepped aside and started for the door, but Matthew gripped my hand. "Stay here. No one will bother you in here."

Mr. Doyle pushed the door open, and Matthew went out into the hallway. Then Mr. Doyle looked me over from head to toe and shook his head before stepping through the door himself. I noticed he didn't close it all the way. Had that been on purpose?

I'd never been one to mind my own business very easily. As a child I'd had a bad habit of eavesdropping on my parents as they talked into the night. I hadn't quite defeated that little vice, and my curiosity stirred as I heard the mumbles between Matthew and his daddy. I crept over to the door and stood just to the side of the crack, trying to make out the harsh words coming from Mr. Doyle.

"...despicable behavior. It's an embarrassment to your family and position in this community."

Matthew's response was low, and I couldn't understand what he said, but it was clear his tone was angry.

"Do you have any idea what this is doing to your mother?" Mr. Doyle asked.

Another muffled reply from Matthew.

"I most certainly care about your mother's well-being, and I resent your implication otherwise. I won't tolerate you speaking to me that way."

"Fine!" This time I heard Matthew loud and clear. "I don't want to speak with you anyway."

Matthew moved into my line of sight, reaching for the door. But a hand grasped his arm. "She's sick, Matthew." He stilled. "Your mother's ill, and she needs you right now."

Matthew turned around, his back filling the crack so I couldn't see anything else. "What do you mean? What's wrong with her?"

"We're not entirely sure yet. The doctors say she has a weak heart. That she's under a lot of strain. She's taking some medication, but what she really needs is some peace of mind."

"Oh, that's rich. And let me guess what would ease her mind. If I came home and pretended to be the perfect son you want?"

"I've made no secret about my opinions. I'm telling you the truth— what you decide to do with it is up to you. What I do know is this: I haven't seen your mother so healthy and alive as she was when you were home and planning your wedding to Vanessa."

Matthew shook his head. "I cannot believe you're doing this right now. Ruby is facing—"

"Ruby is facing the consequences of her actions. And so will you if you don't get your head on straight. This isn't just about you rebelling against me. You're hurting your entire family by your senseless devotion to that girl. Not to mention how badly you've hurt the Paschals. They are our closest friends, and now every business deal I've made with Mr. Paschal is hanging in the balance because of you!"

"Ah, and now we get to the heart of the matter, don't we, Father? *Money.*"

"Judge me all you want. But don't think for one second that you'll come out of this unscathed. Ruby *will* be convicted, and she *will* be out of your life for good. And you will be left with nothing. No family, no money, no job, and no future."

My stomach turned. How could I have encouraged Matthew to listen to one word from that hateful man?

"You need to think about everything you stand to lose," Mr. Doyle said. "You can still come out of this with a future. And just maybe it's not too late for Ruby either. I can still put in a good word for her. But not if—"

"You have no say in the outcome of this trial. It's in God's hands now."

"No, son. It's in the jury's hands, and the jury is made up of *men*."

"How…you can't possibly…why are you doing this?" Matthew's voice rose with each unfinished thought.

"Because I want what's best for you, and what's best for our family."

Matthew moved away from the door, so I couldn't see him anymore, but I could hear his feet pacing the floor just beyond. "Are you telling me that if I walk away from Ruby right now, and come home—"

"And honor your promise to Vanessa," Mr. Doyle interjected.

Matthew let out a harsh laugh. "Oh yes, let's not leave out poor, heartbroken Vanessa. You're telling me if I agree to all that, you can make sure Ruby isn't convicted? That's insane!"

"I'm not guaranteeing that. Ruby's conviction is all but certain at this point thanks to your stubborn refusal to listen to reason thus far. But there's no need for it to be any more difficult for her than necessary. Convictions can be appealed, overturned."

Matthew's pacing stopped. "It's Richard Moore, isn't it? I recognized his name, but I didn't know where I knew it from. He's in that ledger I saw. The secret one. What does he owe you?"

"Never you mind about that. You have a decision to make, and very little time in which to make it."

"Do you even hear yourself? Do you have the slightest clue how lost you are when you're ready to send an innocent young woman to prison so that you don't lose out on some business deals?"

"She's far from innocent. I heard the same evidence as everyone else in that courtroom, and it only solidified my resolve that I'm doing the right thing by getting her out of your life."

Matthew stepped back into view, his finger shoved into his father's face. "You will *never* get Ruby out of my life. All you've done is removed me from yours."

I stepped away from the door as Matthew came through it, his eyes wild and angry. He slammed the door behind him and immediately went to pacing. "You heard all that, didn't you?"

I nodded. "I had no idea he was like that. I'm so sorry. I shouldn't have encouraged you to—"

"How can he live with himself? I can't believe he's doing this! We have to tell someone. Maybe Mr. Oliver can get a mistrial or something."

"It's too late."

"No it ain't! We go to Mr. Oliver or the judge and tell them my father has someone on the jury—"

"What proof do you have?"

"I'm not going to let him do this to you!" He stopped pacing and gripped my shoulders so hard pain shot down my arms. I winced, and he let go. "I'm sorry. I just...I can't believe this is happening. You're about to be convicted of murder because of my father."

"It's going to be all right," I said. "He isn't in control of that courtroom or the jury, as much as he'd like to think he is."

"I know, I know. God's in control, right? Is that what you're going to sell me right now?"

I stepped back from the sting of his words. "Of course. Because it's true. No matter what your daddy does, God is still on His throne, and He will decide my future. Not anyone else. So don't lose faith."

"That's easy for you to say. You have more faith than five apostles put together." He groaned. "You face tornadoes and...and grown men three times your size...and every person out there who thinks you're crazy 'cause you treat colored folks like...like..."

"Like what?"

"Like there's no difference between them and us! That's what got you into this whole mess in the first place. None of this would've happened if you hadn't gotten involved with Hannah years ago. And now you want to look a murder conviction in the eye and just accept it as the next step in your life!"

He fell into a chair and propped his elbows on his knees, dropping his face into his hands. I knelt in front of him and prayed I could make him understand. "Matthew, there *is* no difference. We're all lost and broken. All in need of saving. All in need of compassion, grace…mercy. We're all the same. When I met Hannah and Samuel, they were alone in the world with no one to help them or show them any kindness. All they knew was the violence Chester doled out on them, and rejection from colored and white folks alike. Can you imagine? Not belonging any-where in the world? It broke my heart."

"Ahh, Ruby," he groaned, moving his hands to my face. "I know why you did it. And even though it makes me crazy, I love you even more for it." He leaned forward and kissed me gently, giving me just a moment of joy. "But what do we do now?"

There was a knock on the door, and Matthew and I stood as Mr. Oli-ver came into the room with a grim frown. "Jury's reached a verdict."

"Already?" Matthew asked. "It can't have been more than half an hour."

"Forty minutes, actually."

Matthew rubbed the back of his neck. "Is that a good sign or bad?"

"Hard to say," Mr. Oliver said. "Guess we're about to find out."

I squeezed Matthew's hand, and he glanced down at me. "It's all right now. It's about to be over. Just have faith."

"You may have to have enough for the both of us," he said.

We followed Mr. Oliver out into the hallway and back into the courtroom, which maintained a low hum of conversation as we squeezed through the crowd. Once everyone was in place, the clerk called in Judge Woods.

As I took my seat, I tried to measure the men of the jury. Most kept their eyes on the judge to their left. The black-haired man near the back stared at the floor; his shoulders hunched forward just a bit.

"Mr. Foreman, have you reached a verdict?" Judge Woods said.

One of the men down front stood. "We have, Your Honor." He passed a piece of paper to the clerk, who passed it on to the judge.

Judge Woods read the verdict, and I thought I saw the slightest rise to his eyebrows. I tried not to make anything of it. "Very well," he said. "Will the defendant please rise."

I stood, and Mr. Oliver rose with me. I was grateful not to be alone. Judge Woods passed the piece of paper to the clerk, whom I hadn't paid much attention to until this point. He was a young man, maybe in his twenties. I wondered if he realized he was holding my future in his hands.

When he began reading I closed my eyes and prayed for strength.

"We the jury find the defendant, Ruby Graves, guilty of murder in the first degree—"

Gasps and rumbles of conversations in the crowd behind me made the clerk pause, but then his voice rose and he completed his duty.

"—as charged in the within indictment and fix her punishment as execution by means of electrocution."

My stomach dipped, and all the commotion behind me seemed to come through cotton in my ears. The room tilted, and I reached for Mr. Oliver's elbow to steady myself. Somewhere in the distance, I heard my mother crying.

CHAPTER TWENTY

Matthew

Execution? *Execution?* This couldn't be happening. I had to have heard the clerk wrong. But Mrs. Graves had collapsed into Asa's arms. Ruby swayed and clutched Mr. Oliver's elbow. Behind me, people were as shocked as I was.

"Can't believe it..."

"Did that fella say 'lectrocution?"

"...knowed in my heart she done it, but still..."

"Look at her poor mother..."

I gripped the railing as the floor dipped beneath me. It only took a moment for the rage to hit, and all I wanted to do was tear that whole courtroom apart. I turned to Asa and Mrs. Graves next to me. "This is insane!"

Judge Woods rapped his gavel and dismissed the jury. I jumped up from my seat.

"This is insane!" I repeated to no one in particular. I searched around the courtroom for someone to back me up. My gaze settled on Richard Moore, as he made his way along the bottom row of seats of the jury box. Our eyes met, and I pointed my finger at him.

"How can you live with yourself?" I yelled.

His face flushed red, and he jerked his gaze away from mine. He shuffled quickly past the remaining chairs and out the side door of the courtroom. I started to take off after him. What I planned to do, I had no idea, but I wasn't thinking straight.

Ruby turned around and grabbed my arm. "It's all right, Matthew. Look at me." She squeezed tighter as I watched the door close. "Look at me!" I found her eyes, but I could barely look at her. This was all my fault.

"Matthew," she said again. "I'm all right."

"We'll fight this," I said. "I promise. I'm going to make this right."

The sheriff walked around to Ruby's side and took her by the arm. I started to rip his hand away from her, but she squeezed my arm again where she still had hold of me.

"Don't lose hope," she said. Then she leaned toward me and stared into my eyes like she meant business. "Don't trade your faith for me."

Sheriff Peterson pulled her gently toward the side door. She let go of my arm, and I thought my chest would rip apart.

"I love you," I choked out.

"I love you too," she said, her voice steady and calm. She looked over at Mrs. Graves as she followed the sheriff. "I'll be all right, Mother. Don't worry."

Mrs. Graves nodded, but couldn't get any words out. Asa squeezed her shoulders and answered instead. "We'll be down to see you as soon as they'll let us."

She nodded, and then she gave me one last glance as she went through the door. As soon as the door closed, Mrs. Graves turned into Asa's chest and let out the sob she'd been holding back. I turned to Mr. Oliver for some kind of explanation.

"I'll get started on an appeal immediately," he said, raising a shaky hand to his forehead. "We have plenty grounds to file under."

"No, we have to do something *now*. That jury was rigged!"

Mr. Oliver put up a hand to calm me. "I know it may seem that way—
"

"No! Listen to me. It was actually rigged. My father as much as admitted it."

Asa stood from his seat. "What? Why...How is that possible?"

"Are you certain?" Mr. Oliver asked.

"Absolutely," I said, looking between the both of them. "Richard Moore, one of the men on the jury, is an associate of my father's. I saw his name in a ledger book he keeps hidden in his office. When I confronted him about it during the recess, he certainly didn't deny it, and he said he could affect Ruby's sentence."

"Why on Earth would he want to do that?" Mr. Oliver asked.

"He's never particularly cared for Ruby, but I thought it was just bluster about our standing in the community. I don't understand all the particulars, but Father has some shady business deals that are tied up in my choices, and choosing Ruby over my family has set him off." I turned to Asa and Mrs. Graves. "I'm so sorry. I'd never hurt Ruby in a million years. I just couldn't believe he had this much reach, or would go this far."

Neither of them looked at me with an ounce of condemnation, which surprised me.

"So what can we do?" said Asa, the steadiness in his voice surprising me further.

"Do you have any proof?" Mr. Oliver asked. "The ledger? Any business transactions between your father and Mr. Moore?"

My stomach sank. "No."

Mr. Oliver leaned back against the table and crossed his arms. He surveyed the courtroom as if he was afraid someone was listening, but by this time the room had emptied. "Without any proof, there's nothing we can do about this particular jury. What I can do is petition for a new trial based on some things that came up. Firstly, the footprint evidence should never have been admitted. The sheriff had no proof, and was simply making assumptions. Secondly, the verdict and sentence are no-where near consistent with the evidence—or lack of it. There are a few more minor details that probably won't amount to much, but if we throw everything we've got in there we might get a new trial."

"Might?" I said. My head was pounding by this time. "How long could all this take?"

"I'll get the paperwork started now. Submit the petition today. You work on keeping Ruby's spirits up."

I agreed, but I knew the opposite was likely the case. She'd be the one keeping my spirits up. And I was going to need it.

Mr. Oliver's request for a hearing to set aside the verdict was granted, but it would be a week before there was room on the Judge's schedule. Thankfully, Judge Woods delayed Ruby's transfer to the penitentiary until the petition was resolved. But still, that week was the most agonizing time of my life.

Asa and Mrs. Graves were kind enough to allow me to stay with them until the hearing, but I barely got any sleep at all. When I did sleep, my nightmare of losing Ruby returned with a vengeance. Only now it didn't end with Ruby simply fading into the wall. Instead, she drifted away from my outstretched arms and into a mangled metal chair with wires connected to it. As I ran toward her, a jolt of electricity buzzed through her, and a blinding light flashed in my eyes, waking me in a cold sweat. Every night.

I tried my best to put on a brave front for Ruby's sake when I'd visit her at the jail. But the combination of exhaustion and desperation set me on edge. Every day I'd walk in and grunt at the sheriff, wait for him to let me through the door, and then skulk down to Ruby's cell. She'd give me her best smile when she saw me, and that would lift my spirits for a brief moment. But not nearly long enough.

We'd talk about the increasingly wet weather, which made me feel terrible since she couldn't see it for herself. Then we'd talk about

Christmas coming just around the corner, and what we loved most about it. But that would lead to thoughts of family and lost loved ones. I'd feel terrible for being the reason she might not be with her family for Christmas. She'd feel terrible for being the reason my family was torn apart. It was an vicious circle we couldn't seem to escape, and we always wound up at the same guilt-ridden destination. Before long we'd either be too depressed to talk, or snapping at each other out of frustration.

The Friday after Ruby's trial, her uncles told us they were heading back to the caverns, and gathered up their things from the barn. Mrs. Graves hugged them all and thanked them. Roy told her to come and get them if they were needed for anything unsavory.

"Thank you for offering," she'd said. "But we're holding fast to our faith that God will provide for Ruby."

Roy had given me a pointed look before adding, "All the same, if you need us, come and get us, you hear?"

I'd walked them out to their trucks with a load of canned fruits and vegetables Mrs. Graves had insisted on sending with them. Once it was loaded, I shook Roy's hand and thanked them all for being there.

Roy had lowered his voice and held onto my hand. "If things get bad...I mean really bad...You come down to the caverns and get us."

"How will I find you?" I'd asked.

He'd proceeded to describe several back roads and turns I was sure I'd never remember. "Then you'll see a run-down gas station on your right called the Tipsy Gin. Ask for old man Harris. Tell him ole Ironside sent ya."

"Ironside?"

"Yep, and he'll ask you if you's lost or somethin'. Tell ya there ain't no Ironside around. You tell him you met ole Ironside in the war, and you need to see him. He'll look at you like you're crazy, but don't waver none or he'll clam right up. You tell him how terrible it was that Ironside got his leg blowed off." I was certain I'd never be able to get all this right, but he kept right on going. "He'll ask you which leg, and you be sure to tell him the wrong one. Say it just like that. 'The wrong one.' And then you take a seat and wait for me."

After he'd climbed in the truck and pulled away, I'd gone through the conversation several times in my mind, trying to memorize everything. But I'd prayed I wouldn't need to. I prayed every single night, as I tossed and turned on the sofa, that God would rescue Ruby. That he'd at least grant her a new trial, and a new chance.

The day of the hearing, I sat in the courtroom, in my same seat behind Ruby and Mr. Oliver, beside Mrs. Graves and Asa, with my head pounding like a drum. I hadn't slept a wink the night before. The pews were only half full this time, with the Calhouns and the sheriff in their same place, and Mr. Adams from the paper just behind them. Only a few spectators showed this time, and Father was nowhere in sight.

We listened to three hours of arguments from both Mr. Oliver and Mr. Garrett, and not once did Judge Woods call for a recess. Not even a lunch break. He seemed determined to press on through to the end, cutting off lengthy arguments and encouraging both attorneys to keep their statements brief.

Mr. Oliver put forth five assignments of error that would warrant a new trial—improper evidence admitted, jurors not having been given the option of finding Ruby guilty of lesser charges, a verdict contrary to the law and the evidence, and finally, that there was no evidence to support the verdict. Most of his arguments centered on the footprints presented by the sheriff, and the failure of the sheriff to eliminate others who had entered the barn. Mr. Garrett did his best to refute every claim made, and forcefully argued the footprints were valid evidence that showed Ruby's intent to cover up the truth of what actually took place.

After a long weary morning of arguments, I expected Judge Woods to dismiss us while he considered his ruling. But he did no such thing. "In the interest of everyone involved," he said, "I will be making my ruling without delay."

Mr. Oliver jumped out of his seat. "Your Honor, may we request a short recess while you consider all the information presented to you here today? I'm sure you must be exhausted, and we could all use a break."

"I thank you for your concern for my well-being, Mr. Oliver. But I am ready to present my ruling. I imagine your client is anxious to know what it is. So I will proceed."

Mr. Oliver sat back down like he'd been scolded. Then Judge Woods looked between the two sides of the courtroom and rested his elbows on the bench. "In preparing for today's hearing, I have carefully studied the transcript of Miss Graves's trial. I have also listened carefully to the arguments presented. I can find only one area where perhaps the evidence admitted was questionable. I concur with Mr. Oliver that the footprints at the scene should have been investigated more closely and compared to the footprints of others who'd entered the barn. This would have eliminated the doubt about the sheriff's claim."

My hopes rose with every word, and my headache eased just a bit. But my brief reprieve didn't last long.

"As to the other assignments of error made by the defense," he continued, "I'm afraid I cannot concur. First, it is not the duty of this court to offer any instructions to the jury that the defense did not ask for in the first place. Furthermore, in regards to whether the evidence supports the verdict, let me remind you that the jury must weigh the evidence it is presented. The jury must decide if a witness is credible, as well as the importance of the evidence offered. It is not up to this court to perform the duties of the jury. Therefore, given the limits to the power and duty of this court, I find that there is enough evidence to support and uphold the verdict."

The pounding renewed in my head, and I rubbed my temples, my vision blurring before me. How could this be happening again? Had God completely abandoned Ruby? None of this made any sense.

Judge Woods announced Ruby would be transferred as soon as possible to the State Penitentiary in Wetumpka, where she would await her execution, and then he dismissed us.

Ruby sat unmoving in her seat. I reached for her shoulder, and she placed her hand over mine. Then her chin fell to her chest, and her shoulders began to shake. It was the first time I'd seen her cry during this whole thing, and it shot through my chest like a bullet.

Mr. Oliver put a hand on her arm and tried to offer some comfort. "We'll appeal to the next higher court. We won't give up, I promise."

"This is all your fault," I growled at him. "If you hadn't convinced her to leave out the option for manslaughter—"

"Matthew, no." Ruby stood and turned to me, swiping her tears from her cheeks. "Don't blame Mr. Oliver. He's done everything he can to help me. I did this. It's my fault." She gave Mr. Oliver a thin, grateful smile. "Thank you for working so hard."

I saw Sheriff Peterson approaching from the other side of the room, so I stepped over the railing and pulled Ruby up into my arms. I pressed her against me and kissed the top of her head. "I ain't giving up, so you don't either."

This time, Sheriff Peterson didn't pull her away. He stood off to the side and let us have our time together. It was a pretty decent thing to do, but I couldn't forgive him for offering up the very evidence that would take Ruby away from me.

Mr. Oliver stepped away from us, and busied himself with papers. Mrs. Graves rubbed her hand up and down Ruby's back. And I gently swayed with her in my arms. I had to fix this. Somehow. I had to make this right.

I stayed with Ruby outside her cell till the sheriff closed up for the evening. We didn't say a whole lot to each other. Mostly just sat there, shoulder to shoulder with the bars between us. I held her hand, and she did her best to keep up my faith along with hers. I had to wonder if even Ruby might falter in her faith at a time like this.

"I'm scared," she whispered.

I closed my eyes and tried not to let in the terrifying images that had haunted my dreams recently. "Me too."

"They're transferring me soon. Sheriff said it might be as soon as to-morrow. Maybe the day after."

My stomach lurched. I dropped her hand and leaned forward onto my knees. "I can't let this happen, Ruby."

"There's nothing you can do. We have to trust that God has a bigger plan for us than this."

"A bigger plan?" I couldn't take it anymore. All this faith in a God of no action! I stood and gripped the bars to steady myself. "There's no plan, Ruby. Except to let you die for something you didn't do. And I can't just stand around and do nothing about it."

I pushed away from the bars and headed for the door.

"Matthew!" she called.

But I didn't stop. I knew exactly what I had to do.

I drove up to my parents' home as dusk fell, screeching into my usual parking place without my usual care. I slammed the door behind me as I jumped out of my car, not bothering to lock it. I took a moment to gath-er my thoughts, deliberately taking the stairs one at a time. But my rage did not subside. I pushed the door open and stepped inside the foyer.

The lights made a gentle humming sound, and I could hear the clink of silverware from the direction of the dining room. I slammed the front door closed, rattling the windows.

"Father! Get out here and face me right now!" I was determined to go no further than the foyer.

But instead of him coming out to see me, it was Mother who rushed out of the dining room. Her eyes were anxious, and she held out her hands as she came to me. "Oh, Matthew. You're home. Come inside. Come eat with us, and let's talk."

I let her hug me, but I moved away as soon as possible. "Where's Father? I want to speak to him right now."

"I'm here, son." He strolled out of the dining room still wiping his hands on a napkin. "What's all the commotion about? Your mother and I are trying to have supper."

"You're going to fix this," I said, marching closer to him. "You're going to contact whoever you have to, and you're going to fix this."

"What's going on?" Mother asked. "Honey, what are you talking about?"

I turned to her, knowing if I could get her on my side, I might actually stand a chance. "He had Ruby convicted of murder, and now they're going to electrocute her!" I turned back to Father. "Do you even understand what you've done? Do you? She's going to die because you can't get your way on a business deal. *A business deal!*"

Father barely moved. "Get control of yourself, son."

"That's your answer?" I screamed. "To control myself? When you're trying to rip my life to shreds?"

Mother came up beside me and laid a hand on my arm. "Patrick, is this true?" He didn't answer, so she turned to me instead. "Honey, your father couldn't have—"

"Mother, stop being so blind! He used Richard Moore to influence the jury for the verdict and sentence he wanted!"

"Now hold on here," Father said. "I did no such thing. You jumped to that conclusion on your own. That jury reached the verdict it did because of the evidence—"

"You are such a liar! Do you even know how to be honest anymore? Tell her the truth!"

The expression on his face darkened. "Listen, I may have hinted that if it seemed a conviction was likely, that he should do his best to convince the others of what he believed. But I did not force him to do anything."

"Patrick!" Mother gasped. "You...you couldn't have known he'd be on the jury."

He looked between us with contempt in his eyes. "Neither of you understands the level of commitment it takes to keep this family prosperous in times like these. Do you see our neighbors? Do you see what's happening around here? Roosevelt has been re-elected, and he is only going to squeeze more and more out of people like us. I'm doing my best to secure your future—"

"At what cost?" I shouted over him. "Ruby's life? Listen to yourself!"

He pushed up his chin and pointed toward the door. "I'm going to finish my supper. If you're only here to parade around and make a big scene, then I'll have to ask you to see yourself out."

"Patrick!" Mother yelled. "What are you doing?"

"I'm eating my supper."

He turned to leave, and panic surged through me. "You win, all right? I'll do what you want! I'll stay here. I'll marry Vanessa. I'll work for you. Whatever it takes. But you have to make this right. You have to contact whoever you can and save Ruby." I walked over to him and stepped directly in his line of sight. "Please. I'll do whatever you want."

His frown deepened as he looked between Mother and me. "It's too late."

"What?" I said. "What do you mean? How?"

"What's done is done. It's out of my reach now. You should have come to your senses a lot sooner, when I still had the power to do something."

Rage shot through me, and before I knew it, I had his throat in my hands. Mother screamed. I pushed him to the wall and held him there. "You are the most despicable human being I've ever known. You are not my father. Don't ever try to contact me again. Don't ever show your face to me again. Do you understand?"

He met my gaze with no sign of emotion. "Clearly."

I let go of him and barged past Mother toward the front door. "Patrick, do something!" I heard her cry.

But I'd slammed the door behind me before I could hear another word. I ran down the steps and flew to my car, sending dust everywhere as I sped away. There was only one solution left.

I lost count of how many wrong turns I made before I finally found the Tipsy Gin. It was basically four walls made from cement blocks—none of them at right angles with any other surface—and a slab of tin on top that looked like it would blow away in a strong breeze. As for it being a gas station, well, it appeared to have had a tank at some point, but the roof over the pump had fallen in on one side so that it was unreachable now.

I pulled in next to the only other car there and got out to look around. The hour it had taken me to find the place had calmed my feverish hatred of Father, but I was still on edge. I stepped up through the makeshift front door, and was surprised to find a fully functioning store on the inside.

Behind the counter was an older man in ragged clothes making notes on a pad of paper. There were five tables scattered around the room, with four men playing cards at one, and two men drinking something not quite clear from mason jars at another. I didn't look too closely. Not one of them stopped what he was doing, but I could feel their eyes on me somehow.

"Can I help you?" called the old man from behind the counter.

"I hope so," I said.

He looked me over, and I was keenly aware of how my slacks and dress shirt must have stood out in that place. I walked over to him and tried to remember exactly what I was supposed to say. "Um…I'm looking for, um…a Mr. Harris?"

The old man went back to writing on his little pad of paper. "Never heard of him."

"Oh, well…I was supposed to find him and tell him old Ironside sent me."

"You were, huh? Well, it's too bad fer ya then. 'Cause ain't no one here that goes by either of them names." He set his pencil down and started digging around behind the counter where I couldn't see. "I can get ya a drink if you like though."

I leaned onto the counter and folded my hands together. "I'm kind of in a hurry. It's very important."

"What's important?"

"That I speak to Ro—old Ironside."

He straightened and lifted a bushy gray eyebrow at me. "Well, then you's outta luck!"

I searched my brain for the rest of what I was supposed to say. "I uh…I met him in the war. Yeah! I met him in the war."

"That's just wonderful. Now can I get you a drink? If not, you need to mosey on."

I slammed my hand onto the counter as the rest of it came back to me. "He lost a leg! I mean…uh, it was a shame about losing his leg and all. Real shame."

This time I could've sworn the old man's mouth twitched just a bit, and his eyes held a hint of laughter behind them. "Sounds like an interesting fella." He came out from behind the counter with a cloth and went to wiping down the empty tables. I waited for him to finish the routine, but he didn't say anything else.

"I said, it was a real shame how he lost that leg in the war." I was about ready to just speak plainly and beg the guy to help me, when he finally stopped wiping and stood up straight.

"Say there, which leg did he lose?"

I nearly jumped in the air. "The wrong one! It was the wrong one."

The old man had himself a good chuckle. "You have a seat young fella, and I'll be back in a while."

He went behind the counter and brought out a Coca-Cola for me before he headed out a back door I hadn't even seen. The other men in the store still hadn't paid me the least bit of concern. I dropped into a chair at one of the empty tables and took a swig of the soda, letting the burn in my throat replace the fire in my belly.

Seemed like I sat there for a good thirty minutes, sipping my Coca-Cola till it was empty, and then watching the four men playing poker. I was fascinated how they played in nearly complete silence. Like a dance they all knew by heart. After a particularly long hand, I turned back to the table and nearly fell backward when I saw Roy seated across from me.

"How bad is it?" he asked.

After I recovered my wits, I found my voice again. "Just about as bad as it can get. Can you help me?"

Roy leaned onto his elbows and lowered his voice. "The boys and I been talking things over in case you showed up. We got some options, but we need to know where things stand."

"The judge upheld her conviction and execution. They're moving her to Wetumpka either tomorrow or the next day."

"That narrows our options. Looks like our best bet may be to derail the transfer and get her over here to the caverns to lay low for a while."

The older man whom I'd spoken to earlier—I figured he was Mr. Harris—set a mason jar full of clear liquid in front of Roy, who took a sip and grimaced. "That's some a our best stuff right there. Want a taste?" He grinned when I shook my head. "Might need a little Dutch courage come tomorrow."

"So what's the plan?"

"Leave the details to us. Best to keep your hands as clean as possible if you're running with her. That way, the law won't be looking for two of ya. Can you disappear for a while? Affairs all in order?"

I nodded. "I got nothing to my name. No job. No family. I can leave now and never look back."

Roy nodded. "Good. 'Cause that's exactly what you're doing." He motioned for Mr. Harris to come over again. "Bring a pencil and some paper, would ya?" he said.

Mr. Harris dropped the pencil and paper at the table and disappeared in the back of the store. Roy wrote something down and then slid the paper across the table. "Sure you're ready for this? Ain't no turning back once this sets in motion. And it ain't gonna be pretty neither."

My stomach knotted. "You're not going to actually...kill anyone...are you?"

Roy sighed. "Look, it's best for everyone involved if no one gets killed. But things don't always go as planned. And like I said, for your part, your hands should be pretty clean. So don't you worry none. The boys and I are used to all this."

My uneasiness grew, and I wondered what Ruby would say to Roy's plan. But who was I kidding? I knew exactly what she'd say. She'd tell me to trust God. She'd tell me to believe that if I waited around and just prayed hard enough, somehow things would work out for the good. But I couldn't do that. I couldn't just wait. And I was pretty sure God wasn't listening, anyway.

"Mr. Harris," I said. "Is there any more of that moonshine left?"

CHAPTER TWENTY-ONE

Ruby

The next morning when Matthew, Mother, and Uncle Asa came in to see me, I could tell something was wrong right away. All three looked as gray as death, especially Matthew. He almost looked sick. Sheriff Peterson walked ahead of them, looking grim as well. He nodded to me and stuck his key in the lock.

"We're heading to Wetumpka in a little while, Miss Ruby. Everything's set to go. You all take some time to visit. We'll come in and get you in about thirty minutes."

Mother, Asa, and Matthew filed past him. The sheriff didn't even bother closing the door. Matthew turned to him and asked, "How far of a drive is it down to Wetumpka?"

The sheriff looked at the ceiling and furrowed his brow. "Well, usually takes a good three hours just to get to Montgomery. Then another half hour or so to get to Wetumpka." He took a look over at me. "It'll be a long day for sure."

Matthew shifted his weight and crossed his arms over his chest. Then he shifted again. "You taking '31 all the way down?"

"I reckon it's the quickest way."

"Would you allow me to follow? I'd feel better knowing she arrived safely."

This seemed to unsettle Sheriff Peterson. He eyed Matthew with a hint of suspicion. "I can't tell you where you can and can't drive, but I'll say this. I'd be mighty uncomfortable with you following behind us. It ain't that I don't trust ya or nothin' but I think it would be best if you waited and visited Ruby in a few days once she's settled in. You can trust that Deputy Frost and I will get her there in one piece."

Matthew ran his hand through his hair and shifted again. "All right. Thanks, Sheriff."

Sheriff Peterson made his way out the door, and Mother was the first to come to me. She wrapped her arms around me and stroked my back as I tried to hold myself together.

"We'll be down to see you in two days," she said. "Mr. Oliver's coming too, and we'll get to work on your appeal."

She let me go, and we took a seat on my cot. Matthew remained near the cell door, his arms still folded over his chest. "What's the matter?" I asked.

"Nothing," he said, moving closer to us. "I just haven't wrapped my head around all this yet. Just don't make any sense, is all." He rubbed the back of his neck. "I talked to Father last night. I tried to get him to make this right. But he says he can't. Says it's outta his hands now. I should've done something sooner, said something when he first made the threats. I just couldn't believe..."

"It's all right," I said. "Thank you for trying."

He paced the floor next to Mother and me. Sweat had dampened the hair around his temples. Asa must've noticed his nervousness too. He shot a glance at me before calling on Matthew to have a seat.

"I can't," Matthew said. "I can't sit still right now. This shouldn't be happening."

"I know this is hard," Asa said. "But Scripture tells us God won't give us more'n we can bear. He knows our weakness, and He wants us to rely on Him for our strength."

Unfolding his arms, Matthew rubbed his temples. "What if He actually wants us to *do* something besides sit around and wait for Ruby to die?"

"Matthew!" Mother said, covering her mouth with her hand.

He cringed. "I'm so sorry, Mrs. Graves. I'm sorry, Ruby. This is making me crazy inside."

Asa went over to the little table beside my cot and took Daddy's Bible in his hands. "Why don't we read some Scripture together? I'm sure we can find some comfort in God's words."

"That's a wonderful idea," I said.

Mother nodded. Her hands shook a little as she reached for mine. "What would you like to hear, honey?"

"I want a miracle," I said. "When Jesus walks on the water." Asa gave me a warm smile as he sat down and began flipping through the pages. "Read it from Matthew," I said, glancing over at *my* Matthew. "That's my favorite."

Asa turned to it and began reading:

"And straightway Jesus constrained his disciples to get into a ship, and to go before him unto the other side, while he sent the multitudes away. And when he had sent the multitudes away, he went up into a mountain apart to pray: and when the evening was come, he was there alone. But the ship was now in the midst of the sea, tossed with waves: for the wind was contrary. And in the fourth watch of the night Jesus went unto them, walking on the sea. And when the disciples saw him walking on the sea, they were troubled, saying, It is a spirit; and they cried out for fear.

"But straightway Jesus spake unto them, saying, Be of good cheer; it is I; be not afraid. And Peter answered him and said, Lord, if it be thou, bid me come unto thee on the water. And he said, Come. And when Peter was come down out of the ship, he walked on the water, to go to Jesus. But when he saw the wind boisterous, he was afraid; and beginning to sink, he cried, saying, Lord, save me.

"And immediately Jesus stretched forth his hand, and caught him, and said unto him, O thou of little faith, wherefore didst thou doubt? And when they were come into the ship, the wind ceased."

"Why is that your favorite?" Matthew asked. He'd finally stopped pacing and had been listening to Asa intently.

"Because it's about me," I said. "There have been many times when I was terrified of the storm I was in at the moment, but Jesus called me out of the boat. It doesn't make any sense to step out onto crashing waves in the midst of a storm. Reason tells me to stay in the boat where I'm safe. But Jesus looks at me and says, 'Come.' So I go to Him. It's all I know to do."

Matthew leaned his back against the bars and slid down until he was seated on the floor. It was a while until he spoke. "I don't know how you do it. Does your faith never waver? Do you ever doubt anything?"

"Of course I do! Every day. I'm just like Peter. I step out of the boat and get swamped by fear and doubt. I start to sink. But I call out to my Savior, and He rescues me. That's how I can face this. My Savior loves me."

Matthew's tortured gaze met mine. "Then how can He let this happen, Ruby? What good does it do for anyone? Your sacrifice will go to the grave with you, and then what difference will you have made? No one will ever know what you've done, except me. I'll get to live with it."

A wave of understanding passed over me. I stood and walked over to him, kneeling in front of him. "Whatever you're planning...don't do it."

His eyes widened. "Wh-what do you mean?"

"I don't know exactly. I just *know*. I see it all around you. The fear. The doubt. There's darkness all over you."

"I'm *afraid* for you."

"No, you're afraid for yourself. Of a life without me."

"You said you were afraid too."

I took his hands in mine. "Yes, but I dealt with mine. I prayed for courage. Yours is the kind of fear that can leave you broken and lost. Don't do it. Whatever's going on in your head...just pray...ask for wisdom and courage. Please. Don't lose your faith."

Matthew

Don't lose my faith. How many times had she said that to me now? Seemed like she was more afraid of that than losing her own life. Looking at her there as she knelt in front of me, I could almost grasp ahold of what she was saying. Maybe we were in a boat, in the middle of a storm, in the middle of a great sea. And maybe Jesus was calling on us to step out of the boat. But what I couldn't catch onto was: What was I supposed to do? Was it exercising my faith to sit back and wait for something to happen? Or was there greater faith in taking action?

She looked on me with so much peace in her eyes. That same way she'd looked on me all those years ago, the night God had healed me. Ruby had this presence with her that I couldn't understand, like a bubble of *something*—love, grace, and fire all wrapped into one—that made me love her all the more, and yet kept her separate from me also. I didn't deserve someone I couldn't begin to understand. But I couldn't imagine living one day without her, either. Did that make me selfish? Was I to be judged for considering my own needs also?

"Miss Ruby, it's time," Sheriff Peterson said from the door of her cell.

I jumped to my feet, shaken out of my reverie. Ruby and I stood, and she took my hand. "All right," she said to the sheriff, "I'm ready." Then she turned and gazed up at me. "Don't do anything out of fear. If there's no peace, then wait for God."

I wrapped my arms around her, wishing I could slow down time until I could figure out what to do. "I love you," I whispered.

Then I released her, and she hugged her mother and Asa one last time. We followed her and Sheriff Peterson into the lobby where John Frost was waiting.

"We'll need you folks to step out now," he said. "I'll get all the information from Wetumpka for ya, and pass it on so you can go visit as soon as you'd like."

He looked at us with expectant eyes, while we all looked around at each other like we couldn't comprehend what was happening. Finally Asa spoke up. "All right then. Let's go." He wrapped his arm around Mrs. Graves and ushered her out the door into the parking lot. I followed behind, still weighing my options. I took one last glance over my shoulder at Ruby before I went out the door. She met my gaze and held it until the door closed between us.

As soon as I couldn't see her anymore, my heart started to race. I had to decide, right then, what I was going to do. If I did nothing, and Ruby went to Wetumpka, there was still a chance her appeal might work, and she'd be released. But how long would that take? And what if it didn't work? I could lose her forever. If I waited, and trusted the system to work, I could miss the best chance possible for saving her.

If there's no peace...

There was no peace with either option. No peace within my own heart. I only knew that living one day without Ruby would be the most awful existence I could imagine. I couldn't wait. I couldn't hope and pray for something that might never happen. Wasn't that exactly what I'd done all this time? Hadn't I hoped and prayed God would intervene? He hadn't shown up.

I can't wait.

As Asa helped Mrs. Graves into his truck, I ran past them towards the end of the courthouse, turned the corner, and headed across the street to the café. When I pushed open the front door, the people at the nearby tables stopped mid-conversation and stared at me. I reckon I was panting and seemed a bit crazed. I straightened myself up and moved to the counter on my right.

A gray-haired woman eyed me as I approached. "Can I help you, young man?" she asked.

"May I use your telephone?"

"Ain't got one. You might try the office next door. Think they got one last year."

I thanked her and hurried out the door. Looking to my left, I saw a small clothing store and a law office. I decided to try the law office. Maybe if they overheard something, they'd be less likely to repeat it.

I pulled open the door and went to the first desk I spotted. A young man in a suit looked up at me in alarm as I rushed toward him. "Is there a telephone I can use? It's an emergency."

"Um, sure." He pointed to the black box on the wall behind me.

I thanked him and picked up the receiver. I took a quick look at my pocket watch. It was just after ten. A female voice came on the line asking for my connection. I pulled the piece of paper that Roy had given me the night before out of my pocket and repeated the numbers.

"Just one moment," said the voice.

I glanced out of the front windows and saw the sheriff's car pull out of the courthouse parking lot and onto the main road heading south toward Hanceville.

"Hello," an unfamiliar voice rasped on the other end.

I tried to speak, but it felt like I had cotton in my mouth.

"Hello?" said the voice again.

"Yes, hello. This is...um...Henry Graves calling for Tipsy. I'm just leaving now, so I should be there 'round ten-forty or so. I'll bring a friend with me, so there'll be two of us."

"All right then." There was no wavering, just an acknowledgement of my coded message. "We'll make two places at the table for ya."

"I'm running a bit behind," I said, indicating the signal that the sheriff hadn't allowed me to follow. "Gimme a few minutes."

"All right then. See you soon."

And I hung up the receiver. I thanked the man behind the desk and ran out the door, across the street and back to my car. When I climbed inside, I cranked it and rested my hands on the wheel. *Lord, I pray I didn't just make a huge mistake. But there's no turning back now. Please keep Ruby safe.*

I drove out of the parking lot and turned onto '31, heading south toward Hanceville. I had just over thirty minutes of my life as Matthew Doyle left.

Ruby

At first, I kept my eyes closed and prayed as we traveled along Highway 31. I couldn't look at Hanceville, even though some part of me wanted to. I reckon some folks might want a last look at their home if they were in my position, but I didn't. I already knew every tree along every road, knew the "S" would be missing on the sign at Ashwander's produce store, knew that old man Tucker would be in front of the gas station, winning at checkers. All I wanted was to feel God's presence.

So I opened my heart to him and poured out my fears of the future, my longing to be free, my heartache at seeing Matthew's faith so shaken. I prayed my Mother would stay strong, and I thanked God for bringing Asa back into her life. It was such a comfort to know she wouldn't be alone.

I did my best to stay positive, to avoid questioning why this was happening, or asking for God to take away the lonely ache in my chest. I wanted to face my future with the same courage the apostles had when they were thrown in prison for their faith. Maybe God would give me the opportunity to tell others about Him while I was in there. But I also thought of John the Baptist, and I wondered if he had a moment of weakness as he faced his execution. Did he wonder if God had abandoned him?

I thought about what Matthew had said, about how no one would ever know what I'd done, and that it wouldn't change anything. I prayed he was wrong. I prayed that somehow my tiny, brief existence would be like a pebble tossed in a pond. I prayed that small example might eventually ripple out toward others, and someday people wouldn't look at skin color as a way of measuring a person. Maybe someday we'd figure out how to see into a person's heart without even noticing the pigment in their skin.

Rain was beginning to tap insistently on the windows, the noise disturbing my reverie and making me feel unsettled. I opened my eyes to discover we were well past Hanceville, driving past muddy brown fields, broken up occasionally by patches of woods with only a smattering of green pine trees in them. The dark cloud overhead seemed a perfect companion for my trip. Soon, I saw a sign ahead for the little town of Blount Springs, and I realized it was the first time in my life I'd been that far away from home. Seemed sad really. Here I was about to leave Cullman County, after dreaming about getting out of there for so long, and it was in the back of a sheriff's car headed for the state penitentiary.

In the seat ahead of me, I heard Sheriff Peterson ask John, "You see that?"

"Sure do," John said.

I slid to the middle of the bench I was sitting on so I could see too. Up ahead of us, just in the bend of a turn, a car had run off the road and crashed headlong into a tree. Steam was shooting out of the engine, and a man's body was lying in the ditch a few yards away from the open passenger door.

Sheriff Peterson slowed down. "I reckon we ought to check on 'em."

Another man stumbled out into the road from in front of the car, waving his arms for help. Our car came to a stop about thirty feet behind the wreck. The stumbling man fell to his knees. He seemed familiar somehow, but it was hard to see through the rain, which was heavier now, and beginning to fall in sheets.

"I can help," I said. "I've been trained to take care of injured folks."

"You stay right where you are," Sheriff Peterson said. "Something about all this don't feel right." He opened his car door and stood behind it. "Sir," he called to the man in the middle of the road. "Sir! Are you all right? What's happened here?"

The man in the road moaned loudly, lifting his head. Beneath the brim of his hat, I saw my Uncle Roy's face, and my heart jumped into my throat. "I...I lost control," he said. "Hit the tree there. Can you help my friend? I think he's hurt."

Sheriff Peterson glanced at John. "Get Jefferson County on the radio and get some help out here."

"We ain't crossed into Jefferson County yet," John said. "Still Blount."

Sheriff Peterson swore under his breath. "Get Blount then. It'll take 'em five years to get here, but ring 'em up anyhow."

"Yes, sir." John reached for a large round speaker that looked like a huge sucker. He twisted some knobs until it hissed and called Blount Sheriff's department, explaining the situation and our location to a crackly voice on the other end. I kept my eyes on Roy, wondering how in the world I was to keep this situation from turning bad. My initial concern for injured strangers had been replaced by a horrible feeling in the pit of my stomach that things weren't as they seemed.

"They're on their way," John said to Sheriff Peterson.

"All right. You keep an eye on this one while I check out the one in the ditch."

John climbed out of his side of the car and took a position behind his door, his left foot propped up on the running board. Sheriff Peterson approached the man in the ditch, who I assumed was another one of my uncles. He knelt down and felt my uncle's neck. Roy rocked back on his heels, moaning again. "I don't feel so good," he said.

Sheriff Peterson called from the ditch. "He's alive! Beat up pretty good though."

Roy fell onto his back, splashing down hard into a puddle. "Oh Lordy!" he hollered as he landed.

John bent down and met my gaze. "Just...stay here. Don't move, all right?"

"John, listen—"

"Just stay where you are."

He darted over to check on Roy. I was staring at the car and Roy, trying to figure out what was going on, when there was a light tap on the passenger side back window. It startled me, and I jumped.

A face slid up into view. It was Franklin, his hair plastered to his scalp by the driving rain.

"What are you doing?" I whispered.

He slid in the passenger side door where John had just left. "Getting you outta here. What else?"

"No! You're going to get someone hurt...or worse. Now get out of here before one of them sees you."

"There ain't no time to argue, now come on."

"No," I insisted. "It's illegal!"

Franklin took a quick look at the Sheriff and deputy still tending to the supposedly injured men. Then he turned back to me. "Look, did you kill anyone? Tell me, Ruby, for real. Did you kill Calhoun?"

I was tired of lying at this point, and something about Franklin told me he wasn't interested in spreading anything I said to the police.

"No." I sighed. "I didn't kill him."

"I knew it." He shook his head, stealing another glance toward the wrecked car. "Then there ain't nothing wrong with you getting out of this car. You didn't commit no crime. So there ain't no punishment you need to pay. You shouldn't die for something you didn't do."

I had to admit there was a good part of me that agreed with his reasoning. At this point, if I disappeared, it wouldn't cast any suspicion on

Samuel. But my heart was racing too fast for me to find peace with that decision. "You might be right, but breaking the law here don't fix nothing. I can't do it."

"Then you're condemning all of us, including Matthew."

"Matthew?" I nearly shouted. "What is he doing?"

That was when all hell broke loose. Glancing up at the sound of my voice, John spotted Franklin in the passenger seat and sprang to his feet. "Hey, get away from that car!" He took about three steps towards us before the blast of a pistol sounded.

John fell to the ground. Sheriff Peterson jumped up and tried to pull his gun out, but another blast sounded. He fell face down against the wet gravel. I couldn't tell if he'd been hit or if he was dodging a shot. Franklin swore and jumped out of the car, pulling a pistol out from his belt. I couldn't believe what I was seeing. He peered around the passenger door, took two steps, and fell to the ground when another blast of gunfire sounded.

"Franklin!" I shouted.

I climbed over the seat and out the door. Franklin had gotten back up and was stumbling off the road into the dead stalks of corn just below.

"Ruby, get back in that car!" Sheriff Peterson called from the ground. He had his pistol pointed straight at me. I dove back into the car, peering over the hood as Sheriff Peterson crawled over to John, who was groaning on the ground. Sheriff Peterson helped him sit up, and they started sliding backwards toward the sheriff's car.

Another blast came from the front of the wrecked car, and the Sheriff fired back. He and John continued to scoot backward until they reached the open passenger door. I reached down and helped pull John into the car. Then Sheriff Peterson stood and ran around the back of the car to the driver's side, while I took a quick look at John's condition. The bullet had gone through his back and out his chest. He coughed up blood and groaned.

Sheriff Peterson leaned against the door, pointing his gun over the top at the other car. "Ruby, get in the back of the vehicle!"

"I can stop this! They won't shoot at me."

"Who are they?"

"I...I think it's my uncles."

Sheriff Peterson's knees buckled, and he fell against the door. That was when I noticed the blood staining the front of his shirt. I climbed past him and out into the open.

"It's me!" I shouted. "Stop shooting!" I kept moving toward my uncles' car. "Please stop!"

"Ruby," a gruff voice called from the front of the car. "You all right?"

"Yes, I'm fine. But please stop all this. The sheriff's hurt, and so is Deputy Frost. I have to help them. You all need to get out of here!"

I reached the side of the car and could see Roy and Eddie crouched down with their guns drawn. "Come on," Roy said. "We gotta get outta here."

"They could die!" I shouted, pointing back to the sheriff's car. "I have to help them. We have to get help!"

I turned to run back to help the sheriff, when I saw another car approaching. Just before it stopped, I could see Matthew's worried face come into view.

CHAPTER TWENTY-TWO

Matthew

My stomach churned as I approached the two cars ahead of me. This wasn't what I was supposed to find. The sheriff's car was parked to the side of the road, both doors flung open to the elements. Sheriff Peterson sat on the road, leaning against the running board. Ruby stood between the two cars, her face ashen and eyes wild.

I jumped out of my car and met her as she raced for Sheriff Peterson. "What's going on?"

She knelt beside him and placed her fingers on his neck. "Roy and Eddie are over there. I think they staged some kind of wreck or something to try to get me to escape. But then everything went crazy and they all starting shooting at each other!"

"Are you all right? What can I do?"

"I'm fine, but we've got to help them." She pointed inside of the sheriff's car where I saw John Frost laid across the seats. "They're hurt pretty bad. Can you go around to the other side and see if John's still alive? Then check to see if Roy and Eddie are hurt. We need to find Franklin too. He's around here somewhere."

I stared at her for a moment, not registering everything that was happening. This wasn't at all what Roy had explained I'd see when I drove up. They were supposed to be gone. They were supposed to have lured the police into a chase after Ruby had already been taken from the car. I was supposed to pick her up.

She pulled open Sheriff Peterson's shirt and wiped away the blood spurting out. At least he was alive. Then she closed her eyes and lifted her face to the stormy sky, prayers tumbling from her lips.

The hair on my arms stood on end as I realized what she was about to do. I was suddenly crushed by the weight of how badly this had turned out. I got my feet moving and ran around to the other side of the car, climbing in as best I could to check John. "Still alive!" I called out.

Then I backed out and jogged over to the car in front, finding Roy helping Eddie nurse a wound to his forearm. "How did this happen?" I asked as soon as I realized they were all right.

Roy shook his head. "Sometimes things don't go according to plan. You have to improvise."

"Improvise? You may have just killed two policemen. And now this whole thing is going to blow up in our faces!"

Roy finished tying off a piece of cloth around Eddie's forearm, then he came around the side of the car and took a look over my shoulder. "We can still get everyone to the caverns and hide out until this blows over."

I couldn't believe what I was hearing. Was this all a bad dream? "Murdering cops don't blow over!"

"He's right," Eddie said, coming around the car. "This is bad, Roy. There's gonna be cops all over in a few minutes. We gotta get out of here. Forget all this. I ain't going to jail."

Somewhere up ahead and around the curve, I heard a car engine roar to life and a loud honk.

"We can't just leave Ruby in a mess like this," Roy said.

"I'll get her out of here and meet you at the same place we agreed to," I said.

"Don't you let no cops follow you now," Eddie said. "Cops get on your tail, and you're just gonna have to keep going."

"Hush up, Eddie," Roy said before turning his glare on me. "Don't come straight to the cave. Backtrack if you can, drive around the back roads, and stay off the highway. Get to the cave by dark, though."

Another honk. Roy ran around to the driver's side of the car and pressed down on the horn. A second later, a black Ford came barreling around the curve and swung around in front of us. Thomas jumped out of the driver's side and ran around the car. "Frankie's hit!"

As Roy and Eddie ran over to check on Franklin, I ran back to the sheriff's car. Ruby was inside now, with John. She was on her knees on the floorboard, bent over his chest, and weeping.

"What's wrong?" I asked.

"I can't do it," she said, leaning back and looking over at me with eyes that seemed lost. "I've been praying for God to heal them, and it just...it won't work. Just like Chester."

Tears rolled down her cheeks as I reached for her hand. "Come on, Ruby. We can't fix this. We need to get out of here."

She pulled back, her eyes wide. "Matthew Doyle! We are not leaving them here to die!"

The way she looked at me, with such disappointment and shock, was like a jolt of electricity. Who was I? What kind of man had I become that I would leave two innocent souls on the side of the road? I was just as bad as Father.

"You're right." I leaned into the car and made sure I had eye contact with her. "Listen, I believe in you. Whatever your gift is, whatever you do, or God does through you, I believe. You're just scared, and everything's going crazy. Just take some deep breaths, calm your spirit, and talk to God. You can't do this, but He can."

She closed her eyes and took a long, slow breath. Her hands steadied, and she moved them in a small circle over John's chest. I was certain I was witnessing something holy that I had no business being a part of, but I couldn't move. Then she opened her eyes and reached for my hand.

Her skin on mine was like fire, and everything around us seemed to go perfectly still. All around me the air prickled the hairs on my body, like a fiery breeze coming into the car. Except nothing moved, and nothing made a sound. A wave of love and peace washed through me, and I could've sworn, if I hadn't been braced by the car door, it might have knocked me over.

And then as quickly as it had come, it was gone. Ruby let go of my hand and opened John's shirt. She closed her eyes again. "Thank you, Lord," she whispered.

I backed away, still reeling from the experience. She tightened his shirt around his chest and then climbed out of the car and ran around the front. Through the open doors, I could see her kneel down beside Sheriff Peterson on the other side.

Off to my left, I heard the roar of approaching cars and turned to look. Police cars—two of them—were coming from less than half a mile away.

"It worked!" Ruby called.

I was already running around the car and took her by the arm, pulling her away from the car. "Then they're all right?"

"They should be." Her eyes looked past me at the approaching cars.

"We have to go," I said. "This is our only chance to keep you out of the electric chair. Especially now. There's no way to explain this."

"No, if we just—"

A gunshot spilt the air by my head, and she screamed. There was no time to argue. I dragged her to my car and pushed her inside, diving in and slamming the door. Just as I cranked it up and pressed the gas, a police car slid to a stop beside me. I yanked the wheel to the right and took off into the field. Dead corn stalks flew everywhere as I plowed through, with no idea where I was headed. My wheels dug into the wet mud, spinning in the ever-deepening puddles, but somehow the car kept moving.

"Matthew, stop!" Ruby said. "We're only going to make things worse!"

Furiously I pressed the gas pedal into the floor, swerving left to try to find the road again. The back window of my car shattered, spraying glass all over the back seat, and Ruby screamed again.

"Stay down!" I yelled.

Up ahead I could see the ridge of the road. I burst out of the cornfield and jerked the wheel again to straighten us out on the road. Then I floored the gas again. A moment later, I took a quick look behind me. One police car was still coming.

Ruby

I closed my eyes and prayed with all my might as Matthew slung us around the winding highway. *Lord, please protect us. Jesus, please be with all of us. Don't let anyone else get hurt.* I repeated the prayer over and over. I grabbed the door and the seat as we took another turn, my knuckles turning white.

"Where are we going?" I asked.

"I don't know," Matthew said. "Roy told me about a cave where we should meet him, but that ain't till later. And I got to lose this cop first."

"So you *were* involved?" My mind reeled. "This is crazy, Matthew! What possessed you to do this?"

"I told you, I ain't gonna let them execute you for something you didn't do. I can't lose you like that!"

I slid up a bit until I was sitting in the seat. A quick glance behind us showed the cop car still hurtling down the road after us. Matthew jerked the wheel, and I tumbled sideways as he turned onto a dirt road.

Lord, please let us lose this cop so we can stop and find our sanity again. I couldn't even think straight, just bounced from one side of the car to the other as I tried to hang on. The road was fairly narrow and boggy, and the tires slid as we took every curve. On the other side of Matthew, I could make out a large creek that seemed to be following our same path. The heavy rain was causing it to overflow, and parts of it were nearly up to the road.

"Hold on tight!" Matthew yelled.

Up ahead, was a fork in the road—a curve to the right and a bridge to the left. As Matthew turned the wheel of the car, time seemed to slow down, and I saw everything that was about to happen in one hideous instant of clarity.

I braced myself against the dashboard as the wheels slid sideways along the road, gliding out into the rushing water for half a second before rolling onto its side. I screamed as I crashed into Matthew, and felt a surge of pain shoot through my head. Everything went black.

When I could see again, it was hazy and cold. Freezing cold.

We were moving. The car was drifting down the overflowing creek, bumping along as it hit rocks on the bottom and sides. Matthew lay beneath me against the driver side door. His head had hit and cracked the window. He was bleeding, and he was unconscious.

I shook him, pain shooting like a web of fire from my shoulder. "Matthew! Matthew! Wake up. Wake up!"

He groaned and shifted. His eyes fluttered open. *Thank God.* Water seeped in all around us, its freezing cold fingers sliding along my legs and feet.

"We have to get out of here," I said.

He pushed against the door and managed to half-way sit up. "Are you hurt?"

"Yes, but we have to get out of this car."

He took a look around, squinting groggily. Water seeped in through every crack. It rushed around the trunk, pouring into the back of the car through the smashed window. Then the car lurched and came to a stop, wedged against something. The back end lifted for a brief second before the water began to gush in even faster. It was already waist high.

Matthew pushed his way to the back seat and tried to get through the window. He managed to get his head and shoulders out, but the car dislodged and started moving down the stream again. He fell against the broken glass, cutting through his shirt.

"Watch out!" I yelled. My head throbbed, and my vision blurred.

He pulled himself back into the front seat and tried to stand against the driver's side door. I steadied him as he reached up for the passenger door. He pushed it up, but it fell right back into place. He took my hand and pulled me up beside him. "Come on. Climb on my shoulders and push the door open."

The water was up to my chest. I crawled up his back and put my knees on his shoulders, using the seat to my right to steady me. Then I pushed up on the door until it fell open.

"Climb out!" Matthew yelled.

I put my hands on the sides of the open door and pulled myself up as Matthew pushed from below me. Climbing out onto the side of the car, I got my first view of what we were facing. Only a few feet ahead lay a wide waterfall. I only had time to yell Matthew's name.

Matthew

"Matthew!" Ruby screamed.

I looked up at the hole she'd climbed out of. Her face was there for one instant. Then the bottom dropped out, and she disappeared. The car tipped forward, and I slammed into the steering wheel and dashboard. A sharp pain shot through my ribcage as the car hit the bottom of the fall.

And then it sank.

Water poured in from the top, the back, the sides. Everywhere, filling up past my head before I even had time to take a deep breath. And as the car fell beneath me, my head swam with confusion. Which way was up? I couldn't breathe. I couldn't see. Darkness surrounded everything. I pushed on every surface, trying to find the hole again. Nothing budged, and panic took over.

I fought. I hit my fist against everything. But I couldn't find the hole. I couldn't find the hole!

Be still.

The voice in my head wasn't my own. I couldn't think clearly. I slammed my hand against one thing after another. The steering wheel, the radio, the dashboard. The side of the car. And then I realized why I couldn't find the hole. The door had closed when the car went over the waterfall.

Be still.

I felt for the door handle, pulled on it, but nothing budged.

Be still.

It was so dark and cold. I quit fighting. I couldn't breathe. I was going to drown. This was it.

But then a small hand grabbed my arm. It pulled me, and I found my way past the seat and into the back of the car. The hand slid down into mine. Pulled again. I reached forward and felt the shattered glass of the back window. The hand pulled me forward, tugging insistently. My lungs were about to burst. I couldn't hold my breath any longer.

My hand slipped from Ruby's grip.

Ruby

I must have hit my head on something as I crashed to the bottom of the falls, 'cause all I saw for a few moments were brilliant flashing stars in my vision. The car sank away beneath me, carrying Matthew with it. Once I was able to register a thought, I dove under the water, reaching for any part of the vehicle to grab onto.

It took too long, and I was nearly out of breath as I reached it. I couldn't see anything. I had to feel along the back window for the opening, slicing my hands as I did so. I pushed through the opening, praying God would lead me to Matthew. I could feel the water moving as he thrashed around, so I reached out and was able to find his arm.

I pulled him toward me, found the hole again, and pulled him toward it. But his body seemed to go limp. I moved around him and pushed as hard as I could. My lungs burned. *Lord, please. Jesus, help. Save Matthew.*

I pushed again with everything I had, blowing the last drop of air out of my lungs. His body floated up and away from me, toward the light. I could see now, a dark image of him drifting away from me as I sank lower. I reached for the hole in the glass. My hands slipped. Another slice of pain. Then the light spread out before me, like a brilliant sunrise, sparkling in the drops of water. And my lungs didn't burn. And my skin wasn't cold.

I drifted toward the light as it spread down around me, wrapped around me like a warm blanket. Someone called my name.

Ruby...

CHAPTER TWENTY-THREE

Matthew

I came to, spluttering and coughing up the water in my lungs, for a moment thinking I had not been healed from tuberculosis after all, and I was choking to death. A figure leaned over me. A man. Rain dripped off his hat. "You all right, fella?"

I bolted upright, taking a deep breath in the process. My lungs were clear, but a new panic surged through me. "Where's Ruby?"

The man stood up and someone else knelt beside me. It was a policeman. "Young man, where's the girl who was with you?"

I tried to jump up, but my head swam and the policeman grabbed my arm. "Whoa! Just hold on there. You ain't going anywhere till all this gets straightened out."

I looked around, frantic to find her. "The car...it sank...she grabbed my hand and pulled me out. But I...I passed out. Where is she?"

The policeman straightened up and yelled to someone further away. "No sign of the girl. Keep looking!" Then he looked back down at me. "You better start explaining, son."

I couldn't think of anything but Ruby. "Please, I promise I'll cooperate. But I have to find her. I need to look for her."

The policeman bent down and helped me stand. I looked out over the water and could see nothing. No sign of my car or Ruby. "Where is this?" I said. "Where are we?"

"That there's Cold Spring," the policeman said. "About fifty feet deep this time of year, especially with all the rain we've had recently."

I shivered as a cold wind swept over my soaked clothes and body. "The last I knew of anything, Ruby had my hand and was pulling me out of the car. We have to find her!" I turned away from the policeman and called as loud as I could. "Ruby! Ruby!"

"Listen, son," the policeman said. "We'll do everything we can to find her. But I need to know what's going on here."

I couldn't explain. I couldn't think. All I could do was feel Ruby's hand in mine, pulling me through the water. She was there! She had to be there!

"Ruby!" I called out to her, over and over. I dropped to my knees, praying she wasn't still at the bottom of that spring. My chest tightened and burned where I'd cut myself on the back window. My heart thundered in my ears. I couldn't lose her.

I made my way back to the water, intent on diving back down to the bottom. The policeman grabbed my arm again and pulled me back.

"I have to find her," I choked out. "She's right there! Someone just has to go in after her. We have to get her out!"

"The water's too cold for anyone to—"

"I'm going back out there!" I yelled. "Ain't nobody gonna keep me from finding Ruby!"

I waded into the water, still calling her name. I swam out to the middle, but I couldn't even remember where the car had sunk. It had to be closer to the falls. I swam toward them. The freezing water felt like a thousand needles piercing my skin. But I kept on. I swam to the spot where I thought the car had gone down, and I dove under the water. I swam as far as my lungs would carry me, searching with my hands in the darkness.

Nothing.

I came up for air, but went straight back down. I thrashed against the cold needles of pain, against the fear overwhelming me. She couldn't be gone. She just *couldn't* be gone. I came back up for air. Went down again. And again. And again.

Nothing.

I dove down over and over, until I passed out. At some point, I woke up in a hospital room with my arm handcuffed to the bed. I tried to sit up, but it felt like my chest ripped open with the effort, and I fell back against the bed. Pain seared through every part of my body, and I must have passed out again.

When I awoke a second time, it was dark except for a small lamp beside my bed. I was in my room at my parents' house. The handcuff was gone. Or had I imagined that? As my surroundings came into view, I remembered where else I'd been. I tried once again to sit up.

"Easy," came a deep voice from the end of the bed. Father moved beside me. My heart thudded against the burn in my chest.

"Where's Ruby? Did they find her?"

"No, son, they didn't."

A gut-wrenching moan worked its way up my spine and out of my throat. "No!" I cried. "She was right there. She was *right there.* I had her hand."

Mother came around the end of the bed and took my hand, tears spilling down her cheek. "Are *you* all right, honey?"

"I have to go help look for her."

Father frowned and he cleared his throat. "They found your car, but there's been no sign of Ruby yet. Police are going to keep looking tomorrow. They're expanding the search to the surrounding areas and the creek that flows out of the spring."

I couldn't lie still. I couldn't breathe. My whole body revolted against the pain coursing through it. I couldn't have lost her. Not after everything! I shook and moaned again. Forcing myself up to the side of the bed, I shook my hand out of Mother's grip.

"I have to help find her!"

Father grabbed my arm. "Now, you listen to me, young man! I've had just about enough of your foolishness. You have endangered your life and the well-being of this family. And this is the last time I'm going to step in and save you from yourself!"

My reason slowly returned to me, and I remembered who I was dealing with. "What have you done now?"

"Oh, that's rich! I kept you out of prison, is all. Not that you'll ever thank me for it. I explained everything to the Sheriff from Blount County, *and* talked to Sheriff Peterson, *and* Judge Woods. I had to tell them how distraught you've been over everything. Explain how you wanted to drive down and see Ruby immediately after she was moved. That you only *happened* to be coming down the road after the gunfight with those...those hoodlum uncles of hers. I explained that you would never do anything to help her escape. She must have somehow talked you into going for help, and you had an accident. End of story!"

"And how much did it cost you this time, Father? To buy two sheriffs *and* a judge?"

"Matthew, please," Mother whimpered. "Don't push us away again."

"You're lucky the sheriff and that deputy are going to be all right," Father said. "If they'd died, even I wouldn't have been able to save you."

"I'm lucky?" I yelled. "They're lucky Ruby was there! She saved their lives."

Father closed his eyes and pinched his nose between his fingers. "If you mention one word about that wretched girl healing them, I swear—"

"I can't do this right now," I said, pushing myself up to the edge of the bed. "I have to go help look for Ruby."

"This is ridiculous," he muttered. "It's pitch black and freezing. You're an hour away from the scene."

"I'm not staying in this house."

Mother sobbed on the bed beside me. I couldn't look at her. I couldn't feel anything for her. Everything inside me for either one of them was completely numb. I stood, steadying myself before opening the closet. It was empty. I'd already moved out. And everything I owned was in my car. At the bottom of Cold Spring. I couldn't go anywhere.

Slamming the closet door, I turned back to Father. "So I suppose I'm trapped here? No car or even a shred of clothing."

"Perhaps it's best—" Mother started.

But rage exploded through me, and I tossed over the armchair in the corner of the room, stumbling with dizziness. "Don't you get it? I have to find Ruby!" They both looked at me with wide, shocked eyes, which only made me angrier. "None of this would've happened if it hadn't been for you!" I flew at Father, punching him square in the jaw.

He stumbled back a couple of steps and fell against the bed. I stood over him and watched the disbelief spread over his face. He touched his hand to his jaw, worked it from side to side. Then he stood and straightened his coat.

"If you are so eager to leave, then I will make sure you have a car...*in the morning*. You will go nowhere tonight." He looked down at Mother, now weeping into her hands. "And you will apologize to your mother."

Then he calmly walked around the bed and out the door.

The next morning, there was a car waiting for me. I didn't bother thanking him, 'cause I knew as soon as possible I'd be returning it. But even if it meant relying on Father, I had to have the car for the day, so I took it and drove to Cold Spring.

A large number of people were busy searching the area around the spring and the creek, including some folks from Hanceville who had heard the news. I kept my distance from most of them, not wanting to answer any questions. The water level was still uncommonly high from all the rain, and midway through the morning, the skies opened up again. More than half the volunteers went home, but I couldn't. I walked up and down the banks calling Ruby's name until I lost my voice. I knocked on doors of houses, asking if anyone had seen her and giving out the Sheriff's phone number.

By the time the sun hung low in the sky, I was about dead on my feet, and a pretty serious cough had taken up in my lungs. I trudged through the rain back to the car, and drove back up '31 toward Hanceville. I wanted to go to Asa's place and find comfort with people who would understand, but I was terrified Ruby's loved ones would blame me. What if they wanted nothing more to do with me?

I argued with myself for a few miles, but in the end, I had to go. It was the only place I was sure I'd be able to feel her presence. As I drove down the long dirt path that led to the farm, I spotted several cars and wagons in the yard. It shouldn't have surprised me, but it just hit home that Ruby was missing, and the knot in my gut twisted.

I parked my car and walked up the front steps. The door was open, so I could see inside. Several people were milling around, mostly neighbors. On the other side of the living room, I spotted James standing beside Emma Rae, who held a baby in her arms. Anger ran unchecked through me, and I thought to storm across the room, meaning to lay him out. But I caught myself. I was just as much to blame as anyone else.

Instead I stepped into the doorway and looked around. I couldn't see Asa or Mrs. Graves anywhere. Only a bunch of people I didn't know. Then across the room, the door to the bedroom opened, and Asa and Dr. Fisher came out. They closed the door behind them and continued talking, so I decided not to interrupt them.

I turned to my left and headed into the dining area and kitchen, stopping in my tracks when I saw Henry seated at the table. He looked up at me from a plate of biscuits and leapt to his feet.

"Is there any word?" he asked.

I shook my head. "When did you get here?"

"Just today, 'round lunchtime." He fell back into his chair. "I didn't get Ruby's letter till about a week and half ago. Then I couldn't find a way to get here. Wound up hitch-hiking and jumping on a train or two." His shoulders sagged, and he picked at a biscuit on his plate. "Still too late, though."

I fell into a chair at the table with him and nearly came apart. Ruby would be so happy to see her brother. I could picture the joy on her face, and that hurt more than anything else had so far.

"You been looking after Ruby real nice, from what I hear," he said. "Can't tell you how much that means to me."

"I didn't, though. I didn't take care of her yesterday. I did everything I could, and it wasn't enough." I rested my elbows on the table and dropped my head into my hands so I wouldn't have to see the pity in his eyes.

"Sounds like you nearly got yourself killed trying to save her."

"I have to find her," I said. "I have to go back out there. If she's hurt or…"

"I'll help you. I swear, if she's…we'll find her."

The murmur in the living room stopped all of a sudden, catching my attention. A low, deep voice filled the house. "Is there a Mrs. Graves here?"

I turned around in my seat as Ruby's mother stumbled out of the bedroom door. Asa took her arm. I stood and moved into the living room, followed by Henry. The voice was coming from a deputy I didn't recognize standing in the doorway.

"Mrs. Graves, I wanted to let you know that the search for Ruby has been called off."

"They found her?" Mrs. Graves exclaimed.

The deputy looked stricken. He took a step toward her. "No, ma'am. There's still no sign she ever made it out of the spring. The Blount County Sheriff's office is calling off the search, saying they've thoroughly covered every place they could look."

Mrs. Graves's eyes swam. "Does this mean that they're declaring…that she's considered…dead?"

My knees nearly buckled, and I leaned against the wall behind me. *Dead.* The word sat in the pit of my stomach, churned up the bile. She wasn't dead. There was no way. I would know. Somehow, I'd know she wasn't in the world any longer.

Henry went to his mother and held her while she wept. The deputy shifted his weight, looking increasingly uncomfortable. "Ma'am, I ain't sure about that part. I was told to tell the family that the search was being called off. I'm sure someone will let you know about...the other part soon." He tipped his hat and backed out the door.

Asa came toward me and wrapped an arm around my shoulder. "We're glad you're here, son. Come on in here." He guided me into the bedroom and showed me to a wooden chair near the bed. Mrs. Graves and Henry followed, with Dr. Fisher coming in last and closing the door behind him.

Mrs. Graves fell onto the bed and began sobbing. I thought the sound might split me in two. "I'm...I'm so sorry," I said.

"No one here blames you," Asa said. "We all know how much you loved Ruby. And you did everything you could to save her."

"You about drowned yourself trying to get to her from what the officers said," Dr. Fisher added. "You feeling all right?"

I must have looked terrible. I sure felt it. I coughed and rubbed my hand over the stitches in my chest. "I reckon I'm all right. I just...I can't give up. I have to find her. Me and Henry, we're going back out there tomorrow."

Dr. Fisher came over and knelt down in front of me. He peered at me the way he used to when I was sick with T.B. "How do your lungs feel?"

"Fine. I just have a bit of a cough."

"Sounds like you're getting sick." He felt my forehead. "Fever, too. You better rest. You could get pneumonia, and with your history, that could be deadly."

"I don't care."

He raised an eyebrow, then reached for my shirt. "You mind if I have a look?"

I unbuttoned my shirt and opened it. "It won't make no difference. I'm not quitting till I find Ruby."

"You've pulled some stitches loose. And you're well on your way to infection." He pressed gently on the wound. "Let me take care of this, and get you in a bed. Then tomorrow we'll talk about what you should or shouldn't do."

I'd run out of energy to argue with him, but I knew I was going back out there the next day. And the next. And the next. As long as it took to find her.

The Graves family put me up again. And every morning for the next three days, Henry, Asa, and I set out for Cold Spring. We walked around it, searched up and down the woods, the road, the tiniest branches that weaved away from the spring. There was simply no trace of her.

By that Sunday, my body simply gave out. I was ravaged by a fever, infection in my chest wound, and a cough that brought back terrible memories of the searing pain of tuberculosis. That morning, I lay on the Graves's sofa wanting desperately to go back to the spring and search again, but I couldn't move. All I could do was lie there and cough, choking on my misery.

Henry stood at the window across the room, gazing out at the rain. Next to me, Asa stoked a fire to keep me warm. He set the poker against the wall and took a seat in the rocking chair near my head. The gentle sway and creaking of the chair lulled my eyelids to close. But every time they drifted shut, I saw Ruby sinking away from me into the murky depth of that freezing water, and they'd shoot back open.

I forced myself to sit up, which was more of a sad sort of leaning sideways against the back of the sofa. Asa stood and rubbed the back of his neck. "Can I get you some coffee?" he asked.

I shook my head. I hadn't eaten much of anything. I'd been surviving on coffee the past three days, and I was ready to puke just thinking about it.

"How about some food?" Asa asked.

"No, thank you."

He sat down and went back to rocking. "You're going to have to find a way to move past this, Matthew," he said. "Ruby's gone."

I rubbed my face and tried to keep the rage inside me from overwhelming me. "She can't be. I can't face that."

"Yes, you can. You have to. When all the dust settles, and you're looking at the days ahead, you'll need to come to terms with what got you here."

"And what's that?"

"Fear." Asa stopped rocking, leaned forward, and looked me right in the eyes. "Doubt. A lack of faith in the One True God. You lost your center, lost your faith. And you took matters into your own hands. I know a little something about that myself. There are always consequences."

"I can take my own consequences," I spluttered, waiting for a fit of coughing to pass. "But Ruby? She shouldn't be punished for what I did. She didn't want any part of it. She was the one telling me, over and over, to hang on to my faith. I failed. Not her. Why should she suffer 'cause of what I did?"

"Listen, son, death ain't a punishment. Ruby...if she's...if she's gone, she's in a better place, with no suffering at all. She's praising Jesus, not being punished. Those of us left behind, we're the ones who suffer."

He was right about that. I looked over at Henry, who was still lost in thought by the window. My actions had hurt so many people. All 'cause I didn't believe God was doing right by Ruby. If I'd just been patient, maybe her appeals would've worked. I'd never know now.

"Henry," I said. "Are you going back out there today?"

He didn't answer for a moment. Just stared out the window with his hands shoved in his pockets. "No," he finally said. He turned to face me. "Ruby wouldn't want you to do this to yourself. She wouldn't want you to kill yourself trying to find her. She's…she's all right. She'd want you to find a way to move on with your life."

I shuddered. "Move on with my life? I don't even know how to begin to do that."

"It starts with accepting that she's gone," Asa said. "She ain't coming back."

For the first time, I considered that he might be right, and that Ruby was really gone forever. My insides shattered, and all I wanted to do was crumble away and die myself. A life without Ruby? Why had I ever thought I could save her? I was no savior. I was the reason she was…*dead.*

And I deserved the pain of living with that.

Sitting through Ruby's funeral service was an inescapable nightmare. It was bad enough I was still coughing from whatever illness had taken over my lungs. But every kind word from those who knew her, every reminder from Brother Harbison of Ruby's care and sacrifice for others, *every moment*, was an individual nail driven into my chest. By the end, I could barely breathe.

I went outside to the cemetery where a small stone slab had been placed in the ground next to her father's headstone. The wind blew right through me, chilling my bones and making me shiver. I wrapped my coat around me, thankful that at least the rain had let up for a time. Ruby deserved a beautiful day, and she'd gotten one.

I knelt next to the sad little marker, touching her name on the stone. It still didn't seem real. Something inside of me was still connected to her, and it refused to believe she was really gone. I couldn't see how I could ever let go of her completely until I knew for sure what happened at that spring.

I felt someone approaching from behind, so I stood and turned around. Henry tipped his hat and came up next to me. He'd seemed surprisingly calm most of the day. I couldn't understand how the Graves family managed that inner peace that always eluded me.

"She deserves better than this," I said.

"She already has it," Henry answered.

"Soon as I can make some money, I'll replace it myself. She should have a proper headstone." Henry didn't say anything. "I mean, I know the family doesn't have much, and this is the best they can do for now…I just meant…"

"It's all right. I know what you mean. And I understand. But like I said before, Ruby don't want you agonizing over the past. What's done is done."

Even Henry seemed to have a hard time talking of her in the past tense. I wondered if he realized it.

"What will you do now?" Henry asked.

"Not sure yet. But I have to get away from here. Maybe I'll head west or something. Maybe north. You're doing all right for yourself. What do you do?"

"You don't want the life I have. Trust me. Moving from place to place for work in the winter. Hoping a team will pick me up for the spring and summer. It's not a life I'd recommend to anyone else."

"Actually, it don't sound so bad. There's nothing left for me here."

"What about your family?"

I shook my head. "I don't care to ever see my father's face again, long as I live. I reckon that means the rest of my family as well."

Henry kicked at the loose rocks by his feet. "Listen, I know guys all over the country in several different Conservation Corps camps. They're not paid much, but it's work. And it's a start. Kept me fed during some hard times."

"I'll keep that in mind. But I'll probably try to get back to building things. That was all I dreamed of for a time."

I couldn't help but remember the day I'd done my best to leave Ruby Graves behind, when I'd come to her after Hannah was healed. I couldn't bear the way she'd looked at me, like I could be so much more than who I was. Instead of working to become that man, I'd pushed her away. She'd been hurt. I could see it in her eyes. But she had still looked on me with the gracious love that shone out of her, even back then.

Matthew, I will be fine. God has a wonderful life ahead for me, and a wonderful life ahead for you. There's no need to dwell on this anymore. You go on and finish college, and build those skyscrapers you dream of. I just hope that one day you come to understand that God wants so much more for you than you could ever dream of for yourself. I do see more than what's in front of me. I see the man you could be. A man who builds a little home in the woods for a colored woman and her son is a much greater man than the one who builds skyscrapers for the wealthy.

I reckoned it was time for me to be that man. I didn't have any idea what that meant, but I knew I would find some way to serve others the way Ruby had. With my whole heart and soul. And maybe then I could find some small measure of the peace she'd found.

I turned to Henry and took hold of his hand. "Thank you for...well...for being here. And for the advice. Ruby loved you like crazy. I can see why."

"Good luck to you," he said.

I turned to go, but only got a few steps away when Henry called out to me. When I turned around, he was turning his hat over in his hands. "One more thing. Do me a favor, would you? When you get to wherever you're going, you stay in touch."

"All right," I said.

"I mean it. Write me and let me know how to reach you. You know...just in case."

"In case of what?"

He shrugged. "I...I don't know. Just, don't forget. Let me know where you are."

I said I'd do my best, and waved goodbye. Then I walked across the empty cemetery back toward town. Everything I owned was either on my back or in my pockets. I had barely enough money to catch a train north.

But I had hope, and I was determined to make something out of myself that would make Ruby proud.

Ruby

I coughed. Water spluttered out of my lungs. Something pounded on my back, and I coughed again. "That's it, honey," said a low, gruff voice.

Rocks pressed into the side of my face. I heard my name from far away. I fell onto my back, and the sunlight pierced my eyes. A dark figure moved above me, blocking the brightness for a moment. Rough hands felt my neck and pushed up my eyelids. Then the darkness returned.

When I woke again, the first thing I noticed was the earthy aroma of potatoes and onions. I opened my eyes and found myself in a strange bed, in a house I didn't recognize. I was covered in several quilts in the corner of a small one-room house. A fire blazed across the room from me in the fireplace, and a large pot sat on the stove nearby. Potatoes. My stomach tightened with hunger.

I tried to sit up, but pain shot through my head, making the room sway. Nausea replaced my hunger. *Not another concussion.* I refused to let it get the better of me, so I forced myself up to sitting on the side of the bed. Looking down at my body, I saw a dress I didn't recognize. Where was I?

The door opened, and a stocky man with a load of wood in his arms came inside. He set the wood by the fireplace and stoked the fire. I couldn't see his entire face, just a sprinkling of gray in his dark side-burns. When he turned around to see me, his eyebrows shot up. "Well, thank the Lord. I was afraid you was done for."

"Where am I?" I asked.

"This here's my home. I'm George. George Harper."

I gripped my stomach as another wave of nausea hit. "I'm...I'm Ruby. How did I get here?"

"Brought you here myself when I seen you and that boy crash your car into the spring. I was fishing for my dinner."

"Matthew!" I gasped.

"Oh, he's all right, far as I could tell anyhow."

I said a silent prayer thanking God for saving Matthew. "Mr. Harper, how...what happened?"

He scratched his chin. "Well, like I said, I was fishing for my dinner yesterday, minding my own business—" He stopped and pointed at the pot on the stove. "Say, you hungry? Let me fix you something to eat." He went over to the stove and dipped out some of whatever was in the pot into a small bowl and brought it over to me.

"Thank you," I said.

"Careful now. It's hot." He went back to the stove to fill another bowl while I investigated the soup. It was mostly water, with a few potatoes and onion mixed in. "Now, like I was saying," he continued. "I was minding my own business getting some dinner when your car came hurtling into the spring. I jumped up and hurried over to the shore clos-est to where the car went down. Then I seen you diving down into the water. A couple of minutes later, I seen this boy floating up to the sur-face like a dead body or something. He drifted over to the other side of the spring, and a couple of police officers drove up to that side. They pulled him out and started trying to get him to breathe."

He sat down at a tiny wooden table near the stove and blew on a spoonful of soup, then shoved it into his mouth. I was so hungry, I ignored the burn in my mouth and kept shoveling down spoonfuls without bothering to blow.

"That was when I noticed you floating along toward me. So I waded out into the water and pulled you over to the shore. I thought you was dead. Wasn't breathing or nothing. I hit you a couple of times on the back. You coughed out some water, garbled something I couldn't understand, and then passed out."

He took another couple of spoonfuls before continuing. "I seen those policemen, and I didn't want no trouble. But I couldn't just leave you there to die neither. So I carried you off to my home here. Reckon I'll be paying for that soon."

"What do you mean?" I asked.

"There's a big commotion going on all over the place. People looking for ya, I reckon. Police too. I went back down there this morning. Lotsa interesting stories floating 'round about ya already."

I took another mouthful, unsure of how to respond. Mr. Harper eyed me with suspicion. "You kill a fella? That why you running?"

I didn't say anything.

"I know something about that, is all. I won't tell 'em where ya are if they come looking for ya."

"Thank you," I said. I hesitated, wondering just how well I could trust this man. "And I didn't kill anyone. They just think I did."

"Innocent, huh? Well, they all say they're innocent. Maybe ya are; maybe ya ain't. Don't matter one way or the other to me."

He went back to eating, and I finished off my soup. The warmth of the room and my full belly made me sleepy. I figured some rest wouldn't hurt nothing. Maybe after I got some sleep, I could figure out what to do next. Matthew was probably going crazy.

"Do you mind if I sleep a little longer?" I asked. "I still don't feel so well."

"Sure, sure. I won't disturb ya."

I curled under the quilts again, and drifted off to sleep. I must have slept clear through the night, 'cause when I awoke again, there was a sliver of dim light coming through the windows, and Mr. Harper was tending to some sizzling bacon on the stove.

I felt even worse than I had the day before. I was soaked through with sweat, and my body ached from the top of my head to my toes. In fact, my head hurt so bad, my vision was blurry. I coughed, and Mr. Harper came to my side. His huge hand rested on my forehead.

"Lordy, girl. You might've been saved from drowning, but looks like you caught your death all the same."

I couldn't speak. My throat was on fire. I closed my eyes and prayed for relief, finally drifting off again.

The next time I awoke, I heard knocking. Pain shot through my head again when I tried to roll over and get a look at the door. Mr. Harper pushed himself out of a rocking chair near the fire. He went to the front door and cracked it open. "Can I help you?"

From the other side, I could hear a male voice. It sounded familiar. "...young girl went missing two days ago near the spring. 'Bout this tall. Brown hair and eyes. Name's Ruby."

Was that Henry? Surely I was dreaming. I moaned and tried to call out to him.

"What was that?" Henry's voice asked.

Mr. Harper didn't move. "What's this Ruby girl to you?"

"She's my sister. Sir, please, have you seen her?"

I called again.

"Is that...Ruby?" Henry called. Mr. Harper pulled the door open the rest of the way, and a blurry image of Henry rushed over to the bedside. He put a hand on my cheek. "Ruby? Are you all right?"

I tried to tell him I was, but my voice didn't cooperate. I was so tired. All I could do was close my eyes.

"She's not doing too well," I heard Mr. Harper say.

"Can barely feel her heart at all." Henry said.

"I'm all right," I squeaked out. But I was still too tired to open my eyes.

"I need to get her to a doctor, but..." Henry's voice trailed off.

"But you don't want her going back to jail," Mr. Harper finished. "Don't worry. I was a medic in France back during the war. I can care for her as well as any doctor at this point. And I won't be telling the law where she is."

I floated away from the voices. Floated away from everything. Prison. The electric chair. Matthew. All of it. All I wanted was sleep.

The End

ACKNOWLEDGEMENTS

As always, I must thank my family for their love and support. Without their patience and encouragement, there would be no story. Thanks to my husband, for finding creative ways to entertain the kids while I write, and to my kids for enduring "Grumpy Mom" after late nights of writing.

Thank you so much to Bryony Sutherland, an amazing editor who can take my stories and polish them until they shine. A huge thank you to Amy Hobbs for once again designing a cover that makes me swoon.

I also couldn't have put together such a realistic story line without the work of Sharon Hatfield in her book, *Never Seen the Moon: The Trials of Edith Maxwell.*

And most importantly, I must give thanks to God for His inspiration and comfort through all my self-doubt and fear. It's still amazing to look through a story I've written and see His hand throughout. I'm so thankful He called me to writing.

Historical Fiction:

Healing Ruby, Volume One of the *Healing Ruby* series

Breaking Matthew, Volume Two of the *Healing Ruby* series

Saving Grace, Volume Three of the *Healing Ruby* series (Coming 2016)

Contemporary Christian Romance:

Love's Providence

ABOUT THE AUTHOR

Jennifer Westall loves writing Christian fiction as a way of exploring her own faith journey. *Breaking Matthew* (2015) is the second volume in the *Healing Ruby* series. The first in the series, *Healing Ruby* (2014) was inspired by events in the life of her grandmother, and explores the mysteries of faith healing. She's also the author of *Love's Providence* (2012), a contemporary Christian romance novel that navigates the minefield of dating and temptation. She resides in southwest Texas with her husband and two boys, where she homeschools by day and writes by night, thus explaining those pesky bags under her eyes. Readers can connect with her at jenniferhwestall.com or find her on Facebook and Twitter.

CPSIA information can be obtained
at www.ICGtesting.com
Printed in the USA
LVOW11s1603060617
537124LV00005B/885/P